THE SUSAN EFFECT

ALSO BY PETER HØEG

Miss Smilla's Feeling for Snow

Borderliners

The Woman and the Ape

History of Danish Dreams

Tales of the Night

The Quiet Girl

The Elephant Keepers' Children

Peter Høeg

The Susan Effect

TRANSLATED
FROM THE DANISH
BY
Martin Aitken

Harvill *Secker*
LONDON

1 3 5 7 9 10 8 6 4 2

Harvill Secker, an imprint of Vintage,
20 Vauxhall Bridge Road,
London SW1V 2SA

Harvill Secker is part of the Penguin Random House group of companies
whose addresses can be found at global.penguinrandomhouse.com

Penguin
Random House
UK

First published by Harvill Secker in 2017
First published with the title *Effekten af Susan* in Denmark by Rosinante in 2014

A CIP catalogue record for this book is available from the British Library

penguin.co.uk/vintage

ISBN 9781910701294 (hardback)
ISBN 9781910701300 (trade paperback)

Typeset in 11.25/15.25 pt Sabon LT Std by Jouve (UK), Milton Keynes
Printed and bound in Great Britain by Clays Ltd, St Ives PLC

Penguin Random House is committed to a sustainable future
for our business, our readers and our planet. This book is made
from Forest Stewardship Council® certified paper.

MIX
Paper from
responsible sources
FSC
www.fsc.org   FSC® C018179

PART ONE

1

WHOEVER MIGHT WISH TO PUT IN FOR THE CARLSBERG Honorary Residence in Valby, 850 square metres with a full cellar and a park, free and for life, may profitably begin by securing the Nobel Prize in Physics. Andrea Fink did so at an early age and was therefore able to take on the house after Niels Bohr sometime in the 1960s, and to go on living in it for over fifty years.

Now she is preparing to vacate it. She is dying.

Most of us approach death reluctantly. Personally, I will face it screaming and with thrashing limbs. Andrea Fink proceeds towards it like an operatic diva might approach her final performance.

It is to be a charity event. She has given everything away. The room into which I enter is utterly bare, save for her hospital bed. All that is left on the walls are cream-coloured oblongs where paintings hung.

Not even a chair remains. I step up to the bed and lean on my crutch.

Her field of vision has diminished. Not until I am quite close does she see me.

'Susan,' she says, 'what are you going to do to get your children back?'

'Everything.'

'You'll need to.'

She unfolds a translucent hand resting on the covers. I put my palm to hers. She has always needed to touch whoever she is speaking to.

'You're thin.'

I can feel her empathy quite physically. Bohr once said of her that she was the only celebrity he had met whom fame had not corrupted.

'Dysentery. But I'm having treatment.'

Something is pressed against the back of my thigh, a chair mysteriously produced from nowhere. The magician withdraws in a wide arc to safety, on the other side of the bed.

He is a small, elegant man with a robust belief.

What he believes in is having the best of tailors and the strongest possible apparatus of government. His name is Thorkild Hegn, and apparently he was once Permanent Secretary at the Ministry of Justice. It is the second time he and I have met.

The first time was two weeks ago, in the Tula prison in Manipur on the border of Burma, in what they referred to as the visiting room, a windowless burial vault of concrete.

The first thing that strikes me as they seat me opposite him is that this is a man who has succeeded in suspending the second principle of thermal dynamics. In a city and a room in which everyone and everything perspires, he is cool and comfortable in white shirt, jacket and tie.

'I'm from the Danish Embassy.'

Of course, he is not from the Embassy at all. His complexion is pale and delicately opaque. He has come directly from Denmark.

'Where are my children?'

'Your son is under arrest in Almora, a small border town close to Nepal. Charged with attempting to smuggle antiquities. Your daughter seems to have run away with a priest from the Kali temple in Kolkata.'

We stare at each other. The twins are sixteen years old.

'Your husband—'

'I don't want to know about him.'

He places something on the table between us. The visual disturbance I've been experiencing means that, to begin with, I can't see what it is. Then a copy of *Time* emerges into focus.

Four people are on the cover: a man seated at a grand piano, against which two children lean, each with a violin. Slightly behind the man, with her hand on his shoulder, stands a woman who callous individuals have talked into donning the academic regalia of cape and mortarboard.

The children are flaxen-haired and blue-eyed, and look as if they are winning everyone's hearts and are about to receive disbursements to study at the finest conservatories abroad. The man has warm, rather sorrowful eyes, and a smile that suggests that whatever might burden his soul it is certainly not scant self-confidence.

The caption beneath the photo reads: *The Great Danish Family.*

The children holding the violins are my children. The woman in the mortarboard is me. The man at the piano is Laban Svendsen, my husband. The family my eyes are struggling to keep in focus is mine.

'Your husband has gone off to Goa with a maharaja's daughter. Aged seventeen. With the entire southern Indian mafia on his heels. How are the standards of comfort in this place?'

'Impeccable. Fifteen square metres to thirty women. A pedal toilet in the corner. Rainwater in a barrel, and a bowl of rice a day to go round. They fight with razor blades in the night. I haven't seen a solicitor in three weeks. I've been passing blood for a week.'

'We can supply medicine. We can take the girl into our custody. We're working on having the boy released. We may even be able to find your husband before the mafia gets to him.'

He talks of performing Vedic miracles. Of neutralising the prevailing chaos of Indian case law. Circumventing extradition agreements, finding a person who has disappeared in the great

5

ocean that is India. And yet the question that imposes itself is not whether he can do so, but why he would wish to.

That tiny part of the Danish population that has yet to serve time in prison believes such institutions to be silent places, weighed down with remorse and self-examination. The theory is false. Prisons are as raucous as the cages of predatory beasts at feeding time. But the walls of the visiting room are solid and thick, a barrier against any high-frequency modulation. Here, the noise is more vibration than sound.

In this relative silence he ought to have stood up and gone already. But he has not. Something he cannot quite gauge is keeping him.

'The charge against you is assault with intent to kill, an assault carried out with your bare hands. An assault upon a man who, if the police report is anything to go by, is one metre and ninety centimetres tall and every bit as athletic as a Greek hero. How would that make sense?'

It's no wonder he's bemused. I'm more astonished myself. If I manage to regain what the last few months have taken out of me, I might just make the sunny side of sixty kilos.

The shift inside him is made plain by the fact that he is unable to conceal his curiosity.

'The casino have told the police you tried to purchase chips by promising them his organs.'

'I was joking.'

'The casino didn't look at it like that. Nor did the man in question.'

At that moment he realises he is losing his grip. That he is revealing to me a part of himself he would prefer not to. The shock of encountering an unfamiliar weakness in his constitution passes fleetingly over his face. Then he gets to his feet.

Here in the honorary residence, two weeks later, that shock has yet to fully recede. Moreover, Hegn is not a man to make the

6

same mistake twice. He makes sure he has the hospital bed between us.

In his hand is a cardboard folder. And the same issue of *Time* he showed me in the prison.

The head of Andrea Fink's bed is pushed up against a wall of glass. On the other side of the wall, trees and shrubs brought home from foreign climes stand in ten centimetres of grubby, melting snow, looking as if they might, like the rest of us, be wondering what on earth they're doing in a place such as Denmark at this time of year. From somewhere in the park comes the sound of children's voices. Her face lights up. Perhaps it's her grandchildren, perhaps she is gathering the family around her for the home stretch.

At that moment I sense the presence of the twins.

It's an irrational feeling, rather than a response to any physically quantifiable stimulus. I get to my feet and crutch my way across the room to a pair of double doors and push them open.

Thit and Harald, the twins, are the first thing I perceive. But they are not the first thing I look at. The first thing I look at is the man at the piano: Laban Svendsen, my husband, the children's father.

Regarding his singular first name – *rascal* or *scamp* to any Dane – a good many opinions have been voiced over the years. I know the authoritative explanation. His mother told me she had given him the name because from birth he so closely resembled a Baroque angel that her maternal instinct informed her of the necessity of thrusting a well-directed stick into his wheel at the earliest possible age.

He still looks like an angel. But now he is forty-five and has had the Indian mafia after him.

I'm pleased to note the experience has marked him, though sorry it has failed to mark him more.

The fact that I look at him first is down to a very firmly entrenched agreement. Even before the twins were born, both he and I knew we ran the risk of being consumed by them. So

7

we set out some rules. Rules by which we still abide, no matter that the family is disintegrating. The first of those rules is this: in any encounter between us at which the children are present, we adults will first acknowledge each other's presence.

In a distant past we did so with kisses and hugs. Now it's with pensive glances signalling lifelong resentment and everlasting sanctions.

The twins are standing next to the piano, albeit without violins. And the violins are not the only thing they have lost since posing for *Time*. Something else that is gone is part of the innocence some might claim was visible in that photo.

They run forwards, I stagger, and we meet in the middle of the floor and hold each other tight.

Our reunion is on the outside only. Inside, I lost them a long time ago. Perhaps already at birth. Which, though brief, was difficult. The doctor wanted to give me something for the pain. I must have said something to him, because when I saw him again on the ward forty-eight hours later, he was still pale. But I wanted the whole experience.

As soon as I put the twins to my breasts, the bubble in which we had been living during the pregnancy burst. From the moment they enter the world, children are deserting their parents. They turn towards the nipple, but somewhere deep inside their nervous systems they are already in the process of leaving home.

Nevertheless, I feel tremendous relief. And overwhelming anxiety. Most laws of nature may be formulated as energetic equilibriums. Anyone who gives birth to a child will thereby be dealt a meticulously measured balance of love and fear of losing. And anyone who has twins will be dealt double. On both sides of the equation.

The exhaustion I have until this point suppressed is now suddenly released. The room spins, and the twins ferry me to a chair.

Thorkild Hegn is standing in the doorway. With his grey folder. And his copy of *Time*.

'To a great many people the two of you are a symbol. The artist and the scientist. Cultural ambassadors to UNESCO. Co-responsible for the largest EU-funded educational project ever implemented outside Europe. We will endeavour to protect that symbol. We believe we can appease the Indian police. Avoid trial in Denmark. Prevent the oriental demons whose sensibilities you have offended from tracing you here. It will take some weeks. We have turned on the heating in your lovely house. We have stocked the fridge. And we have a car waiting outside to drive you home.'

Laban and the twins acknowledge him with gratitude. They think he's the good fairy.

But this is an error of judgement, on account of their upbringing. Laban was born to be fêted and loved, and massively sponsored from the cradle to the grave. The twins have reached their sixteenth birthday suffering no harder blows than the odd gentle pat to their powdered bottoms. They have yet to suspect. They think life is a gift shop and everything in it is free. Even Laban, who ought to know better, thinks so.

It's always been me who has managed the family's finances. Not only because I've got a flair for figures, but also because I'm the only one among us who actually knows what things cost.

What things cost is what now becomes apparent.

'There is a small favour we should like to ask in return, Susan. We want you to put a question to someone.'

He places the grey cardboard folder on the piano.

The room falls quiet, apart from the distant children's voices and the spiritualistic interference that always whispers in the vicinity of a piano. Now even the twins are cottoning on to where we are headed.

Thorkild Hegn remains silent. He does not threaten us, or pressure us in any way. Without saying a word, he merely allows reality to bear down.

'There's a telephone number on the inside flap. For when you've good news.'

He withdraws, stepping back through the door and closing it behind him. At the other end of the room another door opens. We look out into a hall with a glass exit. Through the glass we see a waiting car. The Svendsen family's audience in the Carlsberg Honorary Residence is over.

2

I'M STANDING AT MY COOKER, PREPARING A CREAM OF tomato soup with fresh herbs. It's a small industrial cooker that runs on natural gas. I converted it myself to attain an operating pressure of twenty-nine millibars, thirty per cent above the legal maximum. I like the flames to hiss.

I won't have induction in the house. If Maxwell had known what misuse would be made of his equations he would have kept them to himself. The home fires do not consist of a magnetic field, but of open flame. I want to see the flame's blue kernel of vaporous hydrocarbon. I want, as now, to hear the wood-burning outdoor pizza oven whistle in the drizzle.

The twins are sitting on the sofa, Laban at the piano. Three-quarters of an hour have passed since we stepped over the threshold and we have yet to say a word to each other.

The house was a dream. A dream that collapsed.

It was Laban who envisaged it, I who made it real. That was the division of labour. It consists of 300 square metres framed by rendered, whitewashed walls and enclosed by an arching zinc roof whose underside is clad with timber like an aeroplane hangar from the First World War.

The feeling that it all may fly is reinforced by large expanses of plate glass from floor to ceiling, opening out onto a green jungle.

We built it from materials that, like our marriage, were going to last five hundred years, preferably into eternity. The floors are solid oak. Laban cut the plugs, while I levelled the joists. And we built it in such a way that the solidity of the place would not compromise our sense of freedom. From inside, it looks like the whole structure is suspended somewhere above the treetops in a temperate primeval forest.

It isn't. The address is Evighedsvej in Charlottenlund – Eternity Street to those unversed in our singular tongue. Fifteen minutes from the centre of Copenhagen. On a good day.

The idea that houses are living organisms is a strategic research axiom I have yet to present to the Royal Danish Academy of Sciences and Letters. But I shall. I'm waiting for the time to be ripe.

Our house breathes, though only just. We've been away for six months. That fact in itself lends a sense of abandonment to the place. And then there is what we have brought back to it. An atmosphere no building material on earth could withstand in the long run.

Some people believe a felicitous family life comes of successful compromises. This is not true. Love is without compromise. Happy families come from solving koans. Or rather: dissolving them.

I'd thought we'd solved ours for good.

I should have known better. Nothing in the world is for good. The laws of nature are temporary. No sooner has physics contented itself with one picture of the world than the picture dissolves and turns out to be an exception in some greater paradigm. One of the first things Andrea Fink told me was that she had heard John Bell say at a seminar at Amherst College that in its very foundation quantum physics holds the seed of its own demise.

Thus, the Svendsen family's good years have now revealed themselves to be but a temporary state of harmony in a much wider chaos.

At least we tried. And one of the puzzles we solved was the issue of how four extreme individualists, all of them solitary creatures by nature, may live together in the same house.

Like, for instance, the kitchen and the lounge, which are one big room. Without a single argument we agreed on the furniture, the piano and the white walls. And we concurred that the only picture that should hang on those walls was a photograph of Andrea Fink.

'I'm glad to see you.'

Thit breaks the silence.

Some would consider this to be an encouraging start. But not us. Ever since kindergarten her friends have approached her with caution. Introductory sweetness is often followed by something more caustic. Like now.

'I was collected by a woman from the police. Her name was Irene. She took me all the way on the plane. She said Harald's looking at eighty years, Mum at twenty-five, because the man's a famous Bollywood actor. I think we need to look around us. Not think of the family we used to be. More the family we've become. Without really having noticed. Mum's interested in young men.'

'He was twenty-five,' I say.

'You could have been his mother.'

I make no comment. In purely biological terms, she's right.

'Dad's interested in young girls. Harald wants money. And I . . .'

We hold our breath.

'I want a house by the sea. Six horses to ride. And people to do the cleaning for me.'

We breathe out again. Respectfully. Not many girls of sixteen have the courage to peer so deeply inside their souls.

I lift the dough from the mixing bowl. My Mettler weighing scales have measured the flour to within one hundred thousandth of a gram. Few housewives would be able to outshine me there. Water and mechanical manipulation have created elastic peptide chains.

The worktop is Corian, made from stone that has been crushed and then glued together again. The textural quality is once again a koan solved, an impossible task, a physical paradox: the unification of marble, plastic and porcelain.

I've had the edge rounded. I let the dough hang down over it and stretch itself wafer-thin. We experimental physicists do not merely picture our formulas, we feel them with our fingers.

'What game were you playing, Mum?'

I don't answer.

They all look at the wall behind me, at the photo of Andrea Fink.

3

OVER TWO DECADES HAVE PASSED SINCE I STOOD FACE TO face with Andrea Fink for the first time.

It was in the main auditorium of the H.C. Ørsted Institute of the University of Copenhagen. Her visits to Denmark were seldom, her lectures more seldom still. The auditorium seats eight hundred. Two thousand had turned up. People were standing in the corridor.

She spoke on Riemann's geometry. When she finished she disappeared in a split second, as though she had dissolved on the spot. Later I found out it was to avoid the hordes wanting to give her a letter, shake her hand, kiss a corner of her cape. Or tear off a button for that special souvenir.

No one could leave the room even though she was gone. They weren't going home.

After three-quarters of an hour the place had reluctantly emptied. Everyone was gone except me, I was the last one there. And then she appeared in front of the blackboard.

The auditorium's acoustics are such that two individuals placed at any random distance from each other will at any time be able to conduct a whispered conversation. When Andrea Fink spoke, she did so softly, and yet I had no trouble picking up her voice on the back row.

'You wrote to me. I've read your letter. And your thesis. Interesting. But I'm afraid I don't accept mentees.'

She stepped up the stairs towards me.

'I especially noted the bit where you say that what makes you most happy is the knowledge that natural laws exist. Quite a statement for such a young woman. At that point I asked myself: Is a girl who would say such a thing not simply neurotic? Is she?'

She came closer. She spoke as if she meant someone else.

'You're in touch with the body. That's something I look for. The deep insights never come from the brain alone. You've a flair for mathematics and physics. You've got looks. So what's the problem?'

'Men.'

My letter hadn't mentioned anything about problems.

'What about them?'

'They're scrumptious. Like apples. It's hard for me to stop myself. Afterwards it's a mess.'

She sat down on the seat in front of me.

'What is it you want?'

'I want to get into physics. The university is a prep school, a waiting room. I don't want to sit in a waiting room, I want to go inside, where you are. I must. I've known all along, ever since I started reading the first articles. When I was twelve someone showed me the periodic table and I understood it immediately. It was the happiest moment of my life. I understood the existence of natural laws. The way they balance out the chaos. But I don't want to understand physics from the outside. You can open the door.'

She put a hand on my arm. It was the first time I experienced the touch I, with time, would come to realise was indispensable to her. It was not merely a gesture of kindness, it was explorative. Her fingers were trying to orient themselves in my system.

'You say you're preoccupied with group field theory. And that you have personal experiences. What do you mean?'

'I evoke sincerity.'

'In what way?'

'When I'm waiting for the bus, it only takes a few minutes and the man in front of me in the queue starts telling me about his wife's illness. Once I'm inside, the woman on the seat next to me tells me how much she loves her dog. The boys getting off at the same stop as me tell me how worried they are that they won't make the first team, and then all about the girls they're secretly in love with.'

She unbuttoned my sleeve, rolled it up and turned my arm over. Her fingers explored the scars.

'I always wanted a daughter,' she said.

As soon as the words left her, she stiffened. The sentence was completely out of place. As was my reply:

'I always wanted a mother.'

People who experience it for the first time are usually taken aback. But not Andrea Fink. Her astonishment was mild. Beneath it lay an intense curiosity.

'I didn't intend to say that,' she said. 'Nor to roll up your sleeve. It was something inside me. Something strange.'

We looked at each other. When she spoke, her words came out slowly. Inside, she was scanning her own system.

'It feels like losing one's footing. As though we are no longer supported by the conventions that govern ordinary conversations. Do you have a word for it?'

'Where I grew up they called it the Susan Effect.'

She rolled down my sleeve and buttoned the cuff.

'It's not normal research. Nothing will be published. All results will be confidential. Funding will come from a separate grant. It would be an odd direction for your career.'

'I've got scars,' I said. 'I'll be a difficult pupil.'

She leaned her head back and laughed. Her laughter was a joy to her surroundings, even to the empty auditorium.

She stood up.

'Come and see me next week. I've got three sons. You're to leave them alone.'

We looked each other in the eye. Deep sincerity is always

accompanied by a feeling of the future emerging. Perhaps she and I both sensed that within six months I would have been to bed with all three sons. And a year later with her husband.

Perhaps we both knew that, given the forces that were now activated between us, I would suppress anything that might stand in the way of getting closer to her.

'Consider it carefully, Susan. And whatever you do, don't burn your bridges.'

I said nothing. Speech was unnecessary. There was no return. Not because the bridges behind me were burned, but because they had lost their relevance.

4

THERE ARE WOMEN WHO KNOW FIVE YEARS BEFORE THEY get pregnant that they're going to have two girls and a boy, and that these offspring will attend the International School and grow up multilingual and be voted Face of the Year in 2027 and study law and marry members of the Council of Ethics.

The only thing I knew was that I would have children and that I would end up cooking for them.

Which I've just done.

We eat in silence. It may be our last meal together. Even so, I assume it's okay to enjoy it.

I never enforced mealtimes. When the twins were little and thought of meals only as fuel replenishment, preferably to take place in mid-air so as not to be compelled to put feet to the ground and interrupt their games, I tended to wait and let them get on with it, to come to the table when it suited them. I think they were nine before we had the kind of immersion we've got now.

Together we savour the light tang of the salad. The sharp bite of the dressing. The pizza base, so thin it's no longer bread, just an intense taste of grain from the Italian flour, an ethereal crispness beneath the stable-like aroma of melted cheese, the tartness and sweetness of scalding-hot tomatoes and the corpulent bitterness of olives.

I will never admit it to any living person, but every time I serve the family food I feel a slight contraction of my womb. The same as when I breastfed the twins. In a way it's as if I'm still doing it. And it's not just the children, it's also the solar eclipse that is Laban Svendsen.

It's a prehistoric sensation, with a hint of something Precambrian. It has evolution and millions of years behind it, every single instance of a mammal giving milk to feed its young.

Soon we'll be a family no more. But right now we're together, and no matter how bad the situation may seem, we need nutrition.

Laban wipes his hands on his napkin. We have always used our fingers to eat pizza. Taste is not just a process localised to the palate, it's in the hands too. He opens the grey cardboard folder and lays it out in the middle of the table.

Uppermost is a black-and-white photograph. Of a woman, perhaps in her early sixties. Her hair is thick and wavy, a light shade of grey, her dazzling features striking in the Scandinavian way, a Nordic goddess straight out of Valhalla.

If it hadn't been for the clothes. And the jewellery. Around her bare neck hangs a string of large pearls that even on the photograph shimmer with the kind of resplendence produced only within the largest oysters at depths the word *imitation* cannot penetrate. Her dark woollen jumper hangs silk-like from her frame as only cashmere can.

Underneath the photo is an envelope. Laban hands it to me. I fetch a knife and slit it open. It contains one folded sheet of A4. I read the words out loud:

Magrethe Spliid. Born 1942. MA in History, employed at the Royal Danish Defence College, Department of Military History, since 1964. Consultant for NASA from 1970. US resident 1968–71. Affiliated to Yale and Cornell; US Military Academy; US Air Force Institute of Conflict Research, Michigan. Professor at the Royal Danish Defence College, Second Section, Department of Strategic and Operational Forecasting, from 1971. Permanently affiliated consultant following retirement in 2014.

Underneath, in block letters, a hand has written two telegraphic sentences:

Danish Parliamentary Future Commission – minutes of two final meetings?
    List of Commission members?

That's all.

I open my computer and type Magrethe Spliid's name into the browser's search field. All it yields is a long list of her published articles. And three small newspaper notices on the occasions of her fiftieth, sixtieth and seventieth birthdays. She is now seventy-six, but looks at least fifteen years younger.

Thit and Harald come and stand next to me. Laban remains seated. To him, a computer is a waste product. He doesn't care to touch them, won't even look at one. Most of all, his sophisticated ear cannot listen to a thing they utter.

Danish Parliamentary Future Commission produces zero hits.

I pick up our landline from the table. It's probably one of the last remaining in the country. There's a phone number on the Defence College website. I dial the number and switch on the speaker.

'Royal Danish Defence College.'

The voice at the other end belongs not to some junior office girl, more like a warrant officer of the women's reserve.

'I'd like to speak to Magrethe Spliid.'

'I'm afraid that's not possible. Can I take a message?'

'My name is Susan Svendsen. I'm a professor at the Department of Experimental Physics, Copenhagen University. Can you give me her direct number?'

'I'm afraid I'm not at liberty to divulge it.'

'Is there anything you *can* divulge?'

'I can give you the college email address.'

'That would leave me eternally indebted.'

One of the great advantages of landlines, and the real reason

I've kept ours, is that you can slam down the receiver. Which is what I do.

Laban shakes the envelope. And listens. He has always listened his way through life.

It rattles.

Onto the table he tips out a small photograph. It's a snapshot, in colour, though it must be around fifty years old, from the dawn of the technology. It looks tinted, bleached by the march of time.

But the scene it depicts isn't at all faded. Two women are seated on the terrace of the Café a Porta on Kongens Nytorv, the sun is shining, they are sharing a bottle of pink champagne and have such an air about them that even though the camera has failed to capture the queue of admirers, one instinctively knows it to be there, just outside the frame, and that it reaches all the way along Lille Kongensgade.

The first of these women is Magrethe Spliid. The way she looked in her early twenties. Rather less grave, and without the authority. But her beauty is the same.

To begin with, I don't think I know the second woman. Yet something about her face makes me uneasy.

I glance up at my family. They look surprised. Surprised that the woman is who she is. And that I have failed to recognise her.

'It's Grandmother,' says Harald. 'All sails to the wind, and afterburner ignited.'

I gather the plates.

'That girl,' says Laban. 'Laksmir, the one I went away with. She was actually a student of mine. At the conservatory.'

Thit delivers him a smile, the kind that goes straight through tissue and bone and embeds itself in the wall behind its recipient.

'So what you're saying, Dad, is that your relationship was in actual fact mostly of a musical nature?'

Laban says nothing. He's run out of road. An unfamiliar position for a man whose self-image involves the world lying at his feet.

'Mum, why hasn't Hegn given us more information?'

The question is Harald's. He likes exactness. Economy with information offends him.

I see Hegn in my mind's eye. In the prison. In the honorary residence. The curiosity he was suddenly unable to restrain.

'He's testing us,' I answer. 'Testing me. He doesn't believe in the Effect.'

5

THE FIRST TIME I LAID EYES ON LABAN'S FACE IT WAS partly concealed behind twelve kilos of freshly excavated potatoes that Andrea Fink had commandeered him into peeling.

I was nineteen and had known Andrea Fink for a couple of years, and at that point in time her home was as yet open and convivial. But the dinner parties she held in her honorary residence were not the kind at which one handed one's fur to a servant before sitting down at a resplendent table, unfolding the starched cloth napkin into one's lap and digging in.

Andrea Fink invited people for four thirty, thrust them a pinny in the hallway and led them downstairs into the scullery, in the middle of which was a wheelbarrow full of muddy leeks, and on the table a quarter part of a calf awash in its own blood. Besides the twelve kilos of potatoes Laban Svendsen was busy peeling.

The language has no adequate terms for what occurred inside me when I saw him. In a way I suppose I recognised him. Without ever having seen him.

Sometimes recognition has nothing to do with having seen each other before. Sometimes, as then, it is a sombre feeling of falling victim to an inexplicable and already existing intimacy, the origins of which cannot be pinpointed.

I turned to make myself scarce, but Andrea Fink was standing behind me. She pressed a potato peeler into my hand, and edged me around the table and deposited me opposite Laban. I was stuck.

The potatoes were small, thick-skinned and scabby, with lots of little black eyes that stared at me as if in trepidation at the fact that they were soon to be gouged out. Our hands were reddened and numbed by the cold water. We stood there facing each other, toiling without a word.

And then a young girl came up to us, sixteen years old perhaps, one of the serving staff, in uniform. One should not mistake Andrea Fink's motives. The fact of her guests being made to prepare dinner was not a matter of thrift, for Andrea was nothing if not well staffed, both in her laboratories and at home on the domestic front.

Laban looked up at the girl.

'My mother committed suicide when I was eight,' she said. 'I don't think about it that much any more. I just felt an urge to tell you both, that's all. I feel trust in you.'

Laban stared at her. From the periphery of my field of vision, people came closer. I knew something of what was happening, and yet it happened so much quicker than I had anticipated.

An elderly woman stepped in front of the girl, addressing Laban.

'Excuse me,' she said. 'May I share something with you? The doctors have told me I've slipped a disc in my spine. At the fifth vertebra. I'm so afraid I shall end up in a wheelchair.'

I took Laban to be a couple of years older than me. It was obvious that he had already notched up a good deal of practice in dealing with people's attention. And yet what was unfolding around us was another matter entirely.

'Did you have shooting pains in your legs?'

A well-known physician, a neurologist, had now joined us:

'I did, and ignored them. Man to the last. Nothing was going to stop me clearing an acre of woodland with my chainsaw. Ended up destroying the nerve. Forced me out of the hospital, my professorship.'

He demonstrated his limp. His lower leg dragged at every step, orphaned as it were, bereft of will.

'All this is making me so scared! I've always been so very afraid of death.'

This from a younger woman, otherwise hard at work on the leeks, now sucked into the maelstrom.

Laban looked like a person drowning. I took him by the arm and pulled him towards me, slowly, without turning my back on those addressing us.

We came by a side room. I drew him inside and closed the door. He stared at me.

'What was all that about? What happened?'

I would have liked to have introduced the truth to him gradually, employing the kind of pedagogical, step-by-step verifiability that is one of the traits I so love about the natural sciences. But there wasn't time for that.

'In a room such as that kitchen, in which people are gathered together, normally only a tiny fragment of reality is ever laid out on the table, presented up front, as it were. What happened there was that the rest was starting to come out.'

'Why?'

'It's something that occurs in my presence. It's always been like that. It's the bane of my life.'

The door opened and a waiter came in with a stack of trays. He halted abruptly as soon as he saw us.

'I became a dad this morning,' he said. 'Father to a little boy, at six fifteen. Three point eight kilos. I'm over the moon. His mother and I . . .'

We withdrew backwards out of the door.

'Never turn your back,' I said softly. 'Otherwise they'll come after you.'

Reaching the corridor, we closed the door behind us. Laban thought we had escaped and were safe. All I hoped for was a bit of breathing space.

But we were both too optimistic by half. The stairs up to the ground floor were blocked by a silk dress as expansive as a mandarin's cloak. The garment enshrouded a female Nobel laureate in chemistry, the revered and respected successor to Brønsted. Tears were streaming down her cheeks. As we tried to get past, she grabbed Laban by the wrist.

Her grip was tight, it seemed, for Laban stopped as if he'd walked into a door.

'You want to know why I'm crying. It's because I've been unfaithful to my husband. For years.'

If the look on Laban's face was anything to go by, it hadn't been with him. He was sweating cobs. What's more, it looked like the cold sweat of fear.

We both sensed the woman's suffering. That's the problem with the real world. It's not a stable chemical combination, but a labile solution, a large amount of which comprises anguish.

I decided to intervene.

'You've got a choice. Either leave him or come clean. Believe me, I've been studying men since I was fourteen.'

As I spoke, I held her tightly by the wrist and released Laban by levering his arm in the direction of her fingertips, away from the muscular insertions, towards the point at which her grip was weakest.

'That can't be more than a year, surely,' she said. 'Since you were fourteen.'

It was a good rejoinder, but then they're very picky about who they give the Nobel prize in chemistry to. Nevertheless, I had touched on a point, and something was now clearly sparked inside her.

Having escaped her clutches we went up the stairs.

'How did you do that?'

'When you're me,' I said, 'it's the only survival method there is. Good advice and extrication techniques.'

Between the main course and dessert it dawned on me that Laban was a composer. The source of that realisation was him performing one of his own piano sonatas and two of his own songs, amid breathless silence followed by thunderous applause.

He stepped down and seated himself opposite me.

'What do you think?'

Artists and scientists are normally far too fragile just to step down from a stage or a podium and ask for appreciation. But even at this early stage I had the first inklings of what would later be confirmed to me: that Laban Svendsen was an empiricist; that he simply possessed solid experience to the effect that there could only ever be one outcome of anything to which he put his hand. Things could only ever go well.

'I'm more into easy listening, myself,' I said.

'I was only playing for you.'

'Sorry. It's all pling-plong to me.'

I stood up.

He ducked under the table like a springboard diver and resurfaced at my side, a jack-in-the-box.

'There's something I must ask you. Are you going out with anyone?'

And then he realised what it was he'd said.

People converged on us all of a sudden. A man put his hand on Laban's arm and leaned forward.

'I've had three and a half thousand people through therapy. A lifetime of work. I'm seventy-two. In my experience . . .'

A look of panic appeared in Laban's eyes. He grabbed my arm.

'It's that Effect! Like you were talking about!'

I pulled free. He tripped along behind me into the hallway.

'Why are you leaving?'

'I've got three kids. I'm still breastfeeding the youngest. I promised their father I'd be back by ten.'

Andrea Fink was standing in the doorway of the drawing room. Laban was blocking my way out.

'I'd like to drive you home. Say hello to your husband. Sing the little one a lullaby. Of my own composition.'

I shook my head.

He stepped aside. The next moment I was free and on my own in the nightfall.

It was spring, though misty and dark. I've always been fond of darkness, and I began to run down the drive. The physical motion and encroaching night gave me a sense of having eluded a genuine peril.

6

IN THOSE DAYS, ANDREA FINK LIVED HER LIFE IN laboratories.

Her office and what she called her behaviour labs occupied half the top floor of the Department of Experimental Physics on the Universitetsparken natural science campus. Moreover, she had labs installed in the honorary residence. There wasn't a single room in which a heart monitor had not been casually left or some mobile EEG apparatus set up, or sliding blackboards installed on the wall next to plate racks or the great canvases of Vilhelm Lundstrøm that were even bigger than the boards themselves.

In front of those canvases, ten days later, I saw Laban for the second time. He was seated next to Andrea Fink and she hadn't warned me. It was our usual weekly conference.

At this historic juncture in time, a gravity had arisen in my relationship with Andrea, attributable to certain goings-on between me and members of her family – first her sons and then, more recently, her husband. She and I had yet to tie things up.

She began, as ever, without circumlocution.

'Susan inspires candour. As yet we have no idea why, though we have been conducting tests for the past nine months.'

She turned towards me.

'Laban, it seems, has a similar effect. Differently toned, but much the same. I had been entertaining a theory that the Effect might be augmented if the two of you were in the same room. That was why I brought you together. Of course, controlled observations were out of the question. But I kept my eye on you, nonetheless, in the kitchen and the dining room. I am now quite certain.'

'How have you been testing her?'

Laban was on the edge of his seat. I had remained standing.

'Susan has been conducting interviews for the police, of so-called diehard deniers, people involved in organised crime. Individuals the police had given up on. It was by far the most appropriate line of experiment. In such cases we can be sure of objectified resistance to sincerity. During the course of our studies Susan has interviewed a total of seventeen subjects, each with between twelve and fifty-eight hours of police questioning behind them without having divulged a thing. In our case, twelve of the seventeen came clean after two hours. A further three after four to six hours.'

He counted on his fingers.

'And the last one?'

'She became psychotic.'

Laban stared dreamily into space. And then, for the first time, I was confronted with the acuteness of his thinking.

'What about the ethical side of that? Doing physical experiments by questioning criminals?'

Andrea Fink looked away.

'Funding doesn't come on its own. The Ministry of Justice and the Defence Command are willing to pay for new developments in interrogation techniques. And we get to investigate an important phenomenon.'

Laban said nothing.

'It's humane. The Effect is humane. Unlike many other procedures.'

Laban still said nothing. His silence drew her up from her chair.

'That's the problem of physics. It's always been financed like this. That's what Fermi meant when he said that regardless of what else the atom bomb might be, it was great physics.'

They both looked at me. It was my turn.

'You exploited me and Laban as guinea pigs,' I said. 'Without our knowledge.'

'I did warn you,' she said. 'Right from day one.'

I collected myself and turned to leave. Laban blocked my exit.

'I'll walk you.'

'My husband's waiting for me outside.'

'I've looked into that. You haven't got a husband. And no kids either.'

I leaned towards him.

'Laban,' I said, 'you've seen me for the last time. And while that may seem harsh to you at this moment, I can assure you that in the long run you'll be very, very happy about it indeed.'

He stepped sideways, but kept looking straight at me.

'Aah,' he said. 'So candour's not the only thing in your repertoire.'

The door closed behind me.

There was a briskness in my step as I walked down the driveway. The exchange had left a pleasant taste in my mouth. I'd drawn a line, necessarily so, and put up a warning sign telling people to think again if ever they tried to erase it.

7

IT'S QUARTER TO TEN IN THE MORNING, AND THE ROOM Harald and I enter is at least 150 square metres in area and illuminated by a flood of slanting light that streams in through great, arched windows extending all the way to the floor.

I cling to my crutch. Along one wall there is a bar, some thirty children aged between nine and twelve straggled along its length: boys in black tights and white T-shirts, girls in leotards and grey leg warmers. Next to the wall is a piano, and at the piano sits a young man.

Neither the children nor the pianist pay any attention to Harald and me. Their focus is fully directed towards the woman standing over by the windows.

Above the soft tones of the piano she guides the children through the barre exercises of classical ballet. And as she speaks, gently and yet insistently, she dances.

She is sixty-five years old, and throughout those sixty-five years she has driven her constitution to its every limit, for which reason it is not in the conventional, physical sense that she dances.

But conventional is something she has never been, and dance is at heart not physical at all. Most profoundly, its movements issue from a place far deeper inside us than the physical form, and from that place inside her it flows as yet unhindered, even now, with her physique soon depleted.

We have seen it so many times before, Harald and I, and still we are transfixed, rooted to the spot by equal parts respect and fascination.

The windows face out onto Kongens Nytorv, and we are in the great practice room of the Royal Danish Ballet's children's school.

With a gesture she indicates that the lesson is over. The pupils and pianist applaud, darting looks of appreciative adulation in her direction as they leave the room.

Beneath the odour of perspiration and perfume that lingers in the space they leave behind is a fragrance of fresh apple, and when finally the last of her pupils has closed the door she brings the apples forth.

They are of the sort called Filippa and have been picked, pressed, fermented and distilled by Aqua Vitae on the island of Fyn, and are now an intense, glassy aquavit of some forty per cent proof. She raises her glass towards us in greeting and knocks back the greater part of its contents. Whereupon she glides across the floor and embraces us both at once.

She is a head taller than I, and her body is as hard as polished wood: a frightening sight whenever naked, a bit like an illustrative plate in a textbook of human anatomy, devoid of the subcutis, all muscular fibres and fasciae exposed.

I place my hands against her cheeks, drawing her forehead towards mine.

'Hello, Mum,' I say.

She pulls free and raises her glass again.

'*Skål*, dear. You too, diddums.'

My mother doesn't have a cramped little dressing room like the other instructors at the Royal Theatre. She has an office, into which we now step. The window affords a view across the imposing square with the elliptical parterre of the Krinsen at its centre, and in terms of floor space the room is but a few square centimetres smaller than those of the artistic directors of the theatre's Playhouse and Ballet.

There are two reasons for such distinguished accommodation.

The first is that classical ballet, like deep natural science, is taught in the spirit of the apprenticeship. The Royal Danish Ballet comprises a wealth of excellent dancers, but only a select few keepers of the seal whose artistic capacity and phenomenal memory bear forward the essence of the tradition. As such, there is a direct line of descendence from August Bournonville, down through the great dancers of the twentieth century, to Lander and Brenaa and Bruhn, and through them to my mother.

That's one reason for the office. The other has to do with the way she is as a person. While she may appear to hover transcendentally – as if, unlike the rest of us, she does not have to contend with gravitational acceleration at all, but floats upon the ether when rising from a chair or seating herself in a taxi – there is a deeper part of her that moves upon the earth. Few people would not go to great lengths in order to avoid getting in her way.

'Who's Magrethe Spliid?'

It's a year since we saw each other last. I don't know what sort of opening line she might have been expecting, but it was hardly that.

'Never heard of her.'

I place the photo in front of her. She is seated at her desk. She puts on her glasses. Studies the photo. Puts it down.

'Sorry, I don't recall ever having set eyes on the woman. If I did it must have been a very casual encounter. You know how many thousands of people I run into all the time.'

She looks me in the eye. Then she looks at Harald. Then she savours a long sip from her tall, slender glass.

She's always been an alcoholic. Or rather: she's always been dependent. The alcohol didn't start until she stopped dancing at the age of forty-five. Before that it was pills. And men. And the attentions of an audience.

In a way, her relationship to dance has always been a kind of alcoholism.

'We got into some bother in India,' I said. 'That's why we're home. We're under charges and risk going to prison. I'm looking at twenty-five years.'

'They'll reduce your sentences. For good behaviour. I'll send you parcels, delicacies.'

Sooner or later all alcoholics proceed to comprehensive ethical collapse, when the sheer weight of wasted life tips the cart. But not my mother. There are those who would incline to believe that in her case all is already lost, that no ethics exist to collapse.

'There'll be a big court case,' I say. 'The press are bound to mention your name. What would that do for your position here at the theatre?'

She puts the glass down.

'You're trying to blackmail me!'

I step up to the desk and lean across it.

'I'm Thit's and Harald's mother. Until they're safe, I'll blackmail whoever's around.'

She picks up the glass and takes another sip. Only this time without the savouring. This time she's taking her medicine.

'What have they got you charged with, dear?'

'Intent to kill.'

'Who?'

'A lover.'

'And what did he do to arouse your displeasure?'

'He tried to rape me. I'd finished with him.'

The panes of her office windows must be made of a special kind of glass, since hardly a sound penetrates from the eternal traffic outside.

'Where did we go wrong, your father and I? Since you made do with intent?'

I seat myself on the edge of the desk.

'The goodness of my heart got the better of me,' I say.

We look at each other. She sniggers. I likewise. I'm through to her: mother and daughter understand each other. It feels nice.

36

The office is practically wallpapered with photographs, meticulously framed and hung: Harald Lander, Erik Bruhn, Nureyev, Baryshnikov, Suzanne Farrell, Peter Martins, Peter Schaufuss, Margot Fonteyn. All signed with fluttering kisses of dedication. My mother gets to her feet and steps up to a photo hung at eye level.

It's bigger than the others and shows a young man and a young woman on horseback. Both are tanned, captured in a gallop, radiant with life, and though the photograph itself is black and white and more than forty years old, one has the distinct feeling it could have been taken yesterday. You can smell the woods and the wind, the sun on their skin.

And the money. The picture reeks of money.

It's a photograph of my father and mother. At one of his hunting lodges, seemingly the one at Rold Skov.

My mother likes to dwell on that picture. Especially when I'm here. That's how it is with the great traumas. We keep returning to them. To remind ourselves of how irrevocably too late it is to do anything about them. And yet also to continue looking for some way out.

Preferably, we would like to have witnesses to our tragedies. Especially my mother. If she could, she would sell tickets and gather an audience for everything she did, including going to the bathroom.

'What do you want with that witch Magrethe?'

'There's something I need to ask her. If she can answer me it'll buy us out of the charges.'

'You'll get nothing from her. She's like a clam. It's twenty years since I last had anything to do with her. She was living by the city lakes then, but she's moved now. No one seems to know where. She worked for the Defence Command. Still does, I shouldn't wonder. Never let on about what exactly she did, but whatever it was it was secret. She had an office at the Svanemøllen Barracks. I found out quite by chance. The army had their physical education school there. They ran obligatory courses in ballroom dancing. Only the best teachers were good enough. I used to substitute there for a couple of years, the pay was quite respectable. One day I saw her going into one of the buildings. After that, we met up there a few times, on Friday afternoons when I wasn't rehearsing, and walked into town together.'

'How do I get hold of her?'

She dips into a drawer and retrieves a card bearing her steel-plate-printed initials. A broad-edged pen for that very particular calligraphy when signing photographs or programmes. And then she draws.

'This is the bridge over the railway cutting, leading to the former barracks area. Unless you're authorised there's no entry now, after they built all those company headquarters it's all closed off with a barrier and security. You'll have to get past, one way or another. The building she works in is in the far corner. The sports ground that belonged to the PE school is still there, backing onto it all.'

She draws the swoop of an elliptical running track. Behind it a rectangle. At the rectangle's north-western corner she draws an X.

'She was always quite libidinous about sticking to routines. Precise as clockwork. Up at the crack of dawn to start work at four. Then at eleven she'd be here. Every day, Christmas and birthdays included.'

She hands me the card.

'Am I to be concerned about you, dear?'

Ninety-nine per cent of parents feel guilty about their children's downturns. Their grandchildren's, too. But not my mother.

Nonetheless, I seem to trace a hint of sympathy. It would be sensational.

I put my hands to her cheeks by way of farewell. Her eyes, as ever, contain elements of train wrecks and maritime disasters. And some smidgeon of religious ecstasy.

She looks at Harald. If it makes sense to say my mother has a favourite person besides herself, then he is it. At unguarded moments I have seen her looking at him the way the wolf looked at Little Red Riding Hood. Wishing he were a few years older and that she wasn't his grandmother.

'You've grown, diddums, since I saw you last. And it's not just the year that's gone in the meantime either.'

Harald gives her a toothy smile.

'I'm staring at a four-year sentence, Gran. It's kind of a coming-of-age thing. If you know what I mean.'

We back our way out. She stares as we leave, and I blow her a finger kiss. Then shut the door behind us.

8

A BRIGHT SUN SHINES OVER KONGENS NYTORV. I PAUSE before starting the car.

The car is the only chance a parent gets for communing with the kids. Only when the twins were buckled in and unable to make a jump for it in traffic was there ever any chance of talking to them about life and death.

That came to an end when they got to be nine years old and insisted on taking buses and trains all on their own. Since then I've had to make do with occasional, exceedingly rare moments such as this on Kongens Nytorv. That's why I hesitate to turn the ignition.

'Mum, how exactly do you feel about Gran?'

He's never asked me that before. Nobody has, not even myself.

I start the car regardless, and pull out into the traffic. To ease some of the pressure inside.

The opposite lane has been blocked by a protest. Thousands of people, presumably marching on Christiansborg, seat of the Danish parliament, the Folketing. The traffic is at a standstill and we're stuck in the tailback.

'She was away touring a lot,' I say. 'I never saw her that much.'

He says nothing. And yet he's not letting me off the hook. Eventually, I proffer this:

'I stood waiting for her outside school one day. She'd

promised to collect me, I hadn't seen her for two months. She never turned up. I stood there by the gate, waiting while the school gradually emptied. After three-quarters of an hour I knew she wasn't coming. I began to walk. I walked all the way home to Havnegade, where we lived in one of the theatre's apartments. Along the way I realised something. I realised I still loved her. No matter what.'

The line of cars begins to move. A placard held by one of the protesters says something about the price of milk.

'What's with the price of milk?' I ask.

Harald is the only one in the family who reads newspapers.

'It follows the price of energy. It's gone up a hundred per cent while we've been away.'

We pass the laboratories of the national energy company on Gothersgade, the Department of Geology, the Department of Microbiology, the Panum Institute, the Rigshospital, the Copenhagen University Faculty Library of Natural and Health Sciences, the H.C. Ørsted Institute on Nørre Allé, the Natural History Museum, the Centre for Particle Physics on Jagtvej.

This is how I get my bearings in Copenhagen. The city is a relief map of natural science institutions. They can be trusted.

Never mind about the Folketing, never mind about the media and the arts. Never mind about the price of milk. If one day I should ever come back and find the Niels Bohr Institute abandoned and boarded up, civilisation will surely be on the brink of definitive collapse.

We pass Svanemøllen Station and I turn onto the bridge over the railway cutting. It ends at a barrier and a security cabin, out of which steps a young man wearing a grey uniform, not of the military but a security firm's.

A forest of buildings has gone up since I was here last, vertically aspiring fifteen-storey office complexes that tell us it's not only our family who is doing well, the entire economy is booming and on its way upwards to the infinite universe beyond.

On a little open space is a low cylindrical structure clad with plates of polished steel, one of eight points of service access to the Copenhagen Collider, which, when it gets finished in five years' time, will be the biggest particle accelerator in the world, ten per cent longer and forty per cent more powerful than CERN's Hadron Collider.

I produce my University of Copenhagen ID. Glancing up at the office fronts, I select the first name I recognise and hand him the card.

'I'm due in a meeting about the collider. At COWI.'

He looks down at his clipboard.

'I'm afraid you're not on my list.'

He is a polite and correct young man, at most five years older than Harald. Standing there on the frozen concrete he's as handsome as a prince in a ballet. There's an open book tucked under his arm. Twisting my head I can see it's the sonnets of William Shakespeare. A name that might be familiar to some, but not to me.

'That's a shame,' I tell him. 'Because you can pencil me onto your dance card any day. How about it?'

The bloom of his embarrassment begins beneath his eyes, extends down through his cheeks and vanishes underneath his collar at the knot of his tie. Some women might have been interested in following its anatomical journey to conclusion.

The barrier goes up. We're in.

I can sense Harald looking at me in a way he never has before. And I know exactly what he's doing. He's trying – possibly for the first time ever – to see his mother through the eyes of another man.

'You made him blush, Mum. He was embarrassed.'

'It's only a flesh wound,' I tell him. 'Underneath, he was flattered as hell.'

9

THE BUILDING MARKED ON MY MOTHER'S DRAWING AS
Magrethe Spliid's workplace doesn't look much like a college of
anything. It looks like any other office building, thrown up
with a bare minimum of budget and too little understanding of
the fact that once a building is up the rest of us have to look at
it until it falls down or gets dozed.

The car park, however, tells another story, of no expense
spared. It's as big as a football pitch. Perhaps the Royal Danish
Defence College, Second Section, gets a lot of visitors.

As we cross through it, Harald gives my arm a little squeeze.

The gesture is profound. Harald is not wont to be profuse
with his affections. Especially not with me.

Until he was eight he could hardly do without his mother. If
we watched a film together or I read out loud to him, his hands
would stroke my skin. One day when I picked him up from kindergarten he called the other kids together so they could feel
how soft my cheeks were. I had to kneel down while thirty
children put their hands on me one by one with Harald looking
on, solemn and proud at being able to share out his mother's
warmth.

It all stopped when he was eight. One day I opened my arms
to him the way I always did, but he wouldn't come. He stood
there, half a metre away, looking at me.

A process had been initiated, for which the psychologists
doubtless will be able to provide any number of porous

43

explanations, but whose brutal reality is that there will come a day when a mother will have held her child close for the last time, and when significant evidence will thereby be presented to indicate that love is never deep but merely a Darwinist illusion, made up to make sure parents and other animals take care of their young.

What remains between Harald and me is a very occasional and sudden physical intimacy such as this squeeze of my arm. I know the reason for it. The reason is the excavator.

Any other mother, and most fathers too, would call it a digger, as they would call the excavation it has made a hole, and most likely they wouldn't notice one way or another. But we're not like them. Harald grew up with a mother who knows the difference between a grab crusher and what we now pass by, which from a distance we have already identified as a thirty-five-ton Volvo excavator with a reach of some eight metres, meaning that I don't need to peer into the excavation to satisfy myself that what they're doing is laying sewage pipes with an internal diameter of ninety centimetres and a nominal life expectancy of a hundred and twenty years, and a minimum fall of twenty-five millimetres per running metre.

Harald's squeeze of my arm is wordless acknowledgement of the fact that much may be said of his mother and the rest of his family, but when it comes to the outside world he's been pretty much filled in on what's what.

To the west, the area is penned in by a five-metre-high fence of wire mesh topped by two tiers of barbed wire, an announcement to the effect that the defence college sports ground isn't for just anyone to kick a ball about in.

Even if it is rather inviting. The pitches are mown and rollered, and despite the frosty weather they seem to be bursting with health and chlorophyll.

Five metres behind the fence is a small circle of gravel, and in the centre of that circle stands Magrethe Spliid.

She looks like her photograph. Her body, however, is

surprising. She is the most rectangular person I've ever seen. Her shoulders are right angles, her torso could have been constructed out of cubes. And yet, quite unfathomably, it is feminine.

She is wearing a tracksuit, is standing side on and hasn't seen us. She leans forward, begins to rotate about her own axis, and only then do we see what she holds in her hand. A discus.

Her spiralling acceleration is so fast I've only ever seen the like in animals and machines. Moreover, it is so perfectly centred one can almost perceive a physical, unwavering plumb line descending through the middle of the motion.

She releases the heavy disc by allowing it to slip from the crook of her index finger, lending to it a lateral spin that makes it draw a flat parabola in the air.

It remains there for so long she is able to interrupt her movement, straighten her back into the dignified upright, lift her hand to shield her eyes from the sun, and still have time to savour the final phase of its arching flight.

She strides the long way to the point of impact and her gait is elastic and ground-gaining as a riding horse's. As she picks up the discus, she sees us.

She comes slowly towards the fence, stopping a couple of metres away from it.

'Susan Svendsen,' I say. 'University of Copenhagen, Department of Experimental Physics. I was hoping you could help me with a couple of questions.'

'And what might they be?'

'What was the outcome of the Future Commission's final meeting?'

It transpires that the fence between us isn't merely physical. It's inside her, too. She has locked the doors and barred the windows, and now she peers out at us through the slot of a letterbox. After a moment, she turns away and starts walking.

'I'm in trouble,' I say. 'I've got a prison sentence hanging over me. If I can get my hands on the minutes of that meeting they'll drop all charges.'

Behind me, Harald shuffles impatiently. He prefers the sophisticated approach to life and has been hoping I would tip-toe into this encounter wearing ballet shoes and velvet gloves.

'I'm Lana's daughter,' I say. 'Lana Levinsen.'

She stops and comes back, all the way up to the fence, where she stands and studies me, then Harald.

A flicker passes over her face. The letterbox snaps shut.

'Sorry,' she says. 'Can't help.'

And there she is, on her way again.

'My son Harald here will go to jail!'

I'm talking to the back of her head. It becomes ever more distant with each stride.

'A phone number,' I shout. 'A way of getting in touch! You're our only chance!'

She vanishes into the low, black sheds that edge the running track.

Harald looks at me, mute with unspoken reproach.

10

WE GO BACK TO THE CAR.

I stop at the excavation. The excavator's cab was empty before. Now there's a man in it.

Andrea Fink once said to me she thought there should be a workman in every woman's life.

I disagree with her about that. One can never be enough. I believe there should be at least half a dozen workmen in any woman's life.

I love to watch them do what they do. Men at labour. The way their energy can be so expertly focused and directed towards the job at hand, at the same time as they are unaware, or perhaps have a very slight inkling, that you're standing there watching them, relishing their bodies in their meticulous procedures, their complete and utter oblivious immersion.

Even now I pause and try to make eye contact with the man in the cab. Or perhaps especially now, for I've never believed a woman needs to be done up to relish a man, needs to present herself in a certain kind of packaging, at a certain time of day, with immaculate hair and her heart in the right place. Personally, I can drool over a man anytime. And when one day they whisk me off, I hope the porters at my psychiatric rest home will look just like workmen.

But the man in the excavator isn't looking.

Some people are always searching for signs. As if life were tea leaves in which fortunes could be told. I don't belong to that

47

category. Nevertheless, there's something about his looking the other way that I don't like.

And it's not just my female vanity that's bothered, either. It's my common sense.

I'm three metres from the excavator. At that kind of distance, the Effect can be very intense.

Candour is a scalar phenomenon. From the massive suppressions of truth all of us live with to the extremes of unguardedness that, if allowed to occur, leave behind them a reality in which nothing ever again is the same. Somewhere in between, a few notches along the scale, is the high voltage that exists between man and woman.

That tension is one of the first things to become apparent whenever a woman, however briefly, moves into the vicinity of a man.

It's not that I'm waiting for him to leap down from his Volvo, throw himself in the mud and propose marriage. But he ought at least to turn his head and thereby acknowledge what he and I both know: a woman with an open mind is standing looking at him.

But he doesn't, and the fact makes me pensive. And in that frame of mind I go back to the car with Harald.

It's not on its own any more. On one side of it a lorry has parked, on the other a van.

Both are empty.

Their drivers had the entire car park at their disposal. And yet they parked here, smack up against us. And after that they went away.

We get inside. At that same instant, the excavator starts its engine.

In experimental physics, structure and repetition are closely linked. You hardly ever see the pattern at first blush. It's only at the second or third repetition you realise something systematic is going on.

When the excavator raises its bucket and starts to move, the tea leaves suddenly reveal a pattern. Our car is trapped in a cul-de-sac. We've got a wall behind us and a vehicle on each side.

'Don't shut the door,' I say.

It's been years since I last gave Harald an order, and this is the non-negotiable sort. He leaves his door open.

'When I give the word, I want you to duck down under that lorry next to you. Once you're there, slam the car door shut.'

His face is a blank. The cab of the excavator is situated high up. Eight metres from the car and the driver can't see us any more.

'Now!'

We slither out of our respective doors. The excavator bears down on us. Nevertheless, I manage to grab my bag and crutch. We slam the doors. If we're lucky it'll look like we're still in the car and getting ready to pull out.

The noise is tremendous. It's not from the engine but from the caterpillar tracks, their transverse ribs of hardened steel. The vehicle is so heavy the sheer inertia means its acceleration occurs in slow motion. But the hydraulics of the arm and bucket cylinders are of a different amplitude altogether. The driver has tipped back the bucket and brings it down on our car like an axe, splitting it in two down the middle just behind the windscreen, where seconds ago Harald and I sat.

The motion has a gentle ease about it, as if what was being parted were a 500-kilo brick of freshly patted butter left out in the sun.

The vehicle continues its forward movement, crushing the car beneath it and stopping at the wall before reversing back out. Each of its caterpillar tracks is a metre wide. Our VW Passat has been compressed into a plate of tin and vinyl.

The excavator draws away and comes to a halt. The engine is switched off. The driver gets out.

In that elevated, irrational state of clarity that mortal danger engenders, it's his shoes I notice. If truth be told, they're about the only thing I can see from my vantage point flat out under the van.

They're eye-catchingly new and elegant, in grey leather, snug as moccasins.

He doesn't hang about. That's another thing I notice. He couldn't care less about our car.

Logically I suppose it makes sense. Nevertheless, the fact of it is striking. Not many people in this world wouldn't pause to look back in a situation like this. But he walks away. A car has driven into the car park. He opens the back door and gets in.

I look into Harald's eyes. His face is chalk.

The car pulls away. We watch as it heads off between the office buildings, vanishing momentarily from sight, then re-appearing at the security gate. The barrier goes up, the car sweeps up the bridge over the railway cutting, turns onto Ryvangs Allé and is consumed by the flow of traffic.

We wriggle out on our stomachs, though without getting to our feet. Instead, we sit up and lean back against the wall in the sun.

I feel like saying something, only language seems to have left me.

Ten metres away, a figure is staring at us. It's Magrethe Spliid.

'I suggest we go to my office,' she says.

11

SHE LEADS US NOT TO THE MAIN ENTRANCE BUT TO THE side of the building that faces the sports ground. She keys in a code and presses her fingertips against a biometric sensor, a door opens and we step into a back stairwell. I know I'm going to start shaking, but at that moment I am calm and collected, in some kind of survival mode. All thought is suspended, all senses enhanced. The stairs are cast in terrazzo. I recognise the individual varieties of stone: quartz, granite, marble, little shards of shale. We ascend to the second floor, proceeding through empty corridors lined with rows of closed doors, before coming to her office and being ushered inside.

It's spacious, occupying a corner of the building, windows looking out onto the running track and the railway line. She produces a bottle of mineral water from a built-in refrigerator and pours three glasses. From a shelf she takes a silicone mask mounted on a short, transparent plastic cylinder, inside which is an aerosol canister. She puts the mask to her face, presses down on the canister and breathes deeply in and out.

'Chronic bronchitis. Smoke poisoning when I was a child.'

There's something mechanical about her movements: she is quite as shocked as we. She turns the centre of the discus with a twirling finger, absently almost, loosening a small plate, and from the recess it conceals she removes a number of small lead ingots and places them on the desk. I understand immediately. She trains using a heavier discus than the standard for competition. The realisation tallies with my first impression: this is a woman on the constant lookout for ways of pushing the limits in order to make things work in her favour.

She looks at Harald, gauging his age and mental constitution. Then she nudges a phone across the desk towards me.

'The police?'

'Officially we're still abroad.'

The shakes set in and I feel the need to move about. The office is as big as a living room, tastefully done out in grey. Her tracksuit is grey, too. The only colour in the room comes from the photos on the wall.

They're not of her family. For some reason I know she hasn't got one. Instead, they depict the pyrolytic phenomena commonly known as mushroom clouds. They are photos of the earliest hydrogen bomb tests, before they went underground in 1961.

There are perhaps fifty pictures: some black and white, others in colour, some taken from planes, others from boats, others still from the land. Each is marked with the date, location and explosive yield of the device measured in tons of TNT: *1 November 1952, Eniwetok, 10.4 megatons, of which 15–20 per cent from fusion. 6 August 1945, Hiroshima, 15 kilotons. Bikini, 1 March 1954, 15 megatons. 27 December 1960, Reggane, Algeria, 1.6 kilotons. 4 September 1961, Semipalatinsk, 150 kilotons. 6 October 1962, Johnston Island, 11.3 kilotons.*

'I had NASA make them public,' she says. 'Fifteen years ago.'

Each image possesses a beauty that is at once inhuman and irresistible.

Where the photos end, a glass-fronted cabinet runs from floor to ceiling, and behind its doors are her sports trophies. There must be at least a hundred. In the absolute centre is her Olympic silver medal.

'My Danish record still stands, forty years on. If it hadn't been for anabolic steroids, I'd have won gold in Moscow in 1980. Susanne Nielsson too, in the hundred-metre breaststroke.

They took more than nine thousand blood tests, and not one came out positive. Science has made it difficult indeed to find out what's real and what isn't.'

That's aimed at me.

'I'm a physicist,' I tell her. 'Doping's more the chemists.'

I sense her natural reserve. Normally she wouldn't be talking about herself at all. But it's the shock. And the Effect. Through this breach I try to reach her.

'What is the Future Commission?'

'You mean *was*. It was abolished in 2018.'

'When was it first set up?'

'The early seventies.'

She answers like a robot.

'To what purpose?'

'To advise changing governments.'

Now my legs are shaking. I walk up and down, struggling to regain control of my muscles.

'Why was it secret?'

'To ensure its political and scientific independence. To protect its members against outside pressure.'

'Who picked them out?'

'After a couple of years the commission was self-elective.'

I pause at a noticeboard on the wall, a cheerful collage of photographs depicting burning cities. Cities being destroyed by firestorms. The flames have that white intensity that occurs at temperatures in excess of one thousand degrees centigrade. Below them are names and dates: *Dresden, 13–14 February 1945. Hamburg, 27 July 1943. Cologne, 20 May 1942. Tokyo, 10 March 1945.* Highlights of the Allied bombings of civilians during the Second World War.

She stands right behind me.

'I was there myself. In Dresden. I was three years old. My father was German. He died at the Eastern front. I lived with my mother. It's where I got the bronchitis. Who promised you the charges would be dropped?'

'His name's Thorkild Hegn. Do you know him?'

She says nothing. But I'm through to her.

'Secrecy,' I say, 'is not a very Danish concept. If the idea was to protect the commission's members, then the Economic Council might just as well be top secret, too.'

'It was. In the years before it was established, there were plans to keep it from the public. Transparency didn't come into it until later, in the final months of . . .'

She hesitates as if trying to recall.

'Autumn 1962,' says Harald. 'The chairmanship was Hoff-meyer, Carl Iversen and Søren Gammelgaard.'

She is silent for a moment. The way people are when Harald enters the fray in the great quiz of life.

'He's got a memory like flypaper,' I say. 'Has done ever since birth. You wouldn't believe the stuff he keeps in there.'

'But the idea of a watchdog economic council goes back further,' she says. 'The secrecy was Kampmann's pet idea, from his time as finance minister back in the fifties, to safeguard it by preserving the anonymity of its members. But Kjeld Philip was social-liberal and against any kind of hush-hush. Kampmann wanted no one else but the members themselves to know who was involved.'

My whole body is trembling now. I feel my concentration beginning to wane. I pick up the phone to call a taxi.

'I'll drive you home,' she says.

We climb into her Mercedes in the building's underground car park.

I ask her to stop at the remains of our car. I get out, opening the driver's door of the lorry first, then the van. Levering myself on my crutch, I clamber onto the excavator's caterpillar tracks and peer inside the cab before getting back in the Mercedes, on the back seat next to Harald.

We pass over the railway cutting. My ballet prince looks up

54

pensively from his Shakespeare. Maybe he's wondering why we're not going home in our Passat.

'What were you looking for in the vehicles, Mum?'

'How the ignitions were started.'

Hellerup glides past in the frosty sun, smug and oblivious.

'So how were they started?'

'A lock pick, perhaps. But that would leave lots of little scratches. And the van was a Mercedes. A Mercedes lock can't be picked. It has to have been some other way.'

'Like what?'

I refrain from answering.

'How come you know how to steal cars, Mum?'

We pass the Charlottenlund Fort. Out in the glittering Øresund, a new complex of buildings has risen up. When we left for India the Kronholm Islets were flat bird sanctuaries, like the nearby Saltholm, hardly visible from land at all, but now they're gigantic building sites. One of the structures is as big as a tower block, though twisted, like a seashell of steel and glass. North of the islets there's now a small windfarm.

'I was in care for a few years.'

'You never told me that.'

We park on Evighedsvej. Harald gets out. I lean forward, towards Magrethe Spliid.

'Harald and I almost didn't make it,' I tell her. 'And they've seen us talking to you. If I were you, I'd lock my door tonight and put the chain on. And drag your biggest wardrobe in front of the window for good measure.'

I climb out, but she's after me in a split second. The door inside her is wide open now. There are lots of ways to gain access to a person.

'I'm not afraid!'

'You're afraid to give me the minutes of a meeting of a now defunct commission. Those minutes could be the difference between life and death.'

'You're better off without them.'

'Then you should have told that to the driver of that excavator.'

I rummage in my bag and hand her my card. It's not of normal dimensions, but big as a postcard from a seaside holiday town.

She stares at it.

'Isn't this rather on the large side for a calling card?'

'There's no room for all my titles on a normal one.'

She scans the list: the professorship; the board and committee memberships of the Council for Research Policy and Planning, the Council for Development Research, the National Research Foundation, the government's Growth Forum, Euroscience, the European University Association, Danida, UNESCO.

'That's one reason,' I say. 'Another is that if you want to be remembered in a society that generates twenty petabytes of information per day, and you happen to be a woman and forty-three years old, you need to talk in rather a loud voice.'

'I wasn't there. At the final meetings. I wasn't present.'

She gets back in the car.

'Who does Hegn work for?' I ask. 'What part of the state apparatus does he represent? Police? Military?'

She shakes her head.

'Where does he live? Do you know his home address?'

She slams the door shut.

But then an afterthought makes her roll down the window.

'What you said about a loud voice. That bit's right.'

The window glides up and the big car pulls away.

Harald is standing stock-still on the pavement. He's not looking at the car, he's looking at me. Imploringly.

'The Effect, Mum. We always turned it on others. Never on ourselves.'

I walk past him and into the house.

12

WE'RE SEATED AROUND THE DINING TABLE, WHICH IS A
seventeen-hundred-year-old circle.

More exactly, it's the wood that's seventeen hundred years
old. It comes from an oak my great-great-grandfather found
whilst digging for peat on his property at Raadvad. He had it
sawn into boards and made into two tables, one for his armoury
and another for his dining room, which is the one that has
remained in the family.

He must have been a perfectionist, and he must have loved
wood. The boards are quarter-sawn, the lip exquisitely rounded.
The table has survived a hundred and fifty years without the
slightest warp.

The tannin present in peat bogs turns oak black and ren-
ders it hard as stone and utterly imperishable. The beauty of it
seems almost unreal. When I was pregnant with the twins I
removed the eighteenth-century varnish with caustic soda. Delicately varnished surfaces do not accord with small children,
nor with their parents. Since then I've scrubbed the table once
a fortnight, which has lent the pitch-coloured wood a tinge
of grey.

The table is the only thing I have of my father's. It's the only
thing I want. When your parents take up as much space inside
you as mine, you should be especially careful about filling up
your home with their junk as well.

But I love the table. Its oak is heavy and immovable, resistant to change. Which is an illusory kind of assurance that at least one thing in the world can be relied upon to remain the same.

It's just the kind of assurance I need now.

I've told Laban and Thit about the day Harald and I have had. Whereupon a stunned silence ensued of some length, during which I made dinner and the other three stared vacantly into space.

When eventually I serve the food, they eat nothing to begin with, even though it's fillets of lamb, fried for twenty-five and a half seconds on each side, then let a tablespoon of fifty per cent double cream simmer in the pan. And still they gawp, oblivious. Until eventually, Laban breaks the silence.

'Thit and I have been to the Folketing's library. A sudden impulse, you could say. We looked up the chief librarian there. She's an old friend, appointed by the parliament's Presidium. I know most of them, actually, and the director's another friend of mine. Anyway, it's on the second floor, directly above the main lobby. I told her I'd been commissioned to compose a festival cantata, for the parliament's one hundred and seventieth anniversary. That I wanted to make a head start and begin by looking at some key events in its history. I gave her a list. On it was the phrase *Parliamentary Future Commission*.'

For Laban to tell a lie intentionally is something of a novelty.

I put the mixing bowl with the whisk down on the table in front of Thit. She starts to whip the cream. When her arm begins to tire, she'll pass it on to Harald, as she has always done. I peel the oranges.

'We were received most convivially.'

That's how it is with Laban. If one day he should ever pay a visit to Hell, he will be received most convivially there by the Devil himself and all his hideous assistants.

'The library and the archive deliver information to the entire parliament, on all imaginable subjects. Moreover, the chief librarian is responsible for keeping the archives. She gathers our political history, you could say. She'd never heard of the Future Commission.'

'She heard what he said all right,' says Thit. 'He read out all the different words on his list, and she kept nodding. Only then when he got to *Future Commission* there was no reaction, just mild surprise. She was blank. Completely blank.'

With Thit and Laban at a range of half a metre, even a trained pathological liar wouldn't be able to hide anything.

'She went into the archives,' Laban says. 'She told us they've got everything digitalised as far back as Johan Pingel's speech in 1885 that triggered the failed assassination attempt on Prime Minister Estrup. So she types in *Future Commission*, but nothing comes up. Then she tells us she's going a step further up in the system. The archive is organised in a hierarchy with different levels of confidentiality. At the second level are all the sensitive data on individual persons plus all cases that are exempt from the law on open administration. Certain documents of the Foreign Policy Committee and the European Affairs Committee. She doesn't find anything there either. I ask if she can dig a bit deeper. "We're not really allowed," she says. But nevertheless she carries on. At the third level are documents pertaining to the security of the nation. Limited access even to the Presidium. And there she finds it. But the files are barred. She says there's a kind of upper tier, a fourth level, with information that's privileged indefinitely. But then we sense she gets the jitters, so we back off. Smooth over, and return to the conviviality of before.'

I spoon out the fruit salad.

'There's another little detail,' says Thit. 'While she was searching I was looking at this picture she had on the wall. Old-fashioned, but cool, all the same.'

'Hammershøi,' Laban says. 'Christiansborg seen from Gammel Strand.'

'It was on the wall behind her. So I stand there looking at it with my back to her, doing my make-up at the same time.'

Thit's relationship to make-up is hard to explain. It's passionate, but also exotic. She daubs it on the same way she dresses: extravagantly, especially around the eyes, as if bent on demonstrating that, to her, every day is a celebration of Cleopatra's ascension to the throne. And always she has with her a palette in a compact case in order to touch up the overall impression.

In that compact case is a little mirror. Thit spends a lot of time in front of mirrors. And like anyone else in that habit, she is used to orienting herself in a world in reverse. In her case, she can read a three-page back-to-front email as fast as any regular one.

'I couldn't help noticing her three passwords,' she says.

Laban pauses, spoon in hand.

'Susan. Would you say a few words?'

All families have their little rituals. In ours, the others have always wanted me to present the food, to attach a brief description to each dish. I've done it a thousand times. But no more.

'Sorry,' I say. 'Those days are gone. Gone to the place of eternal memories.'

All three put down their spoons.

'Even in the darkest dictatorships,' Laban says, 'the condemned are allowed a final meal. And some choice words about the menu.'

The few individuals in this world fortunate enough to have been genuinely loved as children inhabit a universe apart from the rest of us and are unable to seriously entertain the notion of rebuttal.

'Any fruit salad comprises a system of coordinates,' I say. 'The bananas are the horizontal, the X-axis, the bass tone. Bananas are earth, they provide a rich, creamy foundation for the sunny fruits, the oranges and the pineapple, that inhabit the Y-axis. Citrus provides upward lift, that tangy, near-displeasurable zest. The strawberries are the Z-axis. They deliver the spatial element. Even now in December they taste so very much of Danish summer. They expand this tropical encounter of opposites into a global project. Acacia honey and whipped cream are the fourth dimension. Both cream and honey add a dash of the animal. They raise this modest little dessert up out of the mire of Newtonian three-dimensional banality into the complexity of Einsteinian spacetime.'

'You forgot the raisins,' says Harald.

'The raisins add bite. Resistance. They remind us of dentures to come. The care home. Spoon food.'

We exchange glances and think about the wrecked Passat. The excavator.

And then we eat.

'I'm going to miss it,' says Harald. 'Not just the fruit salad, but the presentations, too. If you're going to be put away for twenty-five years, Mum, I'm going to wish we'd got some of this on tape.'

Laban has cleared the table.

'What about that priest?' I say. 'From the Kali temple?'

The room freezes. There is a very small handful of pedagogical principles on which Laban and I unusually have always agreed. One of them is to stay well out of our children's love lives.

Until now it's always seemed like the matter of Thit and boys was something that sorted itself, like a train running according to a timetable rather better organised than the one that has shaped the life of her mother.

When she was four years old she brought a boy home for the first time from kindergarten to stay the night. I put an extra duvet out for him in Thit's double bed, thinking that when you're four years old and you've got playmates sleeping over, the nicest thing in the world is to sleep next to each other in the same bed.

Thit cast a single glance at the set-up, before pointing at the floor and calmly and unemotionally, though without allowing even the slightest possibility of contradiction, stating: 'He's sleeping there. On a mattress.'

When she was fourteen and had met her first boyfriend, I once offered my help and advice. We were in the car, of course, because I'd picked her up from school. I took a deep breath.

'If there's anything I can do for you,' I said, 'with regard to Thomas, any advice you need, or guidance, you know you can come to me.'

A stretch of Svendsen silence ensued.

'That's very kind of you, Mum.'

I sensed immediately this was merely a prelude to some more combative reply.

'When you wanted to know about physics, Mum, you went to Andrea Fink, didn't you?'

I didn't answer. The suburb of Ordrup flashed by the windows, snow-covered, neat and respectable.

'And Dad told us how he went to Bernstein with the first musical he wrote. So if you want to know something, you ask someone who knows. Am I right?'

I said nothing.

Then I felt her hand on my arm.

Not in apology, because no living creature on earth will ever hear Thit apologise to anyone. But mildly placatory.

Since then I have not broached this prickly subject. Until now.

Thit stares at me pensively.

'The order he belongs to isn't one of celibacy,' she says, spelling it out slowly. 'So no rules were broken.'

She looks at each of us in turn. Potentially, this is a situation that may evolve in a number of ways, some disastrous.

But then she smiles.

'He was so sweet!'

13

WE BUILT THE HOUSE ON EVIGHEDSVEJ INTENDING IT TO be a quiet place with four separate living spaces. Or rather four and a half, counting Laban's annexe in which he composes: a small structure in the garden with room for a Bösendorfer piano and a Jensen bed, and still enough floor space for him to dance the rumba whenever the feeling of being a genius gets too much for him to be able to sit still, which it does with great frequency.

The four living spaces are separated by doors soundproofed to sixty decibels. Normally, when the four of us have retired to our own quarters, you can't hear a peep.

But tonight is different. I am sitting up in the living room, everyone else has gone to bed, and yet I hear the rhythm of their breathing. It means they've left their doors open, all the way in to their bedrooms.

It's because of all our troubles.

I enjoy the feeling of the house at rest, of Charlottenlund asleep, the more distant city gradually settling down and turning in.

I have switched off all the lights. I like the moon to shine in through the great, paper-thin limewood window blinds. The dissolution of yet another koan: how to sit with a clear view and yet behind lowered blinds.

As on most such nights, I drink a small glass of scalding-hot mint tea, sweetened with honey to the point where the fructose begins to wonder if it ought now to crystallise and deposit itself directly onto the spoon.

Our days are filled to the brim and beyond, with tastes, sounds and smells, with people, and impulses of hope and fear. There is a need for the simplicity of mint tea, for the encroaching stillness of night, geometric shadows cast by the moon on the white-painted walls.

We used clay paint. I mixed it myself. Clay absorbs excess moisture, releasing it again as soon as the steam pressure drops. From the day we applied it we could sense the walls breathing. The texture of clay-painted surfaces possesses an inexplicable beauty, like the surface of a bowl as yet still wet, resting on its potter's wheel.

We painted directly on top of a layer of smooth natural-fibre wall covering. While some structural movement must surely have occurred, the walls remain perfect.

I smooth my hand over the white surface. If a house is a living organism, then there can be nothing wrong with petting it. Indeed, it can hardly do anything but good. I must remember to make a point of saying so to the Academy of Sciences and Letters.

But then I put my mint tea down. Something isn't right.

I run my fingers across the wall again, and encounter a very slight bump, perhaps only a couple of micrometres, invisible in the moonlight, and yet so discernible. The nerve endings in my fingertips are capable of registering irregularities down to a few hundredths of a millimetre.

I pull up a floor lamp, position it close to the wall and switch it on. A faint shadow becomes visible. A straight line running from a metre off the floor to the ceiling.

In my stockinged feet I tiptoe into my own space. In the drawer of my desk I find a Stanley knife, an illuminated magnifying glass and a small Phillips screwdriver. I get the big ladder out of the utility room, the one I use to polish the skylighting. Returning to the living room it takes me a while to find the bump again. It's as inconspicuous as that.

Carefully, I cut along the shadow. The wall gives almost immeasurably, cushioning the motion of my hand. I put my nose to the incision and sniff. It smells of what it is: recently applied acrylic sealant.

I pick at it with the screwdriver, and a wire appears. Not the everyday kind used by your average tradesman, but a tissue-like length of tape, thin as gossamer, a millimetre and a half in width and with a core of copper.

I pull it away from the wall, and find it runs all the way up. I tug, and the finest dust descends from the ceiling, the wire following the arc of one of its arches, camouflaged by a spray-on sealant of exactly the same colour.

The ladder extends like a telescope. I secure the legs and climb aloft. From the top, I can just reach the skylighting. And the light fixture in the ceiling.

I flip off the cover. Inside is a tiny plastic box, less than one and a half by one centimetre. I remove it and climb down, seating myself at the dining table, the box still connected to its wire. I examine it with the magnifying glass.

But then there's a knock at the door. Or rather, a faint pecking. Like a little bird on the birdtable outside the kitchen window. Nevertheless, it almost gives me a heart attack. I cover the device with a cushion from the sofa and go to see who it is.

It's Dorthea Skousen, our neighbour.

'I saw the light was on,' she says. 'I hope nothing's the matter, only we weren't expecting you home for another five months.'

Evighedsvej slopes down towards the Øresund at Skovshoved. Once, back in some pre-history, the road was a narrow right-of-way meandering among half-timbered fishermen's cottages with limewashed walls and nets hung out to dry in the garden. Now the plots are occupied by fancy wedding-cake homes from the time nouveau riche profiteers erected their summer residences along Strandvejen and gave them names like Villa Palermo. Or else by bragging architectural structures such as our own. The only exception to all this is the house belonging to Dorthea and Ingemann. Theirs is still a fisherman's cottage.

They lived there when we arrived, and they will remain there until carried out feet first, which more than likely will be rather soon, he being ninety and she well into her eighties.

Despite all odds, and against all expectations, they have taken us into their hearts. To all intents and purposes they are Thit and Harald's proper grandparents.

People taking you into their hearts always involves some cost. I've never felt entirely comfortable with either of them, but particularly not with Dorthea. Maybe it's them knowing so much about us. They were the ones who looked after the children when Laban and I were going through relationship therapy. When we had to go to the bank and ask for extensions on our loans. It was they who let the bailiff in on the two occasions we've had property seized by distraint.

So they don't just know a bit about us, they know everything, the way people who look after your children always do. And when children are small, they are, by the very nature of things, an open picture book presenting in colourful detail all the entangled and unsavoury innards of their grown-ups.

Besides, both Dorthea and Ingemann are unfathomably different from us. They may be our next-door neighbours, but the reality of the matter is that they belong to another galaxy altogether.

But they understand me, and that's the problem. Dorthea especially understands me, I sense that very strongly. She has this unobtrusive and yet piercing way of scrutinising me. And she's doing it now.

'Everything's fine, really,' I say. 'We just came back a bit early because of some important matters to attend to.'

She stares past me into the hall. I'm afraid she might be able to see into the living room, that she possesses some kind of X-ray vision.

'It was kind of your friends to get the place ready.'

'Very.'

'They even checked the electrics. Ingemann saw them from his cabin. They'd pulled the blinds down, but he was able to see them through the skylight. Not without his binoculars, though.'

She hands me a jam jar. It's full of roasted almonds. She's given us one every year at Christmas ever since we moved in. The almonds are exquisite. Dorthea must surely have access to some very special alchemy. She can make the sugar crystallise into an utterly clear, homogenous film that clings to each almond the way seven layers of immaculately applied marine varnish cling to the spars of a rowing boat.

'There were four men and a woman. Two of them spent half an hour in the garage.'

'They'll have been recharging the car batteries.'

'That'll be it, yes. And while they were at it they mounted a little flat box on the wall behind the first-aid kit.'

She blinks her eyes and peers at me. The worst thing about her, the very worst thing, is that she's a pleb, like me. But whereas I have endeavoured to work my way up and above my station, she has steadfastly remained faithful to hers.

'I'll wish you a peaceful night, then.'

It's her ritual farewell.

'The same to you, Dorthea. And give our love to the captain.'

When I return to the living room, Laban is seated at the table.

14

HE'S WEARING SLIPPERS AND A DRESSING GOWN. AND he's removed the sofa cushion I'd placed on top of the device.

I fetch a set of optician's precision screwdrivers and a pair of tweezers from the utility room. Then I open the tiny box.

I extract the minutest black bead from its mounting and place it on the table. Then, next to it, a grey disc, quite as minuscule, and thin as a printed letter of the alphabet. I examine them with the illuminated magnifying glass. The bead is a lens, the smallest I've ever seen. The disc is a microphone. Underneath it is a colour filter. I remove it with the tweezers. Then come the photovoltaic cells, underneath them the processor, next to which is a transmitter, and alongside the transmitter a circuit board so tiny its details elude me, even in the magnifying glass. One of the conductive traces is a bit longer than the others and must be the aerial. Next to it is a voltage stabiliser. And the two tiniest lithium cells I've ever laid eyes on.

'This is a camera,' I announce. 'And a microphone. My guess is it saves images and sound for no more than a few minutes, before compromising them and sending them as a very short signal. That would make it very difficult indeed to trace, as well as saving energy. Batteries this size tend to run flat rather quickly.'

'How come they didn't hook it up to the light fixture in the ceiling?'

The question comes from Harald. He and Thit are standing

in the doorway in their pyjamas. Laban and I exchange glances.

'Your dad and I installed the electrics ourselves,' I tell them. 'When we finished doing the painting, I realised we'd forgotten to allow for the wiring to be recessed into the light fixture. I wanted to do the whole thing again. But I was pregnant with you and big as a house. So your dad wouldn't let me. He said that if a Zen master had completed a piece of work to perfection, the artist would have to apply an edge. A little dab here, a splodge there. Only the gods are perfect. Perfection is superhuman. It was a night just like this. To begin with we almost fell out about it. But then we settled on a solution. That light fixture has never been connected to the mains. That's the necessary human flaw.'

'They'll have discovered the fact when they installed their device,' Laban says. 'It was meant to give them a full view of the whole room.'

'So they had to chase out the plaster,' I say. 'And then fill in the recess with acrylic sealant. Not the best of alternatives. That was the reason I noticed. They must have been rather busy.'

We've moved three extra beds into Thit's space. Tonight we're all sleeping together, for the first time in years.

I led them all out to the garage, where I unscrewed the first-aid kit from the wall, then removed the flat, black, oxidised aluminium box that was concealed behind it and took it back with us into the house. I disassembled it on the round table, where we discovered it contained a receiver and a powerful transmitter. The little device in the light fitting has only a very short range and limited storage. It sent its data to the garage, from where it was transmitted on. To people of seemingly serious conviction. The aluminium box and its contents have the sort of finish you'd expect of a lighter, updated version of the old Swiss Nagra tape recorders the Niels Bohr Institute used for the dictation of provisional lab reports when I was quite young, and which at the time, in the early nineties, would knock you back fifty thousand Danish kroner a piece.

Laban has made tea and toast. He has cut the bread in thick slices and toasted it to the extent that here and there its surface is charcoal, while inside it remains soft and palatable.

He lays thick curls of cold butter on the hot toast. We are a family of butter-lovers, and Laban's butter curls, cut with the cheese slicer, are at least five millimetres thick. I've never had my cholesterol levels measured. I prefer to put that off until the autopsy.

Only rarely have we as a family ever been awake and gathered together in the middle of the night. But whenever we have, we've always made tea and toast. Last time was when Laban's mother died.

We exchange glances. We've known each other ever since the children were born. But at this moment we are, at the same time, strangers to one another.

Laban and the twins sleep, while I make a final round of the living room. The shadow made by the blinds on the walls has wandered. On the table are the two devices and my phone. I've got a voicemail.

It's from Magrethe Spliid. She doesn't bother saying her name, and the number's anonymous. It's just her deep voice, and no pleasantries:

'Susan Svendsen, I've got something for you. Adolphsens Allé, the last house on the left-hand side, facing the sea.'

The message is from just after midnight. An hour ago. I find the car keys and put on a sweater and jacket.

We've never owned a weapon. But from the toolbox in the utility room I take a small, flat crowbar. It's only forty centimetres in length, yet it weighs approximately one kilo and rests snugly in the hand. For good measure I pick out a chisel, too, with a blade as sharp as a barber's knife.

Some objects are symbolic of the profession, and one selects them accordingly. Bohr had his blackboard and chalk. His droplet of liquid. Andrea Fink has her cardiogram, the physical registration of the heart. Laban has his piano.

To me, the crowbar is the king of all tools.

I drop it into my bag.

15

ADOLPHSENS ALLÉ LEADS OFF STRANDVEJEN AT ØREGÅRD-
sparken. Property prices here are among the highest in the
country: the villas are as big as blocks of flats, with gardens tiny
as flowerpots, and the vast majority have been bought up by
advertising bureaus, Internet firms and foreign embassies.

I park on the next road down and walk along the front, hug-
ging the garden walls.

The last house on Adolphsens Allé is the smallest of them all,
only three storeys. It's also the only one you could imagine
might be a normal house, for human habitation.

All the windows are dark. I linger for a moment by the tall
wooden fence of the property next door, trying to merge into
the environment.

In the open carport I can see her Mercedes. Waves lap gently
at the shore. There's no wind, but the proximity of the Øresund
makes the air cold as frozen breath.

And then my eyes pick out Magrethe Spliid. She is sitting on
the second-floor veranda, looking out across the sound. The
door behind her is open, the room dark.

The garden towards the shore ends not in a wall but in a
rather symbolic, knee-high fence. I step over it onto the property, at the rear of the house.

The snow's reflection of the moon enhances the lux level
by about forty per cent. I sense colours. One of the grand

rhododendrons beneath the veranda has a crimson flower on it. At the end of December.

I reach out and find it not to be a flower at all but Magrethe Spliid's inhaler. I put it back on top of the bush.

The back door is locked, the lock reinforced by means of a steel plate. It's by no means a hindrance to my little crowbar, but a door being jemmied in the middle of the night makes a racket. Instead, I remove the snap-in bead from a window, take out the glazing unit and put it down on the grass, squeeze through the opening, wriggle across a counter, and find my feet again in the kitchen.

The place is so tidy you'd think she was going all-out for an elite smiley from the food-safety authorities. And maybe not just from them, but from the women's guild, too, for the little corridor through which I pass is spotless and smells of the natural soap-suds used to saturate the light, lye-treated floorboards. Not a superfluous item is visible, nothing to distract the eye, not so much as a discarded magazine, a pair of earmuffs or even a car key.

On the first floor is a hallway with rooms on both sides. All is quiet. The house has been renovated from top to toe, presumably only the outer shell of the original building remains. Not a stair creaks. Perhaps Defence Command pays a princely salary, or perhaps Magrethe Spliid won the lottery or inherited a large sum of money.

I continue up to the second floor, where the staircase opens out onto a broad landing and a single door has been left open.

The whole floor has been knocked into one, an oblong space at least 100 square metres in area, ceiling raised to expose the beams, skylighting installed to let in a maximum of daylight.

The room is bare apart from her desk, some bookcases next to it, a pair of comfy armchairs and a sofa, all gathered together in the far corner, where the door opens onto the veranda. The light wooden flooring is as extensive and uninterrupted as that of a ballroom, with the exception of a small, dark, rather unmotivated mat in the corner that looks like it's made of plastic. That and a discus, which for all her neatness she has left on the floor next to the mat.

It could have been a very pleasing room. In a very pleasing house. One of the few houses I could actually see myself living in.

Danish society comprises a massive mainstream. If you follow it, the current will carry you gently along. The only thing required of you is to complete your education by the time you're thirty, get yourself a husband and some kids and a desirable detached before you're forty, moderate your alcohol consumption, survive the mid-life crises, make sure you're on your marks and set for when the kids leave home, then curve into the final straight and the dash for the line in that singular Danish discipline called *Whoever's got most when they die wins.*

And I know what I'm talking about. All my life I've toiled to keep myself afloat in the midst of that current, and I intend to keep at it.

Magrethe Spliid has done things differently. As yet I don't know exactly how, but one of her sacrifices has most certainly been a husband and children.

Getting out of the stream isn't free. Normally it's something only the privileged and losers can do. I'm not sure yet which of these categories she belongs to. But while only a small minority of those on their own have the means to set up a proper home for themselves, this is something she has managed rather successfully. There is a rich atmosphere of life about the place, and a pervasive aura of quality and refinement.

But at this moment, such atmosphere has been overlaid by something else, a smell I'm unable to identify, that reminds me of something for which I don't much care.

I walk through the room and step out onto the veranda.

She's sitting in a high-backed deckchair, her head tipped backwards and resting against its edge, her long, muscular arms hanging limply over the sides. Her eyes are open, the tip of her

74

tongue protruding from between her lips, as though she were blowing a raspberry at the moon.

I take off a glove and place the back of my finger against her neck. Her muscles are as stiff as wood, she is already extremely cold, and my guess is that death must have occurred only a very short time after her leaving the message on my phone. Since then she's been sitting here in minus five degrees.

A slight waft of excrement tickles my nostrils. In death, her sphincter has relaxed and her colon has released some measure of its contents.

I put my glove back on. The police superior with whom Andrea Fink and I worked in the early years of our collaboration once told me the police can recover fingerprints from any surface whatsoever, even human skin.

I go back inside and sit down on her swivel chair, out of the cold and yet able to see her and also to scan the room. Her desktop has been tidied. The only thing on it is another discus.

Fear is the strangest of phenomena. It doesn't just occur in the body and in the mind. It can pervade the physical environment too – rooms and walls, for instance – and can remain for long periods of time. Perhaps this room, this house, will be suffused with the terror of what has taken place here for months or even years to come. My entire system is crying out for me to run and return to freedom.

The twins are the reason I stay. I'm forty-three years old, my best years are behind me. Or at least the chance of having some. But the twins are still just overgrown children. I've made it my intention to do what I can so they can have a future.

After a few minutes I get to my feet, step back out onto the veranda and pull the sleeves of Magrethe Spliid's cardigan back from her wrists, first one then the other. There are haematomas on both, and not from her cashmere being too tight. These are swollen black cuffs of bruising.

I go back in and sit down on the chair again for a few minutes. Then I get up and go over to the black mat in the corner.

It's not a mat. It's blood.

You can't be a mother of two kids like Thit and Harald without having seen blood in abundance and learning at least the basics of first aid, minor surgery and nursing.

And on that account you'll know approximately how much blood to expect from even the smallest graze. But here in the corner of Magrethe Spliid's room we're dealing with something else altogether. This is a pool of blood, whose sickly sweet, butcher's shop smell pervades the room. The reason it looks like plastic is that there's too much for it to have coagulated or seeped through the floorboards.

Here, up close, I can see the wall has been spattered too.

A moment's nausea ensues, I am unashamed to say. There must be some reason I never became a butcher or a surgeon.

I pick up the discus from the floor. It's got little bits of what looks like bathroom sponge stuck to it with glue. I take it over to the door and study it in the moonlight and see that it's not glue but blood, not bathroom sponge but cerebral matter. In the midst of this coagulated mass are tiny tufts of human hair, attached to flakes of what must be someone's scalp.

My time in this house is up. I return the discus to the floor and go out the way I came in, inserting the glazing unit and snapping the bead back into place, hoping the police aren't able to trace fingerprints through alpaca gloves and that my car hasn't been seen.

I walk back along the front and get in behind the wheel.

I sit there for a while.

Something's missing.

I listen to her message again. Her voice is calm.

'Susan Svendsen, I've got something for you.'

And then, suddenly, there are two things I know.

I know why they brought us back to Denmark. It was the only way they could get to Magrethe Spliid. I sense her fearlessness, the way I sensed it at the Defence College. Her integrity. There were no weaknesses. No family they could threaten to take it out on. No job they could take away from her. Not much life left to cut short.

She knew something someone else wanted to know too. And whoever it was knew they were never going to get it. So they used us.

That's the first thing I know.

The second is that she's left it all to me.

I go back to the house.

It's an immense physical effort. I've got nothing left in me for the finer points of burglary. I go straight to the front door and find it unlocked. As I step inside, my feet stick to something on the floor of the hall. I bend down and let my hands investigate. Wild horses couldn't get me to switch on the light: only in the darkness do I feel any semblance of protection. My fingers find a thin rubber mesh of the kind used to stop rugs from slipping underfoot.

I go upstairs to the second floor again, my teeth chattering like they haven't done since I braved the waters of the Jammerbugten with the children in early May – according to them the start of summer, for which reason the sea, in their view, couldn't possibly be cold and they were impervious to any suggestion that we return to dry land.

This time I don't sit down but remain standing.

I'm not practised in the art of body searches, nor is it the kind of experience I'm interested in adding to my CV. But I embark on one anyway.

Beneath the warmth and softness of Magrethe Spliid's cashmere cardigan, the frost has begun to turn her rectangular frame from wood to stone. I pass my hand gently over her body. It's as though I've grown fond of her, especially this past halfhour. Does that make sense? Can one's feelings for a person grow after they're dead?

She was alone most of her life. I sense it strongly now. What then of the desire for affection, that is so much a part of our being human? *Skin hunger.* I pass my hand over her, as though in a long-deserved caress.

77

I find nothing. My impulse was wrong. Or else it'll take too long to verify. Even such a simple room as this contains any number of hiding places, for instance among the books on the shelves.

I cast a final glance at the desk. In physics there's a guiding principle that says that when you've got to choose between different theories, all of which are exhaustive and consistent, you should go with the simplest one. It's not just a rule of natural science, it's common sense too. If she left something behind for me to find, she'll have chosen the most obvious option available.

On the desk is a dark, rectangular item measuring about two by six centimetres. I pick it up. It's a small, solid ingot of lead. I pick up her discus from the desk and unscrew the cover.

Identical ingots line the recess, all pressed into place in their individual rubber-lined slots.

But one of them has been removed and left on the table. In its place is a piece of tightly folded paper.

16

FOR ME, THE ONLY TRULY EFFECTIVE CURE FOR THE jitters is preparing food. It's always been that way.

So when I get home, instead of going to bed, I bake croissants. But only after a light breakfast of two 500-millilitre caffeine tablets, a *café au lait* with four shots of espresso, and a half-litre Coke with ice.

Croissants are an unnatural phenomenon. Theoretically, combining raw puff pastry with bread dough can't be done, they belong to different dimensions. Every time the pastry is folded, the number of separate layers of laminated dough is doubled, the thickness of each layer being reduced exponentially with the number of folds and rollings-out. Eventually, after an hour and a half, and four periods of refrigeration, we're talking about a layer thickness of a tenth of a millimetre. Physically, it's impossible at that level to keep the two things apart.

Empirically, however, it works, and this morning the croissants are a success.

It's only half past four. But the aroma has woken Laban and the twins. They appear in the living room, drowsy with sleep and sniffing the air like animals.

I squeeze them each a tall glass of orange juice and place croissants in front of them. They eat and drink in silence. Not because it's a rule or manners, but because croissants, when they're done well, are a manifestation of great physics, and as such impart to the table a sense of church festival.

'You've not slept,' says Laban.

'There was a message from Magrethe Spliid on my phone. She wanted to give me something, so I went out and got it.'

They glance towards the smoothed-out sheet of paper that I've placed on the counter.

'Once we've eaten, I'm going to deliver it to Thorkild Hegn. If he keeps his side of the bargain we'll be free. Everything will be sorted. Thit and Harald can go back to school. I can start working again.'

They say nothing. All they do is stare at me.

'Susan,' says Laban, 'we're in this together.'

'Thit and Harald,' I say, 'go to your rooms!'

They stay put.

'Mum,' says Harald, 'we're too old now to be sent anywhere, especially to our rooms. We'll soon be leaving home. They're hardly even ours any more.'

I sit down in front of them.

'She was dead when I got there. Someone suffocated her, a short time after midnight presumably, after she left me her message. They used her inhaler. It's got a silicone mouthpiece that shuts off the mouth and nose. All they had to do was press it tight to her face and block the intake. She was strong as a horse, so there must have been at least two of them, one to keep her down, the other to hold the inhaler. It was slow, done in stages. The mask leaves a mark on the skin if it's pressed hard, like a diver's mask. There were several, all identical. They wanted something from her. Information, or some item or other, who knows? So they went straight for her weak spot, her lungs. But whoever they were, they underestimated her. My guess is there were three of them. She took one of them out with a discus. Harald and I watched her practising. Her Danish record still stands. The guy's head was smashed to pieces. There were litres of blood on the floor. The other two dragged him away in a rug.'

They stare into space.

'She gave them something, otherwise they'd have taken the place apart. But she hid what she wanted to give me in the discus she used for training. She knew Harald and I had watched her take it apart. She knew I'd find it. It's a list of members of the Future Commission. And Thorkild Hegn's home address. For some reason she was absent from the final meetings. She didn't have the minutes. We've done all we could do. I'm driving over to Thorkild Hegn's place now. It's over. We're out of all this.'

I get to my feet and gather up my coat, the sheet of paper and the car keys.

'Susan,' says Thit, 'would you mind sitting down again, please?'

17

I'VE DONE EVERYTHING HUMANLY POSSIBLE FOR THE kids to call me Susan. I never wanted to be *Mum*, it sounds too much like an institution to me. I wanted the twins to see me as an individual, for the person I am. At the first parents' evening when they were in kindergarten, there were eighteen mothers and two fathers, one of whom was Laban. The other women introduced themselves as 'Victor's mum', 'Diddums's mum', 'Little Dumpling's mum', and so on, and before long I was writhing with exasperation. Eventually, I got to my feet and said, 'Listen, you've got to pull yourselves together. Being a mother is hard enough as it is. Kids are basically black holes, singularities that absorb all light and energy without giving anything back. If you're going to give up what little individuality you've got left so you can be Blob's mum instead, you're betraying yourselves!'

I never got any further than that. The mood plummeted to well below freezing and Laban and I were obliged to make ourselves scarce in the break. We argued all the way home, or at least as far as Kirkevej, where we got stopped by a patrol car and a well-mannered police officer pointed out to us that there was a new centre just opened called Dialogue Against Violence, and would we be interested in him showing us the way?

Which prompted us to adjust our charm levels. The disagreement, however, continued. At least until reality intervened and came down on Laban's side. When the twins reached the age of five, they at once stopped calling us anything else but Mum and Dad. All that's left of *Susan* and *Laban* is what comes out in situations such as this. Whenever they feel it necessary to have a very serious word with us, they address us by our first names.

So I sit down.

'Kamal,' says Thit, 'my priest. He had a white Rolls-Royce. We drove from Kolkata to the Lake Palace Hotel in Udaipur. We stayed there for two weeks. It's the only time I ever felt I was anywhere near understanding India. After a week I knew I had to put an end to it. When I told him, he broke down. In Denmark, unrequited love is sort of temporary. At some point you dry your eyes and get a grip, maybe find someone new. If you don't top yourself instead. Or go into therapy. In India it's a way of life. It can go on for years. All of a sudden he could do nothing for himself, he was like a child. I had to drive him home, without a driving licence, all the way with a blubbering man on the seat next to me. He hardly slept at night, all he did was cry. After three days I was coming apart at the seams. But I still drove him home.'

She looks at us in turn.

'If you've started something, you must carry it through. And tidy up after yourself. Someone's dead here.'

I get to my feet again.

'Let me tell you all something,' I say. 'Do you know what it is, basically, that I've been looking for in life? A normal existence. That wish has been stronger for me even than getting to the essence of physics, stronger even than the urge to understand the Effect, or to understand anything at all, for that matter. Deep down inside, all I ever wanted was a normal life. With a house, a job, and a husband, kids, and food on the table. Safe in the knowledge that entropy and chaos apply only to closed systems, not to me. But what I want now is a normal separation, a normal divorce, normal on-one's-ownness. You, Thit, and you, Harald, can go on living with Laban or you can live with me. Alternatively, you can move into student

accommodation, or board at whatever college, or else find yourselves a bedsit or a cardboard box. You can do what you want.
But neither you nor anyone else is going to stand in my way of
getting back to normality. That path leads past Thorkild Hegn.
If the papers get wind of what happened in India there'll be
court proceedings, I'll be suspended from the university and my
normal life will be postponed by at least ten years. And in ten
years I could have Alzheimer's or Parkinson's and, no matter
what else, the long haul towards sheltered accommodation and
the care home will have begun. Thorkild Hegn is the only person I've ever met who I think can manage the media. The only
person who I think can keep this secret long enough for the case
to cool off and lapse, and who can afford us police protection
until it's all been cleared up. And to do all that he needs this
piece of paper.'

They've gone quiet. It's a characteristic of the Effect's phe-
nomenology that I've deduced from the empirical evidence but
never understood. It's never lasting. Eventually someone will
say something, or make a gesture that effectively draws things
to a close. I'm assuming their silence is just such a gesture.

But I've underestimated Thit. Her caustic burp now follows.

She's the smallest of us, even more delicate than me. Her features are refined, her voice soft and rather husky, though never
raised, not even now.

'There's one last thing. For me, at least. Someone tried to kill
my mother and my brother. I've got an account to settle with
that person.'

I sit down again.

They stare at me. They know I've given up.

I unfold the sheet of paper once more and place it in front
of them.

On it are six names. Written by hand. Magrethe Spliid was
from a generation for whom handwriting was the only means
when time was of the essence.

It strikes me that she and computers shared a childhood and

a youth. That they grew up together, she observing their development in close connection with the hydrogen bomb.

Four of the names, lumped together in a single row, are the surviving members of the Future Commission. Beneath them is Thorkild Hegn's name and address. And below that a single word, or perhaps a name: *Gaither.* I've googled it in Danish. Zero hits.

Laban and the twins lean across the table. After each name there's a job designation: chartered surveyor, priest, Governor of the Danish National Bank, metallurgist.

The only name I recognise is Kirsten Klaussen, the metallurgist.

A national treasure. Like Bohr. Like Tuborg. Like Danish bacon.

I fold the paper back up.

'Thit,' says Harald, 'how did you know you and that priest of yours weren't going to work out?'

He looks out into the winter's darkness. You can't see the waters of the Øresund from Evighedsvej. But you can sense the way they reflect the moonlight in the low-hanging cloud.

'He was too nice. He wouldn't have been able to stick with me in the long run.'

This is a sixteen-year-old girl talking. About a grown man with a Rolls-Royce and a million disciples to ease his procession through life.

And here on Evighedsvej, we all know how right she is.

I send a text message to the Volvo's fuel-driven heater. It responds with a *Message executed.* The twins have always been fond of a warm car.

It's only just gone five a.m. Andrea Fink once explained to me that the hour between five and six in the morning is the most important of the day. She could cite fifteen hundred scientific papers to corroborate what all of us already know.

She referred to it always as the arsenic hour.

It's the hour during which the human body is at its most relaxed. In that short period, the relation between the REM cycle and deep, dreamless sleep is optimal. In that hour, the vital early-morning sensation of having enjoyed a good night's sleep is founded. It is the hour in which a city is at its quietest, and the pattern of brain waves among a test group spending the night in a sleep laboratory is most likely to approach gamma coherence.

It is lack of sleep in that hour that brings the parents of infants to their knees and breaks the fabric of shiftworkers and newspaper delivery drivers. It is in that hour the authorities send psychologists out to private homes unannounced in order to assess whether a child should be removed from its parents. The phenomenon of stress itself has its issue in that hour.

So, of course, that was when Andrea Fink and I scheduled our interview sessions. And it is in that same hour that all four of us now climb inside a warm Volvo to drive into Frederiksberg and pay Thorkild Hegn a visit.

Unannounced.

18

WHEN YOU'RE A KID WITH TWO AUNTIES LIVING IN FRED-
eriksberg, you think the only people who live in that part of the
city are old ladies.

Then you grow up and go to university and become a quantum physicist and discover there aren't just old ladies there, but
old men too.

In keeping with this spritely demographic, the villas that lie
between Vesterbrogade and Frederiksberg Allé are designed like
mausoleums, with the kind of shrubberies in their tiny gardens
one usually finds in cemeteries.

Thorkild Hegn's house, halfway along Kochsvej, is no
exception.

And yet, on each side of the front door a dark disc of glass
has been inlaid in the brickwork. Not for show, but to conceal
a pair of CCTV cameras.

The panes in all the windows are fine-wired with flat grey
conductors that are most likely hooked up to a security system
monitored by police intelligence at PET as well as the regular
police. Fifty metres from the house, on the other side of the
road, a Ford is parked, and in it are two early risers, both of
whom get out and watch us attentively as we pull up and get out
before proceeding to the front door.

Thorkild Hegn is a man of precaution.

I smile at the glass discs and tap the number he gave me into my phone. I hope my call's going to find him in that most unprotected, dreamless phase of sleep.

It doesn't. He answers immediately, wide awake.

'I've got the names,' I tell him.

'Where?'

'On your doormat.'

The door opens within seconds, no matter that Hegn himself is at least fifteen metres away, in the depths of his desirable abode, in pyjamas and dressing gown. Maybe he's got a remote control. Or maybe the door just respects him so much that it opens on his command.

In his get-up anyone else would appear half naked and vulnerable. But not Thorkild Hegn. He must have a tailor doing his nightclothes. You'd be excused for thinking he was on his way to a palace ball.

He ushers us into a drawing room. I hand him the sheet of paper. He unfolds it, glances at what it says and folds it up again.

'She hadn't got the minutes,' I tell him. 'She wasn't present at the final meetings. I know it's the truth. We've kept our side of the bargain.'

He nods.

'The charges against you in India are dropped. Your house in Manipur has been taken care of. Your personal effects are on their way to Denmark in a container and will arrive next week. The story is, you were called back prematurely due to important business. The Indian authorities will confirm it, as will our own Ministry of Foreign Affairs and the University of Copenhagen. The matter is closed.'

'If only it were,' I say.

I take a seat. Laban and the twins take a seat. Thorkild Hegn remains standing.

It was never the idea that we should turn up at his house. As such, we weren't supposed to sit down in it either. Now he wants us to leave as quickly as possible.

88

'Magrethe Spliid's dead,' I tell him. 'She was suffocated in her home last night. Harald and I barely survived an attempt to kill us. With an excavator. The car was pulverised. We need police protection.'

If any of us had been expecting tears and flowers we'd have been disappointed. But he does sit down, at least.

What's more, he's shaken. To begin with he can't speak. Then, gradually, words begin to form, if only with difficulty.

'Who says she was suffocated? Only an expert can ascertain the cause of death.'

'Go and see for yourself,' I say. 'We can talk about it once you've seen the body. And the bits that are left of the guy whose skull she smashed.'

Hegn's wife appears. She has sensed he needs her. Great men always have formidable wives. The weightiest Nobel laureates have always had an Amazon at their side: Bohr, Fermi, Alvarez, Gorbachev, Sakharov, Schrödinger. And those who didn't quite make the final cut were those whose women backed out: Oppenheimer, Szilard.

One shouldn't be deceived by the fact that the woman now standing in the room with us is half a metre shorter than her husband. Shield-maidens come in small sizes, too.

'What's the matter, Thorkild?'

Her voice has authority. She's as much in the know as he is.

Hegn has now got to his feet and paces the room like an animal in a cage.

'Something's out of control.'

Then he remembers we're still here.

'Perhaps the children might like to stretch their legs outside for a minute,' he says.

'You could ask them,' I say. 'They don't listen to me.'

For a second he can hardly conceal his surprise.

'My grandchildren do as they're told.'

'They've got you for a grandad. Thit and Harald weren't that lucky.'

Thorkild Hegn has cultivated many excellent traits. Unfortunately, he hasn't had time to work on his sense of humour.

He looks at his wife.

'We must get them to safety. Until we get this sorted out. Italy, the witness protection programme.'

A moment passes before I realise he's talking about us.

He's made a decision. Now he turns to face us.

'You must go straight home and pack. Someone will come and pick you up within the next few hours. You fly out today. On the way to the airport you'll be given new passports and the relevant practical information. Everything will be taken care of. You'll be home again in a few months at most.'

He doesn't know it yet, but the Effect is active. One of the first things that tends to happen, as it does now, is that politeness disappears. Human politeness is never anything more than the finest veneer.

In the air of mutual lucidity that has arisen between us, some measure of his physico-chemical history becomes apparent to me.

Some people believe in psychology. I don't. Everything is biochemistry on a substrate of quantum-electric effects. Thorkild Hegn must have been made by dissolving a barrelful of senior civil servants, lieutenant colonels and CEOs in a strongly corrosive liquid. Whereafter the solution was evaporated down to the dry concentrate that now, once again, is seated before us. I've seen men of power, but Thorkild Hegn takes the biscuit.

Nevertheless, he's afraid. Which tells me something about what he, and we, must be up against.

Laban and the twins are stunned. They've come here to get things sorted out. And now they're being sent out of the country.

'We're still jet-lagged,' I say. 'It'd be nice if we could wait a few days.'

He gathers himself. And then he makes a mistake. Calmly,

and in a low voice devoid of any remaining molecule of politeness, he says:

'It's non-negotiable. Together, the four of you are looking at the kind of criminal records that in the future will close off your every professional avenue with the exception of newspaper rounds. You do as I tell you!'

Very few people can handle being cut down to size by a true master. Most of us shrink in the face of such crushing disapproval. At the age of sixty, and world-famous, Bohr, like a naughty schoolboy, stood before Churchill and allowed himself to be torn off a strip.

But a good ticking-off has always had a different effect on us. We don't shrink, we get meaner.

You can't tell by looking at us. That's what a decent upbringing does for you.

We get to our feet.

'We'll go in our own car,' I tell him.

'Out of the question!'

'It's a four-wheel-drive Volvo and cost the wrong side of a million kroner. You'll have to add that to our monthly allowance.'

He swallows visibly. I've touched a very sweet, very deep nerve: like all civil servants, he's stingy as hell when it comes to government money.

'Very well. But you leave tonight! Within the next hour and a half a man will come to your house with temporary passports, credit cards, the relevant addresses and information about what to do once you arrive. Have a nice trip!'

We draw towards the door without turning our backs on him. It's not that we think he's going to come after us and ask for a farewell kiss. It's because backwards is the way you withdraw from a royal court.

As we get to the front door, he and I look each other in the eye for the last time.

At that moment something dawns on him. He remembers the

situation in the prison. He remembers the Effect. Only, by then, we're gone.

Instead of starting the ignition, I pause for a moment in the driver's seat.

Harald grips the overhead grab handle and tries to wrench it from the interior. Once, at school, following a fleeting attack of presence in a history lesson, his classmates gave him the nickname *Hardrada*. After a Norwegian king who wouldn't take prisoners, or no for an answer.

I don't bother turning round, and address the windscreen instead, speaking on behalf of us all:

'We're not going to Italy.'

19

I'VE FOLLOWED WITH PLEASURE AND INTEREST THE increasing role women's sexual fantasies have come to play in the public mind during my lifetime.

What's more, we've only seen the start of this beneficial trend.

Indeed, I believe I have a rather juicy contribution of my own to make in that respect. All I need is to find the right forum in which to present it. I'm considering the Royal Danish Academy of Sciences and Letters.

My own steamy fantasies involve the great physicists, many of whom were scrumptious to say the least, including a number of women. Female physicists have often been titillatingly in touch with their inner masculinity. Marie Curie, Irène Joliot, Cecilia Payne and Lise Meitner are all high up on my list.

My favourites, however, will always be the great male physicists of the nineteenth century. Moreover, they enjoy the very great advantage of being dead. Coveting the dead is a lot easier than lusting after anyone living. I've always been aware of how fortunate it was for Bohr to have passed away before I was born. Otherwise I'd have been compelled to try it on with him. It would only have got complicated.

My number one is Thomas Young. A looker if ever there was one, with the sartorial elegance of a fashion council to boot. They say he danced like a musical puma, was versed in sixteen languages, able to read and write from the age of two and to differentiate and integrate complex functions at five. But most importantly, Young was the first to fully grasp and describe the phenomenon of interference. From the moment Andrea Fink showed me Young's formalisations I knew he must surely have been the first to truly comprehend wave phenomena in the energy flow that exists between humans.

When Laban, the twins and I are positioned correctly, the way we were in Thorkild Hegn's drawing room a few minutes ago, and when for the slightest of intervals there is no dissonance between us, our systems will then be coherent and we will amplify one another in what is perceived as a form of interference. That's what we were investigating with Andrea Fink, it's what we've used and abused throughout our existence, and for better or worse it's what has led us here, into our present situation.

It's also what made Thorkild Hegn say what he said.

The instant he accepted the idea of our driving to Italy in the Volvo, a vortex formed in his system. It happened swiftly, perhaps imperceptibly to him, though to me it was manifest indeed. The Effect can be like an X-ray.

It was clear to me, at that instant, that he wanted to say no. And yet he said yes.

I can think of only one explanation for that. What happened is that a mental representation glanced off the surface of his consciousness and implanted itself in mine: he remembered that when his men installed a camera in our house and a transmitter in our garage, they also fitted tracking devices to our cars.

The reason it was so important to accompany us to the airport and put us on a plane was that only then could he be certain we actually left the country instead of turning back in the departure lounge. But then he realised he still had that security, thanks to the tracking device I'll bet my hat has been fixed to our car.

The question is where.

Laban and the twins are quiet. That's one reason we've stuck

94

together so long, in spite of everything: whenever it's been needed, we've given each other some space.

I was twelve when I conducted my first thought experiment. Without knowing Einstein had created the term and refined the technique. Without even knowing who Einstein was.

I was living in a residential institution called Holmgangen, up in the wilds of Vendsyssel. A farmhouse as far out as you can get in a country as overpopulated as Denmark: kilometres to the nearest neighbour, and virtually off the radar to even the most local tradesmen. The institution was underfunded, too. We had to feed the straw boiler with disused car tyres, and its outer surfaces were coated in a sticky black layer of melted rubber, a compound of such durability that to this day whenever I cough I get a peculiarly vulcanised taste in my mouth, of radials and cross-plys.

Being far from the nearest waterworks, the place had its own supply, and one day the electric pump broke down. They never called a tradesman if it could be helped, and the staff tried instead to fix the problem themselves, only they couldn't. Then someone suggested asking me.

I sat on the manhole cover, peering into the depths of the well. The pump was half a metre down, a Grundfos. Everyone, kids as well as adults, converged around me. No one said a word.

I can't put my finger on exactly what I did. But I know today that I conducted a thought experiment. I'd seen the staff eliminating various possibilities: changing fuses, cleaning the intake filter, checking the riser pipe, adjusting the pressure switch so as to increase the difference between start and stop pressures.

Maybe it shouldn't be called a thought experiment, because the feeling, then as now, is more physical. What I did was simply to allow what I saw to be absorbed into my being.

I sat on the manhole cover and became one, physically, with the pump. And then I knew what it was: the volume of air in the diaphragm tank was too small. So I adjusted the regulator nut.

And that was that. They put the pump back together and it started first time. I didn't say anything, didn't gloat. But I knew it had been a decisive moment. A crystal ball in which my future had just become apparent.

It's the same thing now, in the Volvo halfway along Kochsvej in Frederiksberg.

When I was fourteen I de-restricted my first moped, a pink Puch Maxi. When I was eighteen I repaired my first 2CV: the engine was as simple as a scooter's.

In the case of our Volvo, I can barely work out where to put the anti-freeze.

It's not me who's changed, it's the cars. Today you need a university degree and a million kroner's worth of tools and electronics to understand and repair anything in the kind of tin can in which we're seated.

So I don't bother trying to work out where they put their device. There must be a thousand possibilities and I haven't time to waste on thinking. Instead, I try to become one with the vehicle and the situation at hand.

After ten minutes of silence, it comes to me. The others haven't made a sound.

The fuel-driven heater works. That's what I realise – or my body does.

The transmitter in the heater is in principle a mobile phone. It works using a SIM card bought from my provider. It's got a monthly minimum usage of twenty kroner. We've been away in India for a year. I've remembered to do a lot of things since we got back, but topping up that SIM card isn't one of them. It ought to be empty.

But it isn't. And it's not the provider being exceptionally patient with its customers either. It's because someone else topped it up instead.

I open the little compartment underneath the dashboard to the left of the steering wheel. Inside is the driver's manual, and to the left of that the switch to operate the fuel-driven heater manually. Above it, secured by two Velcro straps, is the combined transmitter–receiver unit.

I pull it out. Increasingly, the world is hidden from us in little compartments, behind computer screens and specialised interfaces accessible only to experts. We've had the car for four years and this is the first time I've held this unit in my hand.

It's a bit bigger than a mobile phone. I open it.

The insides are made up of a rechargeable power supply twice the size of a mobile phone's, and presumably twice as durable. It's charged by means of a cable that must be connected to the car battery. Above the power supply is a small cover which I remove to reveal a starry dazzle of electronics no larger than a wristwatch, but requiring yet another university education besides the one called for by the vehicle itself.

However, it takes no schooling at all to see it's been tampered with. Some very dextrous fingers have positioned a printed circuit board on top of the device's own electronics. And although it's only ten by ten millimetres and one millimetre thick, even a child would be able to tell it was a parasite, a cuckoo in the transistor's nest, placed there in order to feed off the telephone's power supply and other hardware for a single dire purpose, which I'm in no doubt is to transmit a constant geographical position.

The others are completely quiet. I disconnect the unit and place it on the seat next to me.

Then I flick the indicator and pull away.

20

TO THE BEST OF MY KNOWLEDGE, ANDREA FINK HAS never said there should be a long-distance truck driver in every woman's life.

Nevertheless, that says little about long-distance truck drivers. All it says is that even Nobel laureates have their blind spots.

I've always had a thing about long-distance truck drivers, ever since I was little. It's not quite true that everything relevant that can be said about music is contained in the songs of Hansi Hinterseer. There are nuggets to be found in country and western, too. Especially when it comes to trucks and the men who drive them.

We pass the post office depot. Across the railway tracks I can see the DGI leisure centre and the Kødbyen former meatpacking district.

'When I was a kid,' I tell the twins, 'the truck drivers used to congregate over there, at Kødbyen and around the Halmtorvet. Their trucks would be lined up and there were cafeterias where they would have breakfast. My mother used to bring me along here in my pushchair.'

'Why would Grandmother bring you here?'

The question comes from Thit, casually, as if she weren't really interested. But underneath the incurious exterior, she's on tenterhooks.

'My father was doing time in Vestre Fængsel. And my mother

liked to walk. We came this way whenever we went to visit him.'

We've reached the Køge Bugt motorway and pass the first services. It's one good place to find truck drivers. But not the best.

I take the next exit. At first it looks like a mistake that's about to lead us into some godforsaken sprawl. But then all is revealed.

On a sign that might have felt at home in Las Vegas are the words *Oda's Rest Stop*. There must be a hundred trucks parked, of all shapes, sizes, colours and nationalities. The place itself comes into view as we pull in.

Architecturally it's hard to describe. I remember from my childhood that the physico-chemical point of departure was a sausage stand. They must have given it some shots of whatever it is they put in the sausages, because now it's a two-storey structure some fifty metres in length, all of it lit up like a Ferris wheel in a fairground.

'Why don't you come in with me, Thit?'

She stops outside the entrance, as if in reverence.

'Mum, how come you know about this place?'

'My father used to bring me here.'

'You mean when he wasn't in prison?'

'Yes,' I say. 'They actually let him out sometimes. I've been here a few times on my own since.'

'Why haven't you ever taken us with you?'

I pause. We look at each other.

'Sometimes, once a year perhaps, I just want to sit here with all these men.'

She doesn't flinch. She nods.

We go inside and it's as if, for the briefest of moments, everything stops. There are maybe fifty men at the tables, and we're the only females. Apart, that is, from Oda.

She's standing behind the counter, and of course she doesn't recognise me. I've only been here about fifteen times in the course of thirty years.

Like her sausage stand, she's grown. But some women age into wisdom instead of falling apart. And instead of getting fat they just acquire more volume and become a bit firmer in the flesh.

'I need a man,' I tell her. 'Someone going to the south of Italy.'

Never one to hurry, she studies first me, then Thit.

'You've got a decent pair of wheels out there, with a man inside. And even if you didn't, you're not short for the airfare. So you're not looking for a lift.'

I bide my time. She likewise.

'I've had this place forty years,' she says after a while. 'I'm pleased with it. We do the best homemade pork sandwich you're likely to get. We rake in the money. But that's not what's important. What's important is the customers. Some of them have been coming here from day one. Forty years. Do you know what I don't want? What I don't want is to see one of my boys charmed into carrying illegal goods over the border and getting done south of the Alps, banged up inside for eight years for something he got sweetened into by a pair of blue eyes and a bit of lipstick.'

She knows as much about sincerity as I do. Probably more. She's heard every conceivable story humanity has to offer, and has lent her ears and heart on every occasion.

I put the transmitter–receiver unit down on the counter in front of her. Complete with the extra battery.

'We've been sent out of the country. It's a witness protection programme. They're tracking us with this device. We need to win some time. A couple of days, that's all.'

'And what were you thinking of doing in the meantime, love?'

I lean towards her.

'I'm looking for a man,' I tell her. 'A man who did something really bad. And when I find him I'm going to make him say he's sorry.'

She looks me in the eye.

'What did you say your name was?'

'Susan. And this is Thit.'

'Come with me,' she says.

She steps out from behind the counter and leads us down among the tables. I'd never have believed a person could weigh eighty-five kilos and still move like a mermaid through this world of chrome and vinyl, weightless amid its greasy plates and battered fish. But now I do.

She halts by a young man seated on his own.

'Johnny,' she says, 'this is Susan.'

She whispers some explanation in his ear, turns and is gone. I sit down in front of him. Thit remains standing. I put the unit and the battery down on the table. Followed by six thousand-kroner notes, counted out one after another and placed in a little pile.

'This is a tracking device. I want the authorities to think they're following me. I'd like you to take it with you to Italy. Somewhere in Apulia there'll be a garage with a workshop. The place'll be a tip. At the back, among all the junk, there'll be an old bucket. A nice, dry place where no one's going to look for at least a fortnight. I want you to drop this there.'

He weighs the device in his hand.

'How did you know? That I knew a place with just such a bucket?'

We smile at each other. He looks at Thit, then back at me, thinking better of trying to work out the connection. Thit has never looked like she was descended from me. Or descended from anyone. Rather, she looks like she just stepped out onto a stage or materialised from outer space without any incriminating past packed into her luggage.

'I could give you my mobile number,' he says, 'in case you get into trouble. Or want to see the world.'

The suggestion is spontaneous and comes from a place beyond his control. As soon as he realises what he's said, his face turns crimson.

He's not half bad, a kind of twenty-one-year-old version of Kris Kristofferson in *Convoy*. There's a sparkle about him, and yet a darkness in his eyes.

It's a darkness that comes from a longing I'd bet he doesn't even know he's got. A longing for mature female sexuality, with all its flashing lights and sirens ablaze.

Thit's as motionless as a statue. I get to my feet.

'I can't do that,' I tell him. 'At least not yet.'

The darkness in his eyes deepens slightly. Then his face brightens.

He shoves the banknotes back across the table.

'You'll be needing this yourself. For what they give you in witness protection, you might as well be on the dole.'

I take the money.

'My pleasure,' he says.

I turn to leave. Thit comes with me. I stop in front of Oda and put one of the notes down on the counter. She shakes her head.

'I've got more money than I know what to do with, love. I've got three places like this on the E48. I'm only here because I can't stay away. You keep your money.'

I stuff it back in my wallet. It's the second time in five minutes someone seemingly in their right mind has turned down free money. Maybe I'm sleepwalking.

She looks me up and down one last time.

'I'm not sure why,' she says, 'but I'm glad I'm not that bloke you're looking for.'

Thit and I linger for a minute outside the door. In the distance, we can see Brøndby Strand.

'Mum, have you ever been unfaithful to Dad?'

Some people might think there are truths best kept from chil-dren. Those who do know nothing about the Effect. And they don't know Thit.

'Yes,' I tell her. 'Lots of times.'

She says nothing. We go back to the car. Harald gets out and opens the door, first for me, then for Thit.

'Laban's driving,' I say. 'I'm tired.'

We get in. Laban pauses before starting the ignition.

'Why is it so important for us to hide from Hegn?' he says. 'What's his interest in us, exactly?'

From the breast pocket of my shirt I take out a very tightly folded sheet of paper, size A4.

'What I gave him,' I reply, 'wasn't the names I got from Magrethe Spliid. His are made up. The real ones are here. Once he realises, he's going to be rather miffed. And then he's going to come after us.'

21

'we're invisible!'

Laban's in the middle of the floor with his arms raised. He dances the first steps of a rumba.

I'm leaning on Harald for support. I've slept a total of six hours in the last forty-eight.

'Hegn will be tracking us to Italy on his computer. The guy who was after you and Harald most likely got his brains bashed in. So now we're invisible!'

It wouldn't be fair to call Laban a Renaissance man. To do him full justice you need to add that his ability to construct his own version of reality is so powerful that, for much of the time, he actually resides in the Renaissance. Before real-time information collection and digital surveillance. Before big data.

'They could be here any minute,' I tell him. 'We can't be sure they're not monitoring the house. We've got forty-eight hours if we're lucky.'

'Twenty-four,' says Thit. 'I'm afraid it's only twenty-four. Christmas Eve doesn't count.'

Laban stops dead, as if nailed rather abruptly to the floor. I lean heavily against Harald.

Christmas Eve is a demon Laban and I have endeavoured to exorcise for sixteen years. The children keep bringing it back.

Laban and I have never cared for Christmas. The excess of consumerism. The mass psychosis.

The Department of Experimental Physics is less than 400

metres from the Teilum Building and the Department of Forensic Medicine. Occasionally, we'd lend the forensic pathology section a statistician, or computational time on our servers, or some lab equipment. Pathologists work round the clock at Christmas. At no other time of year do they see as many suicides and victims of domestic violence. If anything can work the Danes into a rage it's the singular combination of alcohol, presents you can't afford and a massive collective imperative that requires families to be sweetness and light from the first strains of a carol.

We always went away for Christmas. To the west coast of Jutland or some arid little island in the Mediterranean. Until the kids came along. Then we were trapped. When it comes to loving Christmas, in all their national conservatism Thit and Harald must be somewhere to the right of Ghengis Khan.

'And we have to invite a homeless person,' says Thit. 'It goes without saying.'

Thit is forever on the lookout for needy creatures to take home with her, be they beast or human. At one point we had six stray dogs. And never fewer than eight cats. For some years we had a crow called Kevin that she found with a broken wing in the Charlottenlund Slotspark and brought home with her. It slotted straight in, uppermost in the family hierarchy.

When she was nine, the idea occurred to her for the first time that Christmas isn't Christmas unless spent with someone homeless. By the time she got to ten she was strong enough to enforce it.

Since then we've had at least one – on a single occasion, three – joining us for Christmas dinner every year. The Christmas before we went to India it was a woman touching on two metres tall and smelling strongly of meths. Five minutes into my duck à l'orange, she winked at Laban and said: 'Do you fancy a bit of slap and tickle after?'

'We're barely alive,' I say. 'We've got forty-eight hours, tops. Christmas is cancelled.'

Thit and Harald exchange glances.

'You can do what you want,' says Thit. 'Harald and I are having Christmas. With a tree, and presents underneath, and a homeless person to share the meal. If I die tomorrow then I'm going out with fairy lights. And the satisfaction of being true to my values.'

I hobble off to my room and turn down the duvet. I don't have time to take off my clothes, not even my shoes. All I can do is fall forward. I can't remember hitting the sheets. I must have dropped off before.

22

AFTER I WALKED OUT ON ANDREA FINK AND LABAN IN the honorary residence twenty-four years ago, having emphatically blocked all avenues of approach and dashed any hopes Laban might have harboured – thereby trapping the ball for good, so to speak – three months went by before I saw him next. And it would be a fib to claim that I forgot him in the time that passed, even though I tried.

Then one day he was standing in the foyer of the H.C. Ørsted Institute, waiting for me.

I saw him from twenty metres off and swivelled on my heels. Even then I knew that if you had to run from your destiny, you'd have to run fast.

He was right behind me.

'I've been waiting here for three days. From morning till night. In the hope of catching a glimpse of you. Campus security have been eyeing me up. One more day and I'll be banned.'

We went to the canteen. I filled up my tray and sat down at a table. He sat down opposite.

'I'm not eating. I've stopped all intake of nourishment. I've sworn I won't touch a bite until I've asked you out and we're sitting at a table together in a three-star restaurant.'

'You'll be dead in five weeks then,' I said. 'That's as long as a person can go without food.'

'Tough luck for me.'

It was obvious he meant it, in a way. There, in the Ørsted

canteen, surrounded by six hundred students and professors – all of whom, to one extent or another, were searching for invariable regularities – I sat facing a man who had abandoned structural considerations altogether.

'You don't know me,' I said.

'I'm working on that.'

People passing by with their trays had begun to pause and linger. Those at the neighbouring tables had turned round to face us. It had nothing to do with us. I was nineteen, he was twenty-one. We looked like any other students. It was the Effect. I stood up.

'Don't go!'

'I've got lectures.'

'I'll wait here until they're finished.'

'They go on all night.'

'I'll wait anyway.'

When I left four hours later, he was waiting outside. Security had thrown him out. His lips were blue from the cold.

He walked me over to my bike.

'I'll follow you home.'

'You're on foot.'

'I'll run alongside.'

'Laban,' I said, 'sometimes, the bitter, inescapable truth of the matter is that the woman simply isn't attracted to the man.'

'I know,' he said. 'Isn't it marvellous we haven't got that to contend with?'

Standing there on Nørre Allé, he looked like a person who'd stepped off a precipice and couldn't care less whether he floated or fell, because the step was an absolute necessity.

I couldn't resist him. To this day I still don't know if it was right or not. All I know is I couldn't resist.

What drew me to Laban Svendsen was not his nascent fame, nor his talent. It wasn't his looks either, because at that moment on Nørre Allé I hardly noticed him physically at all. What I perceived was the insane high-diver inside.

'You can walk me to the next set of traffic lights,' I told him. 'Nice and easy. And there we can shake hands and part for good.'

'Three sets of traffic lights!'

'Two.'

We walked next to each other.

What I still keep asking myself is whether I could have done things differently. Whether I ought to have.

I glance at Laban. We're seated at the breakfast table, all four of us.

The others have slept badly, they've got shadows under their eyes. I slept like a baby, ten hours straight, deep and dreamless.

There is mercy in sleep. It is a profound, physiological regularity of human life that if you're sufficiently tired, sleep will wipe away all fear.

Until you wake up again. Then it comes back. As it does now, here, at this table.

I place Magrethe Spliid's sheet of A4 in front of me. I address Laban, in order to take immediate control of the situation.

'We'll go and see all four surviving members of the commission. To find out what all this is about. Once we've done that we can go to Hegn and make a deal. We get our old lives back. Plus police protection. We'll do two each. The children stay here.'

Harald turns the paper towards him and begins to type the names into his phone.

'Forty-eight hours,' he says. 'Minus Christmas Eve. Thit and I are in this, too.'

I couldn't be bothered arguing. Harald's already got the addresses off the Internet and written them down. None of the surviving members of the commission, apart from Magrethe Spliid, has done much to keep themselves hidden.

I go with them to the garage. Follow them out into the road.

Standing there on the pavement as they reverse down the drive, I sense my fear begin to spiral. I don't know what it feels like for anyone else, but with me fear starts in the chest, from where it spreads through the entire parasympathetic nervous system.

More than anything I'm scared of the children dying. It's a fear that comes up every time I say goodbye to them. The first years, I cried just leaving them at nursery school.

Right now, the risk seems greater than ever. As I stand there I've a feeling of being exposed, as though under a microscope, and that Laban and the twins are, too. Someone could be watching us: through binoculars, in a rear-view mirror, through a hedge. And we've no idea who we're up against.

23

KELD KELDSEN, THE SURVEYOR, LOOKS HIS AGE IN THE photo, which is to say just short of seventy-five, though time has allowed him to keep a thick, white head of hair, and his face is thus a pair of gleaming blue eyes beneath a snowy haystack.

According to the web he's not only a professor but principal of something called the School of Surveying. Which unfortunately for me is as far away as Hirtshals. It means I'm going to have to try to prise confidential information out of him over the phone.

The receptionist who answers my call would never have got a job at the Defence College. She presents herself in a motherly Jutlandish as Hilda, and sounds like she wants to bring me a cup of coffee and a wedge of lemon half-moon cake before taking me by the hand and leading me to Keldsen herself. Unfortunately, he's not there.

'I'm awfully sorry,' she says, 'he's not in today. He's over in Copenhagen.'

'How fortunate,' I say. 'I don't suppose you'd know where, exactly? You see, I'm calling from Copenhagen myself and I need to ask him a very tiny question. I'm sure he wouldn't be put out if I could do so in person.'

'I'm sure he wouldn't,' she says. 'He's very helpful. He's at the Eksperimentarium. A board meeting.'

'Hilda,' I tell her, 'some good advice: if you should ever stumble upon a vacancy at the Royal Danish Defence College, Second Section, promise me you won't apply.'

I sense a bashful smile at the other end.

'Oh, I'd never leave Hirtshals.'

'That's the spirit,' I tell her.

I could have walked to the Eksperimentarium in about forty-five minutes along Strandvejen. In any other circumstances I'd have loved it: the sun's come out and the sky is blue as iron.

But instead I'm going to have to disguise myself in sunglasses and a scarf, and crouch in the back of a taxi.

Then something wells up in me. Maybe it's spite, or maybe it's because I remembered about my bike and Laban on Nørre Allé. At any rate, I end up putting on an anorak and gloves and getting the Raleigh out of the garage.

It's spent a year there in solitude and looks sorry for itself: the tyres are flat and it needs some tender care and attention.

I pump up the tyres, lube the chain and talk nicely to it. It's as if it lifts its head.

Bicycles need someone to talk to them. I decide to mention the fact in the relevant professional fora. Though perhaps not the Academy of Sciences and Letters. The profound scientific truths are no different than any other kind: they must be presented in small measures and with the utmost consideration.

One of the phenomena for which no one yet has produced a wholly irrefutable and exhaustive explanation is the peculiar occurrence of serial instances of good luck. The wind's behind me all the way along Strandvejen, all the traffic lights are green, and when I get to the Eksperimentarium's ticket booth one of my students is behind the counter, a girl of perhaps twenty who, once she's got over the shock of realising that one of her teachers, who she hasn't seen in a year, turns out also to exist in some private form outside the auditoria of the Universitetsparken campus, lets me in for nothing and informs me that the board meeting has briefly adjourned for a coffee break but its members will be back in five minutes.

I go up to the first floor and wait at the balustrade, from where I can scan both the entrance area and the exhibition areas.

You can't look out on the great halls of the Eksperimentarium without getting a lump in your throat. All the major set-ups are here: a modern version of von Guericke's vacuum pump; a simplified reconstruction of Michelson and Morley's experiment of 1887 that did away with the concept of stationary aether, thereby lending a nail to Lord Kelvin's coffin; a device demonstrating the conservation of energy by means of perfectly elastic colliding steel spheres that may or may not have been designed by Newton; and a series of photostats as tall as a man, visualising Faraday's electromagnetic induction, as detailed in his *Experimental Researches in Electricity*.

These physical forms have long since vanished from all modern laboratories, yet their depth and beauty live on all around us. I find it inspirational indeed.

'Inspirational, don't you think?'

I haven't seen him, though he's been standing two metres away the whole time. It's because of the physics. People are small next to physics.

Beneath a shaggy white mane, two turquoise beads hold me in their gaze. They belong to Professor Keld Keldsen, principal of the School of Surveying.

He could be Hilda's dad. With coffee and lemon half-moon cake to boot.

The disarming Jutland demeanour provides half the explanation as to why he approached me. The other half is down to the Effect.

'There's only one thing I've always missed here,' I say. 'And that's surveying equipment. Some tripods and ranging poles. Relief maps. A bit of equidistant projection.'

His ruddy cheeks already tell of the great outdoors. But now he positively glows.

'All on its way!' he says. 'At my behest! I'm a surveyor myself.'

'Really? How interesting! You must promise there'll be an historical explanation attached to each instrument. So we lay-men can fully grasp why surveying is so very important.'

He almost flaps his arms in glee.

'Surveying is without doubt the single most important scien-tific discipline if one wishes to understand why Denmark looks like it does today. From the first farming laws around seventeen sixty to the zone legislation of the nineteen seventies, surveyors have been right at the heart of any topographical change of note. There are those who think the landscape's appearance is due to chance. Well, it isn't! It's all been managed, down to the last square kilometre! Denmark is one gigantic demonstration of our interpretation of the right to land ownership. From redis-tribution to the conversion of entailed estates, all the way through to the nineteen fifties, with its sharp decline in the number of holdings, and the modern country of today, Denmark is the result, from arse to tit, if you'll pardon the expression, of the minutest planning, most of it sociopolitically motivated. And in that process, surveyors have been indispensable!'

'Is that why they wanted you in the Future Commission?'

He withers before my eyes. The colour drains from his cheeks. The hearty warmth of Jutland evaporates and is replaced by something else that ought not to be there, something that doesn't fit in with the person he is.

It's fear.

The price for being able to gain a person's trust. The talent to do that isn't just a matter of establishing a sincerity that con-denses and converges asymptotically in the direction of comfort and intimacy. It's also about knowing when you've got through the outer layers of packaging and need to use the tin opener. And if the tin opener isn't enough, there's always the angle grinder.

He turns on his heels, but I grab him.

He pulls free and starts to run. He gets to the lift ahead of me, waves a keycard and the doors snap shut in my face.

I glance around. No stairs leading down.

My student girl is standing behind me. She's not asking questions. Instead, she steps forward and unlocks a door. Behind it is a stairwell.

I've got two hundred and fifty students.

Had got.

It was impossible to learn their names. If it even mattered. Like the rest of us, their identities are uniquely fixed by their civil registration numbers in tandem with the Zermelo-Fraenkel axiom that states that it can always be established whether an element belongs to the set or not.

'There's something I want to say. I want to thank you for your teaching. I love physics!'

Before my eyes stands a model of myself, twenty-five years earlier.

I throw my arms around her and hug her tightly. She's as surprised as I am.

Then I turn and descend the stairs one flight at a time. I can sense her still standing at the top, mobility crystallised into a solid lattice structure. Maybe because of the hug. Maybe because she just saw a professor descend to the next floor down like a gibbon, in two leaps.

Keld Keldsen's car is about to pull away from its parking space. He drives a Jaguar. I stand in the way. If he wants out, he'll have to run me down.

He seems set on it, and accelerates.

I jump straight into the air and land on the bonnet.

He's yet to pick up speed, but still I'm pressed against the windscreen. I spread out flat to block his view. In front of my eyes, on the inside of the glass, is a parking permit from the

School of Surveying. A pair of dividers superimposed on a golden theodolite.

He brakes. His face is less than half a metre from mine, but he's not looking at me. I twist round. At the bottom of the stairs stands my student. Calm, but pensive. In the process of revising her view on university lecturers. And members of the Eksperimentarium's board of trustees.

I'm off the bonnet. I fling open the car door and get in next to him on the passenger side before he has time to do anything about it. The girl's presence has delayed his reactions. As a surveyor he must know, from countless boundary inspections conducted in cases of running dispute between neighbours, the risk of one's petty misdemeanours being witnessed by others. Like running down innocent pedestrians in underground parking facilities, for instance.

From the pockets of his tweed trousers he produces a pouch of tobacco and a packet of cigarette papers. Normally, I would assume him able to roll himself a smoke with one hand – and in his pocket – to shield the business from the tornadoes of Vendsyssel. But at the moment, his hands are shaking. A little oblong of paper flutters from his grasp. He retrieves it, draws out the tobacco from the pouch and rolls a make-do cigarette while staring blankly out through the windscreen. Only then does he notice the smoke detectors on the ceiling.

'Damn it!'

I take the matches out of his hand and light up for him.

'Smoke all you want,' I say. 'We're in a Wilson chamber.'

'What's a Wilson chamber?'

'The single most important piece of apparatus in experimental quantum physics. Together with the Geiger counter.'

He takes a drag.

'Magrethe Spliid's dead,' I tell him. 'Someone suffocated her in her home the night before last.'

He rolls the window down for fresh air. The smoke alarm goes off with a shriek. My student is still at the bottom of the

116

stairs, adding ever increasing layers of surprising detail to her overall picture of the natural sciences' intelligentsia.

'Let's go,' I tell him.

He drives without seeing. I guide him out towards the waterfront. He stops when we can go no further. Behind us is the outer wall of a building, to our right an iron-mesh gate leading to a closed-off area of the quayside. On the wall is a mahogany plate with gilded lettering that informs us the area is the private property of the Kronholm Yacht Club. In front of us, a short flight of stone steps leads down to a jetty.

'What was the Future Commission?'

Next to the gate, in a glass-fronted kiosk, a young girl sits painting her nails with a look on her face suggesting that at the tender age of twenty she has already wearied of life. And the sight of us in the Jaguar makes her even more tired.

A small fishing boat has been moored with its prow towards the jetty. It's rather rusty and looks a bit like a bathtub. This part of the harbour has been turned into Denmark's own little Venice, and the jetty is here so residents can step straight out of their suites of reception rooms into their own private teak gondolas. But maybe they gave a single fisherman a mooring out of consideration for the local folklore. He's standing upright in the boat, tending his nets.

Keld Keldsen has had a little think. He's had a fag, or half of one. His nerves have settled. He leans across in front of me and opens the door.

'Out!'

'I've got two kids in deep shit,' I tell him. 'The boy and I nearly got killed.'

He turns to face me. The cheerful mood of before, with all its promise of lemon half-moon cake, is gone. In its place is something else: the threat of physical violence. Any second now I'll be scrabbling on the ground outside.

'If you'd only allow me to sit on your knee,' I say, and slip immediately onto his lap.

It takes him by surprise. Me, too.

I throw the car into reverse and hit the accelerator.

We're less than twenty metres from the wall and doing thirty kilometres an hour at the most when we hit it. Nonetheless, the impact is considerable. The rear window shatters into a cloud of tiny shards, the boot springs open and we're at a halt.

The girl in the yacht club kiosk stiffens mid-movement, her little brush applicator suspended halfway between the nail varnish bottle and her extended fingernail. The fisherman on the boat freezes like the water around the jetty. Normal reality is momentarily suspended.

'What was the Future Commission?'

He grabs me by the throat. I press him back into the seat, thrust the car into gear and put my foot down hard. The tyres squeal and the Jaguar leaps forward.

Acute peril is a litmus test of how deep a person's outward composure actually runs. As we plunge down the steps, Keld Keldsen starts to scream. We hit the jetty, the hard English suspension making the car bound like a kangaroo. I slam the accelerator down, then move my foot swiftly to the brake.

The jetty is made of smoothly planed planks. They're as slippery as soap. We skid to a halt, the Jag's front end jutting out over the iced-up slush of the waters below.

Beneath me, Keld Keldsen is a knotted muscle. I swivel in his lap so I can see him.

'Keld,' I tell him. 'Look at me.'

He's only partially in touch with the real world. I lower my head in front of his face and point two fingers at my eyes.

'Keld,' I say again. 'What do you see here?'

He stares at me blankly.

'"The Story of a Mother",' I say, helping him along. 'Hans Christian Andersen. You know it, Keld, don't you? The mother who'll give up anything to bring back her child. Her hair, her eyes, her tax-deductible pension plan. That's half of what you see. The other half is the mad scientist. Frankenstein. Mabuse.

Dr Strangelove. I'm a cross between them all. And do you know what? That makes me one mean son of a bitch, as they say. Do you get my drift, Keld? We're talking one step away from a straitjacket.'

He nods.

'I need to know what that commission was all about. And if you're not going to tell me now, I'm going to put my foot down on the accelerator and we're going to take a nosedive through the ice. The water's at least seven metres deep here. With the door open we'll go straight to the bottom. Which is fine by me, I'm a winter bather. Ten minutes every morning, splashing about in the freezing-cold sea at the open-air baths in Charlottenlund. I love it. But you probably won't survive, Keld. Do you understand me?'

He nods again.

'Okay,' I say. 'So talk.'

He has to clear his throat several times. I remain seated in his lap. It shouldn't stop him from breathing properly: I'm well under sixty kilos. Anyway, it means I've still got the wheel and the accelerator.

'Seventy-two,' he whispers. 'It was set up in nineteen seventy-two.'

'Go on – and speak so I can hear you!'

'No one took it seriously. There were six of us, straight out of college. Later we brought in six more.'

'Why seventy-two?'

His mind is wandering. I need to keep him focused.

'It was the fashion then, all of a sudden, to listen to what young people had to say. It's all gone by the board now. But back then it was the order of the day. The kids were everywhere. Students in the governing bodies. A children's council. Student councils in the schools. A children's parliament in the Folketing. A UN plenary assembly for youth. Think tanks were popping up all over. Someone got the idea the government should have a young people's think tank. Everything was in flux. The landslide election of seventy-three, when half of parliament got voted out, was only a matter of months off. So they got us together. Six young people, with Magrethe taking the chair. Shortly after, there were twelve of us. We met several times a year for two years. That's all there is. There's nothing more to it.'

'Keld,' I say reproachfully, 'there's a lot more to it.'

I sense the pre-tension of muscle. He's preparing a desperate counter.

I swivel back, throw the car into reverse and put my foot down hard. The wheels spin before finding purchase and the Jag tears off backwards. We're already doing a fair lick when we hit the steps. Immediately, the rear hatch is lost, the windscreen cracks and showers down on us, the thud of the wheels against each stone step clutches at our insides, and then we're back on the quayside, slamming into the wall and finally coming to a halt.

The fisherman and the girl watch us. Only their eyes move.

'What made you all so special, Keld?'

He clears his throat. Twice as many times as before. He's beginning to understand how serious I am.

'To begin with, no one took much notice. Not even us. We met and talked about the future. Gave talks for each other. Every six months we'd write a report. No one ever read them except us. Or if anyone in the Folketing ever did, they never let on. After two years, someone got the idea of drawing up an overview. By that time they had five reports to go on. The overview listed all our predictions and held them up against reality. It named twenty-four key events, domestic and foreign. Not only had we predicted them all, we'd done so with an accuracy of within three weeks!'

Even here inside the car, with the wind from the Øresund blowing in through the empty space left by the windscreen, he's proud of himself.

'By then, the first American surveys had come in about think tanks and their prognostic accuracy. Ours left the rest for dead! The summary said no other instance came anywhere near. We could tell the future. Like looking it up in a table.'

'You must have known.'

'Of course we knew! But we were hardly out of our twenties. We thought we were champions of the world. But there's always a nagging doubt. At that age. Somewhere deep down, in the murky depths, there's a part of you that's never quite sure. So the overview was what we needed in order to see it was true. And even then it wasn't enough.'

He stops. I put my hands on the wheel to remind him of how easily we can take off again.

'We read it and planned our next meeting as usual. It was always just circumstances that decided where. Sometimes we'd borrow a room at Christiansborg, sometimes at the university. Often it was at someone's flat. Once, when we all happened to be going away on the same day, we met in a restaurant in the departure lounge at the airport. Anyway, this next meeting was scheduled for mid-week, the report having come out on the Friday. Only we couldn't find anywhere to have it. It was the middle of February, Hartling's government had stepped down the day before, so Christiansborg was fully booked. In the end we borrowed a loft at Gammel Dok. It was my turn to make the tea and coffee, so I got there early. When I opened the door there were four men and two women sitting there. It turns out they're intelligence, PET and FET, police and military. Along with a government minister. So there's not going to be any meeting. When the rest of them get there we're told that from now on we're to convene only within the confines of Slotshol-men. There's going to be two observers, security on the door, everything's going down on tape and would we please write down our full names, addresses and telephone numbers on this list? When they're finished, it all goes quiet. We exchange glances. And then we tell them where to stuff it. Their faces turn grey, but what are they supposed to do? They go away again. We decide to forget about the day's agenda and adjourn to Rabes Have where we order fancy *smørrebrød* with beer and aquavit and make plans. Later that afternoon, on behalf of the commission, I write to the Folketing and tell them we don't care, no one's going to tell us what to do, so we're resigning to carry on as private citizens whose discussions won't be any concern of theirs. Less than twenty-four hours after the letter is sent, Magrethe and I get picked up. We were the only ones whose identities they were certain about. I was at the Geodetic Institute's map shop, but they found me nonetheless, drove me round the corner to Slotsholmen and took me upstairs to a room at the top where they'd got Magrethe waiting. So now it's a different game altogether. No police, no demands, just one man.'

'Thorkild Hegn?'

He nods.

'He apologises for the day before, our freedom was inviolable, of course, and was never in question, blah blah blah. Anyway, he'd like us to stay on. Only no longer under the auspices of the Folketing. He thinks it best our work be accorded complete freedom and discretion, so they're going to make a little umbrella for us. A small office, that's all, with a secretary so we won't have the bother of typing and filing our reports. What would we say to that? At that point we'd had the lunch at Rabes Have to cement a mood, so we say up to a point, only we want to be self-elective, we won't be giving up any names, we won't be accountable to anyone apart from drawing up the semi-annual report. And besides that, we want some money. He gives us everything we ask for. And that's when we begin to realise what we've got going on. Because even though we've never seen Hegn before, we sense very strongly that this is a man who, if he wants something done, can be sure people are going to get their behinds into gear.'

I pick up the remnant of his cigarette, place it between his lips, strike a match and light it for him. I have to cup my hands against the wind. From somewhere behind the city's tall buildings, sunlight slants down, spilling over the narrow belt of ice and leaving a twinkling ribbon on the water.

All of a sudden, I sense why he became a surveyor. He loves well-defined boundaries. And now the world is coming apart all around him.

'Keld,' I tell him, 'you've got an erection.'

His face sets. He blushes, a crimson bloom that becomes him. It takes away some of his paleness.

'Not that I take it personally,' I say. 'Most likely it's due to the series of little shocks you've just had to your system. It's a well-known physiological regularity that men in mortal dread often get erections. But it does mean I'm unable to accept your offer of a lift back to the Eksperimentarium. A stiff cock can be so intimidating to a woman.'

I climb out of the car. The fisherman and the girl in the kiosk stare at me. I'd like to do something for them. Those of us with the gift of starting a situation have a certain responsibility to stop it again. I raise my voice.

'Keld,' I say, 'I don't think I need any more driving lessons. I think I'm ready to take my test.'

I turn and walk off.

24

I BIKE IT TO HELLERUP STATION. A LITTLE SHORT CUT takes me down past the bridge over the railway cutting and the entrance to the Defence College's First and Second Sections.

Across the tracks I can see the car park in front of the college and it's as good as empty. The excavation has been filled in.

I cross the road.

Andrea Fink's field theory accords an important role to the principle of verified intuition.

If one day you should find yourself fancying baked anglerfish in a cockle and clam sauce and you get on your bike and pedal over to the quay at Taarbæk Havn, and at the very moment you get there the good ship *Betty* is putting in and Finn the Fish just happens to have with him a bucket of five anglerfish, and another full of cockles and clams, and you get the lot for two hundred kroner on account of Finn always having been a ladies' man and because he can appreciate there must be something in the coincidence of it, even if he hasn't read quantum physics – if all this happens, or something like it, then what you've got is very possibly a rudimentary instance of verified intuition.

Most people would call it an idea that just happened to get lucky. But one of the first things Andrea Fink discovered, she told me, was that when it comes to certain groupings of people, the frequency of instances of verified intuition starts to increase as a function of time – first linearly, then exponentially – until before long, singularities begin to occur, events that go beyond known models of description.

It was my own frequency of such instances that made her force me to sign, in the presence of witnesses at the premises of the Police Licensing Unit, a document to the effect that I would never engage in gambling.

Crossing Hellerupvejen, as I do now, turns out to be yet another of those instances.

The same young man as before is sitting in the security cabin at the barrier. Seeing me park my bike, he blushes and comes out.

'There was something I wanted to ask you,' I say. 'Do you keep a list of vehicles going in and out?'

He shakes his head.

'Only names. And it's not complete.'

'The day before yesterday, when I was here. Do you remember a dark-coloured van? It must have come just after me.'

'It was the next one through. From a building contractor who's doing the digging for the council.'

'Did he show you any ID?'

He shakes his head again.

'We're only here so people can see there's no access. There's no real checks. He did come back, though. Later in the day.'

I'm wearing an anorak and a scarf, woolly hat and gloves, and I'm sweating from the bike ride. Nevertheless, I feel a sudden chill.

'He asked about you. And the boy. I told him I let you in.'

We look at each other. It's a dizzying moment.

'But I never said I saw you leave.'

'Why not?'

He shakes his head for the third time. Like the majority of us, he's essentially unable to explain his actions.

'There was something about him. The guy next to him, too. I didn't think . . . I haven't done anything wrong, have I?'

'You did exactly right. More than you'll ever know,' I reply. 'Were they in a truck with a loading crane?'

He nods.

The remains of the Passat would have been on the flatbed. Naturally, they were decent enough to tidy up after themselves.

To be on the safe side, they enquired about me. And thanks to an almost unbelievable instance of verified intuition, this young god has denied to them my existence. Thereby perhaps affording us a little more sand for our hourglass.

'My name's Lars. What you said, about putting me on your dance card. Does that still apply?'

'I'm in the middle of a divorce.'

'I can wait till you're finished.'

I've got a soft spot for men who, in the face of rejection, still find the means within them to hang around and wait.

'In quantum physics we say that divorcing from a profound romantic relationship takes seven years on average.'

Wistfully, his eyes follow an S-train as it rattles past.

'So even if a person waited seven years, he couldn't be sure?'

'I'm afraid not. It's called Heisenberg's Uncertainty Principle. The best quantum physics can offer is a statistical probability.'

I glance to my right, then to my left. Then I lean forward and kiss him on the mouth.

As I cross Ryvangs Allé, he's still standing there, rooted to the spot.

Stories abound – in art, religion and other such unreliable sources – of people who, during or after some particular experience, find themselves transformed into one or another phenomenon of solid-state physics. If one were to sift through the empirical evidence, one would most probably discover that the reality behind such exaggeration is that the persons in question were given a kiss. A kiss of the most unexpected and paralysing kind.

25

THE FIRST SET OF TRAFFIC LIGHTS ON NØRRE ALLÉ AFTER
the H.C. Ørsted Institute is the one directly outside the Faculty
Library of Natural and Health Sciences, and that's where I
finally managed to get rid of Laban twenty-four years ago on
that cold Wednesday in April.

Or at least that's what I thought.

I ask him to hold my bike while I go in to pick up a book I've
reserved. I walk past the statue of Niels Steensen in his wizard's
hat and his blustering pose before the naked corpse of a woman
on whom he's about to perform an autopsy, then proceed inside
into the foyer, lifting the flap in the counter and continuing into
those most hallowed of vaults.

I've never been on this side of the counter before and I'm not
supposed to be, either, but if a person exudes enough confidence, most doors will open of their own accord. So that's what
I do, and what I've decided is that I'm not going to end up like
the woman on that plinth outside, the poor victim of some
all-powerful male, and although Laban Svendsen at this point
in time is still in his very early twenties and a simple conservatory student of the Royal Danish Academy of Music, I have long
been aware of his wizard's hat and his scalpel.

So I stride through the lending area, and on through the
imposing depots of books and magazines, before opening an

emergency exit and emerging into a garden somewhere behind the Department of Exercise and Sports, from where I slip out onto Tagensvej and walk on up to Jagtvej, hop on a bus going to Frederiksberg, and twenty minutes later I'm sitting in front of Andrea Fink in the honorary residence, convinced that Laban will surely grasp the implications of being so unequivocally stood up.

To bring him to such realisation has cost me a second-hand Raleigh with a floral-patterned saddle, purchased at a police auction.

But one's personal freedom cannot be bought for money.

Standing in front of Andrea Fink I forget all about Laban, the way I always forget the greater part of the outside world, and this time faster than ever because I can see right away she's discovered something.

When Andrea Fink makes a discovery, she goes quiet and becomes more compact in a way. It's as if her density increases and her metabolism drops. She walks ahead of me into the laboratory with small, plodding steps.

This one's in the basement. Between the kids' discarded skis and sledges, banks of monitors and computers have been installed, and in the centre of them all is a dentist's chair.

A projector has been set up in front of a screen.

On the screen are two figures. She hits a key and the two figures shake hands.

'Before you and I met, Susan, we had already conducted fifteen hundred days of experiments covering three hundred subjects dressed up in electronics from head to toe. Heart monitors, blood pressure monitors, electrodes measuring tension in the surface of the skin, oximeters registering oxygen levels in the blood, EKGs and EEGs, MCGs to record the electromagnetic signals of the heart. Moreover, in-depth phenomenological interviews of each and every subject after each and every test day.

We've now compared that data with your own sessions. The results came in yesterday.'

The two figures on the screen jump into life again. Next to their hearts, a graphic appears in the shape of a sphere, and then another between their eyes.

'The sheer volume of information is, of course, immense. The mobile EEG on its own delivers thirty thousand cross-section cerebral images per second. For that reason we concentrated on conventional encounters. The ways people have of greeting each other. We isolated those situations in which test individuals shook hands with others. The handshake is a global gesture, there are billions of them occurring every day. Yet no one has ever investigated what actually takes place.'

A thought steals my attention for a second: the number of test individuals. At this point I'm only nineteen years old. I haven't the faintest idea when it comes to research funding. But all of a sudden I get a sense of what it must cost to hire three hundred subjects, dress them up in electronics, monitor them for a whole day and then process the resulting data.

I don't enquire about anything. But this is one of those moments where I get an inkling of the extent of the resources this frail woman has at her disposal.

Her voice slows.

'It seems three things happen. All over the globe, the same three things whenever people approach each other. And none of it ever systematically described. First, a physical connection is established: the touching of hands. Almost simultaneously, the heart's electromagnetic field expands and a subtle increase of activity occurs in the medulla oblongata. We could call this an activation of the heart. Then a change takes place in the mind: arousal and keener levels of attention. This is the physical correlate of the persons involved making eye contact. What's new here is the cardiac activity. The empathetic emotions are mirrored physically by the heart. Trust, gratitude, sympathy. The data here indicates that human interaction, even between strangers, is facilitated by an increase in cardiac interference. Supported by physical contact and borne along by an intensification of focus and heightened attentiveness.'

She pauses for a moment. Both of us are thinking about her sons. And her husband. And me. Everything people can feel compelled to trample on in order to get close to each other.

'It would seem to be a law governing all human fellowship. At every encounter with another human being, however brief and superficial it might appear, we endeavour to reach one another. Primarily through physical adjustments, in the heart and the brain. The process appears to be the same in every instance. The question now is what constrains such encounters? As yet we don't know. But if we look at the twenty-seven hundred handshake situations in our study, then deep, mainly subconscious and yet minutely standardised conventions would seem to be qualitatively determinative. Conventions regulating the length of each eye contact, the extent to which empathetic emotions are liberated. One theory could be that these conventions protect us against what would happen in the instance of an encounter becoming deeper than the situation warranted. It's with that assumption in mind that we've been examining your interviews. They show the same amount of contact time as observed in the case of the police's own interview experts. The same frequency of eye contact. But the cardiac activity patterns are completely different. Both you and those you interviewed displayed strong increases of activity in the region of the pons, as well as more generally in the heart's wider electromagnetic field. Something in your system, Susan, doesn't stop at the normal limit of empathetic contact. With no marked visible or even measurable variance in perceivable physical or cognitive contact, the empathetic opening that occurs between you and others continues to deepen. At least under certain circumstances. And the effect is seemingly transferred from you to your interlocutor.'

Outside the window is a pond full of carp. Graceful, torpid

fish that now and then ripple the surface, the April sun a shimmer in its mirror, a golden chemical combination of water, fish and light.

The pond is covered by a near-invisible, fine-meshed net of nylon. Another koan solved: how to make sure the pond is deep enough for the fish to survive a harsh winter beneath thirty centimetres of ice and at the same time eliminate the risk of your grandchildren drowning.

She puts her hand on my arm.

'The twenty-seven hundred handshakes are nothing. The outer rim of something much greater. The evidence up to now is compelling. We appear to be on the verge of proving that whenever people come together, some deeper relationship is trying to establish itself. Our job now is to proceed to other kinds of interaction. My guess is the results will be much the same. The field effects we've discovered up to now – of which your own is but one – could well prove to be the first steps towards describing something never before uncovered: the laws governing cognitive interference between humans.'

I remove her hand from my arm.

'There's no such thing as cognition,' I tell her. 'Other than as a derivative of physical processes. The Effect has nothing to do with the heart. Differences between people are all down to chemistry.'

She looks out at the pond. It's a way she has of controlling herself. Somehow it gives her peace of mind. The pond was Bohr's idea. The carp species in it were bred to refinement in Taoist temples.

'And what of love, Susan? Is that chemistry, too?'

'Especially love.'

Two blotches of red bloom on her cheeks. I get to my feet.

'Andrea, you're looking for something that doesn't exist. The human consciousness isn't an independent phenomenon. In ten years we'll have reduced it all to psychology, all psychology to biology, all biology to chemistry, all chemistry to physics, and all physics to mathematics, which in turn will be exhausted in a single logical calculus. By then we'll have an algebra providing an exhaustive and consistent description of the regularities governing all human interaction.'

Something about the sight of the pond annoys me. Maybe it's the insipid softness of it. The way they've tried to minimise the risk of accident. Her inveterate belief in what she's doing.

'Susan, you're about to leave in anger. Do you know that half the times you've been here you've done just that: left in anger? It's all about self-control. You'll never let go of the emergency brake if you reserve the right to turn on your heels at any moment!'

Now she's standing too.

'You should see yourself,' I tell her. 'You're as furious as a troll!'

She twitches with rage. We've only known each other a couple of years and she's still getting used to the resistance I've brought into her life.

'And today,' I say, 'I finally got rid of your little composer for good.'

She advances towards me. Any minute now and we'll spiral into our first catfight. We face off, nostrils flaring.

'Leaving like this,' I tell her, 'has nothing to do with self-control. Nothing at all. The real reason is physical. I've always loved slamming doors!'

And with that, I turn and march out. And slam the door so hard the dust whirls in my wake. Bohr's carp dive to the bottom.

I catch the bus to P. Carl Petersens Kollegium, the student halls where I live. Stepping into my room I'm met by the sight of my Raleigh in the middle of the floor.

It's mine, and yet it isn't. The frame, the handlebars and the wheels are mine. But the saddle is new.

My floral-patterned saddle is a worn-out thing of plastic with a crack in it that's been pinching my buttocks for a year. But what am I supposed to do? I live on a student grant and money's tight. You can't be immersed in Boolean algebra *and* have a weekend job in a bakery.

But now the saddle's gone, and in its place is a costly, dark-brown leather job by Brooks. On top of it there's a red rose.

I edge past the bike and sit down on the bed.

What touches me most isn't the saddle or the rose. It's the fact that the bike's been polished. And not just polished, we're talking mirror finish: even the hubs and spokes are gleaming. The green paintwork's been seen to as well. It's been given some kind of wax finish, and is all buffed up like new.

It's easy to tell experimental physicists from the theorists.

Theorists don't want acid on their clothes. They basically don't care for the smell of laboratories, and they certainly don't like white coats and rubber gloves. Practical physics is too much like manual work for their liking. And part of the reason they hide themselves away at universities at all is to avoid that sort of thing.

Laban Svendsen is, with one hundred per cent certainty, the music world's equivalent of a theoretical physicist. I could tell that right from the start. I could read it from the way he handled the potatoes in Andrea Fink's scullery.

What touches me now is that he nonetheless has risen from his scattered sheets of music paper, the ivory and Bakelite keys of his piano, or whatever it is they're made of, and has rolled up his sleeves and polished my bike.

He hasn't left a message. No address, no phone number. Only my shining bicycle, its matt, treated leather saddle and the red rose.

One could be inclined to think it sufficient.

26

ACCORDING TO KRAKS DIRECTORY, THE FORMER MONASTERY of Vor Frue Kloster is situated on the Kratrenden path running through the boggy area known as Vaserne, bordering on the Furesø.

I get there by taking my bike with me on the S-train from Hellerup to Holte, then following the railway north to where the Kratrenden begins.

I'm starting to think I must have taken a wrong turn, because a monastery can't possibly be located on Millionaires' Row. But then I come to a white sign with a pictogram of what I take to be a stained-glass window featuring the Virgin Mary, below which it says *No. 7* and *Vor Frue Kloster*. I follow a long avenue of trees through a landscape too cared for to be woodland, too true to nature to be a park, before eventually the path stops at a cluster of buildings that with all clarity indicate to me that this is not a habitat of millionaires at all, but of multimillionaires, because the buildings and attendant woods extend over at least sixteen acres of land leading directly down to the lake, and the structures themselves are built the way Laban and I would have wanted if only we'd been able to afford it, clad in Norwegian slate stacked up to form a solid encasement and punctuated by great expanses of plate glass so the monks inside can lounge around and enjoy the view.

I park my bike outside. There's no enclosing wall and no gate, and if it hadn't been for the sign at the bottom of the path and the big bronze bell that hangs ponderously in an open wooden construction on the grounds, the buildings could have been almost anything. Anything, that is, with the capacity to generate a seven-figure monthly mortgage.

'Welcome!'

I didn't hear him approach. He's about my age and clad in something resembling a cowl. Gone, it seems, are the days when monks went about in barbed wire. This is class fabric, with an elegant hang and a distinctly modern cut.

'I'm here to see Henrik Kornelius.'

What does a monk look for in a woman before deciding whether to let her into his monastery?

'Do you fancy a beer?'

I must look surprised, the way he smiles.

'We'll go through the brewery.'

He leads me inside and through the largest of the buildings. The main space is as high-ceilinged as a sports hall, with white-washed walls, and throughout its length, each standing on its own concrete platform, are perhaps thirty or forty 1500-litre stainless-steel vats.

'We brew in open vats. It adds an element of unpredictability to the process. Of course, we can't do it during the summer months, because of the high risk of infection from microbe fall-out and wild yeast. But it does lend a unique individuality to each brew.'

The end wall is covered by shelving, on which large, corked bottles are lined up in their thousands. He picks one out, turns it in his hand and shows me the label. It's handwritten. Beneath the picture of the Holy Virgin and the monastery's name, a brewing date has been indicated, along with a specification stating the hop as a sort called *Kaskade* and then a number.

'Each brew is unique and therefore accorded its own particular number.'

He hands me the bottle.

'It's a gift. Monks have been brewing here since before the

Reformation. The Trappists were one of the few orders the absolute monarchy allowed. Because of the beer. However, it wasn't until the forties we started numbering. The hall here is from the big rebuild in 2012.'

We walk through a passage of glass connecting the fermentation hall with another building, continuing along quiet, tiled corridors with walls of exposed brick. There is no adornment here, nor is any necessary. Outside the windows, the snow-covered lawns are bathed in sunlight, and where they end the Furesø begins. It doesn't get much better than this. And that's without the very singular atmosphere of the place, the mood of contemplative silence.

We round a corner and the corridor ends at what looks like the door of a strongroom; in front are two stringently designed sofas on which you can sit and wait until the bank opens.

My guide doesn't knock, and even if he did it wouldn't help much, because no one on the other side would ever know if the world the rest of us inhabit came crashing to an end. There is, however, a button, which he presses, and then we wait for Father Kornelius.

Who apparently isn't in any hurry.

'What's it like being a monk?'

'It's a calling.'

'What about sex? Does the urge go away?'

The Effect has a twist of impudence about it. One must trust in the verifiability of one's intuitions and allow oneself to fall. And hopefully land on one's feet.

Which is what we do. He smiles, his teeth a gleaming white.

'In the secular world the urge is always present. The choice exists in the question of what to do about it.'

It's the first time in my life I've spoken to a monk. I don't know what I was expecting, but it certainly wasn't this kind of frankness.

He pushes the heavy door open and calls out. There's no answer.

136

'Let me go and find him. Back in a second.'

He disappears off down the corridor again. I sit down on a sofa. There are several books spread out on a table, all by Henrik Kornelius. One of them bears the title *Circular Prayer*.

The door has been left open. Somewhere behind it I can hear the sound of a washing machine.

Laban would immediately have been able to pinpoint the electric motor's tone, and its overtones, too. I can identify it as an industrial model with a digital inverter.

The machine is too full, the arrhythmic thud of the drum tells me so, though the outer casing must be stabilised, because there's no attendant noise from any levelling feet against the floor.

I stand up and put my head round the door. It's impolite of me. But time's pushing on and we're already well into our countdown of forty-eight hours minus Christmas Eve.

The door opens into a small entrance containing a second door, on the other side of which is a library-cum-living room, or else a living room-cum-library. At any rate, the walls are obliterated by books from floor to ceiling. And we're talking about a ceiling height of over four metres.

Across the room is another door, this one half-open. Through the gap can be seen a bedroom and a single bed. The sound of the washing machine is coming from behind that door.

And then the noise stops, as if a fuse suddenly blew.

You can get a decent idea of the way anyone relates to the world just by casting a glance at their desk. Laban's, for instance, looks like an explosion, an anarchy of sheet music and coffee mugs, CDs and violins, flutes and inspirational thingamajigs from ancient sunken cities, photos of the kids and, at least until a few months ago, of me – all of it signalling confidence in providence, or some other responsible institution, at some point sending a man to tidy up.

That's not what it looks like here. This place isn't just tidy, it's meticulous, and when whoever's responsible was finished, they sharpened all the pencils and placed the pile of Xerox paper, which has been laid out ready for the next book on the importance of prayer to be printed onto its pages, in neat alignment with the edge of the desk.

A man with such a well-developed sense for the importance of physical organisation does not overfill a washing machine. I step inside the bedroom. Though not without a distinct feeling of being out of bounds. It's one thing for this to be a place where people brew beer and tell things like they are. But quite another for a woman to enter the bedroom of a man who has taken his holy vows.

The bedroom walls, too, are lined with books. A door leads off into a bathroom. Inside the bathroom is another, behind which, presumably, is some kind of utility room. That's where the washing machine is.

Apparently, Henrik Kornelius has his own flat. Again, I'm struck by the superior choice of materials. The bathroom is done out in marble. The utility room likewise. If the brewery business is financing this, there must be some major production facilities hidden away that I haven't seen yet. Thirty-odd vats in a gym wouldn't do it.

I find the switch and turn on the light. Through the glass door of the washing machine, Henrik Kornelius's face stares out at me.

Even though I've never met him, I know it's him. His face is partially submerged in the grimy water that reaches halfway up the glass of the front loader's door.

Time comes to an abrupt halt. My thoughts become rational, calm, oddly exact. And completely beyond my control.

I realise what sort of strength was required to stuff a full-grown man inside a washing machine. The opening is no more than forty centimetres in diameter. They must have smashed his hipbone and his ribcage in the process. I sense the kind of rage it must have taken to start the machine after it was done.

That's as far as I get before real time intercedes. And my real-time thoughts are about one thing only: how to get away.

By the time my smiling monk returns, I'm back on the sofa.

He's slightly perplexed. Yet serene. I suppose that's how you get from silence and circular prayer, a view of the Furesø and limitless supplies of beer.

It's a serenity that before long will be tested.

'We're looking for him. He may be outside somewhere.'

'I'll come back another day.'

He doesn't ask me to wait. It wouldn't have helped any.

He follows me out. I have to control myself so as not to run.

'Can I give Father Kornelius a message?'

I look him in the eye.

'Wish him a happy journey.'

He balks.

'I didn't know he was going anywhere.'

'Nevertheless.'

I get on my bike and set off. Only once do I turn my head and glance back. He lingers pensively, watching as I pedal away.

27

TROPICAL COPENHAGEN IS SITUATED ON THE MARSHLAND of Amager Fælled and consists of eight structures in steel and glass, each tall enough to house thirty-metre palm trees and above them still have enough clearance for a highline system of polypropylene rope bridges from which visitors can look down on them.

The most positive thing that can be said about this establishment is that it's made up of eight regular polyhedra with pentagonal faces, prompting any mathematician to think of Euclid's strikingly elegant demonstration of the dodecahedron's status as the fifth Platonic solid.

Apart from that, the place gives me the willies. You pay three hundred kroner for the privilege of filing through a central African steam bath populated by parrots as noisy as any construction site, constantly having to duck so as not to be upended by flying insects the size of coconuts, and needing an eye on every finger in order to avoid the resident monkeys half-inching your credit cards and lipsticks from your bag. And in the middle of all that, you've got your work cut out trying not to think of the fact that modern technology, underwritten by modern physics – which is to say me – is clearing 1,200 square kilometres of rainforest every day, a tiny speck of which we've got transplanted here on Amager Fælled. Which is another area of natural beauty no one ever got round to slapping a preservation order on, for which reason it, too, is in imminent danger of being wiped out. Then, when finally you reach the in-house restaurant, it's called The Blue Okapi and reminds you once again of something we'll soon only be able to enjoy thanks to the work of taxidermists.

Still, none of this can be helped, because it's here Laban and the twins have decided we should meet. They love the place.

Laban's got a thing about the tropics. He recorded the noise of the parrots here and composed a piece of music around it that he then sold to be used in television commercials advertising the place. And of course Thit is mad about the animals.

They're sitting waiting for me and have already ordered, and the food has even arrived: Ghanaian fufu, a doughy porridge made from plantain and cassava, with a garish red sauce of coconut oil. Normally I find it delish, but today I can't touch a bite. The sight of Henrik Kornelius's face in the scummy hot water of that washing machine keeps swimming about in the air, right in front of my eyes.

'We've been to see Kirsten Klaussen,' says Harald in a voice like the grave. 'She's bought Bagsværd Church!'

They look at me expectantly. As if waiting for me to share their indignation.

'So what?'

As of 2016, the Ministry of Ecclesiastical Affairs started selling off empty churches as part of the kind of income-generating scheme to which we all must resort when there are no more customers left in the shop. Usually I cycle the long way home from the Department of Experimental Physics, via Bispebjerg, and on that route I've had to endure the Grundtvigskirken being put on the market, snapped up and turned into a five-floor cut-price department store. So why should I cry over Bagsværd Church?

'It was designed by Utzon,' says Laban. 'It has the most magnificent organ.'

Harald grips the edge of the table as if to pull it out of its wall mounting.

'She's hung rocket parts up on the walls! The walls of a church! And a machine gun!'

Religion is one of many issues on which our family have yet to reach consensus.

I believe in the laws of physics, which isn't faith, but experimentally verified, rock-solid knowledge. Laban believes in anything that can provide him with inspiration, be it Buddhism, Kabbalah or the philosophical concept of Music of the Spheres, as long as there's a new twist to it every six months.

Unable to establish a common ground, we've therefore agreed to touch upon this delicate subject as seldom as possible in the presence of the children, who for the same reason have never been christened and whose viewpoints on the world have always been allowed to emerge naturally and spontaneously.

Thit turned out to be the born heathen. Once, in Year 7, as a way of kicking off confirmation classes, her school took them to one of the churches apparently yet to be sold off, where a priest introduced them to the tenets of Christianity. I sat in the car and waited for her outside, firstly because Thit has always been used to having her own private chauffeur, and secondly because I had the feeling it was going to be the kind of day on which she might need to express herself to someone.

She got in beside me and slammed the door. Any day now, those mapping the human genome are going to turn up the DNA strand carrying the genetic code for slamming doors, which Thit very obviously inherited from me.

We sat there quietly.

'Mum,' she said after a while, 'it's a load of rubbish!'

Ever since then – until today – she has refused to set foot in a church.

In brazen binary opposition to this standpoint we have Harald, who has always been passionately fond of the scriptures. If it makes sense at all to speak of Harald being passionate. He loves Jesus, loves churches, loves his biblical history.

When he was four years old and witnessed the christening of

Laban's sister's infant child, an unsettling silence fell upon our house that evening. Silence is the worst thing for a mother. When the children are babies you're scared their silence means they've died in their cot, and when they're older you fear that silence forewarns of them doing something secretive that's going to explode in their hands at any moment. That evening, I discovered them in the bathroom. Harald had found what to him, among all the furniture and fittings, most resembled a baptismal font, which is to say the toilet bowl, and was now well underway christening the latest litter of Thit's homeless kittens. One by one he held them under the water, and while I stared in disbelief, he rattled off what snatches of the ceremony he could remember:

'This creature,' he said, 'we baptise in the name of the Holy Spirit.'

From then on, the kitten was called Holy Spirit, and no one could convince Harald otherwise, not even Thit.

So his outrage at the soiling of Bagsværd Church has a long history behind it.

'How did you get in?'

Laban and the twins exchange glances.

'We turned left,' says Thit.

Laban and I are perfectly clear on the division of our labour with respect to Thit and Harald: I've done eighty-five per cent.

Which is fine by me and always has been. It means I've spent eighty-five per cent of our time together with them, so in a way the split has been reward in itself. What can get me riled, though, isn't the raw division of man-hours, but the qualitative difference in their content.

Laban took weekends. And left the day-to-day running to me.

So I'm the one who made their packed lunches and did all that needed doing to get the twins to school on time or thereabouts. I'm the one who made sure their appearance was such that they at least would not bring shame upon the family after passing through the school gates. Whereas one day a week

Laban might suddenly exclaim something like 'I just finished a symphony' or 'I just finished a string quartet, so I'll drive the kids today'. And very often on such a day, instead of driving to the kindergarten or school, they turned left.

Turning left is something Laban and the twins hit upon a good many years ago, and the game was all about them looking at each other in the car and bursting into giggles, and then saying, 'Turn left!' Whereupon Laban would make a hazardous U-turn, thereby rendering the entire world open to their every most fanciful whim.

The world lying open in this way meant two things: either they would go to the Tivoli Gardens or to a restaurant, or else they would buy toys or in some other way spend money we didn't have. But only after they had finished what turning left was really all about: bluffing their way into some place where entrance otherwise was strictly prohibited.

'We knew nothing in advance,' says Laban, 'but when we laid eyes on her two dogs, a pair of big black dragons like the hounds of Hades, and the way she's rebuilt the church, the outdoor swimming pool she's had put in that leads inside through the vestry, I felt I could sense some measure of her self-importance.'

'She thinks she's the queen,' says Thit.

And Thit knows a queen when she sees one.

'I introduced myself,' says Laban, 'but she'd already recognised me. I told her I'd always wanted to show the children Bagsværd Church. The fantastic light inside. As though the divine were on the very verge of manifesting itself. I told her I'd dreamed of letting them hear the organ play.'

'Most of the interior's taken up by her living space and workshop,' says Harald. 'She boasted about that. She's got bits of a hydrogen bomb hung up on the wall!'

'Fragments of the outer shell,' Laban explains. 'She told us she'd developed shell elements for the American nuclear-energy agency, as part of their maintenance programme. She said she was on the scientific panel that advised the US Department of Defense during the Vietnam War. A frosty lady, and rather full of herself, that was our impression. Only then she thaws and gives us a guided tour of the place. She must have spent a fortune on it. The nave's all split-level now. Then there's the pool coming in from outside, like it was the Alhambra. The mood suddenly becomes very convivial.'

'Until we ask her about the Future Commission,' says Thit. 'Then the fun's over.'

'She wanted us out,' says Harald.

He picks up his knife and tries to flex the blade.

'I was obliged to use my charm,' says Laban. 'I reminded her about my dream that the children might listen to the organ. I told her they'd be traumatised if that promise were to remain unfulfilled. Reluctantly, she backed down. And then I played five-sixty-five.'

Laban has always spoken of Johann Sebastian Bach as if the two of them had grown up masturbating together and been inseparable since nursery school. He talks about Bach's works as if he'd co-composed them, and assumes everyone knows that *five-sixty-five* is the Toccata and Fugue in D minor, work No. 565 in the *Bach-Werke-Verzeichnis*.

'And as I play, I'm talking to her.'

Laban has this trick of playing something hypnotic to the accompaniment of his own voice-over. It works like a siren song: all human defences, including the immune system and the faculties of common sense and scepticism, shut down immediately and one is left abandoned to his despicable devices.

'I'm thinking to myself: The woman's seventy and famous all over the globe. Her self-esteem extends like a great front bumper into outer space. What kind of thing would occupy a woman like that? Answer: her posthumous reputation. So while I play, I'm telling her I'm writing an opera commissioned by the University of Copenhagen. About the great scientific discoveries of the last fifty years. How I'd been hoping to include the work of the Future Commission. I sense I'm getting through to her. She opens her mouth. Only then she shuts it again. Impossible, she says, but lets slip that all the information has been secured for posterity. So I tell her that as a composer I know how vain information can be, especially digitalised information. Compact discs deteriorate, computer memory degenerates with time. Then she gives me this sneaky look and tells me it's not digital, it's all on paper. Paper, I tell her, gets damp. It rots, and can burn. Ink will fade. Not in this case, she says. The notes are in ink, but everything's stored in a temperature-regulated, humidity-controlled environment. You're an expert in metals, I say, you know full well even a safe can burn at sufficiently high temperatures. It's not a safe, she says, it's a concrete vault. Eleven metres underground. No access to anyone. But when it's all released, ninety years from now, heavy volumes will be written about it, and some people are going to be very surprised indeed. And that's when we leave.'

Laban is incapable of keeping a secret. He's forever giving me and the children our Christmas presents three weeks early.

'Spit it out,' I say.

'As an important composer, I'm part of this country's cultural heritage. I've got an arrangement with the Royal Danish Library. They get all my notes. And another with the National Archives. They get my letters.'

For a moment I'm at a loss for words. It's the thought of all the things he and I have written to each other, and more particularly the fact that it hasn't all been burned as would be fit and proper, but will instead find its way to the National Archives, where it will lie and simmer, its neutrons bubbling away, waiting for criticality.

'Not your letters, of course,' he says. 'Nor indeed those of the other women I have known.'

'I'm pleased,' I say. 'On behalf of the National Archives. It means they've saved themselves a packet on extra storage capacity.'

But he's unruffled. He's about to get one over on me.

'As destiny would have it,' he goes on, 'I am thereby well informed as to declassification dates on restricted information in this country, and there is only one archive in the whole of Denmark whose contents may be withheld for ninety years. That place is the National Archives Annexe, located somewhere underneath the Folketing.'

I glance around the restaurant. At the tables, diners are enjoying aromatic dishes whose spices come from countries in which large parts of the population survive on less than a thousand calories a day. On the walls hang diplomas awarded to The Blue Okapi by the Glutton Club, and enlarged photocopies of restaurant reviews according the establishment six meat pies or six enema syringes or whatever unit of excellence the newspaper in question employs. Denmark is in many ways a remarkable country.

'I found Henrik Kornelius,' I say. 'Someone stuffed him inside a washing machine and turned the dial to boil wash.'

Thit and Harald are only sixteen. I must have nurtured a dream once of protecting them and giving them a better life than my own.

That dream is an illusion now. If you're dead lucky you might just be able to shield your kids from assault and abuse. But you can't shield them from the real problem. Because the real problem is life itself.

Maybe Laban and I kept them away from reality for too long. We – or at least I – have always had time for them. We selected their kindergarten with the most meticulous attention to detail. We picked out the best primary school. We gave them enough pocket money to defer their encounter with that most dreadful fact of life: work.

Here, at the restaurant called The Blue Okapi, I wonder if we might have done them an ill turn. Because sooner or later, the reality of life will become plain to them. And now, facing one particularly hideous aspect of that reality, the thought occurs to me that we may perhaps inadvertently have stunted their resiliance.

Laban can't talk. His lips have gone white.

But Thit can.

'How do you get a man inside a washing machine?'

I look her in the eye.

'By exerting sufficient pressure per square centimetre.'

Slowly, she puts down her knife and fork. I'm glad I was able to put this off a bit. At least they could enjoy some of their meal.

28

IT'S AFTERNOON. OUTSIDE, THE WINTER'S DARKNESS HAS descended. The twins have gone off to Jægersborg Allé to buy the last of their Christmas presents and look for some duck for the dinner. Laban and I are sitting facing each other at the round table.

'We need to get into that archive,' he says. 'It needs to be tonight.'

Denmark was once an open country. Where a dentist on Amager Torv, an admirer of Thorvald Stauning, the country's first social democratic prime minister, decided he wanted to tell of his affection to the man himself, for which reason he stopped by the prime minister's office on his way home from work and was asked in for coffee, after which he performed an extraction of one of the beloved statesman's teeth, on the spot and without charge.

Those days are gone. The courtyard of the Rigsdagsgården, housing the National Archives, is no longer open to motorised vehicles.

'How are we going to do it?'

'We turn left, Susan. You and me.'

During the last dozen years or more, Laban and the twins have turned left and conned their way in to see the crown jewels at Amalienborg Palace, the city's sewer system and the headquarters of FET, the Danish military intelligence agency, at the Kastellet. They have, moreover, visited the Panum Institute's department of pathology and its rather unappetising collection of tumours and sexually transmitted growths preserved in formalin. They've been round the Technical University of Denmark's National Laboratory for Sustainable Energy at Risø and – on what until now I thought would be their final outing – the vaults of the National Bank.

It was there they were finally collared, their combined powers of persuasion eventually falling short. The police were called, and a phone call made to me. God knows how, but they'd succeeded in getting themselves let in to view the nation's gold reserves, and that's where their luck ran out. It was only because I used my police contacts and referred to the rounds of questioning I'd done for them, which at that point had been some ten years previously, that I got them back home at all.

That evening I subjected them one at a time to interrogation. Harald cracked and spilled the beans about turning left.

'Weren't there any limits?' I asked him. 'No rules?'

'Only one,' he said. 'There's only ever been one rule for what we do with Dad: *Don't tell Mum.*'

Laban and I came close to divorce that night. The only reason we pulled through was because he swore he'd never turn left again. And now here he is, wanting me to go with him.

'There are security checks,' I tell him. 'I've seen it on TV. At the entrance to the Folketing. Magnetic barriers, like at the airport. Guards round the clock.'

We look at each other for a moment. Then we get to our feet.

We walk towards the garage. I've got my toolbox with me. I feel oddly nauseous.

Then I stop at the gap in the hedge leading to Villa Chez Nous, Dorthea and Ingemann's house.

'Dorthea used to be in charge of Sightseeing Day.'

Laban stares at me blankly. He grew up in the kind of

environment that has traditionally set store by not knowing about Sightseeing Day.

It was a popular annual festival. The Sightseeing Day catalogue used to be sold in all the newspaper kiosks, and the money went to shoes for the children of the poor, or a stay at some colony for weaklings, or whatever. Moreover, it allowed the general public, on that one day of the year, Sightseeing Day, access to all sorts of places that were normally out of bounds: the Svanemølle power station, the storage depots of the Arsenal Museum, the nuclear laboratory at Risø, the Holmen naval base, the Flakfortet sea fort in the Øresund, the winter quarters of the Benneweis circus.

And the city's hidden underground: its sewers, the casemates, the vaults of the Børsen Exchange.

We squeeze through the gap.

I ring the bell and Dorthea comes to the door.

'Dorthea,' I say, 'we've got a problem.'

Without a word she steps aside. We enter the hallway and she closes the door behind us.

Neither she nor Ingemann ever went to college. He was a fisherman most of his life, until the night he saw an angel. He was sailing in the North Atlantic. Off the coast of Greenland, on a night of fog, in a small, thirty-foot, copper-bottomed wooden cutter sailing at full speed, he suddenly saw an angel in the bow pointing ahead. Immediately, he stopped the engines, and the very next moment an iceberg the size of the cliffs at Møns Klint loomed up out of the fog, seventy vertical metres of sheer ice. Seconds later and the boat would have smashed into it, the bow would have been matchwood, and they would have sunk and drowned in an instant.

He told us the story once, in a matter-of-fact sort of way. The twins were with us, and it was obvious he wanted them to listen. He's never mentioned it since.

After that he went ashore for good and became a road mender. Dorthea came from seven years of schooling to the

Copenhagen city hall, where she worked her way up to departmental manager, back in the days when that sort of thing was still possible and the civil administration looked at what people could actually do rather than just at their exam certificates.

What unnerves me about them is that they're a bit like angels themselves. In all the years Laban and I have been tearing each other's heads off at regular intervals, I've never heard a cross word between them. They love Thit and Harald like their own grandchildren. Their garden is an unorganised paradise, with Ingemann's laid-up cutter in the middle and a sea of flowers all around. Before arthritis got the better of him, all but confining him to his cabin, as he calls his room at the top of the house, Ingemann planted what he refers to as – and what indeed is – a lovers' walk, with roses arching on high, where one might stroll arm in arm with one's beloved, and feel oneself transported to a different and better world.

So, basically, they're beyond me. Too good to be true by half.

'We got ourselves into trouble,' I tell them. 'In India. All four of us, though each in our own way. But then we got this miraculous offer, from the government. They asked us to get them some information. In return, they would make sure all charges against us were dropped and our civil liberties reinstated. We agreed and got them what they wanted. Only now it's all going wrong. People are getting killed. Someone tried to do away with me and Harald. So we've decided to go into hiding.'

Dorthea glances across at our house.

'At your home address?'

She's got a point.

'They think we've gone to Italy, on a witness protection programme. Some other people think we're dead. At least we hope they do. The fact of the matter is we're in limbo. We think we've got two days. We're trying to figure out what it's all about before we give any information up. What we're trying to get hold of is a document. A report. We think it's kept somewhere in the vaults of the Folketing, in a restricted archive.'

She tips her head to one side and peers at us.

'That'll be the National Archives Annexe. It's the only archive there besides the Folketing's own, beneath the lower level. A sub-basement, if you like, underneath the information support centre, the postal unit and the printing rooms. It's a series of tunnels, really, dating back to medieval times. You can cross the entire Slotsholmen. If you've got the guts.'

'Dorthea, would there be the slightest chance of getting in there?'

She tips her head to the other side. From the hall where we're still standing, a narrow staircase leads up to the first floor and then to the top of the house, to Ingemann's cabin. On the wall at every third stair is a framed, coloured print of a girl in different regional dress, so by the time you reach Ingemann every outpost of the country has been represented in traditional folk garb. The staircase itself is lined with a red carpet with polished brass stair rods. The doorknobs in the hall are polished too. The windows are polished. Everything in Dorthea's house is spick and span, meticulously neat and clean.

'It's all closed off. Has been since the bombing of the prime minister's office in Oslo, right next door to the Norwegian parliament. And the riots. All the doors are wired. If anything gets activated, the alarm goes off simultaneously at police HQ, the Folketing's security unit and Securitas.'

She peers at us again.

'But of course you can get in.'

29

THE CURVE DEPICTING OUR RELATIONSHIPS WITH OTHER people as a function of time is close to being a straight line. Meaning that when it comes to being in a relationship, one day is pretty much the same as the next. We might experience the odd little downturn, but basically it's all much of a muchness. Those instances in which we might apply differential calculus and discover the tangent line at a given point x to display a positive slope, thereby indicating that we are approaching each other, are few and far between.

And even more seldom are the moments in which the function becomes discontinuous and performs a leap.

By the looks of things, Laban and I are approaching just such a moment with Dorthea Skousen.

She's sitting in the passenger seat next to Laban, and in her lap is an unfolded map of the system of underground corridors beneath Christiansborg Palace.

It's a photocopy, seemingly from the infancy of the Xerox machine in the 1960s. The paper is yellowed, the image grainy, and since the machine could apparently only handle A4, the map comprises five or six separate sheets glued together. And where the glue has come apart it's been fixed with Sellotape.

Each sheet has been rubber-stamped with the word *CONFI-DENTIAL*, originally in red ink, now mostly a faded grey.

There's always been a bit of municipal management about Dorthea. Not just her cleaning and the way she keeps house, but also the care and attention to detail by which she and Ingemann, without fail, have always cleared the snow on the pavement outside their house and gritted by the book. And outside ours, too, because we always forget. Not to mention the meticulous manner in which they have driven and continue to drive their old Volvo, a vehicle manufactured in the 1960s and thus formally, one would think, a veteran, yet kept immaculately running by their kind words of encouragement, a heated garage and fifty years of accident-free motoring, not to mention the general atmosphere of kindness and conviviality that comes with its owners.

It's a side of Dorthea I understand only too well. I'm municipal myself, the way ninety-five per cent of all science is. A comprehensive set of rules administered by university-educated bookkeepers.

But the Dorthea we see now is different altogether: completely calm, despite being quite as aware as us of what those smudged stamps of confidentiality actually mean. They mean that she is in the process of doing something she must once have agreed in writing never to do. She is about to violate her obligation of professional secrecy.

'The corridors underneath Christiansborg featured in the Sightseeing Day catalogue eight years on the run. To begin with I acted as tour guide myself. I was office manager, so who else was supposed to do it? It was only the Folketing's caretakers who even knew they existed and who would have any kind of business there. A lot of it was blocked off due to the danger of collapse. We couldn't ask the caretakers to show anyone round, so we had to do it ourselves. The system starts underneath the Thorvaldsens Museum and leads through the crypt under the Slotskirken. After that, there are branches leading off under the royal stables in one direction, while another lot run under the casemates, the cellars housing the exhibition of what's left of Absalons Gård. From there, they carry on under the Folketing, all the way over to the Royal Library. Narrow tunnels, dug out by hand. Full of heating pipes and cables now. In the seventies, a group of youngsters broke into a locker room and some security guards' uniforms were stolen. After that, the underground passages were mapped and sealed off, but one arm was kept open to be used as an archive – an appendix, if you like – running under the old Landstingssalen. They kept all the treasures there from the Arnamagnæan Manuscript Collection while there was all that fuss going on about their being transferred back to Iceland. *Njál's Saga*, and all that. They were afraid they'd be vandalised. The earliest copy of Saxo's history of the Danes. *Codex Holmiensis*. The most valuable incunabula. Besides those documents kept under what we in the public administration called permanent protection. Which is to say ninety years. Occasionally longer in the case of documents concerning the security of the nation.'

Laban drives us along Nørre Voldgade and H. C. Andersens Boulevard before turning down Stormgade. After we pass the National Museum, Dorthea points and we veer onto the square that is Prins Jørgens Gård. She signals for Laban to pull in. In the gloom of December, the Thorvaldsens Museum is a solid slab of grey.

She gets out, goes away, then appears again, waving us across the street and down onto a narrow ramp. She's opened the gate, and we pass through into a small underground car park beneath the museum. The lights go on automatically and the gate closes behind us.

We get out of the car. I take the crowbar with me and a small head lamp. The car park contains some twenty-odd parking spaces, the rest of the area taken up by marble statues in storage. Dorthea keys in a code, deliberately, so I can memorise it.

'I'm still on the committee,' she says. 'The friends of the museum.'

The door opens.

I've always avoided museums. Even the Technical Museum at

Elsinore. It's enough trying to come to terms with my own past, without being lumbered with society's too.

Dorthea lets me enter the code and another door opens. We descend to another level, this one clearly older. No one's found it worthwhile to render the walls here: at first it's all raw concrete, then medieval brick and stone. I switch on my head lamp. Dorthea has brought a little torch, a splendid thing made of metal, from an age when flashlight electromechanics was still young and innocent. Its power comes from a dynamo she activates by rhythmically squeezing the handle, causing a flywheel to spin inside. The sound it makes is pleasant and soft, like a mechanised erotic moan. We come to a third door and Dorthea stops.

'This is as far as I go. Ingemann will be needing me.'

I open the door and she points down the tunnel.

'Seventy-five metres further on you'll come to an exhibition room. Pass through and the tunnel carries on. Another hundred and fifty metres and you'll see three steps up to a door on your left-hand side. Use the same code. If you get caught, there's a three-year sentence. Ingemann and I will look after the twins, if worst comes to worst.'

There's something I want to say to her. Something like *thanks*. Something about never truly knowing your neighbours until they've helped you commit a break-in carrying three years in the slammer. But I'm mute.

She peers at me.

'Susan. What's wrong with you is you never believe people actually like you.'

And with that, she turns and leaves.

Laban's about to speak. I shake my head. There's no more to be said on the subject.

We go through the door and come out in the exhibition room a bit further on. I was here once as a child, on Sightseeing Day. I can't remember if Dorthea was our guide, but what I do recall is the bleakness that resides among the historical remains of the medieval city. The present day might not be that cheerful, but the past was worse. To me, the brick foundations whisper not of romance and adventure in the colourful Middle Ages, but of disease, dungeons and rape, and an average lifespan that would have me long since dead. Not to mention a cuisine that peaked with salted herring and gruel.

Next to the toilets is another door opened by the same code, and behind that a staircase, at the bottom of which the service corridors begin. From here we must hug the walls as we proceed, the bulk of the space occupied by great air-duct systems, heating pipes and bundles of cables led through the tunnels in open stainless-steel troughs.

I count our paces. After a hundred and twenty-five we reach the steps and the door on our left.

Only it's not a door. It's a sheet of steel without a handle or lock. They've sealed it off.

We walk another fifty metres, then fifty metres back. There's only the one entrance.

Laban thumps his fist against the metal. The sound it makes is dull and solid as a railway sleeper.

'The room on the other side will be equipped with sensors,' I say. 'Monitored round the clock. The place will come alive with security.'

'We'll be hog-tied,' says Laban.

'They'll call it terrorism and give us ten years instead of three. By the time we get out, the twins will be twenty-six.'

'We should give up.'

'Turn ourselves in,' I say.

But then I insert the chisel end of the crowbar between the steel and the brick. Laban lends a hand, and we heave. The sheeting is ripped from its frame and crashes to the ground, a clattering supersonic cacophony.

Just as we thought, it's hooked up to an alarm: a red lamp flashes inside the doorway and a siren begins to wail.

The alarm mechanism – and the siren with it – is housed in a

158

casing that looks like it's made of hardened steel. I raise the crowbar as if it were an axe, and bring it down with all my strength.

It gashes open, the red lamp goes out, and everything is at once quiet.

In that silence we wait. For sirens and guards, a sudden stealth attack in the dark. But nothing happens. The room behind the door is pitch black, and quiet as the grave.

We step inside.

In the light from my head lamp we see we've entered an enlarged tunnel area, perhaps four by seventeen metres, much of the ceiling raised in the form of an arching vault of rendered brick.

Seventy-odd square metres isn't much, but the space is crammed solid with documents. Its walls are lined with shelving, with hardly a centimetre vacant. The air is heavy and catches in the throat. The sheer volume of paper, most likely combined with a climate-control system, has drained the atmosphere of moisture.

We say nothing, but each of us knows what the other is thinking: we've got no plan for how to localise a file in this chaos. We pass along the shelves. Ring binders, magazine files and book spines are numbered using a decimal system unfamiliar to me, presumably unique to the National Archives. Behind me runs a section of shelving housing six-sided metal canisters, each one locked and sealed by means of a fastener. They must be capsules, for the sensitive stuff, they too marked only by a six-digit number.

I sense a certain desperation. I consider splitting each capsule apart one by one with the crowbar, and try to gauge how many there are: at least three full sections, seventeen times ten metres, seven capsules per running metre, three thousand capsules minimum, impossible.

We inch further and my head lamp picks out a small desk, on top of which is a monitor. I switch it on and the screen comes to life. A box appears asking for a password.

I pull my phone from my pocket. Laban says nothing. I call Thit. I've no idea if a mobile signal can pass through eleven metres of concrete.

She answers straight away.

'Thit! The code. For the Folketing's security levels.'

'What do you want that for? Where are you, anyway?'

She rattles off the digits.

'We've got eight ducks. Organic. Only I've forgotten what you stuff them with, besides apples and prunes.'

I feel dizzy.

'TNT,' I tell her. 'Besides apples and prunes, we'll need some TNT.'

'Is that in the refrigerated section?'

'Yes,' I say. 'And get some detonators while you're at it.'

'How do you spell it? Where did you say you were?'

I hang up.

I enter the first combination. The screen says *Happy Christmas and welcome to the National Archives Annexe*. I enter the second combination. Then the third. *Parliamentary Future Commission*. A number appears. And a plan of the archives indicating the capsule's placement.

It's at the bottom of the final shelf, furthest from the entrance.

We find it immediately, remove it from its place and put it down on the floor. It's as heavy as a barrel of plutonium.

There's a combination lock. I wedge the crowbar in at the seam and apply my full weight. The capsule springs open.

At the same moment, the lights go on.

The entrance door opens. I switch off my head lamp.

Laban leaps into action. He points to the shelf from where we've taken the capsule. Here, at the archive's furthest extremity, a couple of shelf metres remain unoccupied. There's just room enough for me to crawl in.

Normally, Laban would never issue an order. And normally, I wouldn't obey one.

But Laban is a conductor. In that capacity he possesses an

implicit authority otherwise overlooked in what his admirers refer to as his rakishly fanciful demeanour, and which I refer to as his ability to bamboozle the world by underplaying himself to the point where he's got such a good purchase it's too late for anyone to get away.

He straightens up and strides convivially towards the open door.

At the same time, a woman enters. By her elegance and self-confidence I recognise her instantly as the chief librarian of the Folketing. Tripping in her wake is a man I realise I know and yet have never met. In a split second, this rather paradoxical state of affairs unravels itself, and it dawns on me that the man is Falck-Hansen, Denmark's Minister of Foreign Affairs. People you've seen that many times on television and in the papers will often leave just such an impression, and induce perplexity and surprise when suddenly one sees them in real life.

He and the woman step aside, and a group of perhaps a dozen men come piling in. The three at the front are Chinese.

I recognise several of the faces, in the same strangely unreal way I recognised Falck-Hansen's. They belong to members of government, both European and Asian.

I sense their power in the air, even as I cower on my shelf. They're certainly dressed to look the part, in suits or jacket-and-skirt combos that look like they were specially selected for each of them by Anna Wintour so that they might appear on the cover of American *Vogue*. And maybe they were.

Moreover, there's a mood of community about them. I realise without any doubt that they are here for some kind of summit. But who would call a summit the day before Christmas Eve?

They halt in their tracks as they clap eyes on Laban. The librarian is standing right in front of him.

You don't get to be chief librarian of the Folketing without being able to keep a cool head in the face of even the most extreme circumstances. Her features reveal no emotion, as if she were at a card table, in the midst of a game of high-stakes poker. But even from my hiding place I can sense the questions queuing up in her mind.

The first concerns the matter of what Laban might be doing here. The second is about why he hasn't switched on the lights now that he is.

Yet these issues remain unarticulated, because Laban immediately takes charge.

'How marvellous to see you! Delighted, I'm sure!'

I feel a pang of combined annoyance and fascination at the same time. The mere fact of Laban telling anyone he's glad to see them usually sends them into raptures, as if they'd won the lottery and he's the one presenting them with the cheque. It's impossible to explain in rational terms, but it's got something to do with his version of the Effect.

'I can reveal that I have been commissioned to compose a festival cantata for the Folketing's anniversary celebrations.'

He places his hands on the shoulders of the chief librarian and the foreign minister simultaneously, and gently propels them backwards.

'There's something you really must hear, my distinguished ladies and gentleman. And the acoustics are so much better out here in the corridor.'

The door shuts behind him.

I'm just about to emerge, only then I freeze. Measured footsteps cause the smallest of vibrations to travel across the floor, and a pair of highly polished leather shoes stops in front of my refuge.

Perhaps it's the fabric of my clothing that interests him. At any rate, he goes down on one knee, putting a hand on the floor for support. His face appears in front of mine. We stare at each other.

Most of us have heard of Chinese politeness. For the majority of Danes, such behaviour remains merely a hypothesis. But for that hypothesis I am now given performative proof.

For a few seconds he remains motionless. Who wouldn't?

How would anyone interpret the discovery of a woman hiding on a lower shelf of the National Archives Annexe, eleven metres underground on the day before Christmas Eve?

But then he bends forward, the exact number of centimetres required for his nose to nearly touch the floor, thereby completing what would seem to be the impossible physical feat of performing a bow whilst almost lying prone.

I put a finger to my lips. Then fold my hands under my cheek, the universal sign for sleep.

That does the trick. A broad smile of understanding lights up his face. Without a word, we have established international rapport. He knows exactly how it is, after a long day at the Politburo's Central Committee, to sneak down into the archives and grab a bit of shut-eye on the bottom shelf.

He gets to his feet. I watch his shoes as they move towards the door. As quietly as he can, he closes it behind him.

30

THE LIGHTS GO OUT. I EMERGE, SWITCH ON MY HEAD
lamp, and turn my attention back to the capsule. On the other
side of the door, voices break out into song. First Laban's, then
others too. I recognise Falck-Hansen's. Then a couple more
Danes, maybe security guards. The husky alto of the Folketing's
chief librarian joins in. And then the first Chinese voices. Italian
and Spanish. An English female.

I've witnessed it many times before. Laban can make anyone
sing: funeral processions, lifetime prisoners, whoever.

The capsule is full of documents. I spread the folders out in a
fan on the floor. The papers they contain seem to be drafts,
bundles kept together by sheets of paper folded around their
middle, variously yellow or green. My guess is they're Kirsten
Klaussen's own notes, saved for posterity. Calories to feed her
posthumous reputation.

The bottom folder is different. More meticulous, held together
at the spine by two bulldog clips. On the front it says: *Memorandum, Parliamentary Future Commission, 12 September
1974.*

It looks like the report Keld Keldsen told me about.

I remove the clips and run my fingers over the pages. They're
written on an electric typewriter, the individual characters
stamped one tenth of a millimetre into the paper. I go to the
last page.

I read the two signatures:

Andrea Fink and Magrethe Spliid.

Several planes of reality converge.

One is that of the corridor outside, in which people are singing, contrary to all reason. Another is that of the city and its supermarkets, Father Christmas and roast duck, and half a million weary credit cards.

A third is one autumn forty-six years ago. When the world was younger and more innocent than today. And yet awakening. When a group of talented young people were put together to meet informally, without anyone taking them seriously. Until two people wrote a report.

I roll the report up and put it in my inside pocket. I return the metal canister to its place, and manhandle the steel sheeting back into the doorframe. And then I run.

Back in the underground car park beneath the Thorvaldsens Museum I open the exit gate. Part of me expects a score of plain-clothes police waiting to receive me, but Prins Jørgens Gård is deserted.

I drive the car up the ramp and close the gate behind me. I'm out.

I think about Laban. About how long it'll take for them to break him. For all his casual attitudes, he possesses a frightening amount of stubbornness. You have to get close to discover it. When you do, it's something you won't forget in a hurry.

What I have to do now, what he has bought me the time to do, is to find Thit and Harald and make ourselves scarce. Check into a hotel, or maybe head up north to break into a summer house and read the report before figuring out what to do.

I get into the car again. I ought to turn left along Vindebrogade, but something I can't explain makes me go right instead, to Christiansborgs Slotsplads. I pull up on the cobbles, get out, and walk up to the security booth under the archway leading to the Rigsdagsgården courtyard. I flash my uni ID.

The Rigsdagsgården is sparsely populated. Governments need Christmas, too. There's not a police car or taxi in sight, not even that many lights on in the windows. Four or five limos are parked at the kerb, along with some sombre-looking escort vehicles with tinted windows and a couple of motorcycle police.

The entrance door of the Folketing opens. Laban emerges backwards. His hands are raised in the air. At first I think it's in self-defence.

But I'm wrong. What he's doing is conducting. After him come the foreign minister, the Chinese visitors, the chief librarian and the rest of the delegation, and behind them several members of the Folketing's security staff. All are singing.

He brings the movement to a close and everyone applauds. Laban bows, passing the honours on to his choir. They bow in return. Again, I feel a dizziness akin to seasickness.

Laban is about to give everyone a hug by turn. He always hugs the people he performs with. Even the most untouchable of individuals, who would rather commit murder than have anyone approach them physically – people like Herbert von Karajan, Dick Cheney, former KGB head Vladimir Kryuchkov. I've seen Laban hug them all.

It happens the same way, always. He tips his head coquettishly to one side and beams imploringly. As if to ask if it's really all right for him to do what he has always dreamed of doing, which is to embrace them. And, at the same time, to say that as the chivalrous nobleman he is, he would accept their refusal in good spirit.

I've yet to see anyone who could turn him down.

And so it is now. One by one, the Chinese step up and are engulfed in his arms, followed by their fellow delegates. Eventually, it's the turn of the security guards. They're as stiff as tin soldiers and chuckle with goofy embarrassment, but it's obvious he's made their day.

And with that, Laban skips down the steps towards me, as if he'd known all along I'd be there waiting for him.

We walk through the barrier and back to the car. I start the ignition and pull away into the traffic. He leans back in the seat and sighs with satisfaction.

'Wonderful voices! Such musicality! Marvellous people! Give me three days with them and we'd have something for an audience.'

I grip the wheel. Five minutes ago I was sure I'd seen him for the last time.

'What are they doing here, Laban? Obviously they came from a meeting. And with that calibre of delegates, we're talking Cabinet level. Two days before Christmas. It doesn't make sense.'

He's still absorbed in the experience of conducting a choir in a subterranean corridor. Only reluctantly does he return to reality. Helpless as a child.

'You didn't see any memorandum? A note of any kind?'

He shakes his head.

And then his face lights up.

'She was carrying a route map. Klara, I mean, the chief librarian. They still had one stop to make. I noticed because at one point she diverted her attention from the song, and I peeked at what she was looking at. It was the last bullet on her list. The old Radiohuset, the broadcasting house on Rosenørns Allé. You remember . . .'

I remember all too well. Laban's second and fourth symphonies were premiered in the Radiohuset's concert hall.

'What's there now?' I ask.

He shakes his head.

'It's all rented out in units. Cosmetics companies. Solicitors' offices. I think the concert hall itself is a storage facility. The Graphic Design School has the rear premises. None of which can explain why a summit would end up there.'

'Unless,' I say, 'it's a kind of pilgrimage. To the scenes of Laban Svendsen's greatest triumphs.'

He tosses his head as if to laugh. But deep inside he doesn't find it funny at all. He thinks a pilgrimage would be very fitting indeed.

31

IT'S CHRISTMAS EVE. UNFORTUNATELY.

Some years ago, I tried to clear myself some space in the deathly inertia that presides over Christmas by suggesting a vegetarian dinner.

I was a vegetarian until the twins were born. I couldn't sink my teeth into a chunk of meat without tasting the slaughter that had gone before.

Needless to say, I was overruled. Laban and the twins are cannibals. They want their tournedos dripping with blood. They want their lamb chops rose-coloured and edged with the thickest slabs of fat, with the bones sticking out at the sides. They want soup bones they can crack open with a mallet and suck the marrow from.

One year I drove to the Lammefjord and picked up two live ducks. I made Laban and the twins watch from the first row while I chopped off the heads of the fowl with a woodsman's axe and the separated bodies involuntarily waddled around the chopping block before collapsing in a blood-oozing heap.

It had no effect, though Laban did have to withdraw for a moment in order to be sick. Thit and Harald, however, plucked and scalded the ducks and removed the innards, and when it came to evening they each ate a triple portion as if the pleasure were all the greater for their devouring new friends.

Since then I've never bothered. And the food is only a small measure of my overall discomfiture.

Another is my mother. Ever since the twins were born I've tried to avoid having people over on Christmas Eve. But I've never been able to avoid my mother and her entourage.

In the mid-nineties, Andrea Fink and I designed a series of experiments showing that the ideal group consists of no more than five individuals, if any kind of evenly distributed, undistracted togetherness is to be maintained over a length of time.

The results tallied with my own experience. In private contexts I feel ill at ease in any group larger than five. But my mother comes from a large family, and brings a considerable section of it with her every Christmas. We've never been fewer than fifteen for dinner, and it's beyond me how I can be forty-three and still allow my mother to overrule me in such pivotal situations.

This Christmas she's brought what she calls her most decent cousins, which is to say three women with husbands, and children the age of Thit and Harald.

And of course her own husband, Fabius.

Fabius is a successful, homosexual designer whose age remains unknown to the general public, though it's perfectly clear that he's younger than me. My mother married him seven years ago without notice. I took her aside at the wedding, pinned her into a corner and asked: 'Why, Mother?'

A silence descended upon us. The moment turned deep, yielding such vast amounts of data that seven years later I still haven't finished processing it all. Then she said: 'Do you know what, Susan? God presented us with a dilemma and it goes like this: we all want to have a husband. And we all want not to have a husband. Fabius is the solution to that dilemma.'

I nodded. That far I could follow her.

'Then there's the money. Fabius is rolling in it. And he likes to share.'

I nodded again, still following. But then came the bit I've yet to fathom: 'And then there's love, Susan.'

In defeat and behind enemy lines, one must make do as best

one can. I have at least found a way of surviving the caramel potatoes of a Danish Christmas: I boil them in just the right amount of sweetened meat stock, so that at the very moment they reach the desired consistency, the liquid has evaporated and the proteins and glycogens caramelise into a perfect, golden glaze.

This Christmas Eve there's nineteen of us for dinner.

That requires eight ducks. Laban and the twins have an axiom that goes: *One duck is too much for two, but too little for three.* What it means is that I've had to get the outdoor pizza oven going and ask to borrow the cast-iron wood-burning stove Dorthea and Ingemann have got built into the wall of their utility room.

A single duck is one thing. Two would be manageable. But eight is a different kettle of fish. The table looks like a genocide. The earliest respite I'll get is when it's all over and we've danced around the Christmas tree, which is another unavoidable horror, and everyone's unwrapped their new smartphones and iPads – or why not simply shrink-wrapped bundles of crisp, new five-hundred-kroner notes, seeing as how that's what all of us would really prefer?

Once we're that far into the evening, I'll go out into the garden and stand in the darkness with the brightly luminous snow all around me, and breathe in the inexplicable peace that somehow, and despite everything, descends upon the earth on Christmas Eve.

The mood at dinner is tolerable. My mother calls her three cousins decent because they possess at least some of the normality the rest of us spend our lives yearning for. They've had the same jobs for years. They're well liked and respected. They've never been divorced, and their children are bright and polite. By means of strategic intelligence and a great many compromises, they have managed to settle into lives that are just about bearable.

Of course, they've always been slightly nervous about Laban, the twins and me. But their fears are generally put to rest by that rule of existential geometry that says that where there's a relatively stable midpoint in which to plonk oneself, there will always necessarily be a more unstable periphery. As long as the radius is great enough, restricted to Christmases and birthdays, everything should be all right.

That said, Thit's homeless person is of course a rather niggly detail. A couple of years ago it was a university lecturer who'd lost his job and been kicked out by his wife. When Thit ran into him he was begging on the Metro, and on Christmas Eve at ours he recited French poetry once he got drunk enough. The year before that, it was a former nobleman down on his luck. I had to frisk him when he left in order to get my silverware back.

But this year's model looks like the real thing. Behind his unkempt hair and shaggy beard is a man presumably in his fifties, though he looks twenty years older. His name is Oskar, his fingers are yellowed from tobacco, he smells dismal, and when I pour him a glass of chilled Grenache, one of the few grapes not to tremble at the sight of eight ducks, he peers anxiously at it, then leans towards me and says: 'I don't suppose the lady would have a teeny-weeny bottle of Bavarian pilsner hidden away at the back of the pantry, by any chance?'

All in all, then, there's a decent chance we might get to the *ris à l'amande* in one piece.

Only we don't. And the reason why is the Effect.

Laban, the twins and I have done everything right by sitting together. In that way it's as if we form a sealed container, inside which the Effect works like a standing wave, imperceptible to any outsider.

On the list of all the many kinds of intelligence, there is one that modern psychology has overlooked, and that's dinner-party intelligence. Laban has it. He can converse with a whole table in such a way that the youngsters feel respected, the men admired and the women tickled behind the ears by an invisible hand.

At the same time, it's as if he erects a safety barrier along the precipice we all know to be the peril of any dinner party, so that everyone is aware, without having need to be told, that they can only go so far and no further.

Inside this rectangular, meticulously chalked-up court this Christmas Eve, we discuss economics and nice new cars, and how well the children are doing at school, and we are asked politely about our time in India, to which we reply evasively though to everyone's satisfaction, and I'm just beginning to relax a bit when Harald puts down his knife and fork.

'Grandmother,' he says, 'why did Mum get put into care?'

My mother carefully dabs the corners of her mouth with her napkin. She's a solo dancer. From the age of eighteen, until she was forty and gradually moved into teaching, she danced more than a hundred performances a year. So she's got plenty of training and is more than canny enough to improvise, even if the orchestra by accident should suddenly play a few bars of a requiem in the middle of *Swan Lake*.

The problem now is that we're not talking about accident.

'It was a residential institution for young people. I couldn't manage her. I couldn't, the schools couldn't.'

'How long was she there?'

He's not asking me. He knows I'd put a lid on it.

'I don't quite recall.'

It's all gone quiet around the table. All families have their contaminated areas: dumping grounds for old waste, radioactive isotopes or skeletons still with residual tissue. They are places all of us avoid, out of politeness or anxiety, or simply because dredging an entire life, taking it apart and putting all the bits through an autoclave, seems so insurmountable.

We've now ventured into just such an area.

Harald turns to face me.

'How old were you, Mum? When they put you away?'

I look him straight in the eye. To make him stop.

'Twelve.'

'When did you go home again?'

'I didn't. I moved into student accommodation when I was sixteen.'

'How come?'

Frankness has its own timetable. I don't know who manages it, but I do know that once it's started and has got to a certain point, it's very difficult indeed to stop.

And then there's the build-up of pressure. From too many Christmas Eves, the small talk of too many family get-togethers. Too much putting a lid on things.

'It was a place called Holmgangen,' I say. 'There was a young staff member there who used to have sex with the girls. Most of them didn't mind, they wanted the contact. But not me. I spent four years avoiding him. I was the one who repaired things and kept things running. He was afraid of losing my expertise. But then one day it was my turn. He'd got me putting down new decking over at the small house they rented out to him not far from the main building. We were on our own. The others had made themselves scarce, they knew what was going to happen.'

I look at Thit and Harald by turn.

'He threw me to the ground, tore off my knickers and penetrated me. I made my body relax completely. I could hear myself crying, but mentally I kept calm. Inside, I was almost serene. I wrapped my legs around his torso and squeezed as hard as I could, trapping him so he couldn't get free. On one side of me was an electric drill driver. A twenty-four-volt Dewalt, new on the market. On the other side was a box of stainless-steel deck screws. They cost nearly a krone a piece, even then. Eighty millimetres in length, with an auger point to prevent splitting. Fifty millimetres of sharp-angled thread to drive the screw downwards. Then twenty-five millimetres of square thread, meaning that once it's in, it's going to stay there until the timber's rotted away. I picked up the driver in one hand and a deck screw in the other. And as he pumped away inside me I felt along his spine

173

until a point I gauged to be somewhere around the kidneys. I put the screw to his back, turned the driver on full and drove it into him. There was no resistance, so it didn't pass through bone. These days I know it takes a surgeon to drill through the spinous process. But it did go through the erector spinae like it was butter. He tried to get away, but I kept him in a thigh lock while I picked up the next screw.'

Laban looks away. My mother looks away. The others want to look away, but can't.

'Again, I went for the spine, only again it glanced off through the muscle. At that age I didn't know where the organs were, but today I'd have gone a couple of centimetres further down. I was only sixteen, all I knew about was physics. Now he was almost paralysed. I wriggled out from underneath him. He tried to get up, but couldn't. I screwed his hands to the deck, one after the other, then sat on top of him, straddling his back. There was no hurry after that. I picked up a screw and located the medulla. That was where I was going to put the last one in. He'd have been finished then. I pressed the point against the base of his skull and switched on the driver. But I couldn't do it.'

I look across at Fabius. He can't even blink.

'The next day, social services came. I told them either they moved me into student accommodation in Copenhagen and gave me textbooks on physics or else I'd spill the beans and get the others to witness. Not that it was a threat, they had to understand, but a promise. The day after, a temporary guardian came in a taxi and took me back to the city.'

The room is a hush.

After a bit, my mother gets to her feet, goes into the hall and puts on her fur coat. Fabius slinks after her. After a few more minutes, one of her most decent cousins rises and announces that they'd best be making tracks, after which the two other cousins likewise get to their feet, followed by their children and husbands.

Laban, the twins and Oskar remain seated. I see our guests

to the door. I find their unopened presents under the Christmas tree and put them into carrier bags, and insist on giving them doggy bags to take home, and a special treat of freshly chopped apples and walnuts in crème fraiche, my way of getting round the Danish tradition of red cabbage with the duck.

As a final gesture, I also give each of them a tightly sealed, heavy-duty freezer bag filled with duck fat, which they accept mechanically with a lifeless look in their eyes. Nonetheless, I feel sure they'll appreciate it in the days to come. You can make a banquet out of finely chopped onions, potatoes and beetroot, if only you fry it all together in duck fat.

I check and make sure they haven't forgotten anything before walking them out to their cars and waving goodbye.

By the time I go back in, the table's been cleared and the living room's empty apart from Oskar. In the fridge I find the bottle of beer I was given by the Trappist monks of Vor Frue Kloster. I pour it into two glasses and hand one of them to Oskar.

Now it's my turn to savour the peace and joy of Christmas, albeit a bit earlier than planned. I step outside, beer in hand.

32

LABAN IS SITTING ON THE BENCH. HE HAS SPREAD OUT A throw on which to sit, and made room for us both. I sit down beside him, he grabs another and we wrap ourselves up. We've done it so many times before.

He points up at the moon. It's almost full, a shining disc edged by the opal-coloured rainbow phenomenon commonly referred to as the circle of the moon.

'Susan, what do you see?'

'Refraction. The supernumerary bow.'

He nods pensively. We've done this before, too. It's an old game of ours, going back to the time we first got to know each other. Laban picks out some physical phenomenon and we describe to each other what we see.

We never saw anything the same way.

'I see an emotion. A feeling of destiny. Inevitability. In that inevitability there is also harmony.'

I refrain from comment. What can I say? Correlating concepts of destiny and harmony with a refraction phenomenon is not the kind of procedure that would garner support at the Department of Experimental Physics.

'Where was your father in what you were telling us, Susan?'

'He went away when I was eight.'

'And never came back?'

I nod. He gives himself time to take it in.

'How come you never told us before?'

I try to gauge my feelings. I don't think I've intentionally held anything back. I've just avoided having to be precise.

'You wouldn't understand.'

'Try me.'

I search for an explanation, but none is forthcoming. What comes to mind is an image, a recollection.

'The last time I saw him was one day in summer. He had a hunting lodge on the edge of the forest at Rude Skov. He loved hunting and had several cabins dotted about the country where he could go. There was a stream running through the property. I was playing about with rocks, building a channel so I could investigate the current. He came up to me. There was something he wanted to tell me. Somehow I knew it was the last time I'd see him. He sat down. I couldn't make myself look at him, so I looked at the whirlpools in the stream instead. Then he said: "Susan. Make sure your bite is as hard as your bark." I hugged him for the last time. I sensed his despair and embraced him the way a grown-up embraces a child. Then he stood up and went.'

Laban has closed his eyes while I've been speaking, the way he always does when listening intently. Now he opens them again. We look up at the forty-two-degree angle of deviation, the rainbow angle, of which he's never heard, and Alexander's band, the dark area within the incandescent circle. The phenomenon begins to fade, and in less than a minute it's gone.

Rainbows are fleeting.

We've gone back inside. I've put some wood in the stove and we're sitting at each end of the sofa.

Oskar is over by the Christmas tree, staring dreamily into his glass of beer. The bubbles that rise to the surface are tiny and ascend in little trains, like champagne. I study him, and at the same time it's as if I forget about him completely. That's how it is with castaways. We've all had a lifetime's training in getting them to merge with the paintwork.

Laban lifts one of my feet onto his lap and rubs it gently. I allow him to. If the world is nothing but an illusive convention anyway, as modern quantum physics would seem to suggest, what difference does it make to insist on sticking to your limits?

He must have massaged my feet like this hundreds, perhaps thousands of times. Whenever I got home from the endless meetings of the academic council, or came traipsing in at dawn after a night in the labs with Andrea Fink. Even if I crept straight into my own room, he'd still come out in his dressing gown and make me tea, and we'd sit down on the sofa here with my feet in his lap.

I never knew beforehand how much I needed it. But after a few minutes, and always to my own surprise, I realised how tight and numb the surface of my skin felt. And then it was like the tips of his fingers brought something dead to life again. Usually I'd be talking, an insistent flow about the experiments we'd been doing. He can't ever have understood much of it, but he never protested once and always gave me my head.

Now, too, I feel my skin gradually loosening up.

'Susan,' he says abruptly. 'When did it start to go wrong for us?'

We look back. Across the years.

33

I WAITED A WEEK AFTER THE DAY I DISCOVERED MY Raleigh in the middle of my room at halls. There was a concert on at the music conservatory, students of composition were putting on their own works. Laban was on the bill. I sat in the front row.

As soon as he took his seat at the piano, I knew I should never have come. I should never have given in. None of the great physicists ever got anywhere by being soft.

When the interval came I made off. He must have taken a short cut, because all of a sudden there he was in front of me on the stairs, blocking my escape.

'Your admirers will be expecting you,' I said.

'I'd give them all up for you.'

'That might turn out to be a rather foolish exchange. I'm worse than you think.'

I could hear the murmur of voices, the shuffle of footsteps on the landing above us. Laban threw out his arms and lifted his voice, exploiting the stairway's acoustics to the full.

'You and I, Susan, we are lost! But at least we are lost together!'

We walked our bikes home together, he beside me as we went. It was spring, the Tivoli Gardens were full of revellers, and the chestnut trees that lined H. C. Andersens Boulevard were thinking about coming into leaf.

'I've got a suggestion to make,' I said. 'It's the only offer you're going to get. We rent a cabin in the middle of nowhere and spend a month there together. There'll be no touching unless absolutely necessary. And no telephones or computers either. All we're going to do is see what happens.'

We cancelled everything and took off the very next day. We'd found a place by the Limfjord, dirt cheap, with no electricity and an outside loo. It was on a steep slope some twenty metres above the fjord, across whose gigantic waters we could look out towards the neighbouring Skive Fjord.

We slept together in a narrow bed, on a straw mattress, and for the first three weeks we never laid a finger on each other. When eventually we did, he was impotent the first two nights. That was what finally made up my mind: the fact that deep down he was so besotted that his normal functions had been put on stand-by.

We talked about children, as if we knew they'd come, and we promised each other never to let them take over. We told each other about previous love affairs. It hurt me to sense how hard it was for him to hear me tell of such things, and how he stuck it out nonetheless, for just a tiny morsel of my life from before we met.

We didn't have any money. I cooked pasta and vegetables, and we shared our dreams about the future. He'd always seen a house in the country, with an annexe to which he could withdraw to compose, from which he could emerge in the evenings to rejoin a woman who stood preparing dinner while four children tugged at her skirts. I told him I'd always seen a flat in the city, to which I could return home late from the labs, to a man who looked after the kids.

In our final days there, the Effect began to kick in, or maybe it was just our being together, and by the end we were able to see each other the way we were. And we realised how difficult it was all going to be.

He told me that ninety per cent of all music has love as its theme, albeit only in one of two ways. Either the couple have just met and walk off hand in hand into the future together, or else they're separated forever, with violins weeping all over the place. But the love that lies between those two extremes, he said – true love – is never even touched upon.

I told him about Wheeler's use of Schrödinger's equation to describe a universe in which everything hangs together.

The day before we were due to leave, the Limfjord was colder than the air. He pointed out into the fog and asked me what I saw. I told him radiation fog, its upper boundary sharply delineated over the land on account of inversion. He laughed and told me he saw a world in which we were the only living creatures, floating in a state of timeless invulnerability.

We'd used up all our money, and somewhere along the line we got an idea, both of us at the same time, though neither of us articulated it at any point. We got on our bikes and cycled to the shop.

The shop was on a square across from the church. There were white tables outside, on a decking with a little white fence all around. It was the middle of the day, though hardly anyone was out. There was nothing remarkable about our appearance, apart from our glowing with newfound emotions, but passers-by turned and stared.

We waited until there was no one else in the shop but the shopkeeper and us. It was a good and well-assorted store, with a look of care and attention to quality. Most likely they catered for the well-to-do segment of summer-house owners in the season. The counter was a right-angle. We positioned ourselves in such a way that an invisible line ran in a triangle from Laban through the shopkeeper to me. With such coordinates, the Effect becomes most intense. Later, we would employ the same model in our experiments.

'We've run out of money,' I told the shopkeeper. 'We're young and in love. Do you mind if we put a flyer up on your noticeboard looking for a sponsor?'

The shopkeeper was a friendly sort. He chuckled, and we chuckled back. So far we were still within the boundaries of normality.

And then the Effect kicked in. Without him realising, without him having any chance of knowing what was going on, it propelled him beyond a threshold he no longer even recognised.

He reached up to the wine shelf. 'Oh, but we couldn't possibly,' said Laban. 'Though if you insist, a bottle of champagne would be very nice indeed.'

'I'm vegetarian myself,' I said. 'But Laban loves meat. So for dinner tonight, which in a way is a kind of engagement celebration, I would so love to do him a roast. Is that tenderloin of wild boar you've got there in the freezer?'

The weather was typical May. In the garden behind the shop, a Danish flag fluttered from a white flagpole. It was a peaceful, idyllic scene. But somewhere in the space between the three of us, a sense of fate and inevitability prevailed.

We biked home again with baskets laden. I cooked and we feasted. Only once during the course of the evening did a cold front seem to glance by, though we felt its chill:

'I wonder,' said Laban, 'if we might not have been a trifle too audacious.'

I let it pass, and mentioned Rutherford to him. Despite the Nobel Prize, despite a matchless list of discoveries in physics, he ended up running his lab into the ground, losing his best students, and missing out on the discovery of fission. And all because he wouldn't think big and was too proud to allow himself to be sponsored.

Recollections will often come in bundles, like some quantum memory. I recall all these things as Laban massages my feet and asks me where it started to go wrong. And I know the same recollections come to him, too, in exactly the same way. He's not asking because he expects an answer. He's asking in the hope of finding support to cope with what both of us know.

Which is that ever since that evening our relationship has carried with it the whisper of a question, so faint as to be barely heard at all: What does it cost to abuse a special talent?

34

WE'RE SEATED AT THE ROUND TABLE.

I put the report from the National Archives down in front of me. It runs to about thirty pages. The twins haven't looked me in the eye since dinner.

I flick through it, but only to give my hands something to do. I know it off by heart already.

Twelve exceptionally intelligent individuals, from twenty-five to thirty years old. First six – then, after less than ten months, twelve. An economist, a chemical engineer, a theologist, a chartered surveyor, a priest, a psychiatrist, a painter, a geologist, an historian, a physicist and two statisticians. Their first meeting took place in the summer of 1972. The overview report builds on this and the meetings that follow, and was compiled in December 1974.

To begin with, they convene every six months or so, but then they seem to be seized by enthusiasm and their meetings become more frequent. The beginnings are termed *loose*. Young people sitting around talking over dinner, a glass of wine. Playing at being important. Budding specialists within their fields. But this isn't about areas of expertise, this is broader, and at the outset the mood is relaxed and informal. *Amateurish*, is how they describe it. They hardly bother to take notes, barely believing there will be anything to report.

What they've been asked to do is to give their take on the future: their *professionally justified prognoses*. But to begin with, these are few and far between. What they come up with might at best be called creative sketches, the report says. But then it takes off. At first they note the occurrence of a special kind of mood, which they describe in detail. A sense of mutual understanding arises, a deeper feeling between them, a prevailing consensus, which in the course of the following year becomes more profound than any of them have ever before experienced. It's as if the future presents itself to them. And at that point they start writing things down in detail.

The beginning of the report is a summary of the commission's notes from the first eighteen months of its existence, divided into three groups: predictions of individual events, predictions of wider delimited phenomena of collective significance, and predictions of trends. Each prediction is specified in terms of accuracy. The misses gradually cease to occur: the prognoses that didn't match up, and the wild guesses that had indeed been many. But now information is coming at them, clearly intuitive, and only seldom are they able to provide a more rational kind of reasoning, not to mention hazard a guess at where it might be coming from. And yet it is all so unfathomably precise. Even today, with the knowledge at our disposal, it's baffling. And utterly without organisation, a mixture of vague suggestion and intimation.

For instance, the case of the landslide election of 1973. As early as the minutes of their first meeting in August 1972, at a point where they haven't even officially convened as a group, they note down that they see a political upheaval about to occur, a complete turnaround articulating forces that have been at work within the population since at least the end of the Second World War, but which until that point had yet to find any definite form of expression. Moreover, they predict, what was about to happen – within eighteen months – would be the subject of much international attention. It is hard, the report concludes, not to see this as a very exact prediction of the general election of 4 December 1973.

At the next meeting they turn their radar abroad, noting the severe likelihood of tension in the Middle East triggering acts of aggression that will involve several nations and have major consequences for world energy supplies. They foresee the attacks on Israel by Egypt and Syria in October 1973. Attacks that would go on to trigger the first oil crisis. They write that the world has misunderstood the progressive development of the Cold War. There is no real détente: Kissinger's diplomacy shrouds a massive build-up of arms on both sides, American as well as Soviet. This is couched in somewhat vague terms, but all of a sudden there is something very exact: *In August 1974, a humiliated American president will fly home to California having been forced to resign from office.* That's what it says, in black and white. As if it were a horoscope, or the prediction of a fortune teller. Nixon! And right out of nowhere! They had no way of knowing, not even the slightest indication that anything remotely like it could occur. And there's more, much more. Events great and small, domestic as well as foreign. The ruling of the Danish Supreme Court in the so-called contraceptive pill case. The split in the Danish conservative party. The culmination of Soviet stockpiles of intercontinental ballistic missiles. They even get the number right: sixteen hundred.

'Prophets are bound to get lucky sometime,' says Harald. 'A meteorologist can predict a dry summer. An economist can foresee a recession.'

'This is different. Once they discover how often they're getting it right, their self-confidence grows. They realise they need to document it. Their figures are collated in tables. It all speaks for itself. During the first two years they've got twenty-four major prognoses where they hit the bull's-eye, and forty minor ones besides that. As the report says, no other think tank even gets near.'

'Who wrote the report?' Harald asks.

Now's the time to tell them. They have to know.

'It's signed Andrea Fink. And Magrethe Spliid. They drew it up together.'

They stare at me like statues.

'Andrea had won the Nobel Prize only a few years previously,' I say. 'She was one of the most famous people in the country. Her words carried a colossal amount of clout, and have done ever since. She knew what it would mean to give her stamp of approval.'

'How did she get to know about the commission?'

The question's from Harald.

I get to my feet. I'm hungry. We all are. When circumstances force a person into forgetting themselves, at some point they will realise they need food. And we never got round to the duck.

'She didn't get to know about it. She knew all along. She and Magrethe Spliid put the Future Commission together. It was their work.'

There's one duck left in the pizza oven. I'm in the garden, allowing myself to savour the cold air for a moment, the moonlight reflecting in the snow.

Before we know it we'll have moved on. The house will be sold and other people will be living in it. I put my hand to the outer wall. I hold affection for the building, as if it were a person.

The peace and stillness are tactile.

People will be returning even now to these suburban streets, to find their homes ransacked by thieves: burglars who have taken everything, ripped the stereo cables from the walls and left not a fingerprint behind. Now, at this very moment, the waiting room of the A&E at the Gentofte Infirmary will be full of casualties: battered wives, but also their beaters, sated with festive spirits, whose victims have retaliated with the frying pan, though not before heating it up to 280 degrees on the ceramic hob.

A few kilometres away, in the dismal flats of Vangede, single mothers will be celebrating Christmas with aid parcels from the Salvation Army.

And yet it must be okay to stand here for a moment and enjoy the peace.

Laban seems to have sat down at the piano. But the music sounds so faint and distant all it can do is highlight the silence.

Then all of a sudden Oskar is standing by my side.

I don't know if any biomechanical studies have ever been done of the way homeless people move. But one certainly does not imagine them to float about the concrete jungle like ballet dancers on pointe. Nevertheless, that's how he must have come, because I for one didn't hear him.

'You'll be picked up tomorrow,' he says. 'And taken to a safe place.'

What strikes me is not that he no longer looks like he's homeless. Nor that he has somehow ceased to smell. What strikes me is an abrupt sense of powerlessness. The feeling of never being able to escape.

I follow him round the side of the house to the front. He stops at the gate.

'You're not going to do a bunk, are you?'

I step up close to him.

'Suppose there was something I wanted to say to Hegn in person. Before we're taken away. Where would I find him?'

I don't really expect him to answer.

He looks up at the full moon.

'He's playing golf tomorrow.'

'In the snow?'

'Where he plays they've got heated greens. Out on the Kronholm Islets.'

And with that he's gone. I go back inside.

'Thit,' I venture, 'where did you actually find Oskar?'

'Outside the riding school.'

'Mattsson's Riding School,' I say, 'isn't exactly the sort of place you'd expect to find a homeless person.'

'Maybe not. But there was something about him. I could just tell he was down on his luck.'

I let it drop.

35

THIT AND HARALD HAVE GONE TO BED. TONIGHT THEY'RE
sleeping in the same room: Harald's.

They've done so once in a while ever since they were little. I
open the door. The sight of them asleep together has always
filled me with joy and sadness at the same time. Joy at the way
they seek each other's company. Sadness at the fact that it's
always prompted by some threat from outside.

The moonlight shining on them makes their skin seem almost
transparent. Without me being able to do anything about it,
Grosseteste's cosmogony of light, *De Luce*, comes to mind, and
Newton's theory of light as a material substance in his *Opticks*,
then Euler, Young, Maxwell, followed by Planck and Einstein,
and finally Andrea Fink's collaborative research with Grangier
into quantum optics. Five hundred years of science, the sum of
which is that we still don't know what light actually is.

But then I realise. And the answer comes directly from the
moonlight on the faces of my twins.

Light is touch.

I put on my coat, find the car keys, and take the crowbar from
the toolbox. I switch the lights off in the living room and shut
the blinds. A short way down Evighedsvej, a BMW is parked
at the kerb with Oskar behind the wheel.

I walk through the house to the utility room and open the

back door. Suddenly Laban's behind me, in his bare feet and a kimono.

'I've got to go and see Andrea,' I tell him.

I go through the garden, through the gap in the hedge, through Dorthea and Ingemann's garden, past the laid-up cutter, through the hedge at the far end, and after that the little park, eventually emerging onto Hyldegårdsvej, from where I walk down to Kystvejen – the coast road.

I grab a taxi within a minute and tell the driver to let me out on Gamle Carlsberg Vej. I continue on foot, past the place where the Carlsberg physiological, chemical and biochemical laboratories were housed in the sixties, back when Andrea Fink was a professor there and scientists from all over the world were falling over themselves to get a look-in. Word was you couldn't see a hand in front of you for Nobel laureates. Andrea told me she saw Bohr celebrate passing his driving test there. He drove a stately lap of honour around the grounds, and the laboratory staff hung out of the windows to watch him steer straight into one of the stone pillars flanking the eight-metre-wide gateway.

She told me this without a smile, adding, as if by way of explanation: 'Susan, one must bear in mind that the natural sciences are concerned only with a very narrow section of our human experience.'

Carlsberg owns several very large properties here, and I pass their tall gates with their security systems and walk along beside the railway cutting before arriving at the honorary residence. Here again is a heavy-duty fence and a security entrance with an intercom system and a guard doing the rounds who comes by every twenty minutes. I circumvent it all, as I've done hundreds of times before, by taking a key from a hollow tree stub and opening a small welded-mesh gate in the fence.

There are no lights on in the house. I go to the front door. It's never locked.

The hall is brightened by moonlight, Andrea's hospital bed a rectangular silhouette against the glass front facing the snow-covered gardens. The air is simultaneously fresh as ozone and filled with the sweet fragrance of pine needles and burning candles. A great Christmas tree stands against the wall, presumably moved back from the middle of the floor: her children and grandchildren have been and gone.

Now she's alone. I walk up to the bed. My chair's in the same place as it was three days ago. As if everything has been put in the deep freeze, and time suspended.

I sit down. She doesn't turn her head but reaches out, and I put my hand in hers.

'Your crutch, Susan?'

'I'm much better now.'

Death feels very near.

Our years together wander by. One particular time stands out, perhaps because it's Christmas. The first time she took me with her on one of her trips was during our first year of working together. We went to what was then the Soviet Union, flying on from Moscow to a military base called Belbek, near Sebastopol on the south-west coast of the Crimean Peninsula. There we met with Gorbachev, at the dacha he called Zarya, meaning *dawn*. The Soviet government had spent twenty-five million dollars building the place on a rocky outcrop overlooking the Black Sea. He was still president, his country's eighth and last leader. Two years previously, Andrea had been commissioned at his request to hold classes in group decision-making processes for the six individuals whose orders the Soviet warning systems required to be coordinated in order to authorise the use of nuclear weapons.

Present were Gorbachev himself, Andrea and me, Gorbachev's wife Raisa and their daughter and two grandchildren. An army officer in full uniform stood by one wall, guarding a small briefcase. Andrea told me afterwards this was the *cheget*, the Soviet equivalent of the US president's football, the portable doomsday device required to launch a nuclear strike.

I'd never seen anyone as tired as Gorbachev. He looked like

what he was: a man who had shouldered responsibility for the welfare of an entire nation and its people, and whose time, after six years – only half of his allotted period – was drawing to an end.

He and Andrea Fink conversed like old friends. He wanted her help putting together a unit to draw up guidelines for the establishment of a federal Soviet Union bestowing wide-reaching independence on its member states.

Within the first minute I realised she knew it wouldn't work. After ten, she told him.

His power was a very physical presence. There was a hum about him, like a giant electric motor. I sensed his bewilderment.

So I got up and took his head in my hands and placed it between my breasts. The room went quiet. The guard stiffened, the children fell silent. Andrea Fink just stared.

I wanted to give him something. Sexual healing, perhaps. I tilted his head so he could look up at me.

'Misha,' I said, 'if only we could have been on our own together.'

That opened things up a bit. They knew I meant it. His wife knew, and his daughter, and the army officer with the doomsday device – even the grandchildren knew. As long as you time things right, kids can cope with anything.

'Susan,' he said.

He pronounced it *Zoozan*.

'I am unused to being touched by my advisers.'

'That's because you're not yet familiar with the Copenhagen School of Quantum Physics,' I told him.

We said our goodbyes. We all knew it was over. We went out past a fifty-metre pool and along a private beach that stretched for kilometres in the direction of the Foros resort, before arriving back at the car. Two weeks later, on Christmas Day 1991, we watched him announce his resignation on national television from that very same room. And we saw him hand over control of his little briefcase to Boris Yeltsin. That's twenty-seven years ago now.

I recognise Gorbachev's fatigue from that meeting and that television transmission now, in Andrea's face. It's the fatigue of a person who, unlike the rest of us, has not contented herself with earning her daily bread, but who instead has been driven by a vision. And who now must see it crumble.

'You and Magrethe Spliid. You put together the Future Commission. She's dead now.'

She knows.

'Henrik Kornelius is dead, too.'

Her hand is cold. When death approaches, it draws all bio-electric energy away from the surface of the skin and inward towards the body's core. She may die tonight. Or maybe this is another instance of her flouting the rules that apply to everyone else.

'Magrethe and I were both unaware of the full potential of the group dynamic, Susan. But we were on the right track. I'd known her for years. Her position was unusual, a pacifist working for the military. They took her on for the sake of legitimacy. Woman, civilian, German background, yet unstained by the war. After only a few years they couldn't do without her. They made the job permanent in 1964, the same year the first female cadet joined the officers' academy. But even before that I'd noticed her articles. I put myself in touch. She was interested in getting people together, placing them in contexts that would bring out the best in them. Bohr excelled at it. We were worried about the direction in which society was heading. There wasn't much ground for optimism. What we were after was realism, realistic prognoses. The Cuban missile crisis was a turning point for both of us. Magrethe was sent off on a tour of inspection with the air force, to the Ramstein Air Base in Germany. It was October 1962. She wasn't yet twenty, yet they'd selected her. The first week was uneventful, but after that things hotted up for her. Magrethe was fond of men, a bit like you in that respect. She initiated a dalliance with Air Force Europe's second-in-command. Part of his responsibility was being in charge of their forward-based deployment, the bomber planes that would be the first to fly in over the Soviet Union if a nuclear war broke out. He told her he had a minute and a half to get them airborne, their bases being top-priority targets in the case of a Soviet strike. He had pilots sitting in cockpits in shifts round the clock. And they knew their mission was one-way. There wouldn't be a Germany left to come back to. The weeks she spent there were pivotal for Magrethe. They shook her very foundations. Some of her hair had turned white when she got back, like Christmas Møller when he came home from London after the war. From that moment on we were scouting for potential subjects. Individuals to be part of a group. But it took us another ten years.'

'What did you tell the Folketing?'

'That they were specialists. Which was true.'

'You knew they could predict the future.'

'No one can predict the future. It doesn't exist until it becomes present. It's a multi-dimensional field of virtualities. We knew they were excellent prognosticators. That was one of the criteria by which they were selected. We looked at how many of their published predictions had turned out true in each case. But it was only after the commission's first two years, when we were going through the reports, that we realised how incredibly exact the material was. The group's ability to see beyond the horizon of events was formidable indeed.'

'And Thorkild Hegn?'

'Magrethe and I didn't show our report to the Folketing. It would only have given rise to panic measures. The politicians were jittery enough as it was, scared that the media would harangue them for employing fortune tellers. Worried that other experts would criticise them for the young age of the commission's members. But we knew that what we had on our hands was a phenomenon far more powerful than we'd ever imagined. We went to the security services, and military and police intelligence. They tried to take control of the commission, but ended up having to back off. We decided to set up a group that was to monitor and evaluate the commission's work. Hegn was at that time a head of department in the Ministry of Justice. The youngest ever. We put him in charge.'

'At some point you realised you'd lost control of him.'

A flicker of grief passes over her features.

'The commission insisted on anonymity. They wanted to be self-supplying. They distanced themselves from me. Hegn took over. I'm not a politician, Susan. I've never fully grasped that particular power game. He uncoupled me. From the most successful experiment I've ever conducted.'

'And Magrethe Spliid?'

'She kept me informed. But we had to be very careful. Eventually, it became near-impossible to keep in touch. But there was something else, too. It was as though something about her changed . . .'

I lean towards her.

'They got greedy, Andrea. Even Magrethe did. And you knew. I've seen some of the places they live in. They got rich. Far richer than any of their civilian professions would allow. They found a way of cashing in on their talent.'

'Like you, Susan.'

For a moment, my whole body hurts.

'Yes, but I wasn't that smart. I never got rich.'

There's a kind of Lorentz contraction that applies to honesty. As you approach full clarity it's like everything contracts and starts to resist. That's when to press ahead. That's where your chance lies.

'What did Hegn do about it?'

'He left the ministry. After consultations with the government, who for their part had secured the support of key politicians across the Folketing. They gave him the green light to keep it secret. Exemption from the rules of open administration. Offices all over the place, most recently at the former Radiohuset. The commission hated him, but at the same time they couldn't do without him. They knew that what they had on their hands was comparable to Los Alamos, a kind of radioactivity, only in information instead. They were scared. Magrethe admitted as much. They knew they needed government protection, help to keep things out of the public eye. To assess what predictions were actually coming true. Many were little more than feelings in need of verification. They needed guidance to find out what could be made public and what couldn't. Once they got started, I became superfluous. But not Thorkild.'

Now I'm able to identify her fatigue. It's not only hers. It's also the disillusionment of the natural sciences. At having made such discoveries, delivered such opportunities for the world to advance, provided such great tools. Only then to see itself out-manoeuvred, by government, the police, business.

'You and Magrethe created a little monster. And then you lost control of it.'

It's quiet all around. Anyone else in her position would be surrounded by doctors, nurses, priests, backslappers telling her what a monumental legacy she'll be leaving behind. But not Andrea Fink.

'Thorkild came to me a month ago. I hadn't seen him in twenty years. There was a piece of information crucial to him: the minutes of a meeting. He asked my advice. I told him about you. Was that wrong of me, Susan?'

My feelings for her well up inside.

'They're being killed. Harald and I only just survived an attempt on our lives. Did Hegn have anything to do with that?'

She can't bear to hear it. All her life, she has looked only into the eyes of kindness.

'I don't know, Susan. I'm not a part of it any more. But he turned the Institute of Future Studies into an independent organisation. He severed all links to the Ministry of Justice.

Until the end of the seventies he was referring directly to the incumbent government. That's long been a thing of the past. It's harder now to control him. Governments come and go. The civil service is what guarantees continuity. There were always the decent heavyweights. Erik Ib Schmidt. Seirup at the Directorate of Social Affairs. But then there were the dangerous exceptions too.'

There's something more she wants to say. Something she's hiding.

'You and I,' I say. 'We started out like mother and daughter. But we've come a long way since then. It's what I always dreamed about, in life as well as in physics. To proceed to the very limit, to the place where all knowledge comes to an end. And then to step out into empty space. We can go there now, Andrea.'

She turns her head away from me. I get to my feet.

The moon has vanished. Christmas Eve is over.

I flag a taxi on Pile Allé. The traffic is a flow of people returning home from family and friends.

As we pass the bridge that arches across Maglemosevej, the taxi's interior is engulfed by the flashing blue lights of a police car. A motorcycle officer waves us over to the oncoming lane, and on the other side of the bridge we pass the wreck of a car.

It's wedged between two trees, the roof peeled back so whoever was inside could be extricated. An area of road is cordoned off, and police are busy measuring skid marks.

The car is a Jaguar. Its windows are smashed. But in the lower corner of the windscreen I see the characteristic parking permit. I can't read what it says. But I can see the emblem. A golden pair of dividers superimposed on a golden theodolite.

The house on Evighedsvej is dark and still. I take off my clothes and stand under the shower. At Holmgangen we had to take cold baths, yet another trauma for life. Long hot showers are the one luxury I'd have difficulty doing without.

There are two shower heads in our shower, hooked up to two different heat exchangers, both equipped with boosters, an unlawful installation I put in myself. Whenever my work at the lab didn't keep me too late, Laban and I would shower together. Standing there under our separate shower heads we would talk softly, the door ajar in case one of the children should wake up. It was like a ritual cleansing. First we'd tell each other what kind of day we'd had, as if to rinse away its pollution. Gradually we'd make contact, and the hot water and the Effect combined to wash away our protective layers, until finally we were naked together.

He knocks on the door. I know it's him, I know the way he knocks. The same way as he introduces himself: softly and apologetically, and yet impossible to ignore.

I wrap myself in a bath towel and open the door. His hair's all over the place and he's drowsy from sleep. But he heard me come in and wanted to get up and greet me.

'The Future Commission was Andrea's work,' I tell him. 'Once it was established, it got the better of her. She knows nothing about the killings. It was she who picked me out for Hegn. There's something she's not telling me. On the way home I saw Keldsen's car, or what was left of it.'

He nods. I stroke his cheek. His eyes investigate behind my back.

'What?' I say.

He steps away, towards the door.

'Just checking, Susan. To make sure you haven't got your drill driver and deck screws handy.'

36

IT'S CHRISTMAS MORNING, THE TIME A QUARTER TO FIVE: fifteen minutes before the arsenic hour.

Less than half an hour ago I squeezed through the hedge and crouched in the cold, waiting to make sure there were no signs of life on Evighedsvej. And then I drove here, to Holte. In Dorthea's Volvo.

Andreas Baumgarten, former Governor of the National Bank, resides at something called Rudersdal Manor. I turn off Kongevejen down a gravel track that winds its way between snow-dusted fields and patches of woodland, before arriving at a wall and a set of tall, wrought-iron gates. The gates are open. On the wall is a *For Sale* sign.

I carry on down a dark avenue of trees that seems endless and yet eventually reaches a conclusion in front of the main house, which looks like a castle.

All the lights are on. Steps lead up to a large set of doors at the foot of a tower. In front of the steps is a Bentley. A man dressed in black is busy loading suitcases into it. Stacks of removal boxes line the outside wall. The windows are without curtains. The place is being vacated.

A woman in black trousers, a black pullover and riding boots comes towards me. She looks stand-offish, as intransigent as a road block.

'I need to speak to Andreas,' I say. 'Tell him it's Susan from Fanø. I've been to the doctor. I'm four months gone. I need to speak to him about what we're going to do. Is he going to marry me or what?'

She swivels on her heels. I follow her through a hall and into a drawing room as big as a ballroom. Down a staircase from the first floor comes Andreas Baumgarten.

His thick grey hair is like the mane of a lion. He himself is the lion king.

'I've brought you a Christmas card,' I tell him. 'From Magrethe Spliid. It's the last thing she wrote before she got throttled.'

He didn't know. He halts in his tracks, albeit briefly.

'I'm on my way to the airport. Can you come with me?'

We go outside and down the front steps. He puts out a hand for my car keys and passes them to the man in black. We climb into the Bentley. The woman in the riding boots gets behind the wheel. The cockpit of a car is a kind of laboratory and she's a specialist: her movements are few and economic. The car doesn't run, it floats.

'Henrik Kornelius is dead,' I say. 'Keldsen too, probably. I saw his car yesterday. It was totalled.'

The snow in the fields brightens the dark. Following on behind us in my car is the black-clad lugger of suitcases.

'And who might you be?'

'Susan Svendsen. I'm a physicist at the University of Copenhagen. I've got a lot of experience in questioning people. Thorkild Hegn asked me to question Magrethe Spliid. About the last two meetings of the Future Commission.'

His face is expressionless. But I can hear the whirr of mental calculations. He doesn't need an abacus.

'I've seen Andrea Fink's report,' I tell him. 'Her summary of the commission's work. Kirsten Klaussen had it hidden away in the National Archives. I retrieved it. I need to call Hegn within the next fifteen minutes. Otherwise there'll be an army waiting for you at Kastrup.'

He says nothing.

'I've got a prison sentence hanging over my head. They offered to drop all charges if I could get hold of the minutes of the last two meetings.'

'And what crime did you commit?'

I gauge his systems. And proceed on a hunch.

'Grievous bodily harm. Against a lover.'

For some reason it does the trick.

'Nothing was written down. Nothing at all from the final meetings. The prognoses were too gloomy. Our point of departure was a hundred global risks, divided into six categories: economics, environment, geopolitics, society, technology, global resources. We picked out five main issues: chronic financial imbalances, greenhouse gas emissions, unsustainable population growth, extreme income inequality and a shortage of resources that would give rise to highly volatile prices for energy and agricultural products.'

We hit the motorway, passing Lyngby and Denmark's Technological University.

'We drew a picture of a future world in which attempts at global leadership have been feeble and failed. A world in which the Western welfare-society model has partially broken down as a result of national debt, and where young people under the yoke of mass unemployment are saddled with the burden of looking after history's largest-ever elderly population, a billion and a half people over the age of sixty by 2020. Where social unrest is rampant. Where education systems are failing because their programmes are still facing backwards, preparing students for twentieth-century jobs and economies that don't exist any more. A world in which everyday lives are lived in the shadow of metacatastrophes like the great oil and chemical leaks of the twentieth century, only now with the further complication of microorganisms and nanomaterial that can't be contained because response capabilities are inadequate and outdated. A world in which resource shortages lead to neotribalism and war. A world that still retains a nuclear capacity equivalent to one thousand tons of TNT for every man, woman and child on earth. Even the smallest tactical strikes, for example in a border conflict between India and Pakistan, would release at minimum one thousand times the explosive force of Hiroshima. The ash from the burning cities alone would spark off a new ice age across the northern hemisphere.'

We pass Herlev.

'No one's infallible,' I say. 'Your sums are wrong.'

He smiles. It's a physiological smile, restricted to the facial muscles.

'Europe's a comfort zone. We live in a cinema with family entertainment projected onto all four walls. The collapse isn't some far-off future. It's already started.'

'Imbalances will be corrected.'

'They haven't even been acknowledged yet. Look at the day-to-day reality. Politicians jostling for position. Interest groups fighting for a slice of the cake. The media, who know the truth, but can't get it across because no one's listening. The problem isn't *outside* us. The problem *is* us. Our overconsumption and borrowing.'

We're nearing the airport. I start to sense his anger beneath the smile, behind the elegance.

'We've been saying all this for forty-five years, and no one's batted an eyelid! There isn't a single politician in Europe who isn't talking growth. But growth in its present form isn't viable any more. It's past its use-by date.'

'What's going to happen?'

The car swings into an area of the airport I've never seen before, passing through a gate and pulling up in front of a low fence. On the other side of the fence is a Lear jet. Two stewardesses and two uniformed pilots stand to attention by its steps.

They're waiting for Andreas Baumgarten. When he gets out of the Bentley they salute.

'We gave them six different scenarios of collapse.'

Two airport staff open the gate for him. There's no ticket procedure, no boarding pass, no security check.

He goes through the gate, turns and comes back to the fence.

'There's a detail you might like to think about, Susan. All six scenarios involve more dead than in the First and Second World Wars put together.'

His tone conceals a glee I find hard to comprehend.

'Guesswork,' I say.

He smiles again.

'It's quite simple. You don't need any Future Commission. All you need to do is ask yourself the following question: What impact did two world wars have on global leadership? What impact did sixty million deaths actually have? They left one mark: the UN. The weak and infirm, US-dominated United Nations. That's all. Humankind has carried on in exactly the same way, as if nothing happened. So it's bound to go wrong, isn't it?'

He glances back at the plane. His suitcases are being loaded.

'I had a colleague at the National Bank once. He was on the chairmanship of the Economic Council, too. One of Scandinavia's brightest minds. We were considering him for the commission. But he had a drinking problem. One night out, in November, he climbs onto the quay at Nyhavn to urinate into the canal, only he falls in. At the same time, a police car happens by and they fish him out. He's in a coma for two days, but miraculously he makes a full recovery. A couple of months and he's back at the bottle. Two years later, in November again, he climbs onto the quay at exactly the same place, with the same purpose, to piss into the canal. He falls in. Only this time there's no police car. They found him the next day, sunk to the bottom. The Western world is that man. The future isn't our learning from our mistakes. It's our denying there ever was a mistake.'

I picture Thit and Harald in my mind's eye. And millions of other children like them.

'There's a choice,' I say. 'There's always a choice.'

'Didn't you say you were a physicist? Free choice is an illusion. We are biological creatures. We've evolved through competition.

Our nervous systems are programmed into securing as much as possible for our own benefit. No matter what.'

He turns and starts to walk towards the plane.

'True,' I say. 'And you seem to have made a point of it.'

He stops, turns slowly and comes back.

'We tried getting it across for forty-six years! We presented two thousand absolutely precise predictions of trends and individual events of national and international significance. In us, Denmark possessed an instrument the likes of which no government, no nation, had ever seen before! And we were ignored. Smothered by Thorkild Hegn and the security services. Fobbed off with subsistence allowances!'

His injured vanity has a particular ring to it, one with which I am familiar. From our rounds of questioning. From the university. From everywhere in society's upper echelons. And most of all from myself.

'You sold out,' I say. 'What was your share?'

He steps up close, the regal aura now stripped away.

'The manor,' I tell him. 'The Bentley, the jet. Kirsten Klaussen bought Bagsværd Church. Henrik Kornelius built a monastery to the tune of a hundred million. You bagged more than you were ever worth. You're the ones indebted, not us.'

At short range he's got the speed of a cat. I've no time to react before he's got me by the throat and pulled me towards him, against the fence.

'Crawl back, Susan,' he says calmly. 'Crawl back to your little wormhole. Put some family entertainment on the DVD player. Wait and see.'

My movements are measured. It's something I learned early on and later refined in the labs, among the pipettes and the radium salts, the Mettler weighing scales. Seamlessly and without a fuss, I unbutton his jacket, slip my hand down his trouser front, inside his underpants, and take hold of his testicles. They are thick with hair, like the skin of lion.

Then I squeeze. Hard.

His knees buckle, and he lets go of my throat immediately. The woman in the riding boots and the man who drove my car are already stepping towards us.

I squeeze again.

'Tell them to stay back,' I say.

He can't speak, but raises his hand. The man and the woman halt. I lean forward into his face.

'Where did the money come from, Andreas?'

He says nothing. I squeeze.

'Enough, *please*!'

'The money, Andreas. Where did it come from?'

His voice is a whisper now:

'Gold.'

'How?'

'We predicted the price of gold would go up.'

'Explain. The only gold I know is my wedding ring.'

'The Nixon Shock. Nixon suspended the convertibility of the dollar into gold. Gold had been the international standard since the Bretton Woods Agreement in 1944. We knew the price was going to skyrocket. So we bought. And waited. And then we borrowed, and bought again.'

Now I understand.

'It must have been the easiest thing in the world,' I say. 'If you'd played the stock markets or speculated in property investment they'd have been able to trace it all back to you. But this was easy. How much did you make, Andreas? A billion kroner? Ten billion?'

The next moment, two things happen that only he and I register. The first thing is that his eyes glaze over. Like my caramel potatoes the instant the liquid evaporates. The second thing is that he gets an erection against my forearm, like a cylinder of granite heated up over a Bunsen burner.

'Come with me,' he says.

At first I can't hear what he says, and when he repeats the words I can't understand him. Everything around us is as if turned to stone: the woman in the riding boots, the man in black, the airport staff, the Lear jet, Kastrup Airport.

'Where to?'

'Brazil.'

I stare into his face. And then I cotton on.

'What you want, Andreas, is for me to go with you now, and once a week hang you up between two palm trees, wind a twine tightly around your balls and thrash you with a rhino whip. Is that right?'

He nods and emits a gasp.

I've worked with candour all my life. Nevertheless, one can always be surprised.

'Andreas,' I say, 'regrettably, I haven't the time. But having met you, I will say that across the globe – even, I'm sure, in Bahia – there will be women who will be more than pleased to help you out without charge.'

His eyes clear. He returns to reality.

I release my grip. He staggers backwards, but remains standing, rooted to the spot, as if unable to leave.

And then it all recedes. I keep my gaze fixed on his. How will he take his leave? People react in different ways when they've laid themselves bare: some with anger, some with shame, others by pretending it didn't happen.

He runs a hand through his lion's mane and smiles. This time it's a deeper smile. Of relief, almost. Perhaps even gratitude.

'Farewell, Susan Svendsen.'

And with that, he turns and strides towards his plane.

I go up to the man in black and put out my hand. He places the car keys in my palm.

I turn to the woman in the riding boots. Two women whose hands have gripped the same hairy bollocks in the space of twenty-four hours owe each other a sisterly nod of acknowledgement at least.

'What happened to your pregnancy?' she says.

'Do you know anything about quantum physics at all?'

She shakes her head.

'Quantum physics operates with a function it calls *psi*. It doesn't stand for any physical phenomenon as such. It's used in calculations, and once it's worked its little miracles it disappears again.'

I get into the car.

Behind me, Andreas Baumgarten's Lear jet taxis towards the runway.

37

I'VE PICKED LABAN AND THE TWINS UP AT THE HOUSE ON
Evighedsvej, and in the car I've told them about my encounter
with Andreas Baumgarten. The tale has made them silent and
pensive.

We pull up at the gate outside the private area between
Svanemøllen and Tuborg Havn, where less than forty-eight
hours ago I conversed with Keld Keldsen.

The same girl is sitting in the glass-fronted kiosk.

One cannot help but notice that the alertness Keldsen and I
awakened in her has failed to persist. She looks bored to death.

I get out of the car. On the other side of the gate I catch a
glimpse of four Rolls-Royces and a greater number of Mercedes
than I've ever seen before in one place, not to mention a Ferrari
and a Lamborghini, two Lotuses and a Morgan three-wheeler
with wooden coachwork.

'We're looking for someone to take us out to the islands,' I
tell the girl.

She looks up and recognises me. Her deep-seated fatigue
instantly gives way to panic, which, while hardly a pleasant
experience for her, nonetheless seems more in keeping with her
tender age.

She glances at the Volvo. Presumably to see who my new
driving instructor is.

Laban and the twins get out and smile. Laban's smile is the
broadest. He steps towards her window, as if he just bought the

car park and all that goes with it and is now brimming with the pride of newfound ownership.

'My name's Laban Hegn,' he says. 'Thorkild Hegn's son. A pleasure to meet you.'

The girl's paralysis abates. She returns his smile.

'Allow me to introduce Thit and Harald. Thorkild's grandchildren. It's his seventy-fifth birthday today. We're arranging a surprise for him.'

Thit and Harald shuffle dutifully towards the glass front, penning the girl in behind three smiles as wide as a football field.

She lifts a trembling finger and points at me.

'What about her? I've got to account for everyone who goes in.'

'This is Susan,' says Laban. 'Our driver. And caddy.'

'But she hasn't got a driving licence.'

The information mystifies Laban somewhat, but he nods reassuringly.

'Thank you so much for telling us,' he says. 'We'll make sure to keep her off the roads until she has.'

The gate opens. We get back in the car with Laban at the wheel, and roll gently in among the thoroughbreds to park discreetly at the far end, as if the Volvo might somehow be embarrassed. Behind us is a Bentley with room enough inside for someone to put it on chocks and use it for a bungalow.

'Caddy, indeed!' I snort.

'We're in the middle of divorce,' says Laban. 'I'm practising social intercourse as a single. How come she thinks you haven't got a licence?'

I say nothing.

We get out. A little green speedboat is already waiting for us. On the jetty is a uniformed boatsman, rigidly standing at ease.

Something tells me to turn round and go back to the girl in the kiosk. She nods, on her guard and yet friendly. Laban has shouldered responsibility and promised her we live in the best of all worlds.

'Which car is Hegn's?'

'He flew in today.'

'In the helicopter?'

'I think I saw his little jet.'

'He must have been in a hurry,' I say. 'To get his presents.'

She gazes dreamily in the direction of Laban.

'He must be gorgeous to work for.'

'Absolutely lush,' I tell her.

The Kronholm Islets lie between the Middelgrund sea fort and the island of Hven, in the Øresund that separates Denmark and Sweden. Their name has always been familiar to me. But it's only now as we approach that I actually see them.

Most conspicuous is the wind farm, and then the so-called Conch, a seashell-like structure of five twisting storeys that looks like it was washed up onto the beach. Beyond are hangars, storage facilities and a small control tower. Two large cranes preside over an area that looks like it's being filled in.

I refrain from asking questions. Our boatsman doesn't seem like the tour-guide type. Laban believes that what fuels the march of history are the works of the great composers. I believe it to be natural science. Everything else going on in society is mere diversion.

But still the matter remains in the air. And of course it is Harald who fills us in.

'I did an Internet search. The Kronholm Islets were sold off to a consortium when Danish conservation laws were changed and the protection of coastal areas was relaxed last year. Since then the birds have been told to move, huge areas have been filled in and construction projects carried out, including a landing strip, the wind farm, the buildings we can see and a golf course. The case goes all the way back to 1988. The Ministry of the Environment set up a committee to control the selling-off of waterfront areas by Copenhagen City Council. One of their aims was to prevent the sale of the Øresund islands. In early May 1989, the committee tabled a report containing an absolutely brilliant proposal, one of the most carefully crafted in the history of Danish government, according to Wikipedia. It concerns the administration of forty-two kilometres of quayside and forty kilometres of coastline over a period of thirty years, and included plans for sixteen thousand new homes and twenty-five thousand jobs, as well as securing access to the city's watersides for ordinary Copenhageners. But the proposal was rejected. The council went forward with its investment projects, a process that peaked with the repeal of coastal protection laws and the selling-off of the Kronholm Islets. The very rich are few and far between in Denmark. They need reservations. Kronholm is intended to be just such a place. The price was four billion kroner, making it the most expensive piece of land in the country in terms of cost per square metre.'

We gawp at him. There is a part of every parent that never quite recovers from their children learning to walk and all of a sudden being able to construct and utter two comprehensible sentences.

A golf cart is waiting for us. It, too, is green, as are the uniforms worn by its driver and the man next to him. The road rises steeply from the harbour. The islets are naturally flat, so the hills are artificial.

Close up, the Conch no longer looks like it was washed up. Rather it looms, a five-storey construction of steel and glass, with a ground plan approximating the superellipse.

The golf course starts right outside the building and occupies the whole islet. Its trees are so tall they must have been planted fully grown. There are several kilometres of flowerbeds, and little Japanese bridges arching over shallow streams. From where we stand I can see two temple pavilions that presumably will offer tea to the weary golfer, served in delicate little cups from the Ming dynasty on which will be written some choice words of wisdom such as *True wealth is in the heart*.

But the islets and the golf course have one more thing about them which I note: lots of green men. On the narrow ribbon of asphalt that runs alongside the beach I can see three jeeps, each with two men inside, slowly cruising as if to admire the view. At the Conch's entrance are two security guards with their hands behind their backs. In the distance, where the golf course ends, I can see a little harbour facility and a short causeway leading to a landing strip, and everywhere – along the jetties, on the causeway itself and dotted about the landing strip – are little green men.

Their uniforms are the same colour as the grass of the golfing greens. Maybe they're only here to pick up litter and look after the visitors, and to make sure the birds don't come back and splatter the Conch with their droppings. But somehow I doubt it. For all their casually luxurious air, the Kronholm Islets seem to be massively monitored.

Thorkild Hegn is standing fifty metres away with his back turned. The golf cart is electric and silent. He hasn't seen us yet. He is at the centre of a small group, as he would be at the centre of any group, regardless of its size.

He steps up to the tee and prepares his drive. For the first time, I sense his physical strength.

Maybe he has a sudden inkling of our presence. But whatever it is, he straightens up and faces about.

Physiologically and for legal purposes, the five individuals in his company – three women and two men – are people just like us. And yet they look at us as if we're from another universe altogether.

They're wearing loose-fitting leisure clothes made for all weather, of the kind of quality you never find in shops and which Coco Chanel might have made exclusively for them if she'd been able to keep herself going another fifty years.

These are people who can pay their way out of having to

associate with the likes of us, which is exactly what they've done. But now that we've slipped through their finely meshed net, they reveal themselves to have far too much class to let their disappointment show.

I step forward and give Thorkild Hegn a peck on the cheek.

'Many happy returns,' I say. 'And the best of wishes from those members of the Future Commission who are still alive. There aren't that many left. Two more have shuffled off the coil in the last twenty-four hours.'

He looks across at the two green men waiting at the cart.

'We've written you a birthday song,' I tell him. 'Laban's put music to an excerpt from Andrea Fink's report on the commission's prognoses. Would you like us to sing here? Or should we go somewhere else, out of the way?'

He hands his club to a young female assistant. Her skin glows, a warm ochre. But her eyes are cold. A fetching hard-liner, a Danish-West Indian version of Condoleezza Rice, hard as a coconut.

He strides off and we follow, his assistant tripping along behind.

We ascend through the Conch in a glass elevator. The two lower floors are empty, apparently not even furnished yet. But as we pass through the two above I glimpse what I estimate to be about thirty or forty people working in open-plan offices.

Working on Christmas Day is something I approve of, having done it myself on plenty of occasions. Experimental physics doesn't much care for public holidays. But the thirty-odd people we now pass on our way up are hardly physicists. For that reason, one can't help but wonder what exactly they're doing and why.

The elevator stops at the fifth floor, the seashell's upper spiral. We step out into a room approximately eight by eight metres and constructed completely of glass, the curved walls meeting at a point some six metres above our heads.

The room commands a 360-degree panorama view taking in Copenhagen's harbour, Hven, Malmö and Falsterbo. The Øresund is calm, the light as sharp as a knife. It feels like you could see all the way to Poland and Oslo if you looked through the tripod telescope at the window.

In the middle of the room is what looks like a large bubble of clear plastic. I sense the surprise of Laban and the twins, but I'm familiar with the construction from dozens of meetings with Andrea Fink. The monstrosity is standard inventory in all American embassies, from where, in the way of global community and increasing understanding between peoples, it has spread to laboratories throughout the world. It's a security chamber made of Plexiglas, coated so as to reflect electromagnetism and mounted on a block that eliminates 99.9 per cent of all acoustic transmission from within the chamber. It's a capsule for those wishing to conduct conversations without anyone else listening in.

Hegn's assistant opens its door, and we step inside and seat ourselves at her request. The bubble contains chairs by Hans Wegner, a conference table, three computers and near-silent air conditioning.

This time Hegn doesn't suggest the twins go for a walk. Maybe he's lost all hope of it helping. Maybe he doesn't want them to churn up the fairways. Or maybe we've simply reached a point where it's too late to protect women and children.

'I've spoken to Baumgarten,' I say. 'He told me about the final meetings. They were seeing the end of the world. Nothing was written down.'

He stays silent.

'They were speculating in gold. I don't know when they started, maybe not until somewhere near the end. But you lost your grip on them. You got them round the Folketing, only then they got away. So now you know, Thorkild. And now we're staying put, here in Denmark. I'm going to resume my work in the department. We'll find a good school for the kids. You're going to replace our flattened Passat. Life's going to go on as if nothing ever happened. Apart from one little detail: we'll need protection. A man posted outside the house in a car. He'll drive the kids to school for the first few months. A bit like our friend Oskar. Who killed them, Thorkild? It wasn't you, by any chance, was it?'

He grips the edge of the table. His assistant bears down on him, placing a hand on his shoulder. Her most important function becomes clear. It's not taking down dictation on his lap. It's stopping him before he gets himself worked up.

She succeeds. He exhales deeply.

'I'm the one who takes care of the housekeeping in our family,' I tell him. 'It's given me a keen eye for financial anomalies. For instance, I've been wondering how you were able to raise what it must have cost you to become the king of Kronholm, complete with helicopter and private jet.'

She squeezes his arm tightly. By some superhuman effort he restrains himself. But he's foaming at the mouth.

'I've put it all down in writing, of course, Thorkild. Deposited everything with a solicitor. It'll all be sent to the press in the event of anything untoward happening to us. The guy who tried to kill me and Harald. Was that one of your people? Someone you couldn't control any more? The processes of democracy have always been lengthy. But bypassing them is a risky business. Look at what happened to us in India. Is that what happened to you, Thorkild? Is the load about to tip?'

I stand up. For all his rage I sense a degree of self-restraint. Not that it puts me at ease. It's as if he's got something in reserve.

Laban clears his throat.

'One last thing before we go. Might the good people of Kronholm, this marvellous place, be interested in commissioning a piece of music, by any chance? Something tasteful: a choral work, for instance? Or perhaps something more extravagant, for the grand opening? I've got an idea based on the sound of a golf club striking a ball for that perfect drive down the fairway.

Combined with the rush of the sea inside a shell. The cry of gulls.'

It takes guts to produce your order book when on the brink of extinction. But it's no surprise to me. I've seen Laban haggling to offload stock goods onto the board of the university during the banquet when they awarded him their music prize.

Thorkild Hegn stares blankly.

'I'll suggest it at the next board meeting.'

'I'll do you a good price.'

Hegn nods. Laban and the twins get to their feet.

38

WE'RE BACK IN THE GREEN SPEEDBOAT, ON OUR WAY TO
Copenhagen. Laban and I are sitting next to each other.

'Hegn,' he says, 'Baumgarten, Kirsten Klaussen. All more
than seventy years old. And Magrethe Spliid. And Kornelius.'

'Andrea Fink once said to me that the greatest threat to
democracy comes from people not letting go of their power
until it's too late.'

I nod towards the quay. Laban and the twins stare ahead. At
first they can't see what I'm getting at. Then they notice all the
anonymous cars that don't fit in.

To begin with, the area seems deserted. But the second we
step ashore they're everywhere, women as well as men. Some
possess that discreetly irremovable air reserved for plain-clothes
police. They congregate silently around us. A van is backed
along the quay towards us, the kind used by security firms for
transporting valuables. The rear doors are flung open.

There's a man standing right behind me. Whereas the others
exude anonymous authority, he seems almost flamboyant, even
though he is dressed in grey. Clearly he's not the police. And at
that instant I realise there are two forces present: the state as
represented by the arm of the law, and something else.

'I want to speak to a solicitor,' I say.

And then he kicks me.

It's the kind of kick a footballer might employ from range when
driving a low volley towards goal. His foot strikes me hard in the

seat of the pants, the sheer force propelling me into the open van. My face hits the floor, but I don't feel a thing. My vision is clear, but my body is without feeling, nervous system numbed.

Laban lands next to me and remains on his back staring up at the roof, unable to move.

I manage to clamber onto all fours and turn my head.

The man in grey has lifted Thit and Harald into the air. He's got them by the neck and holds them outstretched in front of him, one in each hand. Their feet dangle, thirty centimetres off the ground.

Harald weighs at least seventy kilos, Thit probably around fifty-five. And the man isn't even big. But still he's able to lift them up without exerting himself. His face brightens, as if out of interest.

Harald tries to kick him. The man responds immediately, slamming Harald's face against the van door. He stares into Harald's eyes, as if searching for something he might find there. Then I realise what it is. He's looking for fear. The way a bee looks for nectar.

For a moment his attention has been diverted from Thit. She writhes and wriggles, squirming enough to somehow sink her teeth into his hand, the flesh between his index finger and thumb.

He turns his head and studies her. Looks at his hand. She bites down hard and draws blood. It doesn't trickle, it squirts and splatters her face.

Yet the man shows no sign of pain, only intense curiosity. He drops Harald to the ground and moves his free hand to Thit's throat. I feel certain he's going to kill her. And I can't move. I can't do anything about it.

I notice his shoes: moccasins of grey leather. The guy who operated the excavator.

And then four men converge on him. They're only just able to release her, though he doesn't seem to resist in any way. All he does is stand there facing her.

I realise he killed Magrethe Spliid.

Thit and Harald are lifted into the van. The doors slam shut and we pull away. I stay lying down, unable to move my legs. But still I manage to produce a paper handkerchief from my pocket and hand it to Thit. Slowly and deliberately, she wipes his blood from her face.

They drive us to Evighedsvej. They help us to our feet and take us inside. They have to carry me. The house has been ransacked. The windows are covered with plastic sheeting, floodlighting units have been rigged up and the place gone over in meticulous detail. They worked from the outside in, towards our desks and offices, dismantling everything as they went. The sockets have been removed from the walls; the extractor in the kitchen has been taken apart, its various parts laid out on the floor. The sofa cushions have been slashed open and their insides shredded with the sharpest of instruments: not even a wayward piece of fluff has found its way onto the rug. Everything has been done with surgical precision.

When they got to the gas cooker they found what I'd hidden away: the report and the list of names, concealed behind the protective plate that covers the convection oven's fan motor.

Seated at the round table is Oskar, and behind him stands Thorkild Hegn's assistant. She must have come by helicopter. She hands us each an aluminium suitcase, slightly larger than cabin-size. I glance around in search of the man in grey, but can't see him anywhere.

'You've got fifteen minutes to get your stuff together.'

'Oskar,' I say, 'I've got copies of all documents deposited for safekeeping with my solicitor. You'll be on the front page of every newspaper in the morning.'

He looks at me dolefully.

'You've been under surveillance round the clock. You haven't been to any solicitor. You wouldn't be able to afford one, anyway. It costs five thousand kroner just to send a solicitor a Christmas card.'

'I took care of it over the Internet.'

He places a hand on my laptop on the table in front of him.

'We've been monitoring your online activity ever since we brought you back from India.'

'What's going to happen?'

He turns away without answering. I'm led into my private space by two women who watch as I pack. They take away my mobile phone and my spare computer. They want the crowbar too.

'It's my lucky charm,' I tell them.

They let me keep it.

Only one of the women is from the police. Which makes it easy enough for me to deduce that we're still dealing with two groups of people here. Moreover, there's some kind of polarity between them.

We're taken out to the van. The doors are opened. At that moment, a voice calls out:

'Susan!'

It's Dorthea. Our guards stiffen.

'Are you off again so soon? Thanks ever so much for the presents. Where is it this time?'

She tips her head to the side and peers at me. We didn't give them any presents. She's trying to tell us something.

The woman at my side tightens her grip on my arm.

'Just a little getaway,' I say.

'How nice! And so many friends to go with you! Have a lovely time now, won't you?'

She spreads out her arms and hugs me. Her fingers wriggle to untuck my shirt. I feel something cold and flat against the small of my back. It slips down over my buttocks and lodges itself in my underwear. Then comes a cable. No verification is necessary, I know right away it's a mobile phone and a charger.

'Don't forget to write!'

She blows a finger kiss to Thit and Harald and retreats.

PART TWO

1

WE ARE DRIVEN FOR AN HOUR AND A HALF ALONG THE motorway before taking an exit, continuing on for another thirty minutes, then turning off onto an unmade road and stopping at what presumably is some kind of gateway. Words are exchanged. We drive on another fifteen minutes, until the road peters out into what feels more like a rutted track, and then the van stops and the rear door is opened, our blindfolds removed.

In front of us in the moonlight is a small black-timbered house next to a dilapidated barn. Both buildings are set on an inlet. A small jetty extends into the water, and on the opposite shore the contours of a castle ruin can be picked out, at which point the inlet opens out towards the sea.

The man who has accompanied us opens the house up. The place is freezing and comprises four small bedrooms, a living room, kitchen and bathroom. I turn the tap and nothing happens. The mains are frozen. The man produces a fan heater and directs hot air onto the plastic pipes. I get a fire going in the wood burner.

'Where are we?'

He says nothing.

Laban and the twins have found duvets and linen. The man points through the window to a narrow track.

'Follow the track for a kilometre and you'll come to a farm. Pick up and order provisions there.'

He gets back in the van and drives off into the night, leaving us on our own.

We each find a room and sleep as if comatose. When we wake up, the ground is covered with snow.

We spend four months in the house.

On the first morning we go down the track together to pick up our provisions. After one kilometre we come to the farm. The main house and the farm buildings form a quadrangle. Outside the quadrangle is an extensive complex of industrial greenhouses. Some have tinted glass, others are illuminated by grow lights. In the closest of the greenhouses I see subtropical plants, citrus trees and flowers, absurdly colourful against the backdrop of snow. Ripe oranges hang from one of the trees. In another greenhouse, under grow lights, I see low palms bulging with barrel-like bunches of green bananas.

A man approaches. It's Oskar. He's wearing a suit of green overalls like a surgeon, his hair covered by a hygienic cap, and what looks like a surgical mask dangles around his neck. He leads us into a utility room where there are fridges and crates of milk. He hands us forms on which to make out our orders.

As we turn to leave, I glimpse an adjoining room: a plant physiology lab, white-tiled, with microscopes, petri dishes, grow cabinets, a million test tubes, chemicals. A window affords a peek into another space, where trays containing hundreds of plants, all seemingly tropical or subtropical, are set out on low stainless-steel tables. The tiles are dripping with condensation.

The next day most of the pain has gone from my body. I put on my coat, hat and gloves and stride out in a westerly direction. I walk for an hour and a half without seeing anything but forest and open fields. I'm about to give up when I see a tall barbed-wire fence ahead. Before I get to it, a man appears. He's wearing hunting gear and asks if he can help me. His voice is friendly but firm. He suggests I stick to the paths, for the sake of the wildlife.

The next day I march south. After an hour, I see the fence up ahead. A minute later, the hunter's twin appears out of nowhere.

Two days later I head north, past the greenhouses and the plant lab, through deep snow. I cross two asphalted roads with no traffic on them. After three-quarters of an hour, I reach the fence and another guard.

The week after, when I arrive to pick up provisions, Oskar is suddenly standing in the doorway behind me. I didn't hear him come in.

'Susan, I understand you've been checking the perimeter.'

I say nothing. I carry on putting the groceries in my backpack.

'As it stands, you're guests here, under our protection. It's for your own safety while our investigations are ongoing. Once they're concluded you can go home.'

He steps up close.

'But one wrong move and we'll find a container for you, with four bunk beds, a chemical toilet and eighty square metres of exercise yard surrounded by electric fencing.'

To pass the time I bake bread. I order yeast and cultivate a sourdough starter, thereby turning my attention to one of the twenty-first century's great unsolved scientific puzzles: how to balance out the elastic protein chains of the culture and the low pH value of the lactic acid that dissolves them.

Harald asks to order books, but they won't let him. Instead, he stumbles upon a stack of *Reader's Digest* issues in the attic. They go back fifty years. Thit discovers they keep horses at the farm, perhaps for the fertiliser. She's allowed to borrow a dappled gelding and a chestnut alpha mare along with a saddle, and from then on she's off on her own for much of the day.

Laban builds musical instruments in the disused barn, from

steel wire and wooden crates. Perplexed, I watch my family settle down as if having accepted things the way they are.

It gets colder. The frost of winter grips the landscape, the inlet freezes over, and beyond it the sea. One night I wait until the others are asleep, make myself a packed lunch and fill a plastic bottle with water. I write them a farewell note and strike out over the ice. After an hour I reach the frozen sea. I carry on another 300 metres before encountering open water. I follow the edge of the ice northwards, passing the farmhouse on my left. After another hour and a half, two men appear in front of me.

I don't bother to make conversation. I turn round and go back. Three hours later I'm asleep in my bed. The next morning, when I tell Laban and the twins what I did in the night, they stare at me as if I'm speaking a different language.

Temperatures drop further still. One morning the ground is covered by ten centimetres of powdery snow, weightless as fog and offering as little resistance: the walk to the farm feels like walking on feathers.

When I get there, Oskar's nowhere to be found. I look in the windows of the lab, but the place is empty. I go round the side of the building, to the first of the greenhouses, and all of a sudden I'm less than fifty centimetres away from him. He's sitting in a chair on the other side of the glass, his back turned, unable to see me.

In front of him, hanging over him, is a peach tree, its fruit as yet unripe, a branch drooped to the ground under the weight of some black-red mass the shape and size of an American football. Beneath this mass, between his knees, is an open beehive. The football is a swarm of bees, thousands upon thousands, crawling on top of one another, small and drowsy-seeming with black and red stripes, a species I've never seen before. Perhaps they're tropical. The greenhouse is illuminated by grow lights. A film of moisture coats the panes.

The bees must have swarmed in an artificial summer. The thermometer outside our wooden house said minus fourteen degrees Celsius when I went out.

In his left hand Oskar holds a tiny box, a few cubic centimetres in volume at most, made from a kind of netting. Cautiously, he inserts his right hand into the swarm, then his arm, almost to the elbow. After a few moments, he pulls out. Between his thumb and index finger he holds a bee, more than twice the size of the others: the queen. He places her inside the box, then carefully puts the box inside his mouth and leans towards the swarm.

Like a single organism it seems at first to extend its slender pseudopodia towards him, the writhing mass then spilling onto his face, smothering his features, obliterating eyes, nose and mouth, hanging from his chin like a beard.

He is completely still. Even from where I stand, behind two layers of glass, I can hear the hum of myriad insects, deep as a turbine engine: the overwhelming energy of the swarm.

He sits there for perhaps three short minutes, motionless, immersed in the consciousness of the swarm against his face. On the border of vivid existence and most painful death.

Then he lifts his right hand, draws it gently across his mouth to clear his lips, removes the box and, without yet being able to see, extracts the queen and places her inside the hive.

As if by some biological magnetism, the swarm follows her. First a few individuals, then more, until the entire seething mass pours itself into the wooden hive. Some hover for a moment in the air above the opening. Oskar waits, motionless, until they too descend into the hive, allowing him finally to close the lid.

He straightens his shoulders, as if returning slowly from another world to the one inhabited by the rest of us. And then he sees me. With half a metre between us, we look at each other through the glass.

2

I TAKE HIM ONE OF MY FIRST SUCCESSFUL LOAVES, WITHOUT quite knowing why. When I get there he's standing in the laboratory sharpening a knife. The blade is a concave curve. To sharpen it he uses a cylinder held in his hand, made of a white ceramic material, matt, like unpolished ivory. I bring him the bread wrapped in a tea towel and put it down on the table next to him.

I stay there a few minutes. His procedure is meticulous, movements unhurried, yet swift and economic. At one point he pauses and passes the blade over his thumb, placing it at an angle of ninety degrees against the nail and exerting gentle pressure. A tiny curl of keratin blooms against the metal.

'A grafting knife,' he says. 'The incision has to be precise.'

During the following weeks he is absorbed in the systematic work of grafting. Sometimes he's in the lab, other times at the tables in the greenhouses. Now and then I linger and watch. The trees on which he works look strangely unfamiliar, and occasionally their bark has a scaly or shaggy appearance, like coconut palms. He works painstakingly in the high temperatures, humidity close to a hundred. Apart from exchanging details about our grocery orders, we do not speak.

We receive what we order. One day, after two months, there are books for Harald, though no explanation.

*

The end of February brings a period of unexpected spring. The sun warms everything up. In three days the snow is gone, except for the drifts that remain in the shadows. After five days the sea is free of ice. Gradually, the ice in the inlet breaks up.

One morning I wade out until the water reaches my thighs, then submerge myself for a moment before climbing onto the jetty in front of our house, towelling myself dry and sitting down in the sun to sense how greedily the skin soaks up its light.

The next day I see Oskar swimming.

I've come earlier than usual. The farm, too, lies on the inlet, and as I arrive I spot him straight away.

He's at least 100 metres from the shore. The water must be around freezing. At first I mistake him for a seal, but as I get closer I realise it's him.

He's doing the butterfly. I've thought him to be in his late fifties, yet his swimming is powerful, thrusting and explosive.

I stand and watch, fascinated by the elegance of his movements. Amazed he can spend such time in water so cold. Only when he wades ashore do I turn and leave.

As I pick up the groceries he comes into the utility room. He holds a photograph up in front of me. Monochrome, taken from above, some twenty metres perhaps, from a light aircraft whose shadow is visible on the ground below. One sees the corner of a building. Outside the shadow are three people, two men and a woman. They're looking up at the camera, the woman is alarmed. One of the men is wearing a white, wide-brimmed hat. He is the eldest of the three. The other man is in a grey three-piece suit. The sight of him brings pain to my body. This is the man who kicked me into the van. But he's a lot younger in the photo. Boyish, almost.

Oskar says nothing. He waits.

I hand him back the photo.

'You're a physicist,' he says. 'What's that at their feet?'

I shake my head.

'And their identities?'

Again I shake my head.

'Where's it taken?' I ask.

He slips the photo back inside a worn notebook.

'The Kalahari Desert.'

'When?'

'Nineteen seventy-seven.'

He turns and leaves.

For some weeks, Harald has been engrossed in his reading. When he's not reading, he seems distant. That evening after dinner he fetches a stack and puts it on the table in front of us.

Bound volumes of various magazines. My eyes catch a few titles: *Army News, Journal of Strategic Studies, Journal of Military Studies, Foreign Affairs*.

'Magrethe Spliid's articles. Twenty of them. All are about mass killings. She employs a concept she calls man-made violence: the violence humans inflict on one another. Between one hundred and one hundred and fifty million people were killed by human hand during the twentieth century. Perhaps some fifty million in the Second World War, fifteen million in the First World War. Ten to fifteen million as a result of Stalin's Red Terror. She calls it unprecedented in world history. Only the great infectious diseases and natural disasters have ever claimed as many lives. Her articles are an attempt to understand why. She says the history books count losses as the number of soldiers killed in action, but this amounts to only a quarter of the actual fatalities. The remaining three-quarters is made up of the elderly and the sick, and women and children dying of hunger, disease and cold in the wake of the fighting. She introduces a concept she calls public security, which she compares to public health. She says that in view of the fact that we were able to so emphatically increase standards of public health during the period eighteen eighty to nineteen fifty, primarily by improving hygiene and gaining an understanding of and then eradicating many major infectious diseases, and given that we were able to improve poor public health by directing reason at its causes, why then haven't we been able to do the same in respect of man-made violence? The reason, she suggests, is that violence comes from a place impervious to reason. It issues from human anger. This, basically, is what all her articles seek to illuminate. All end with her posing the same question: What is the root of our anger? That's what she was trying to understand.'

'And what answer did she propose?'

The question is Thit's.

Harald shakes his head.

'I've only read a third at the most.'

'Harald,' I ask, 'what happened in the Kalahari Desert in nineteen seventy-seven that someone might have found interesting enough to take a photo of? Something having to do with high explosives?'

He searches his singular memory. In vain.

He shakes his head.

'Why high explosives, Mum?'

'I saw a photo,' I say. 'There were cable trenches in it, cast in concrete.'

The next morning, a learning curve begins. I'm watching Oskar repotting when he stops and hands me the sharpening cylinder and a grafting knife.

I work an hour a day in the potting room. It takes me days to learn how to make the blade sufficiently sharp. It's a technique significantly different to the one required for the twenty-degree blades of kitchen knives, and indeed for the slanting sharp edge of a chisel.

Oskar shows me how to select the wild stock. He's working

on Danish fruit trees now. He teaches me how to tell apart what look like seemingly identical twigs he places in the soil. He is a patient instructor, allowing me time to memorise their classification numbers and properties. MM 106 yields seventy per cent bigger apples than average, but requires good soil. M 7 is a hardy variety, akin to the crab apple. M 26 puts out small roots and is best suited to espalier, yet is a healthy sort. M 9 produces a very small tree with a short lifespan, though is quick to bear fruit.

From the very first time I saw him handle a plant, I have seen gentleness and care.

He shows me the shallow-angled incision of the whip and tongue graft. How, immediately after the incision, to avoid oxidation and the risk of germs, the stock and the scion are married up and sealed with tape and wax. In his hands, it is a process of surgical precision. The first time I see one of my own grafts produce buds it feels like a little miracle of birth.

As I arrive home one day and stand washing my hands at the sink, Harald looks up from his reading.

'I found it, Mum. What you said about the Kalahari Desert. I found it in one of Magrethe Spliid's articles. Photos taken by a Soviet satellite above the Kalahari in August nineteen seventy-seven uncovered the fact that South Africa had its own nuclear weapons programme.'

I let the water run over my hands. The stiff bristles of the nail brush flay the epithelium beneath my fingernails.

'Were there other photos? Taken at closer range, like from an aircraft?'

He shakes his head.

I put the nail brush down. Here and there, blood trickles from my fingers. But the nails are clean.

I sit down at the table. Laban comes in and sits down opposite me.

'In nineteen seventy-two, Andrea and Magrethe Spliid put together a group of individuals,' I begin. 'They've been working on the idea for about ten years, though we know little about their exact reasons. They're given the support of the Folketing, their proposal coming at a time when think tanks are all the rage. The group is officially dubbed the Future Commission. Official, but secret. Its purpose is to put forward scenarios. For the first time, the welfare state is worried about where everything's headed. To begin with, the commission comprises six young specialists in key fields. Soon, their number is doubled to twelve. Every few months they deliver a report. Only no one takes any notice. Andrea and Spliid discover that in its first two years the commission has struck an unprecedented prognostic seam. Perhaps by chance, or perhaps because of what Andrea knows about structuring collective intelligence. Maybe a combination of both. She draws up an overview, a summary of the group's results showing a predictive precision without parallel. We don't know who saw this report, but what we do know is that police and military intelligence services were informed. They try to assume control of the group, but fail. They're afraid of losing it, so a monitoring unit is set up under Hegn's command. For over forty years that monitoring unit removes itself to some extent from parliamentary control. It's been seen before in Denmark. At the same time, the commission itself retains a certain independence. Presumably they realise that being able to predict the future might be a rather perilous ability. At no point is Hegn informed as to the identity of the commission's members, or indeed of any subsequent changes to its make-up due to members passing away, or whatever. At some point along this timeline, the commission decides it wants to earn money. Big money. That much appears obvious. But then come the riddles. The commission believes a comprehensive global collapse to be imminent. It decides to discontinue itself. Without giving Hegn the minutes of its final meetings. Hegn isn't pleased. So he tries me, having heard about me from Andrea. We're brought home, only something goes wrong. The killings of Magrethe Spliid, Kornelius and maybe Keldsen too are not of Hegn's doing. Nor is the attempt to do away with Harald and me. Which means there's another factor involved. The people who brought us here weren't police. Our psychopath on the quayside certainly wasn't. We're dealing with a different category of people. The man in grey. He was in the photo Oskar showed me. From the Kalahari Desert.'

Thit looks at me.

'Mum, might we suppose the commission, in striving to make a packet, ran up against a very specific issue? About where to draw a line between use and abuse of a special talent?'

3

TOWARDS THE END OF MARCH, OSKAR SHOWS ME A MORE complex graft, particularly suited to more delicate scions: *Bøghs citronæble*, Ballerina Obelisk, Red Astrakhan.

'Oskar, what exactly is this set-up?'

'It's a plant-physiological experimental facility.'

'Why is it so big? Ten by ten kilometres, most of which is fallow land?'

'There's a minimum requirement for grafting experiments. To prevent cross-pollination.'

'We're in the south of Sjælland,' I say, 'aren't we? The northern part is too densely populated for this.'

He doesn't answer me.

'Who does it belong to?'

He doesn't answer.

The next day I'm alone in the laboratory when the postman arrives, in the same little van as always, the one that also brings in our groceries and Harald's books. The letters are left in a basket inside the door, and the van drives off.

Oskar is nowhere to be seen. I skim through the envelopes. Most seem to be catalogues, addressed to the *Plant Physiology Research Centre*. The postcode is 4720 *Præstø*. The last envelope is addressed to *Oskar Larsen*. It's from the Danish Defence Special Forces.

*

There have been a number of nights now without frost. Oskar tells me it's time for bud grafting: the insertion of single buds of particularly attractive varieties directly into the stem of already-bearing stock plants.

He stands side-on. In his left hand he holds the green bud, with his right he makes the incision: a single, exact movement.

'Oskar,' I say, 'why no woman?'

He puts down the knife, turns and walks away.

In early April I lend a hand planting spinach.

After an hour I break off and tell him I need to go to the bathroom. The field is 400 metres from the lab. From the building I can see the arch of his back.

At the far end of the lab is a door I've never seen open. I open it now. Behind it is another, edged with a rubber seal some ten centimetres in width, like an airlock.

The room has no windows and is dark, but a dim red safe-light goes on automatically. Cupboards line the walls. I open one, it too is fitted with a rubber seal. Inside are what look like small jam jars, hundreds of them, tightly packed.

All are three-quarters full of grain. Each has a label stuck to it. I read: *Barley. Landrace. Scandinavian Gene Bank No. 3071. Barley. Landrace. Scandinavian Gene Bank No. 12.440. Rye. Landrace . . .*

On the floor is a wooden crate measuring a metre by one and a half. I remove the lid. It's sectioned up into compartments with thin plywood dividers. In each compartment is a jar. The crate contains more than a thousand, each carefully packed with wood wool.

'What's a landrace?'

Harald is engrossed in his reading. He doesn't even look up when he answers me.

'Cereals selected in the normal way, by picking out the best seeds. They yield less than modern varieties but are much hardier. A bit like you, Mum.'

'Harald,' I say, 'don't be so precocious. You're not vanishing into books in order to avoid girls, are you?'

A moment passes before he glances up. The look he sends me is one of despair.

The next day I'm seized by enthusiasm for the job of planting the spinach. I find myself working in a rhythm, as if on a good day in the physics lab, an inner metronome driving me on, row by row, heart pumping steadily as I concentrate.

Returning to reality, I realise I've worked four hours without a break.

I go back to the farm and into the laboratory. Oskar's sitting at a microscope with what look like tweezers in his hand. He doesn't look up. I stand next to him and watch.

'We remove the outer group of cells from the shoot, Susan, for propagation. In order to eliminate such organisms as carry disease, which are further inside.'

'That photo,' I say, 'from the Kalahari Desert. Was it from the South African nuclear test site?'

'Vastrap Weapon Range. That was the name of it.'

He still doesn't look up.

When I get back to our wooden house I hear music from Laban's instrument. I go into the barn and find him seated. He throws me an icy glance.

'I know you've got something going on with him.'

When he's really hurt, his features don't alter at all. It's his skin. It changes colour.

He gets to his feet.

'Oskar's the old gardener,' I tell him. 'He's ancient.'

'He's a man in the prime of life. I sensed there was a spark the first time I saw you together. And now here you are, obviously returning from some sexual tryst!'

Jealousy is an interesting chemical combination. One minute we're big-hearted and generous, the next we've snorted 0.25 milligrams of the stuff and are transformed into despicable gnomes.

'Brazenly, in front of our noses! Mine and the children's!'

'Laban,' I say, 'get a grip.'

And then he hits me.

He hasn't got the slender hands you'd expect of a piano player. They're broad and strong.

Not all his life has been spent at the piano either, for that matter. His mother once told me he was a boy with a temper, always on the lookout for bigger boys on whom he could vent his aggressions. When Thit and Harald were younger I put a climbing frame up for them in the garden on Evighedsvej. It's years since they grew out of it, but Laban still swings about on it like an ape.

He's never hit me before, so it comes from nowhere, and he hits hard. Even though I go with the punch, it still knocks me to the floor.

But I follow through, rolling out of the fall and back onto my feet.

Laban has to mount the wooden crate of his instrument to reach out and grab me.

'I know you've had sex!'

'You're right,' I tell him. 'A good old romp in the haystack, among the apple trees. The only thing that made us stop was *that.*'

I point behind him and immediately he turns to look. The way 99.9 per cent of the world's population would do in the same situation.

And then I kick the crate from under him.

I judge it to be about thirty centimetres high, and his centre of gravity is thus a metre and a half above the ground at the moment his fall begins. He lands flat on his back, his head snapping against the concrete a nanosecond later.

For a moment he's unconscious, a few seconds perhaps. Long enough for me to snatch a garden fork from the wall and put its prongs to his throat.

We glare into each other's eyes. I press the fork down lightly and see something begin to dawn on him, an insight of the kind that's rather difficult to arrive at in any ordinary family idyll: the realisation that it's not just everyone else who's going to die, but oneself, too, and moreover that it's likely to happen any second now.

But then Thit and Harald are standing there staring at us.

We've gone back into the house and are sitting down in the kitchen. The left side of my face is swollen, my eye partly closed. Thit has cleansed the wound at the back of Laban's head and made a bandage out of a tea towel. He looks like an oil sheik on his last legs.

Our hands are shaking, his and mine.

'We've never had a fight before,' he says. 'There's never been any violence between us. It's my fault entirely. It'll never happen again.'

'There are other kinds of violence, aside from the purely physical,' Thit says. 'Harald and I remember tensions between you all the way back to when we were in kindergarten. We've often talked about the way we had to gauge the mood when we came into the living room, whether it felt safe. Children are like small animals. You listen out for danger. Grown-ups think about the punch-ups, the arguments, perhaps. But not the tension. The tension is like poison. And you never managed to make it go away.'

We sit quite still. In the impotent understanding that she's right.

'I had an idea,' says Laban. 'A wish, if you like, or a dream. When your mother was pregnant with the two of you. It was the only thing I could think about. It had nothing to do with anything I could teach you, and nothing to do with music, either. It was something else: I wanted you never to be lonely. The way I was as a child.'

Laban has two brothers and a sister. He grew up in a loving family environment, with parents who were understanding. They wrapped him up in cotton wool. None of us ever thought of him as lonely before.

'There can be something inside a child. Something very hard to see that's looking for a kind of response, sympathy. The child can't say so himself. And though he might be surrounded by well-meaning adults, there's a part of him that's overlooked. And until it's seen and recognised, he won't ever be able to thrive and grow.'

For the first time, I see inside Laban a little boy lost.

'It went away when I met your mother. But there's a price to be paid. If another person really perceives who you are, and if you feel yourself to be truly fathomed by a woman, it triggers a kind of madness. You crave to be recognised again and again. To feel completely understood. You want her to make up for all the years she wasn't there. And what's more: once you've opened up, you can get really, really scared of losing her.'

I'm standing up, at the sink, with my back to them.

'When my father disappeared,' I say, 'the world split apart. Until then, I'd been living at the centre of a sphere. That was how it felt, like the universe was a sphere that surrounded me. The day he went away, it changed shape. From then on, I was living on a plane surface. With no protection above, and the constant fear of falling over the edge. My mother felt the same way. She'd had other men while they were still together, and she had other men afterwards, too. But she never got over it.

There was a certain unity that came apart. After that, she and I lost our bearings. We were all over the place. Even if she did manage to keep the flat, to stay on at the theatre and carry on with her dancing, she was an itinerant from that day on. She was thirty years old, and a meanderer inside herself. So when I got pregnant with you, I had one thought only, the idea that we would share our meals together. I saw myself preparing food for you all. And to bring that idea into being meant embarking on a long-term project. I realise that now: I decided I was going to stay with Laban until the two of you could look after yourselves.'

I scald out the teapot. Measure out the tea leaves. Pour on the boiling water. And then I turn round and look at them.

'We did our best,' I say. 'Laban and me. And very often it wasn't good enough.'

We eat in silence. Eventually, Harald pushes his plate away.

'The stories I told when I was little,' he says. 'They weren't to do with you.'

Harald told fibs for years. At school, to us, to his friends. We felt guilt-ridden. We tried to talk to him. We talked to the school. We took him to counselling. Nothing helped.

We gave up when the other parents started calling us. Harald had convinced his classmates that our entire family came from a distant galaxy and that we'd hidden our spaceship in the Charlottenlund Slotspark.

After yet another phone conversation with yet another concerned mother, Laban and I looked at each other. Laban said what both of us were thinking:

'Boys tell stories about the dog they haven't got. The air rifle they'd love to have. The kiss they dream about from the girl of their fancy. They don't go around telling everyone their family are aliens. This is a different category. And still one can't help thinking it commands respect.'

243

One day it just stopped. There was never an explanation. Until now.

'No matter what you might have done back then, it would never have been enough. I wanted the world to be bigger. I wanted to *make* it bigger. I realised this in Nepal when I tried to smuggle those antiquities over the border at Almoeda. I could have speeded up. I could have made it across. But I didn't. It was like something inside me held me back. I realised then that the wish is okay. Only the method was wrong.'

That night, I can't sleep. In my mind I gaze out over the twins' childhood. Trying to understand it. To understand them.

They slept with me, sometimes with Laban, until all of a sudden, at the age of eight or nine, over a period of little more than a few weeks, they began to sleep in their own rooms. But before that, I watched them wake up a thousand times.

Until they were seven they smiled as soon as they opened their eyes. Those eyes in the early morning would for a few seconds be without comprehension of what universe they were in. And then they would recognise the bed, each other, and the grown-up next to whom they lay. That was when they smiled. As if out of the deepest confidence and trust in life.

It came to an end when they were seven. Within a few short months there was a shift in their waking eyes. It was as if some new materiality had begun to peer out from inside. A new administration that had begun to realise there was a price to pay for growing up.

I think about Laban. I've always thought he woke up like a citizen of the world, a Renaissance man. Now I look at him differently. As if what he said at the table has thrown a new interpretation backwards in time. As if the present could change the past.

4

I WAKE UP AT FIVE IN THE MORNING. I CAN ONLY SEE OUT of one eye. The other throbs. I go outside. Laban is sitting on his haunches on the decking, singing softly. Less than a metre away, two young hares have paused to listen. As I stand quietly in the doorway, he reaches out and strokes the one nearest, running his hand gently down its back. It sits motionless. Then it notices me and both hares scatter in fright.

Laban looks up and sees my eye. He flinches.

'Animals react to the animal within us,' he says. 'To our aggression and fear. A person singing and making music enters a different state of consciousness. That must be what Francis of Assisi discovered.'

'Yes,' I say. 'And the Pied Piper of Hamelin.'

The sun tinges the clouds with dark purple from below. It hasn't reached the horizon yet.

'Thit has confirmed my estimations,' I tell him. 'From her riding trips. The area's a square, ten by ten kilometres. The perimeter fence is equipped with sensors all the way round, and from whatever way you approach, a guard will always appear. They've got us in a high-security prison.'

He says nothing.

'The farm's a gene bank for cereal varieties. The orchards contain hundreds of different kinds of apple trees. Oskar does grafting experiments with tropical and subtropical plants.

There are bees there, of a kind no one's ever seen in Denmark. Oskar's a soldier. What is this place?'

The hares, which had gradually approached again, turn and scurry away at the sudden volume of my exasperation.

'There's an investigation going on, Susan. As long as that's the case, we're safe here. We've got everything we need. Thit's got horses, Harald's got books. We're managing. Everything's going to be all right.'

The sun appears.

'I was shut away from when I was twelve until I was sixteen,' I say. 'When they moved me away from Holmgangen I promised myself it wouldn't happen again. And if it did I would make sure that situation changed. I didn't want to be kept prisoner ever again.'

He says nothing.

'There's a kind of muzak, Laban. Not just here, but everywhere else in Denmark, too. I've always been able to hear it. It's a song that says everything's all right, we can relax and take things easy, we've got everything we need. We're being looked after, the splendours of life are without end, all we have to do is lean back and enjoy. But it's a siren song, Laban. It makes us forget we occupy the smallest window of time, open only for the briefest of moments. It makes us forget a deeper-lying hunger. But not me, Laban. I'm forever hungry. Do you understand?'

'You've tasted everything, Susan. And none of it satisfies you.'

Later that morning I see Thit ride off into the forest and decide to follow her. I find her sitting by a small lake. The water is clear as glass. From the bottom, springs issue forth, cylindrical curls rising to the surface.

We amble back to the house together. The mare follows her like a dog. Thit has always talked about animals as if they were people. She had her first menstruation whilst out riding. She was twelve years old, we'd bought a summer house in north

Jutland that spring and couldn't make the payments. It was sold off by court order that same autumn. In between, we managed to spend a marvellous summer in anticipation of future grants. Nearby was a farm where there were horses. Thit rode a black stallion every day. It was as big as an elephant. The day it happened, she came riding up to tell me, beaming with pride as she patted her horse.

'He knew,' she said. 'He knew even before it came.'

Animals react to our trust by acting like they are people. The mare tags along behind us like a respectful member of the family.

'Mum, you know those bedtime stories I never wanted to hear?'

I keep walking, albeit on autopilot. We're touching on another family enigma, another pain spot.

I always tried to tell the children a story when I put them to bed. It was for the same reason I took them to kindergarten in the mornings, and later to school, accompanying them on their way towards adulthood, to soften the blow of having to let go and allow them to get on with things themselves. In the same way, I tried to usher them into sleep with a story.

When I was a child myself, I was frightened whenever sleep approached. I would lie in the dark, waiting to succumb, but then fear would come instead. And though I lay still, I travelled. The darkness grew, and there eventually, at journey's end, was sleep.

The fear stopped when I grasped the periodic system. There's no more to say. I looked at the table of the elements and understood it immediately. It was a guarantee. A map of a higher order.

That was what I tried to pass on to the twins. At first I read from a children's book, with the two of them at my sides. Then I turned off the light. And in the darkness I would tell them one last story before they slept.

It was always about physics. About Zajonc's box of invisible light, and Faraday's blindly intuitive genius. About the whole world lined up for the confirmation of Einstein's general theory of relativity at the meeting of the Royal Astronomical Society at Burlington House in November 1919.

I wanted to provide them with a bridge of order and regularity across which they might pass into sleep, a diagram of the only things in which we can truly believe. I wanted to show them you can take a grown-up by the hand and proceed along a shining path to the very place where sleep embraces us.

It didn't work.

Or rather, with Harald it did. His eyes would be turned towards my face in the dark while he lay there motionless. As I spoke, I could sense his attentiveness, and the increasing relaxation of his body. And eventually, when I stopped, a few seconds would pass and he would give in to sleep.

It was different with Thit. She didn't make a protest. But whenever I got up to turn off the light and she realised I was going to tell a story, she always climbed up into her own bed.

I tried asking her why, but she never told me. Without a word, she would turn away and leave me and Harald on our own in the dark, retreating into her domain to fall asleep.

It always pained me. To see a little child, three years old, let go of your hand and withdraw alone to a place to which a mother might have led her.

Occasionally, in the years that have passed, I've ventured to ask her about it. She's never replied.

But now she stops. The horse draws to a halt. The world likewise. The forest holds its breath.

'When you told us those stories, you were trying to build a room for Harald and me. I could hear that, and not just from the words. You were trying to build a room that was full of light. A perfect room. Physics tries to build perfect rooms, you told us that. Perfect lightproofed rooms, airproofed rooms, weightless rooms, sterile rooms. You and Dad, you tried to build that kind of room around Harald and me. And that was always clearest to me when you were telling us those stories. You were good, and almost succeeded. But I didn't want to go into that room. Because if I did it would have been very hard to leave it again. That's the problem, you see. If a person can build a place where no suffering exists, the world outside becomes that much more dangerous. Because you want to stay in that place for ever.'

I hear what she's saying, and at the same time it's like I'm plummeting. As if the bottom has fallen out of the forest.

'You wanted to alter the world, Mum. The way you alter a physics report.'

We go back to the house.

I serve dinner. Harald puts down his knife and fork.

'In nineteen sixty, the United States and the Soviet Union together possessed a total nuclear explosive force equivalent to three thousand kilos of TNT for every man, woman and child on earth.'

I close my eyes and hope he's going to leave it at that. But he doesn't, he carries on.

'Magrethe Spliid describes how powers very close to the American president applied pressure to implement a surprise nuclear attack. When permission remained unforthcoming, they bypassed the president and the American government and carried out a number of provocations towards the Russians to force them into war. In one article she goes through every single one of the local wars in which the superpowers have been involved since the Second World War. Not one ended in clear victory. The Korean War is a case in point. Millions dead, the entire North Korean society in ruins and that close to escalating into nuclear war. And yet the whole thing ends in stalemate. She sums up the research into the decision-making processes of the Cold War. The massive increases in atomic capabilities that occurred weren't occasioned by any strategic or foreign-policy imperative. Instead, they were pressured into being by the weapons industry and more aggressive elements within the military and administrative sectors. Both in the Soviet Union and in the US. And Denmark was involved all the way: a small, hesitant, yet nonetheless unequivocal pillar of support within NATO.'

I realise he's pointing the finger at Laban and me.

'Laban and I weren't even born then,' I tell him. 'Besides, your dinner's getting cold.'

He holds his tongue and begins to eat. I glance across at him, my appetite gone.

Again he puts down his knife and fork.

'She states that research indicates that anger builds up collectively, and very slowly. It's like there's a reservoir of rage, a toxic waste dump, and when it's filled up and starts to run over, war breaks out. She considers that waste dump to consist of the sum of the anger generated by each and every one of us. She believes it to be measurable. Not mechanically, not with a measuring rod or weighing scales. But some people, she writes, will be able to sense the dump filling up. And they'll know when it's about to run over. By predicting that, by pointing out that we're now on the verge, and by being seen to be right, they'll encourage societies to turn the other cheek, to look away from perceived enemies in the external world and instead focus on their own internal anger. And when they do, things will start to change.'

A silence ensues. Eventually, it's broken by Thit. Her voice is soft and gentle.

'That's a very beautiful thought. But it's naive, Harald. You only have to look at the four of us.'

All at once we notice Laban. He's staring into space as if he's seen something.

'The Future Commission,' he says. 'That's what she wanted it for. She and Spliid. That's what they envisaged, right from the start. They thought that if they produced correct predictions, of wars and other widescale acts of violence, people would become aware of the deeper underlying mechanisms.'

He gets to his feet, all eyes upon him. He circles the table. We've seen him do this before, at times of creative inspiration. His eyes gaze into something far away.

'It *is* beautiful in a way. Very humanistic. And yet there's something not quite right about it. It's the conspiratorial side of it, the secrecy, that bothers me. The wish to exercise power, however benignly. It's like they were wanting to creep up and spring a miracle on us.'

He halts and stares at us. Suddenly, I understand him. And I realise why he understands Andrea and Magrethe Spliid. Because basically, it's the same thing he's been trying to do all his life with his music. He's been trying to creep up and spring a miracle on us all.

'It's not on,' he says slowly. 'It's not enough for the plan to be good. There's the motives to consider, too. And if they're not . . . genuine . . . if one in some way wants to coerce others, coerce the public, or the politicians . . . then it's bound to fail.'

He looks at me. I look away.

5

THE NEXT MORNING I WATCH OSKAR SWIMMING AGAIN.

A thin band of advection fog drifts in over the inlet from the sea, settling on the still surface like a delicate mantle of cloud, the swimmer's body visible only in glimpses as the sine wave of his butterfly stroke reaches its apex.

The moment I pass the spot on the shore where he has left his clothes, a blood vessel inside his brain ruptures.

What I see is that his shoulders and upper arms appear out of the fog and vanish beneath it again. I wait for the movement to be repeated, only nothing happens. I go to the water's edge. Advection fog always moves sideways. A gap appears in the water vapour and I see his body at the surface. No longer extended flat, but slanting. And as I stare he tips and goes under for the first time.

I tear off my clothes without a thought. I gauge the water, the temperature and the distance to this drowning man with my body alone. I've taken the twins to the swimming baths and the beach hundreds of times. Anyone with that experience will no longer assess bathing safety with the brain. Instead, you project your physical capabilities out across the surface of the water, and feel within your muscles how far away you can allow the children to go, how fast you'd be able to get to them.

I know as I plunge into the water that this exceeds the limit by far. And yet I plunge.

In the sequences of compressed time surrounding mortal

danger, the realisations that suddenly occur to a person can be astonishing. I realise, deep within myself, that the twins are old enough to get by without me. And that in spite of everything, I trust Laban enough to take good care of them.

The second the water sheathes my body, my skin becomes numb. I sense the cold begin to close upon the very core of my being. I know I've got minutes at the most.

He's about 100 metres from shore. It'll take me less than two minutes to reach him. When I'm halfway there he goes under and doesn't come up.

I find a point of focus on the opposite shore and draw a line of sight. I follow it and count the seconds. When I think I'm at the spot, I dive.

The water is surprisingly clear, blue-green, as yet too cold for the chemistry of decay which in a month's time will begin to colour the still water brown.

On my way down I encounter a cloud of bubbles.

It is the final exhalation of a drowning man. After it, in a matter of seconds, will follow a series of involuntary, retching gasps that will fill his lungs with water, and fungus will infect his mouth and gullet: milky proteins, like whipped egg whites.

Twice during my time at Holmgangen I helped pull people out of a disused marlpit. One was drowned, the other survived.

I find him at a depth of some four or five metres. I grab hold of him under the arms and feel for the bottom with my feet. At first they find only eelgrass and silt. But then a flat rock.

I launch myself upwards. We ascend in slow motion and break the surface.

His eyes are open. I think he can see, but his body is limp. I turn him over and lay his head back against my chest, only our noses and lips above water, to spread his weight.

And then I begin to tow him towards land.

I know I won't make it. I realise as much even with the first feeble strokes. The water is too cold, the chill already too deeply entrenched within my muscles. The nerve pathways will soon

253

be cut off. My body has already in part stopped doing what I want it to do.

I feel the fatigue I've read about, a gentle urge to give in to an increasing drowsiness.

And then my fear of sleep kicks in. After thirty years of absence. At once, I am scared stiff of the darkness that looms. My panic gains us fifty metres.

But it's not sufficient. There's still another fifty to the shore. Anyone can drown quite easily in the shallowest of waters. Six metres is an outrageous luxury. Nevertheless, I feel an inexplicable, paradoxical satisfaction: I'm dying the way I always said I would, with as much resistance as possible.

Then a pair of arms wrap themselves around me from behind. They belong to Laban. He hasn't had the presence of mind to take off his clothes and has swum out in his trousers and sweater. It's an unintelligent way of going about the matter, if ever there was one. But before unconsciousness turns out my lights, I decide not to make an issue of it.

6

OSKAR'S GONE A FORTNIGHT. WE DON'T KNOW WHETHER he's alive or dead.

The farm is locked up, though our deliveries continue. Twice a day, a man in overalls attends to the boiler and the greenhouses. I tell him I've promised Oskar to weed the rows of spinach and take care of the grafting. He shakes his head, but that's all.

When Oskar comes back it's by ambulance. He's in a wheelchair, but after a few days he starts using a walker with big, chunky tyres that can handle the fields.

A routine is established.

The cereals, the apple trees and the planting work are taken over by taciturn men whose vocabularies do not extend to greetings. I carry on with my weeding. Oskar sits in a camping chair and watches. A week goes by before he opens his mouth and speaks for the first time.

'It was a blood vessel at the back of the brain. In Denmark it happens to twenty a year. Less than ten per cent survive.'

Just telling me obviously requires a monumental effort. Several days pass before he can add a conclusion:

'If it hadn't been for you, Susan, I'd have drowned.'

*

The Effect works in silence. I reach the end of the spinach rows one afternoon. The wind off the sea is cold. I always loved the crispness of early spring. The sun feels new. Its presence soothes and nourishes, though as yet it is feeble, the moist air still to be misted by its warmth.

'Oskar, why isn't there a woman in your life?'

'I'm a soldier.'

'Even soldiers have women.'

He looks away.

The following week I dig holes for the strawberry plants, fill them up from the wheelbarrow with three parts topsoil and one part compost, add water, place the plant in the hole and pat down the soil. Affixed to each plant is a plastic label stating the name of the variety. Most are unfamiliar to me.

Oskar comes and sits down beside me.

'They inserted a camera into a vein in my groin and passed it all the way up through my neck into the brain. I watched it on a screen.'

A bumblebee buzzes about in search of a place to settle. A trout leaps in the inlet. A woodpecker flies past with a naked fledgling in its beak, amid a clamour of alarm calls. Nature unfolding in all its splendour and horror.

'Susan, I want to show you something.'

I follow him back to the farm buildings. We pass through the grafting area and the laboratory to the room I have entered only once. He opens the door and the red safelight goes on.

'We've got a complete duplication of the Nordic Gene Bank. In an underground facility. It was set up in spring nineteen eighty, immediately after the Soviet invasion of Afghanistan.'

In the middle of the floor is a wooden crate, the same as the one I saw when I was here last. He removes the lid and hands me a jar from inside.

'It looks like rice,' I say.

'It is rice.'

He hands me another. Rice again, but this time the grains are longer. I decipher the labels: *Short Stem Nimrog, Singapore Genetic Bank*.

He's trying to show me something he's unable to tell me directly. But the message isn't getting through. I don't get it.

'I spent two years with the Danish Defence Intelligence Service. On Sunday, 7 August 1977, I was on duty when a call comes in from the Pentagon. Later comes a sequence of film the Russians have taken over the Kalahari, from a Cosmo 932 low-orbit close-look satellite. It shows the drill holes where the atomic devices were to be tested, the instrument trailers, the buildings. TASS goes public with the information on the Monday. The reason we're briefed the day before is because the CIA knows we're in touch with the building contractors, SecuriCom. Jimmy Carter received the pictures from Brezhnev the day after they were taken. He orders the area to be overflown by a plane belonging to the US military attaché in Pretoria. They take pictures and footage from a height of thirty metres. You can see faces quite clearly. The plane flies over while there's an inspection going on, conducted by Armscor, the South African government's own arms manufacturer. And the armed forces. And representatives of the building contractors. We're presented with the photos, on my watch. I recognise the three men in them immediately. The guy in the hat we knew as the Duke. The second guy, the elegant gentleman in grey, is called Jason Alter.'

He puts the photo down in front of me, the one he's already shown me once. I try not to look at it.

I note that Oskar suffers from a singular obsessive disorder. Whenever he's feeling tense, he spreads out his fingers and studies them. The red safelight makes it look like he's got blood on his hands.

'These are the guys transporting the crates. On behalf of Holmens Kanal 42.'

'What's at Holmens Kanal 42?'

'The Ministry of Defence. And the Danish Defence Command. But the crates are driven to the docks. Loaded onto a boat. And sailed out to Kronholm.'

7

THAT AFTERNOON, LABAN GIVES A CONCERT.

Just as it's about to begin, Oskar arrives. I look at Laban, he looks at me. Oskar's there at his invitation. Perhaps in order to make up for our altercation, perhaps because people kept in isolation band together, even with their keepers. Or maybe just because Laban will always seek to maximise his audience.

He's managed to stretch some steel wire out across a beer crate that he has equipped with a funnel. The funnel channels the wind, which in turn sets in motion a length of brass curtain rail set up with elastic bands, bringing it into contact with the steel-wire strings. It's a kind of wind harp and it makes a sound like tortured souls trapped in a rubbish skip. He accompanies this rising-falling tone by striking with a stick a series of lemonade bottles filled with various amounts of water. And by playing a kind of homemade violin – the body of which is an empty two-and-a-half-litre tin that formerly contained peeled tomatoes – with a bow made of a bamboo flower stick to which he has attached a metre's length of nylon tape.

Somehow, inexplicably and wholly contrary to nature, he nevertheless succeeds in making it sound like music.

We sit down in the kitchen. I've made cauliflower soup. Laban puts his spoon down on the table in front of him, instilling in me an immediate feeling of dread. He addresses the twins:

'Just after you were born, a professorship became vacant at the conservatory in Copenhagen. I knew it would land me work

259

abroad, as well as providing financial security. We invited the conservatory's rector and two of its teaching staff for dinner. The three of them together would make up a majority on the assessment committee. Your mother prepared the meal. And then we let loose the Effect. It doesn't only occur spontaneously, we can release it too, and by that time we had a lot of experience from the interviews and our collaboration with Andrea. We knew what was going to happen. First, whoever is on the receiving end will feel a confidence inspired within them, a sense of being understood and embraced. People react to such confidence by unconsciously opening up, automatically almost. Then comes a kind of attraction. They are hooked, and can no longer escape. The art is to navigate within that landscape. To interrupt at the right times. To give people back to themselves. If you don't, it's tantamount to exploitation and seduction. We went too far that night. In such cases one is abusing the openness of others for personal gain, tainting one's sincerity with darkness. Deferring payment of a bill until some future time. I got the professorship. And it was just the springboard I thought it would be.'

I get to my feet and stand at the window with my back to them.

'That's how we did things for ten years, your mother and I, on many occasions, and mostly with success. Then we tried to make it work with money and our luck ran out. I think this, our present situation, is payback for those years.'

I turn to face them.

'Your dad's a crybaby,' I say. 'Yes, I exploited the Effect for financial gain, so we could live comfortably as a family. It's not something I regret. My own professorship was above board and on the level. But we took advantage of it to secure board memberships. In every case, I've put in work for the money. So, no regrets.'

They remain quiet for some time. Oskar stares ahead as if he's somewhere far away. It all reminds me of our Christmas

260

Eve. The homeless ought to be more careful about who they allow to invite them home.

'What about the costs, Mum?'

The question comes from Thit.

'There aren't any. I wanted a normal life. I got one.'

We eat in silence. Then Oskar places the photo on the table.

He indicates the three people in it.

'I knew them from Greenland. The Danish military had worked with them before on two occasions. First in a cover-up operation, when a US B-1 bomber armed with nuclear weapons went down in the North Atlantic off the Greenland coast. Then when a Danish air ambulance was shot down by mistake during the tensions of the Cold War. SecuriCom salvaged the chopper and doctored the corpses to remove all trace of what had happened. In nineteen seventy-eight, Botha succeeds Vorster as prime minister. He hires help to implement his programme. SecuriCom are part of that. Once again, I'm brought in to take care of the photo documentation, this time for the UN, to give them an argument for tightening the embargo. Later, I run into them again, only this time they're working for the KGB. *Mokri dela*, so-called wet affairs, assassination jobs. Then again, later still, in Alma-Ata in Kazakhstan when I'm over there on behalf of an international committee monitoring radiation levels in the natural vegetation after the fallout from Chernobyl. All of a sudden our contacts are pulled out. It turns out Yasser Arafat is in town, currying favour with the first Islamic state in the world to boast atomic weapons. We hear him address the parliament. Among his entourage I recognise the Duke. And Jason Alter.'

Again he spreads his fingers, and I study them.

He gets to his feet. I follow him to the door and step outside with him to get away from Laban and the twins for a moment.

The night is cold, dark and cloudy. Oskar walks with a stick now he's stopped using his zimmer.

I've come out without a coat. He takes off his oilskin jacket and drapes it over my shoulders. We pause.

'Susan, do you mind if I hold you for a moment?'

I won't say I hadn't seen it coming. But still.

No woman in the world hasn't gone to bed with a man at least once out of pity. I can't deny that's probably true for me, too. And possibly more than once. And why not? Female sexuality is an abundance that may also be shared with the needy.

And in this instance it wouldn't be entirely out of pity. I think of the thrust of his body in the cold water. His feminine meticulousness in caring for his plants. His face crawling with bees.

And yet I know the answer will be no. He knows it too.

Nonetheless, I take him by the arm and walk him home. There's an inexplicable kind of reciprocity between us. In a way, he's the executioner and we're the victims. And in another way, it's the exact opposite.

By the time I get back, the twins and Laban have gone to bed. I can hear them sleeping. I enter Laban's room and look at him. His breathing is deep and measured at the same time, and as light as a child's.

A dark rage wells inside me. A desire to relieve myself of this lust, a wish that there were some pill I could take to make it go away, an operation, a lobotomy that would remove the urge for ever. Perhaps some medicine exists. I tear off my clothes, pull aside his duvet and lie down on top of him. He always wakes up slowly, as if returning from some far-flung corner of the universe. But his erection precedes him. I grip it immediately, straddle him and slip it inside me. I writhe, briefly, a few seconds at most. Enough for the dizzying blur of frenzy to find form and culminate. And then I get up and gather my clothes.

'Go back to sleep,' I say. 'I needed your body, that's all.'

He stares at me, eyes wide. I retire to my own room.

8

THE NEXT DAY, OSKAR COMES OUT INTO THE FIELD WITH his chair. He unfolds it and sits down next to me.

'I'm a gardener.'

My eyes ignore him. Yesterday still lingers in a way.

'Before special forces, I was a gardener. In the summer and autumn of two thousand and nine I was in Afghanistan. Helmand, the Green Belt, between Gereshk and Shurakian. I was there to map the extent of the opium growing. There were three of us, two gardeners and a biologist, working in the fields under protection. One day we came under fire from the Taliban. They came in pickups mounted with heavy 12.7-millimetre machine guns. We eliminated a few of them and forced the rest back to a house by the river. A B-1 came in to give us cover, but they shot it down. In the night, I went into the house and killed eight people with a knife. When I pulled off their headgear, two were women.'

The bees hum. The grass is green. He looks down at his hands.

'Every time I get close to a woman I see them in front of me.'

I finish up the planting work. We're still on the strawberries. Several of the varieties are named after women: Hedy Lamarr, Königin Luise, Zsa Zsa Gabor.

'The war was a mistake. We left a bigger mess when we pulled out than there was in two thousand and six when we went in. The central government in Kabul had no control over the provinces. The Taliban were stronger, the opium trade more widespread. The general level of conflict escalated. Danish soldiers died in vain. The blame has yet to be apportioned.'

I say nothing. What have I done, that everyone should be talking to me about war?

'Seven thousand Afghan civilians dead. Hundreds of thousands displaced within the country's own borders. Fifteen thousand Taliban killed. Eight thousand Afghan police and soldiers. A thousand NATO troops. All to no avail.'

'I don't want to know,' I say. 'Find somewhere else to weep.'

I go over towards the farm buildings. He calls after me. I ignore him, and he comes limping.

I wash my hands.

'Killing is a hard business, Susan. Harder than you might think. Even killing animals is hard. Not many hunters would admit to it, but most are familiar with what they call buck fever. You've got the deer in your sights, and it's as if the body only then realises that you're about to take a life. It protests. The body has its own will. You start to tremble. The more you try to control yourself, the worse it gets. And, of course, it's all the more intense with humans. In combat you immerse yourself in a very particular state. You no longer see the enemy as human at all. In that state it can be done. But outside of combat, without your unit, it's different. That's why good contract killers are so few and far between.'

'Oskar,' I say, 'I haven't had breakfast yet. You're making me lose my appetite.'

'You have to listen.'

He's completely exposed now, as he was yesterday when I walked him home.

'Once in a while, Susan, very occasionally, someone gets to like it. Jason Alter. I've studied him. He likes it. Alter is Danish. Normal background. Nice, ordinary home. But at some early stage he realises he likes killing. First hens and geese. Then larger animals. The dossier on him stemmed from a KGB interrogation in the early eighties. They used chemicals, truth serum. He applies to join the special forces, Navy Frogman Corps. He passes all the tests, but then he takes a chance and slits the throat of some vagrant. They suss him out, though nothing can be proved, and he's dismissed from service. He disappears off the radar for a few years, then turns up in South Africa, working for Armscor under Botha. They reckon that's where he met up with the Duke. Normally, killing is a messy business, Susan. Psychotic. The movies make it glitter, but in the real world it's base and primitive. Alter's different. He's intelligent. Keen. I watched him in Greenland, when those corpses were doctored. He did the last one himself. He'd absorbed the whole technique, could have passed for a surgeon. There's nothing he can't do. Besides speaking any number of languages he's a highly professional photographer – all the photo documentation was his work – and he knows all there is to know about computers.'

Without being aware of it, he spreads his fingers and studies them. Then he passes his hand over the stubble of his skull, above the nape of his neck, the site of his haemorrhage.

'I've never been afraid of men, Susan. Women, yes, but never men. But I'm afraid of Jason Alter.'

'You work with him,' I say. 'I met him on the quayside in Copenhagen. He would have killed Thit. He tried to kill Harald and me. He's a part of this.'

He looks away.

9

THAT EVENING AFTER DINNER I PLACE DORTHEA'S MOBILE
phone on the table in front of Laban and the twins.

'Dorthea slipped me this. Right under the noses of our guards
before they brought us here. There's a charger, too. I've called
the bank. Our credit cards were blocked a week ago.'

They look like they've suddenly turned to stone, the way all
people do when something happens to their credit cards. In the
modern world there's a direct biological feedback function
between people's credit cards and the vital processes of life.

'Who blocked them?'

The question is Harald's.

'The bank says we did. Each one of us. With our own PIN
codes and our secure logins.'

I put the two code cards for my own login down on the table.

'So much for digital security. These have never been out of
my keeping. Yet someone got to them. Or got round them. And
there's more. Three days ago our accounts were blocked too,
then closed.'

They can't keep up any more. Their trust in the state and all
it does is too deep-seated.

'Everyone in Denmark has to have a bank account. Anyone
who hasn't doesn't exist. I called the estate agent on Jægersborg
Allé. I asked if they had anything for sale on Evighedsvej. They
did. Ours. We put it on the market ourselves last week.'

'What's going on, Susan?'

I turn to face Laban.

'Someone,' I tell him, 'is writing us out of the libretto.'

Later that same evening I go up to the farm. I've never been there after dark. I don't even know exactly which part of it Oskar lives in.

I walk round the side. In one of the small windows a light is on. I approach and peer inside. In a room, small and as sparsely furnished as a cell, I see him sitting on a bed reading the Bible. He's wearing boxer shorts and an undershirt. On the table next to the bed is a crucifix. Through an open door I see a hallway leading to a bathroom and a small kitchen a few square metres in area.

I go back round to the front, passing the lab and the utility room. I move swiftly, it takes me less than thirty seconds, but before I reach the door someone grabs me from behind.

It's an expert hold. I can't move, even my feet are locked. I hear a sniff and am released as quickly as I was seized. Oskar steps back. Before his eyes have even adjusted to the dark he has identified me by smell and touch, the way an animal might. In his hand is a knife. It vanishes as if by itself, and yet I have time, even in the dim light, to see it's not a grafting knife. The blade is double-edged and twenty-five centimetres long. A maliciously designed instrument.

We go inside, into his room. He sits down on the bed, I on the only chair.

'Our bank accounts have been closed, our credit cards blocked, and someone's put our house up for sale. Someone's not counting on us going back. I want the rest of the story.'

He looks like someone who's just had a stroke.

'It's all about an island.'

I wonder if his brain might have been damaged after all.

'Denmark has purchased land, Susan. In the tropics. All the specimens here are to be shipped out there. SecuriCom are taking care of the transport.'

'What's it got to do with us?'

He shakes his head. He doesn't know.

'The security's the tightest I've ever seen. There are very few people involved, considering the scope of it.'

'But it's why you're here looking after us?'

He nods.

'Hegn uses as few people as possible.'

I pick up the crucifix from the bedside table.

'I see you've kept your faith, Oskar.'

He gives me a look of defiance.

I sense the masculine stringency of the room. The place is spotless. If there's something both it and the man next to me need, it's the female touch.

I get to my feet.

'There's not much a woman can't forgive, Oskar. Even killing. There's bound to be some tropical beauty awaiting you on that island. All you have to do is forgive yourself.'

'It's uninhabited.'

Nothing is more self-destructive than a man's gloom.

'That's just an excuse, Oskar, for being afraid of women. You'll meet a stewardess on the plane.'

I pull the door to on my way out.

'They're using Atlas military transporters, leaving from Kronholm. There won't be any stewardess.'

'Goodnight, Oskar.'

10

I'M TRYING TO FALL ASLEEP, BUT CAN'T. ALL OF A SUDDEN I hear something outside. Or rather, it's not something I hear at all, more a kind of registration of some subtle change in the atmosphere. The door of my room opens. The night is cloudy and dark, but large expanses of water always give off light. I can't see his face, but the shape is Oskar's.

I put some clothes on and we go into the living room. After a few moments Laban and the twins join us. We sit down at the table.

'I got a call. You're to be picked up the night after tomorrow. An hour after you've gone they're bringing six others in. They'll be here for six hours, to clean up after you.'

'How can cleaning up after us take thirty-six man hours?' I ask. 'We're tidy.'

'They want to remove every trace. Including fingerprints. They'll be very rigorous, so not even a forensic investigation will reveal you were ever here.'

He looks away. Then he puts a key down on the table. When he speaks he's still not looking at me.

'This is for the pickup in the garage building. If you follow the track due east you'll come to a gate in the fence. It's locked with a chain.'

He puts a second key down next to the first.

'Wait in the truck three hundred metres from the gate. There'll be a power outage at 01.15. That's an hour from now.

It'll last ten minutes. In that space of time, all cameras and sensors will be out of action. Once you're out, you'll have forty-eight hours.'

I pick up the keys.

'The children stay,' he says.

The twins rise to their feet, like a pair of cobras. I'm paralysed. It's not physically possible for me to leave them.

Laban spreads his fingers on the table in front of him.

'If your mother and I succeed, we'll come back and get you within thirty-six hours. If we're not back by then . . .'

He and Oskar exchange glances.

'. . . then there'll be another power outage. You'll hitch or take the bus to Copenhagen. You'll go to the Ministry of Foreign Affairs on Strandgade. There you give them my name and say you want to speak to Falck-Hansen. He's a sort of acquaintance of mine. And then you tell him everything.'

The twins can't believe what they're hearing. What Laban has said isn't an order. An order can be ignored, at least in theory. This is a statement of irrefutable fact.

I unfold the copy of Magrethe Spliid's list and hand it to Harald.

'That last name,' I tell him. 'Gaither. There were no Danish hits. Was there anything in those articles?'

His memory boots up inaudibly. But I can feel it.

'H. Rowan Gaither. Former president of the Ford Foundation. Headed up a committee set up by Eisenhower. They wrote a report in nineteen fifty-seven recommending a seven-to-tenfold increase in US atomic capabilities. As well as a forty-billion-dollar programme for the construction of nuclear shelters. They were convinced the US civilian population could survive a nuclear war. As long as there were enough shelters.'

I go into my room and pack a small bag, then return to the kitchen.

Oskar rises from the table and I follow him out. We stand and face each other in the night, outside the door.

'Your plant trials, Oskar. The deliveries they want. Rice and all the rest of it. There must be a figure. You must know how many people they need to sustain.'

'Four thousand.'

And then he is gone.

PART THREE

1

THE PICKUP BUMPS SLOWLY EAST ALONG THE TRACK. I call Dorthea. She sniffles.

'Ingemann died an hour ago. I'm sitting here holding his hand. I haven't even rung the doctor yet. He was just sitting there with his eyes open. He wanted to see the angel.'

'Did he see it?'

'He smiled. He still is smiling. He's so beautiful.'

I hear the love in her voice. It's always been there. She has a way of saying his name, as if it gives her a lump in her throat.

'Your house has been put up for sale. There was a gentleman here on Thursday, said you'd agreed to that witness protection programme. You'd be away for at least a year, he said. We weren't supposed to try to contact you during that time.'

'We're doing a bunk, Dorthea. We're on our way to Copenhagen and will need a place to sleep. Two nights, that's all.'

'The beds are made up in the annexe for you. They have been since you left.'

Nothing was ever too much for Dorthea and Ingemann. It's part of what always made me so unsure. If the kids knocked something over, broke a window, dropped something, there was never a harsh word. And now, with her husband of sixty years dead, his body not yet cold, there's not a moment's hesitation to her hospitality.

'They'll be looking for us.'

'I was a big girl in the final years of the war, Susan. My

childhood home was a hotel for fugitives. Saboteurs, communists, Jews.'

We conclude the call.

Reaching the gate, we wait until seventeen minutes past before I get out and unlock it. Laban drives through. I close the gate behind us and lock it again.

We are silent most of the way to Copenhagen. Laban turns on the radio. We listen to the news. A march on parliament has drawn a hundred and seventy-five thousand protesters. The city centre and the districts of Østerbro and Nørrebro have been hit by riots, the worst since the EU referendum vote on 18 May 1993. Some one hundred and fifty casualties. Cars set alight by the score. Laban turns it off.

'Not long after I was awarded the university's music prize, someone came to see me. At the conservatory. A man from the Ministry of Defence. He asked me for a mobile phone number and wanted me to make sure they were informed if I ever changed it. They had to be sure they could get in touch with me. In case of events unforeseen, as he put it. Military or civil.'

'Did you give it to them?'

'I can't remember.'

'Didn't they ask for my number, too? Or the children's?'

He shakes his head.

'What were your thoughts, Laban?'

He says nothing.

'Your thoughts were the same as anyone else's would have been. That they were up to something. In case of war or something equally nasty they would gather the nation's finest and lead them to safety.'

We approach Copenhagen. More lights, more traffic. Laban exits the motorway in the direction of Bagsværd so as to avoid the congestion of the city centre, and the police who may already have been mobilised. We pass by the detached residences facing out to the ring road. As yet they are in darkness, asleep, with gardens full of trampolines and climbing frames.

'With so many dead,' he says pensively, 'the question is if one would even want to be among the survivors.'

We drive along the lake.

'I never got back to them,' he says. 'I suppose it was a mixture, really, of having the same thought as you and finding it so unpleasant to consider.'

'We'll go to Kirsten Klaussen,' I say. 'She's famous. She can go to the papers with us.'

There has always been a very singular mood surrounding the dead people whose bodies I have sat beside.

I once had an aunt whose corpse at the Frederiksberg Hospital resembled someone very beautiful who had been lost at sea. Laban's mother looked like she had achieved what she came here for, which was to make an effort on behalf of others, and now finally she had been able to close the door and get some peace. The girl who drowned in the marlpit when I lived at the home at Holmgangen looked exactly like what she was: a child who had been calling for her mother without anyone having heard.

Ingemann certainly does look like someone who has seen an angel. His lips are ever so slightly curled, as if he were about to exclaim, 'Blimey, this is going to surprise you!'

We sit for half an hour in silence. I reach out a couple of times and pass my hand across his brow. At one point, Laban gets up, is gone for five minutes, then comes back with a violin. He plays a little piece. The violin has never been his instrument. And yet somehow he makes it sound so very heart-rending.

During the course of this brief half-hour, Ingemann's presence already seems to fade. Perhaps it's the chemistry of decomposition beginning to kick in, or maybe it's just something I imagine.

Dorthea comes in with a tray.

'I got my driving licence renewed. The day before that gentleman came by, the one who put your house up for sale.'

She hands us plates with bread and butter, and pours the tea.

'As soon as he was gone I got in the car and drove after him. He never noticed. Who could imagine being followed by an old woman of eighty-four?'

She puts a jar of honey on the little table.

'A saintly gentleman, as it turned out. And kind to animals. He drove out to Bagsværd Church to feed a dog. A Dobermann pinscher, it was. He brought it raw meat, but it wouldn't touch it. On Sightseeing Day in nineteen sixty-four the police dogs gave a display, at those red prefabs the police college had down on Islands Brygge. They had Dobermann pinschers as well. I remember they put a chunk of meat down in front of them, but they wouldn't move until they got the command. It was the same with this one. It just stood there looking at him. He tried several times. Eventually he gave up. I'm not very quick on my feet any more. By the time I got back to the car he'd gone.'

2

DORTHEA'S ANNEXE CONTAINS TWO ROOMS. LABAN AND I
sleep apart.

I wake at five in the morning. Laban is immersed in deep
sleep and I haven't the heart to wake him.

I step out into the garden. The sun isn't up yet and the ground
is covered with frost. I stand at the hedge and stare towards
our house.

The beech trees in the garden will soon be in leaf. Perhaps
they possess some rudimentary form of intelligence. I've
watched them, year after year. They seem to be able to delay
the moment of their buds bursting open until the final frost
releases its hold.

Fifteen minutes later I'm sitting in the car. At six, as the
arsenic hour draws to a close, I pull up outside Bagsværd
Church.

A fence has been erected around the church and the little
park surrounding it. It looks all wrong. Not because I'm particularly familiar with Bagsværd Church, but because in this
country we're unused to seeing churches fenced off as private
property. The gate is a superior example of TIG welding in
stainless steel. The mailbox likewise. I know instinctively the
work is Kirsten Klaussen's own.

I get a fright when I see the dog, the Dobermann pinscher, a
male, motionlessly alert just inside the gate. It glares at me with
all the insensitivity of a reptile.

There's a camera installed above the intercom system. I step forward and press the button.

Minutes pass.

'Do you realise what time it is?'

Quantum physics has a theory that reality is forever completing itself and making itself whole. The theory is confirmed here. The rust lacking on the gate and the mailbox is on her larynx instead.

I hold Magrethe Spliid's list of names up in front of the camera.

Barely a minute passes before she appears at the door. Still in her nightdress, her hair looking like she's had her hands on a van de Graaff generator.

She calls the dog. It obeys immediately. Its eyes are still fixed on me. It may well be that it only eats on command, but I'd give ten to one it's been hoping for an order to devour me.

The gate opens.

People grab all sorts of things when tumbling out of bed in the early morning. Some reach for their dentures, others a toothbrush, while others will make a beeline for something alcoholic. Kirsten Klaussen has chosen a Havana cigar. It juts from her mouth, and she peers at me along its length.

She looks at me as if trying to establish what kind of alloy I am.

Then she steps aside and I enter the church.

Removal boxes line the walls. Everything seems to have been packed except for the odd piece of furniture and what would appear to be in the region of ten thousand DVDs, a flat-screen TV measuring two by three metres, and a sound system that takes up most of the end wall and wouldn't be out of place in a concert venue.

A narrow channel of water runs in from outside and passes underneath a pair of double doors made of heavy oak. A couple of metres further on, the channel widens, opening out into a large, shallow, asymmetric basin clad in blue tile and illuminated from below. The surface of the water is unnaturally still, invisible almost, the way water only ever is indoors.

Protruding out towards the centre of this pool is a wooden platform on which a complete kitchen has been installed. Here, presumably, she sits in the mornings, tossing toast crusts to her Dobermann.

If, that is, she is at all willing to share. Kirsten Klaussen weighs upwards of 100 kilos. The ankles bared by her nightdress are about the same diameter as Grecian columns.

'I don't suppose you saw a Dobermann on your way? A bitch. She doesn't normally go off on her own, so I'm a bit worried.'

She hasn't managed to ruin the space entirely. It's still incredibly arresting. Perhaps even more so because it's almost been cleared. The organ is the only remaining indication of it ever having been a church. The walls, too, are bare. Apart from something resembling a sewage pipe of bluish aluminium.

'I always wanted to own a building designed by Utzon. By the time I could afford it he was already dead. I know you. You're Susan something-or-other. One of Andrea Fink's little protegées. What became of you?'

She must have a memory akin to Harald's. Or better. It's fifteen years since she saw me last. At the honorary residence, and from a distance.

'I went into administration.'

'Whatever for?'

'To earn a living.'

She nods.

'There's never been any money in science. Not even in metallurgy.'

She lifts the sewage pipe off the wall as if it were made of cardboard. Now I can see it's got a trigger mechanism, a telescopic sight and a muzzle.

'People think of technology as applied science. They think physics precedes technology, when in actual fact it's the opposite. Physics developed as an attempt to provide solutions to problems identified and formulated by technicians like me. Because we're more in touch with the real world. Who gave you those names?'

'Magrethe Spliid. Just before she was murdered.'

'And why did she give them to you?'

'Maybe so the rest of you could be warned. Kornelius is dead. Keldsen too.'

She fondles the weapon.

'A mere five kilograms. Twelve hundred needle rounds a minute and enough muzzle velocity for an adult torso to be torn open by the mere thrust of a single projectile passing by at twenty centimetres. Not only did I design and construct it, I can also hit thirty out of thirty-five moving targets in a minute and a half, at a range of eight hundred and fifty metres.'

'You're not going to get a minute and a half. And you won't see them at eight hundred and fifty metres.'

She doesn't hear me.

'Practical metallurgy begins with copper jewellery. Alloying and soldering skills are developed with the setting of precious stones. Welding and the forging of complex forms begins with Greek statuettes and ritual vessels of the Shang dynasty. Ceramics comes of trial and error with the firing of small fertility goddesses in clay. Glass stems from attempts to embellish beads of quartz and steatite. Most minerals and organic combinations were discovered by painters in search of a pigment. We are artists, Susan. And society has yet to realise the fact.'

She turns, graceful as a hippopotamus, all one hundred and something kilos utterly under control. Her weapon points, as if by accident, at my abdomen.

She smiles. It's a smile that ought to open all doors for her. All the way to a padded cell.

'We members of the commission were paid a pittance. Three hundred and fifty thousand kroner a year by the time it came to an end. A fraction of what any mediocre solicitor would be given for a single annual meeting of one of the major boards. Is it so strange that we eventually decided to make some money on our own? We could have won the country fifteen hundred times the acclaim of Bohr and his sons put together. Not to mention money. Money like water! We foresaw Halk's discoveries. We predicted the mineral finds of molybdenum and uranium in the subsoil of Greenland. As well as the huge oil deposits. But they kept us down. As Hegn, that little shit, used to say: "The public isn't ready to understand this yet. It would be too overwhelming by far. You'd be dismissed as shamans. It would reflect badly on the government and adversely affect your careers." So it all got hushed up. Hegn and his people filtered the information so only a fraction ever got out, in over forty years. Eventually, we'd had enough. Who was that man, the one who was writing a cantata for the Folketing? And those pretty children?'

'Laban is my husband. The children are mine. We found your capsule in the National Archives.'

'So what did you conclude?'

'You were amazingly precise.'

She smacks her lips contentedly.

'We foresaw the collapse of the Soviet Union. Nixon's emergency suspension. Vietnam. The Gulf War. The war in Iraq. We could have given NATO a colossal military advantage. We saw the unrest in the Soviet system years before it came to the surface. But they shut us up. Magrethe did, too. A bloody communist is what she was. A pacifist. A Gandhi disciple. *Ahimsa*, if you don't mind. She considered the liquidations of collaborators during the war to be murder. The way she saw things, the Danish resistance were on a par with Hells Angels. She thought Reagan's advisers, Perle and Cheney, ought to have been tried for crimes against humanity. She was forever harping on about collective ethics. Do you believe in that sort of thing, Susan?'

She has stepped closer. The muzzle of her weapon jabs at my stomach. My hand grips the crowbar in my bag. But the Dobermann will turn any physical initiative into suicide.

'Physics has no definition of ethics. But I'm a mother of two.

283

I want my children to survive. The prognoses aren't good. Someone tried to kill us. Hegn kept us banged up for four months. He's operating with a security firm far outside the boundaries of the law. Yesterday we escaped. You were predicting a major civilisational collapse. Would you have a date on that?'

She returns the gun to its place on the wall, then lowers her hand to the dog, holding out her cigar. The Dobermann slices off the end with a snap of its jaw, like a guillotine. She returns the Havana to her mouth, lighting it with a table lighter made from the shell of a hand grenade.

Once it's lit, she places a fleshy hand on my shoulder. We're friends. Two women in a man's world. She leads me along the water's edge.

'Look at the shape of this pool. Can you see it's the trace of a Eulerian path? Königsberg's famous Seven Bridges. That was the first thing I wanted: a swimming pool. I grew up in a brown-coalfield, a place called Vonge. My mother killed herself when I was three. At fourteen I ran away from home. I emigrated to the States when I was nineteen. Fought my way up. So I'd lost my mother. My childhood home. My native tongue. My social class. My country of birth. Do you know how I managed? By not clinging. I'm a master of letting go.'

'Except when it comes to money,' I say. 'You stick to money like glue.'

She pauses, surveying what opportunities might be open to her. She could get the gun. She could feed me to the dog. Or hold me down in the shallow water until I drown.

But then she roars with laughter.

'Damned right I do! I'm a scrooge, always have been!'

She indicates the ten thousand DVDs on the far wall.

'I love film. Look what they gave Dreyer. Three shorts in twenty-one years. And a three-room flat on Dalgas Boulevard. Even though his desk drawer was full of scripts. Denmark is such a petty little place. I've been involved in the biggest arms projects of the last forty years. I've played a part in winning the Cold War. Now I want some spoils.'

'I want you to come with us to the papers. Tell them about the commission. About Hegn. Your predictions.'

She considers me pensively.

'Susan, I find you attractive.'

'I'm allergic to dog hair.'

She nods. Disappointed, yet composed. The allergy decides it for her. She can accommodate a lot of things, but the dogs are her true companions. Superficial erotic opportunities must yield.

We're standing at the door. She turns and points upwards, at Utzon's arching ceiling where light seems to enter from another dimension. Within the curve of white hangs a large mobile, a kinetic sculptural installation comprising at least three by three metres of coloured metal elements.

'It's made of parts from an F-117A Nighthawk stealth fighter. I worked with William Perry when he was part of the Carter administration. I developed the coating. The beep it gives on a radar is no greater than a sparrow's. During the Gulf War we reduced human losses by factor ten. From one per cent to one per thousand. Only one dead American for every thousand Iraqis. Once you've been in on improving nuclear weapons, you do start to think. Look at Oppenheimer. Szilard. Bohr. They were tormented by conscience. I read an interview with Tibbets once, the pilot who dropped the bomb on Hiroshima. He said, "It was completely impersonal." Do you believe that, Susan?'

I think back. On the thousands of people I've met. The thousands of times I've felt the Effect. And I know I'm not going to win her over.

'Between people, nothing can ever be completely impersonal.'

She won't let me go. She's in her seventies and a multimillionaire. She can do anything, and knows everything. She's got a whole life's work behind her. And yet she's so miserably alone.

'The problem of having to look after oneself at too early an age, Susan, is that one learns never to trust. The others in the commission became a kind of family for me. Even the men. We didn't see each other much, but when we did I felt alive.'

She grips my arm. Not in any patronising way, not as a threat or a challenge. Disconsolately.

'I was in love with Magrethe, of course. We all were. Through all those years. Do you know what unrequited love feels like, Susan?'

'Doesn't everyone?'

'Not for forty years. What do you say to forty years of despair?'

'I can accept a single year of grief in exceptional circumstances, an all-consuming love never reciprocated. But the other thirty-nine seems like pushing it a bit.'

For a moment her eyes fill with madness. Then she laughs again, like a blast furnace sucking in air.

'I don't give tuppence for the papers. And I never trusted politicians. We must all take care of ourselves. I've kept myself indoors ever since Magrethe's death. I get my groceries online, always the same delivery man so I know who I'm dealing with. I've got CCTV all along the perimeter. In a fortnight I'll be gone. I hope they come before then, the people who killed Magrethe. I hope they come.'

I go down the steps.

'You're like a dog, Susan. I saw that straight away. One of those small, ferocious varieties. A dachshund or a pit bull, whose basic instincts have been left intact, despite all attempts to eradicate them through breeding. They wriggle into a hole and come out backwards dragging a fox in their jaws. Maybe you'll find them first. If you do, make sure to come and fetch me.'

3

IT'S STILL NO MORE THAN SEVEN A.M. MOST OF KONGENS
Nytorv lies dark. There must have been clashes here between
police and protesters. Crowd-control barriers have been put up
along the pavements, ground-floor windows have been smashed
in their dozens, and makeshift repairs carried out with tarps
and duct tape. The burnt-out shells of two overturned cars
deface the Krinsen, from which the equestrian statue of Christian V has been removed. The statues in front of the Royal
Theatre are encased in plywood.

But the brass nameplate by the door of the building I enter is
polished and shiny. The first four floors are taken up by various
arms of Fabius's fashion design company. The names at the top
are his and my mother's. She has taken his surname, which is
Magnus.

It's Fabius who comes to the door.

Once or twice in a lifetime, one may be fortunate enough to
find oneself standing before a man so gorgeous as to pain
one's heart. Not pain in the metaphorical sense, but real physical hurt.

Fabius is such a man. His beauty isn't the flashy kind. It's
dark, introverted and mysterious, and exerts the most violent
pull on a woman, an urge to step forward and touch, comfort,
or whatever else might be required to make it known to him
that his refined and complicated soul is understood fully and
without condition.

'Fabius,' I say, 'I am compelled, on behalf of my gender, to express my deepest sorrow at your homosexuality.'

He smiles, like a Chinese mandarin.

'We were told you'd be away at least a year.'

'And yet here I am.'

'Your mum's got a migraine.'

My mother's migraines aren't the same as those borne by frail, cultivated ladies in the manner of a fine hat on Derby Day. Rather, they are a lethal curse that strikes like a sudden fracture of the skull, irregularly and without warning, turning her face the colour of a corpse and making her eyes bloodshot, sucking the very life out of her and driving her into the bedroom, where she will lie for three days and nights with the blinds down and the curtains drawn, without so much as a morsel or a drop of water passing her lips.

And when that time has passed she will appear, weak and staggering, yet resurrected, albeit with an expression on her face to suggest she has been all the way to the kingdom of death and back again.

I have never before disturbed her during such an attack. But this time I've got no choice. What's more, Fabius senses as much. He steps aside.

I haven't entered my mother's bedroom in twenty years. Everyone has a line drawn somewhere, to be crossed by others only at their peril. Everyone, perhaps, except Dorthea. My mother's is located at the door of her bedroom.

I go in without knocking.

The room is dark, its air pervaded with the scent of fresh apples, puffed-up pillows and perfume. I step up to the window, draw the curtain slightly to one side and open the blind just enough to let in a chink of light to stop me falling over the furniture.

The floor space is dominated by the bed. It's antique, resting on claw feet, and has all the stateliness of a grand ocean liner, varnished and gilded, topped by a pink spray of pillows and eiderdowns.

Somewhere within it is my mother. All I can see are her eyes, glaring hatefully at me in the dim light.

'Mum,' I say, 'why did Dad go away?'

Just as we as individuals construct personal narratives to stop us from falling apart, the stories that keep families together are designed to give the impression that these social units are vectors that proceed along the scale of time, to be permeated with both tragic meaning and tearful warmth. The narrative concerning my father has always held that he was a great nomad whose natural wanderlust could not be contained in such a meagre country and a family as minuscule as ours.

I've always known it was a lie.

'I remember him saying goodbye,' I say. 'He didn't go of his own accord.'

Fabius is in the room now, too. He has flowed in, like a precious liquid. My mother gestures to him. From the bedside table he hands her a small bottle of medicine with a plastic straw sticking out of the top. She takes a suck while looking me straight in the eye.

'It's morphine, Susan. The only thing that helps.'

Her voice is a rattle. She was ill when I entered, but now she seems worse.

'I don't know about politics, Susan.'

I wait, merciless.

'He owned a munitions factory. At Raadvad. It was inherited from his father. He invented a new kind of projectile made of some kind of ceramic material. There's always been opposition to arms manufacturing in Denmark. It turned out he'd been supplying countries that were under UN embargo.'

'Like South Africa?'

Either she doesn't want to know or the effort of speaking allows no sound.

'He found out he was going to be arrested and charged the next day. So he fled. It never got out, but they seized everything. All his properties, his savings, the factory, the hunting lodge at Rude Skov. There was nothing left for us.'

Her hatred of the authorities has been unfailing ever since. I sit down on the edge of the bed. She hasn't the energy to protest.

'I've seen him,' I say. 'In a photo. Taken in the Kalahari Desert. I'm sure he must have been in touch with you. Given word.'

She reaches for the morphine. I hand it to her. Next to the bottle is an embroidered handkerchief with which I dab her mouth. She wants to sit up, I help her. Fabius puts a pillow behind her back. She points to the drawer of the bedside table. I pull it out. Inside is an envelope.

'Open it.'

I do as she says and remove the contents. Two photographs of the same man. My father. In the first picture he's older, in the second much older, than I remember him. In both he's wearing the white, wide-brimmed hat.

I turn the photos over. On the back of one of them, in black ink, are the words: *To my beloved Lana and Susan.*

There are no stamps on the envelope.

'The first one came after ten years. Then another ten years passed before the next one came. Since then there's been nothing.'

'How did they arrive?'

'By messenger. The same man both times. A Dane. He didn't say his name.'

'What did he look like?'

She pauses for a moment.

'A physical man.'

Some people notice features, others intelligence. Others still are able to smell the size of another person's bank account at 400 metres. My mother tunes in to people's bodies. With uncanny precision.

'Physical in what way?'

Her hands flutter a picture in the air. A dancer's attempt to describe a reality above or beyond language.

'He made me frightened.'

Only seldom have I heard her express fear of anything other than dwindling audiences.

'But his clothes were impeccable.'

Fabius has sat down beside me now. I sense the tenderness of his affection for her. His love. For a brief second it's tangible, as if there were a physical bridge connecting them.

Until now I've always thought that he was looking for his own mother in mine. Now I see it's the other way round. In spite of the age difference he loves her the way a father loves a daughter.

'How did you and Dad meet?'

'He saw me dance and sent me flowers. A great bunch, as big as a haystack. He asked if he could see me. I declined. He came to seven performances on the trot. Sat in the first row. And the flowers kept coming, after every performance. When the fourth lot came, I asked the theatre not to accept them. So he went to my parents. He had this psychotic charm about him. I was still living at home. One evening he was just there at dinner. A few weeks later I allowed him to take me out.'

Her eyes are distant. She's reliving it all.

'Why did you choose him?'

She looks at me. It's a crucial question for any child.

The answer likewise. To what is one conceived and born? What made one's parents get together?

'It was his *power*, Susan. Brute force. Women love it.'

'And love?'

She glances at Fabius. He nods gently and hands her a tall, slender glass. The apple aquavit. He supports her head as she sips.

'We went shooting together. He'd imported Chinese water deer. The only species of deer with tusks. They can be quite dangerous. In the early mornings, as the sun was rising, we would be alone in the shelter, waiting for the animals to appear. Close together, and without a word between us, while all around us nature was waking up. There was a very strong feeling that if only the world had been different, then perhaps there might have been . . . love.'

I feel a kind of irrational relief. Perhaps it's important for the child in us all to know there was some sort of affection.

'Mum, have you ever received instructions from the Ministry of Defence? In case of disaster?'

In the ensuing silence I hear her laboured breathing. She closes her eyes, trying to worm her way out of the intimacy that has arisen. She fails. We're too far inside.

'It's confidential, Susan. There are two phone numbers. Only the head of the theatre and myself have knowledge of them. Not even the ballet master has them. No one must know. Why do you ask? How do you know about it?'

Now that my eyes have adjusted to the dark, the details of the room become clearer. From the ceiling hangs a Venetian chandelier: antique, mouth-blown, a hovering, lace-like fantasy of glass. The room is sparsely furnished, but each and every item in it is antique and exquisite in a casual sort of way. As if some passer-by with good taste had accidentally on purpose dropped a million kroner outside the door of a well-chosen home.

'An official came to see me at the theatre. It's more than ten years ago now. An intelligent man. He told me that even if the whole ballet ceased to exist, as long as they had me they'd still be able to reconstruct the entire Bournonville repertoire. With new dancers. In another place. It's true, Susan. We won't say it out loud, but it's true.'

'What other place?'

'He didn't say. But it makes such good sense, don't you think? To protect our most valuable citizens, if anything should happen.'

I get to my feet.

'He phoned, Susan. Your father. Shortly after the first photo. He was in South Africa. Mobile phones weren't common in those days. It was the operator who put him through. She said there was a call from South Africa. After a few years he rang again. He asked about you. After that I stopped taking the calls. He wanted to speak to you. It wouldn't have done you any good. We had lives to be getting on with. You and I together. It could have cost me my position at the theatre. They said it would have been one of the great court cases of all time. International crime. It wasn't just arms.'

That's how she is. At heart, she's never been bothered about me or my father, nor even her lovers. All she's ever been interested in is herself and her dancing. I feel tenderness for her. There's something very pure about only wanting one thing in all your life.

'Did he sound like a man in decline?'

'There was no decline. He was on top. At the top of his game, where he always will be. That's how he got to me, Susan. It's how he got to us. It's the way he always approached life, as something to be conquered. Something to power his way through.'

There's a defiant pride about her voice. In a way, she was raped. Maybe it helps to convince herself it was the Prince of Darkness who did it.

She falls back against her pillows. Fabius follows me out. We stop in the hallway and stand for a moment. What exists between us has no words. The place where he and I converge is in our love for the woman lying in that bed. It's a feeling so spooky, language would seem to be at a loss.

'Magrethe Spliid. Did you find her, Susan?'

I nod.

'She and your father were an item. Until he and your mother . . .'

As I descend the stairs, he closes the door behind me, quietly and with delicacy.

At the bottom of the stairwell I see a shadow through the glass pane in the door. I grip the crowbar and step outside into the arch of the gateway. Laban stands leaning up against his bike.

We walk alongside each other to the pickup. He puts the bike in the back. I climb in behind the wheel.

I'm about to turn the ignition, only then I pause. The shop on the corner of Gothersgade has been plundered. Its windows are shattered. Inside, virtually everything's been taken. This happened while I was with my mother.

I start the car and turn in the opposite direction. I've no desire to drive past the vandalised shop. I make a left onto Bredgade. Ahead of me the road stretches from the Royal Theatre and the Magasin du Nord department store, past Nyhavn to the Esplanaden, a sweep through the very centre of the royal city, synonymous with the majestic Copenhagen of old. Now many of the ground-floor windows have been smashed and boarded up. The faint smell of smoke hangs in the air.

'I've called the Centre for Particle Physics,' I say. 'If Denmark's being evacuated, Thorbjørn Halk is the first person they'll bring to safety.'

4

THEY PUT THE FINAL TOUCHES TO THE CENTRE FOR PAR-
ticle Physics while we were away in India.

The visible part of the complex is a four-storey building situated in park-like grounds and enclosed by a high wall, all of
which has devoured some 10,000 square metres of the Fælledparken, the part once called Klosterhaven, on the corner of
Jagtvej and Serridslevvej. We stop in awe in front of the main
steps. The whole thing has cost more than forty billion kroner,
ten of which has come from the Danish government, with the
EU and NASA chipping in with the remaining thirty.

The part that cost so much money is the part that can't be
seen above ground. But the rest is no less sumptuous on that
account. The stairs are granite, the floor of the main hall her-
ringbone parquet. Elegant sofas provide discreet furnishing,
and even the uniforms of the security guards look like something off a catwalk. Official, but without the aggression.

Nonetheless, the men wearing them won't let us in.

'I called,' I tell them. 'I've got an appointment. I'm a professor of the University.'

They refuse to listen. Laban can hardly contain himself.

A woman appears.

'Elisabeth,' I say, 'what's going on?'

She draws us aside. Her voice is hushed.

'I got your message, Susan. But I'm afraid you can't come in.
We're busy. Thorbjørn says to say hello. I understand from him

that you've tendered your resignation. You'll be very welcome some other time.'

There's a little badge pinned to her white blouse: *Professor Elisabeth Halk*.

'So now you're Mrs Halk,' I say. 'And a professor to boot. Nice work, Elisabeth.'

She blushes.

'I need to speak to Thorbjørn,' I say.

'You can't. He hasn't got time. And you're no longer cleared for access. I must ask you to leave.'

I lean towards her and place a hand on top of hers. With the other I grip her forearm. And then I press down, bending her hand unnaturally towards the inside of her forearm in a hyper-flexing wristlock.

The colour drains from her face. Her eyes widen in alarm. Academia is so focused on the mind. It has little experience with physical pleasures and pains.

I maintain the pressure as I lead her towards the lifts. Laban follows hesitantly.

'Elisabeth,' I say, 'there are women who would consider you a scheming little tart, shagging her way up the ladder. But not me. I might say you've speeded up the process a bit, but I'm convinced you'd have got there anyway at some point.'

Her eyes are moist with tears. We reach the lift. The guards eye us with suspicion, but I've angled myself so they can't see our hands.

'Just keep a brave face, Elisabeth,' I tell her. 'Otherwise I shall have to break your wrist. We're going down, by the way.'

The lift descends and stops. We step out into a space furnished like the lobby of a luxury hotel: more granite, more sofas, armchairs in black leather, modern art on the walls. We proceed into a large oval room lined with banks of monitors, at which some twenty or thirty people are seated. A small group stands gathered in front of a large screen in the middle. At the centre of the group is Thorbjørn Halk.

Halk is two metres tall, with a shock of red hair. He is the very reason for all this. His discovery of the so-called Halk Spin while conducting experiments with the giant accelerator at CERN earned him a Nobel prize quite as distinguished as those of Bohr and Andrea Fink, and has moreover enabled Copenhagen to attract the funding for what we now stand gaping at through an open door.

What we see is a concrete tunnel, inside which a cylinder of blue enamelled metal a metre and a half in diameter describes the beginnings of a perfect circle sweeping out at a depth of fifteen metres under the Fælledparken, Svanemøllen, central Hellerup, outer Østerbro, Nørrebro, Valby, the docklands, Amagerbro and Holmen, then back through the city centre to be completed here at the place where we stand: a total distance of forty kilometres, making it the largest particle collider in the world.

It circulates elementary particles through the forty kilometres, accelerating them to a speed close to that of light, creating eight hundred million collisions per second, thereby generating an annual eighteen petabytes of data, an amount that would fill the equivalent of two million DVDs if it weren't for the filter system in whose design I was involved, which from the eight hundred million collisions per second extracts the four hundred most important.

I let go of Elisabeth. She sinks into a chair. I step forward and tap Thorbjørn Halk on the shoulder.

He has difficulty concealing his annoyance at turning round to see me. But behind his annoyance there is fear. His eyes are distracted by the sight of his wife, and his fear intensifies.

'Thorbjørn,' I say, 'I'd like to offer my warmest congratulations. Not only on all this having reached fruition, but on your wedding, too. I'd like you to meet my husband, Laban Svendsen.'

He and Laban shake hands. Without either of them knowing quite which leg to stand on.

Two-thirds of the electronics in the room have been dismantled. A team of men in blue overalls is busy with the rest.

We cross the floor, and a door opens into Thorbjørn's office. Or one of them.

It's like entering a garden: there are plants everywhere. A system of angled mirrors draws light from the Fælledparken down through a light well, creating the illusion of being outside.

The whole of one wall is a system of sliding whiteboards showing diagrams of something that looks like a ship suspended under a balloon. On top of the balloon are mounted what appear to be upended aeroplane wings.

'A new patent, Thorbjørn?'

He can't resist the chance to brag. Especially to me. He swells visibly, as if he were the balloon.

'The plane wingsail is something I borrowed from the America's Cup. It'll go five degrees to the wind. Beneath the sail I attached a small balloon, filled with a light gas. Solar cells deliver energy to expand and decrease the volume of the container. Underneath is a small enclosed cabin of carbon fibre with a long keel. It's a brilliant hybrid, Susan. In rough seas it's a boat that can reach twenty-five knots and sail close to the wind. In fair weather, with a favourable wind, it will fly. It needs no fuel. It's going to revolutionise the transport sector. I'm flying it today, as a matter of fact. An official test flight.'

Mad inventors go back a long way in this country. Ørsted, Mads Clausen with his expansion valves, Krøyer with his polystyrene beads, Thorsen pressing his stainless-steel sinks, Erik Jacobsen, who invented Antabuse. Thorbjørn Halk is another in a very long line.

For a moment he has been immersed in his own merits. Now his wife calls him back to earth.

'She's mad, Thorbjørn! And violent. She nearly broke my arm. Call the police, immediately!'

Halk chews on his lip.

'I have received your letter of resignation, Susan. We're sad, of course. However, we do understand—'

'It's a forgery. Someone wants me off the lists.'

He chews again.

'Why are you dismantling the instruments?'

'Refurbishing.'

'Those men aren't refurbishing, they're dismantling and packing up. Something big is going on. The government's lining up some kind of evacuation. They think society's breaking up. So they're bringing the elite to safety. Tell me about it.'

He's as pale now as his wife was before. He's scared of me. But he's more scared of something else.

'I can't talk about it, Susan. My advice to you is to get out while you can and stay away.'

'I think we should call a journalist,' I say.

'Susan. No matter what you do, no matter what kind of threats you issue, I can't talk about it.'

He's got his back against a wall that won't give. We'll get no further than this. In any case, I've got no documentation any journalist would be able to use. I give Laban a nod. Elisabeth Halk gets to her feet.

'I'm calling the police, Thorbjørn!'

'Shut up, Elisabeth!'

She sinks back into the chair. We turn and leave. As we do so, we note the shock in her voice:

'Why are you so afraid of that bitch?'

The lift doors close behind us.

'I know why he's afraid, Susan,' Laban says.

I am silent.

'I noticed his hands. His limp. He's the man who raped you, isn't he? At the home you were in. The one you nailed to the decking.'

We pass the pensive-looking security staff and exit down the main steps.

'He worked at Holmgangen,' I say. 'To pay his way through university. It was he who introduced me to the periodic table. He was the first person to talk to me about physics. I adored him. He was a friendly grown-up in a world of darkness. Until he became part of it. Despite what happened, I'm still grateful to him.'

Laban stops in his tracks, prompting me to do likewise. He scrutinises me. As if there's something in my eyes he needs to understand.

He might as well give up. Love and affection between two people can never be understood. How close those feelings are to abuse.

I point, and he turns. Three vehicles – a van and two trucks – are parked in front of the building. Lettered on the side of the van is the name *SecuriCom*.

Laban stiffens. I follow his gaze and see two bicycles leaned against a lamp post. Beside them stand Thit and Harald.

5

WE'VE SAT DOWN ON A BENCH IN THE FÆLLEDPARKEN, the least exposed spot we could find.

'We talked Oskar into driving us,' says Thit. 'It took us all night to convince him. This morning he gave in. We stopped at an Indian grocery on Nørrebrogade and bought mangos and lemons. From there we drove to the Defence Command on Holmens Kanal. We go into the Ministry of Defence and ask to speak to someone senior. We tell them we're biologists from the Plant Physiology Research Centre. A woman comes down immediately. She knows Oskar. We say we've got some very important fruits with us that missed the last consignment by mistake. They're a breakthrough, we tell her. Especially the lemons. Absolutely crucial, in fact. But highly perishable. They need to be delivered right away so they can be properly refrigerated. We stand so she's in the middle, under pressure. Eventually she gives in. Oskar's lost his tongue, so we do the talking.'

Laban and I refrain from exchanging glances. We're on the run, and still the twins have turned left, to invade the Ministry of Defence.

'She gives us the address. We ask for her card and she gives us one. We're there in ten minutes. Rosenørns Allé. Nice place, they've even got a statue outside. Oskar's too scared to go in with us. A security guard leads us inside, to four ladies in reception. We close in, with our mangos and lemons, waving the ministry official's calling card. One of them gets to her feet and shows us upstairs.'

The perils from which one wishes to protect one's children exist perhaps not only in the outside world, but also more immediately as forces of darkness within them. In either case we parents have our work cut out. It must be years since Thit and Harald first discovered they could manipulate others. And just as many since they began to abuse the fact.

'His office is on the top floor. It's got the most brilliant view. Out front there's a secretary's office first, but we breeze through. The lady at the desk just looks up and lets us pass. The door opens and there's Hegn.'

'He doesn't recognise us,' says Harald. 'Adults never recognise kids if it's more than an hour since they saw them last. We tell him we're messengers from the Ministry of Defence. We flash our official's business card again and put the fruit down in front of him. And then Thit sits down on the edge of his desk and pulls her skirt up.'

I look over towards the children's play area. Mothers parade their prams in the spring sunshine. Inside the prams, babies coo and gurgle. Not one has even the slightest suspicion of what lies ahead: that in only a very few years from now the girls will be pulling up their skirts and wriggling onto the desks of elderly men, while the boys will be looking at four years in prison for attempting to smuggle antiquities.

'He's got a photo of his grandchildren on his desk. I tell him his girls must be proud of such an attractive grandfather. And then I pretend to have an epileptic fit. I stagger out through the secretary's office. Hegn comes after me. He stuffs his handkerchief in my mouth to prevent me biting off my tongue. It gives Harald loads of time to nose about.'

'I start with his desk,' says Harald. 'But there's nothing there. Predictably, he's got a built-in safe behind a picture on the wall, but it's locked. All the cupboards are locked too. I've only got a couple of minutes at most, so I'm starting to panic a bit. But then there's a door. I try it and it opens. And in the next room there's . . .'

He hesitates, as if still gobsmacked.

'In the next room there's an island. Or at least a model of one, like an architect's mock-up. But this is a whole island, and it's huge. The room is as big as a hall and the mock-up would take up half a handball court. It shows the island above and below the water. There's a tall volcano in the middle, and coral reefs all around. There are two harbours. And what look like military barracks: two separate clusters like little towns. There are swimming pools, and fields full of vegetables. It's all very carefully done. There's a name on it, too. It says *Spray Island*. That's as much as I see before I back out into the office again. Thit's feeling better by then. Hegn gives us a five-hundred-kroner tip. But that would be mostly for Thit, I reckon. We ask to use the phone and call our official at the Ministry of Defence to tell her we've made the delivery. It means we buy time and can be sure she and Hegn won't cotton on for a while. And then we're gone.'

I look out across the park and realise the first beech trees are in leaf, their foliage as yet so delicate, the colour so intensely green the phenomenon seems hardly material at all, more like light than matter.

'It's not even ten o' clock by then. So we find an Internet café and google *Spray Island*.'

Harald closes his eyes, as if retrieving word by word the article he read on the screen.

'Named by Joshua Slocum, the first man to single-handedly circumnavigate the globe, after his home-built yacht, *Spray*. Having rounded Cape Horn, he encountered a storm and ran aground off the island. He discovered it wasn't on any map. Most likely because of an error in the nautical tables, an error that led all the major sailing routes east of the island. Administratively, Spray Island belonged to the Viscount Islands until twenty fourteen, when it was purchased by the Danish

303

government as part of the world's most comprehensive conservation project under the auspices of UNESCO. The idea is to close off and protect a series of island groups in the Pacific and turn them into an international nature reserve along the lines of the Galapagos Islands. Having sorted that out, we go off and tuck into some breakfast courtesy of Hegn and his five hundred kroner. Oskar joins us.'

'Oskar is a man of the system,' I say.

'He helped us escape.'

'That was a moment's weakness: the Effect. He works for Hegn.'

Thit turns to face me.

'Oskar is a man of potential.'

I look away. It's something new that's started these last few months. A time limit on how long I can withstand my daughter's gaze.

'We're meeting him in half an hour,' says Harald. 'He's promised to take us to the pictures. In the basement of the Meteorological Institute.'

6

THE MAIN ENTRANCE OF THE METEOROLOGICAL INSTITUTE is closed. As we approach, Oskar steps out of the shadows. He uses his walking stick for support, his face is pale and deeply lined. He opens a little door for us next to the gate. As we cross the courtyard I make a point of not glancing at my reflection in the windows. I don't want to know what I look like.

We're met by a man at the basement entrance. He doesn't introduce himself. All he does is shake Oskar's hand, and from that gesture alone I know he's a soldier, most likely sent home after some terrible war-zone experience and now living in a bivouac in the woods where he can be alone with the trauma.

He avoids eye contact and leads us through a series of doors he unlocks along the way, until we come to a small auditorium with perhaps fifty seats, equipped with a screen and projector. Everything is set up and ready. The soldier presses a button and the film begins.

It's raw stock, unedited and without sound. It starts suddenly with images of a distant coast shrouded by rain clouds, filmed from a boat tossing on a leaden sea with waves as tall as multi-storey car parks. Some captions tell us in English that what we're seeing is the coast of Argentina close to the 40th parallel south. If the film's anything to go by, it's a place as inhospitable as they come.

The scene changes: now the ocean and the sky are blue, the bow wave and the seabirds white, and out of the swell a violet paradise appears, with coral reefs and the rising cone of a volcano. Suddenly the sound kicks in, a commentary spoken by a voice of the kind every woman on earth would wish could come and sing lullabies to her at bedtime.

The voice says in English that this is Spray Island. That it measures some fifty by fifty kilometres in area, of which a quarter is taken up by the geologically unique volcanic cone. That the island is protected by a conservation order. And then it says no more. Footage passes across the screen without sound. Then comes a computer simulation, apparently demonstrating what the island is going to look like once the biologists have all gone home. All that's left is the jetty, the landing strip, the control tower and a few small buildings dotted about. On the sea is a sailing ship. The camera zooms in. Only it's not a sailing ship, it's the amphibious craft from Thorbjørn Halk's whiteboards. The sail uppermost. Beneath it the balloon. And then the long keel hull.

The animation is over: now we're on a flyover of the island. The volcano seems to rise up out of the sea, its purple tinges turn green, and then we see the azure waters within the reef, white sandy beaches, coconut palms, a small harbour area, a crane. The volcanic cone then dominates the picture, filmed from a helicopter, the shadow of which is clearly visible on the slopes of the peak. Rainforest glistens with dew or rain. It's morning, the sun low in the sky. The light is slanting and intense, casting long shadows.

The voice returns and all of a sudden I recognise it. It belongs to Falck-Hansen, the foreign minister. It says the island has been purchased for a symbolic one billion kroner.

Then comes footage of the island's flora and fauna. Lizards the size of cats, frogs fat as footballs, mountainsides covered by great, unbroken carpets of orchids. Brightly coloured spiders with legs fifteen centimetres long, hirsute as a gorilla.

Some more graphics. There's a caption, though nothing explanatory: *The Atlas Registration*. A square grid is cast across the island, each square 100 metres in area.

I raise my hand in the air. The film stops.

'What's an atlas registration?'

The soldier steps up to the screen and points to the grid.

'This is what's called a UTM grid. In the case of particularly intensive biological surveys of a given locality, a square grid comprising UTM lines is laid out across the area, these lines being used locally in place of latitude and longitude specifications. The survey is then conducted within that grid. In Denmark the technique was first used for a bird count back in nineteen seventy-one. This is the third time. It kicked off last year and won't be finished until twenty twenty-two.'

He looks me in the eye.

'Which makes the Spray Island survey one of the most minutely detailed biological studies ever undertaken.'

The film starts again. The helicopter passes slowly over the landing strip, in the opposite direction this time. Men in blue uniforms are seen unloading a truck, and at the quayside a small container vessel is moored. The foreign minister is standing on the quay. The scene changes, and now he is speaking straight to the camera. At first there's no sound. Then comes the voice. He speaks of the importance of preserving the unique biotopes of the Pacific.

Abruptly, the film ends. The soldier switches the lights back on. He ignores us and speaks directly to Oskar:

'UNESCO are due to launch an extensive documentation study of conservation projects next year. This is to be Denmark's contribution. The educational unit here has been asked to see it through. Most of it's still on the drawing board—'

'I'd like to watch it again,' I interrupt.

What at first seemed whole appears more fragmentary on the second viewing. The film is an amalgam of footage taken at various points over a period of time. Initially, the shadow on the volcano is a helicopter, only then it's a light aircraft. The sun keeps changing position. The first aerial shots of the landing strip show a building that isn't there later on.

'Can we freeze the picture?'

I approach the screen.

'Now slowly forward a bit.'

The camera moves over the landing strip in the direction of the harbour. It passes along the jetty. Furthest out, at the beacons, are six people. A woman in a waistcoat of the kind used by fly fishers, consisting of little else but pockets, stands with a camera on a tripod. Next to her, a man is rigging a boom mic. In front of them, the sleeves of his white shirt casually rolled up, is Falck-Hansen.

The three others, two men and a woman, are walking away. As they do so, they turn their faces from the helicopter to avoid being seen.

The foreign minister speaks. There's something fascinating about multi-talented individuals. Not only is he an experienced and highly regarded politician, his slightly nasal English is also as perfect as a native speaker's. Moreover, he possesses the physical confidence of a trained performer.

'It's a long way from Denmark to Spray Island. This unique and fragile habitat. But my country's resolve to make a difference is unconstrained by time or geography.'

'One frame at a time,' I say.

The camera pans towards the sea. In the bottom corner I see the three individuals from before.

The woman is in profile. Her skin is brown as mocha, smooth and inviting.

The sequence will be cut out of the final film, being nothing more than accidental. Most viewers would take the woman to be a minor ethnic detail. But some would recognise her. And for that reason she will soon be removed.

'That's her,' says Thit. 'Hegn's assistant! From Kronholm!'

'If we could go back a bit . . .'

The film moves backwards.

'And freeze just there. Can we zoom in?'

The image of the three is magnified, gradually beginning to

break up into pixels. Now we can more clearly see the men at her side.

One is in a blue three-piece suit and tie. Hegn.

The other has sensibly donned a wide-brimmed hat, ostensibly to protect against the tropical sun. And yet it has nothing to do with being sensible in warmer climes. We watch as he spots the camera in the helicopter. We see how he retreats, taking Hegn and the woman with him. He says something to them and demonstrates with his hands that they should shield their faces and turn away. They follow his movements as if strings were attached to their limbs and he were their puppeteer. Even Hegn allows himself to be led in this way, however briefly.

I don't need to see any more. I don't need close-ups or a DNA test. The man in the hat is my father.

7

THE SOLDIER ACCOMPANIES US BACK THROUGH THE COURT-
yard. Oskar peers round the main gate, then ducks back.

'There's a car pulled up next to yours. Two men are investigating it.'

He nods to the soldier, who turns round and leads us back
the way we came.

I glance over my shoulder and see Oskar proceed in the direction of our car. There's something ominous and aggressive
about the way he moves.

We follow the soldier inside to the main reception. The place
looks like it's being vacated. Offices stand empty, furniture is
abandoned in the corridors. He opens a side entrance for us. It
faces out towards the National Gallery. On this side of Sølvgade
there's a taxi rank.

Only one taxi is waiting, with a paint job spangled with frac-
tions and integrals. The lettering across the doors says *Maths
Taxi*. I hesitate.

'Science taxis. They started last year. So many academics are
out of work now. You pay the normal fare, but you can ask for
a short popular-science lecture along the way.'

I look at the soldier. And then at Laban.

'Maybe they could do the same for out-of-work composers,'
I muse. 'They could hum a song.'

He doesn't answer me. I open the door of the taxi and we

climb in. The driver makes a U-turn and we head off in the direction of Sølvtorvet.

The driver is silent, hiding himself and his unemployed academic merits behind wraparound sunglasses. Fortunately, he offers no lecture.

We turn onto Evighedsvej. Outside Villa Chez Nous, a hearse and two dark cars are parked. The hearse's engine idles. We're just in time to say goodbye to Ingemann.

I get out and rummage for some cash. To be deprived of credit cards is to feel helplessly exposed and robbed of identity.

Then I see Dorthea. She's standing on the balcony in front of Ingemann's cabin. She sees us, and yet she looks straight through us, without sign of recognition. She raps her fingers twice on the railing. I get back in the taxi.

'She's got company.'

Harald indicates the taxi's display. A message has gone out with a description of all four of us. The tone is objective, undramatic. It ends with a phone number to contact.

'Pull up ahead,' I tell the driver. 'Next to those cars.'

The taxi moves slowly forward. The hearse is empty.

I get out and open the door.

And that's when I make my big mistake.

I do so with the intuitive feeling that we need to keep an eye on the kids. We need to keep them close. But all sense tells me that what Laban and I have to do now is far too hazardous for them to come with us.

I hand Thit and Harald my last thousand-kroner note.

'Take a long ride,' I tell them. 'Until we phone you.'

Laban and I get into the hearse. The taxi is already gone.

8

'KIRSTEN KLAUSSEN IS OUR LAST CHANCE. WITH A BIT OF luck we can talk her into helping.'

Laban just nods.

We pull in and park at the rear of the church.

The former churchyard is enclosed by a wrought-iron fence whose railings are pointed in the manner of spears. We follow the fence in search of a gate. Ten metres on, a Dobermann stands on its hind legs, its snout through the railings.

We approach and its eyes stare lifelessly.

'Oh no,' says Laban.

The animal's head has been pressed down over one of the spears. Its point has entered through the jaw and now protrudes from behind its ears like a little crown.

We find the gate, only it's locked. Laban throws his leather jacket on top of the railings and we clamber over.

The churchyard is overgrown, separated from the church itself by means of a provisional-looking wire-mesh fence. On the other side is the swimming pool Kirsten Klaussen dreamed about in the miserable brown-coalfield of her childhood.

We pause at the edge. The water is the colour of rust. I lean forward over its shimmering surface. At the bottom lies the other Dobermann. Its throat is slit, the head attached only by slender shreds of fibre.

'We could go back,' I say.

Laban shakes his head.

We split up and take different entrances. The doors aren't locked, there's no one here. We converge on the church interior.

Everything is just as it was when I was here this morning. The boxes, the bazooka on the wall. The only difference is the colour of the water. And the slight ripples on its surface.

Laban raises a finger in the air, indicating he wants me to listen. The only thing I can hear is the distant sound of traffic rumbling across Bagsværd Torv.

'There's something dripping.'

We follow the pool, and then I hear it too: a faint, rhythmic plop of droplets as they strike the water. The ripples we noticed are remnants of concentric rings spreading out across the surface.

We look up.

Kirsten Klaussen is hanging suspended from the vaulted ceiling, beneath her kinetic sculpture. Its steel wires have been twisted around her throat, legs and arms. Her mouth and eyes are wide open, arms spread out as if she were some angel of death, a hundred-plus kilos coming in to land from outer space.

We get back in the hearse, Laban behind the wheel.

'I still trust the politicians, Susan. All this must be some kind of mistake. A short-circuiting somewhere further down the lines of administration. I shall have a word with Falck-Hansen. He was minister of culture when I made my breakthrough.'

He starts the engine. I have a feeling of things coming to an end. It tells me that if there's something he and I need to have said, then now's the time.

'Laban,' I venture, 'what's been worst about being with me?'

The reply comes without pause, as if he'd been waiting twenty years for me to ask.

'The affairs have been the worst part.'

He follows the road between the two lakes, Lyngby Sø and

Bagsværd Sø. It's the wrong way if he wants to go into town. And yet we both know it's right for us to take time out for a moment.

'You had one every year, Susan, on average. I counted. When a woman has been with another man, she comes back with his entire energy system brimming all over. His smells, his sperm, his resonance. I could sense the presence of each one of them for a year, even after you'd stopped. And when the resonance was gone and I began to hope that you and I would finally join together, a few weeks would pass, a couple of months at most, and then it would all start again.'

His words are without reproach, spoken in the knowledge that altering reality is a hopeless fiction.

'To begin with I thought maybe I could do the same, make it work for me. And believe me, I tried. Only I couldn't do it. I'm not made that way. The wounds you left could not be healed by any other, Susan.'

We pass through the outskirts of Lyngby.

I put my hand on his arm. There's nothing to apologise for. I did what I had to. We've got fewer choices than any of us imagine.

'That hurts,' I say.

He accepts the acknowledgement. The Effect is active between us. It allows each of us to sense the other's pain without filter. At this moment, I haven't merely the knowledge of hurting him. I can feel it, too.

'What about me, Susan? What did it cost you to be with me?'

'The attention you draw,' I say. 'The fame. The way you couldn't live without it.'

It doesn't need explaining. We both know what I'm talking about. Laban never had affairs. But he always had to have seven women sitting around his piano ready to pounce. Whatever the occasion – in the concert halls, music conservatories, TV studios and ballrooms – barely a moment ever passed before I was trampled underfoot by people clamouring to be in his presence.

And besides the vanity there was his extravagance. Cars we couldn't afford, holidays, the summer house by the sea at Hornbæk, the other one in Jutland, the yacht we suddenly had moored at Rungsted, despite the fact that both of us felt seasick just looking at it bobbing there. Then came the compulsory sales by order of the courts, the emergency loans, the last-minute stays of execution.

'Most self-obsessed alpha males,' I tell him, 'are fortunate enough to find a woman to support them. The woman behind the man. But you were unlucky. You got one like me. And to make matters worse, I humiliated you.'

We turn onto the motorway and head back towards the city.

'Still,' he says with a sigh, 'I don't regret a moment. Not a single one.'

I think I must have heard wrong.

'You're ... fresh as the dew, Susan. That's what you are. Fresh as the dew.'

'I'm forty-three.'

'That's got nothing to do with it. It's the way you always woke up in the mornings. No matter how hard the day before might have been, even if we'd been fighting, even if you'd been up six times in the night to breastfeed the twins, and Harald with his colic – by the time you woke up, you'd shaken it all away. You were indefatigable, Susan. That's what you were. Indefatigable.'

For a brief, fleeting second, I may even understand what he means. That's one of the inherent potentials of honesty – that for a moment another person may reveal to us a true mirror image of ourselves.

And then a flash of recollection appears in my mind. At first it embeds itself in the outer extremities of my perception. Then, a moment later, it engulfs me like a river bursting through a dam. I point to the side of the road. Laban instantly realises something's wrong. He pulls onto the hard shoulder and stops the hearse.

'The taxi driver,' I say. 'The maths taxi. It was Jason, the man in grey.'

Laban shakes his head vigorously. But not because he wants to argue with me. He's trying to get rid of reality.

My phone rings. I answer it.

'Susan?'

I can't speak. My voice has gone.

'Susan. I've got your kids.'

'Jason . . .' I stutter.

'Listen, Susan, you're the one I want to talk to.'

'Where?'

'Not yet. Not until I've finished with your lovely daughter.'

And then he is silent. I can sense him as if he were sitting next to me. He is absorbing my fear through the phone.

In the silence that now shrouds him, far away in the distance, is a sound – a sound I recognise. A whispering movement of air. I know it, but am unable to identify it.

He hangs up.

Laban and I sit for a minute. Inside me it's as if all my powers have been taken away. Something else assumes control.

'Drive,' I say.

9

LABAN STOPS THE HEARSE 100 METRES ALONG STRANDGADE. Outside the swing door of the Ministry of Foreign Affairs, the parking spaces are full.

Once inside we come to an immediate halt. Another reception desk to negotiate. The lobby is busy, a huddle of people seem to be waiting for something.

There have been too many reception desks in my life and I've always been on the wrong side of them. Always, there was a form that should have been filled in, an application made three weeks in advance to gain admittance. It's as if my every endeavour was about trying to pass through to the other side of the desk. I've never succeeded. In any other circumstances this would have made me rather fatigued. But not now. Now I am governed by a state of inner emergency.

The huddle parts, and the foreign minister emerges from its midst. He's on his way out.

Andrea Fink once told me there are three kinds of politician: those who could just as well peddle some other commodity, those with an extraordinary hankering for power and finally the statesmen.

Falck-Hansen is a statesman. Everyone knows he could be prime minister if only he wanted. But his interest in foreign policy won't allow it. His intense passion for development aid, disarmament, international cooperation.

The first time I saw him in the flesh I was still in my early twenties and he was giving a lecture in the ceremonial hall of the university. What struck me then was his natural demeanour. He spoke openly, as if he were sitting at home in your room in student halls. And with such charisma that every woman present wished he could have been just there, in their room in student halls, preferably on the edge of their bed.

That was the first time I heard a politician who did not exploit the opportunity of presenting his own opinions to slag off his opponents. He was quite without aggression, affable and forthright.

And so he is now. He recognises Laban right away and smiles. I step in between them.

'The reason we were in the archives was to gain access to the files of the Future Commission. We're in grave danger. Hegn and his organisation are out of control. Our two children have been abducted.'

The mood in the lobby takes a turn. One shouldn't underestimate the minister's entourage. They're not political groupies. There isn't one of the ten people surrounding us who wouldn't take a bullet for him in the event of an assassination attempt. And that includes the women at reception. Now, suddenly, they view me as a potential threat.

Falck-Hansen and I look at each other. I sense no dismay. He knows all about the Future Commission. He registers and understands the state I'm in.

He takes us by the arm, both at once. His attention feels so intense the rest of the world seems almost to dissolve. It's as if only the three of us exist.

He leads us away along a corridor.

'We need to talk,' he says.

His office faces out onto the harbour approach – which from here seems smaller than one would anticipate – and moreover comprises two secretaries' offices as well as a modest conference room.

He gestures towards a pair of chairs and we sit down. On a small table, a Japanese teapot of cast iron rests in a frame, its contents kept warm by some tea lights. He pours green tea into small cups of wafer-thin porcelain. Neither of us will be able to swallow a drop, but it doesn't matter. What matters is his concern.

'The Future Commission foresaw global collapse,' I say. 'But they kept the details to themselves. Hegn hauled us back to Denmark to get hold of them. We're experienced in techniques of questioning. But something went wrong. Someone's killing off the members of the commission one by one. Our children could be next. Hegn kept us interned at a government research centre in southern Sjælland. We got away last night, the children followed on today. A few hours later they were abducted. What we need is for a search to be initiated right away. And Hegn needs to be taken in and questioned. He's collaborating with an international security firm, SecuriCom, with links to organised crime. The man who's got our kids works for them. He's a lunatic.'

Few people are truly able to listen. But Falck-Hansen is one. He does so in the way only Laban, the twins and Andrea Fink are able. He understands everything, and can accommodate it all.

'There's a plan,' I tell him. 'It's secret, for the evacuation of four thousand citizens in the event of military or civil disaster. To a place called Spray Island. You know it, we just watched some footage of you there. Other Western governments have purchased other islands. Maybe the plan is transnational, a collaboration designed to protect a minimal section of the political, scientific, economic and artistic elites. There are wide-reaching arrangements for the transport of these people, and for the cultivation of the island, energy provision and security. The whole apparatus is about to kick in. Someone must think that disaster is imminent. Was that what your meeting was about the day before Christmas Eve, when we bumped into you in the archives?'

319

He puts his tea down in front of us and pulls up his chair. This is a man who changed the way I look at our democracy. He lives for a cause, the same way as Desmond Tutu, Mikhail Gorbachev, Kofi Annan, Nelson Mandela. Perhaps justice exists, and common sense too, in spite of everything, if only we look high enough up the ladder. Soon the twins will be returned to us. In a moment we'll be cleared, on our way home to Evighedsvej, back to normal.

'No such plan exists. It's unthinkable. I would know about it. In any case, it wouldn't ever happen here. But Susan, imagine Denmark were a ship, a big ship, and you were on board with the twins. I saw that front cover of *Time*. The most delightful children. Suppose you were told the ship was sinking and the lifeboats only had room for certain privileged members of the crew. What would you do?'

I say nothing.

He gets to his feet. Goes over to the window. Looks out across the harbour.

'Consider this. You're on that ship. There's a chance you can save the twins, and yourselves as well. You, Laban, are one of this country's finest composers. If such a list existed, you would be on it. Susan would be too, and the children. Would you be able to turn that opportunity down? Would you even have the right to say no?'

He's not looking at us. I must address his Grecian profile.

'Suppose it did exist, that list. Would it still be possible for our names to be included?'

'You have my word.'

We sit quietly, all three of us. He turns to face us.

'As for these very serious problems society is now up against, we are governing a nation of the deaf. Those who can read saw the writing on the wall a long time ago.'

He goes towards the door.

Even now, with everything lost, I feel the urge to press myself against his paternal integrity, his authority.

'Let me bring in some people. They'll look after you while you consider the matter.'

'The twins,' I say.

'I'm afraid I've a balloon to catch. When I get back . . .'

The door closes behind him. Laban is about to say something. I gesture for him not to.

I take the crowbar out of my bag. And a folded tissue.

The desk drawers are locked. I place the tissue between the wood and the crowbar's metal, apply a small amount of pressure and lift the catch from its recess. The top drawer contains keys, fibre-tip pens, paper clips, USB flash drives, and two wedges of yellow plastic, the kind used to keep doors open. In the next I find writing paper, envelopes, sealing wax and an official seal. The third contains a folder. In the folder is a list, fifty-odd pages, perhaps a hundred names on each. I put it in my bag. That and the two plastic wedges.

I close and lock the drawers again using the crowbar and the tissue.

The minister returns. There are four men with him. Two of them remain at the door.

These are not ordinary men. They are sharks who have come ashore and been clad in tailored suits. They have learned to walk upright and to utter sounds of politeness. Their movements are economical. They step aside and allow us to go first.

On our way out, I pause in front of Falck-Hansen.

'That balloon ride. Does it start from the old Radiohuset concert hall?'

He says nothing. But no words are required. The Effect and I have already registered his system's affirmative reply.

'I hope to repay you for this someday,' I say.

Falck-Hansen is a man with forty years' experience of weathering force-ten gales from the bridge. And yet I sense his unease.

Then, in a moment, we're gone.

The sharks patrol about us. I can feel Laban's tension. But also his readiness. He, too, has been plunged into a state of emergency. We are no longer humans. We are biological machines that will do anything to make sure our progeny survive.

We're almost at the swing door. One of the men cuts in front of me. I prod his shoulder.

'Ladies first.'

He stops in mid-movement. Even sharks once had a mother, who somewhere inside them remains, even after they've grown into very big fish indeed. His mother inside him prompts him to stop.

I enter the rotating space of the door with Laban right behind me. The moment I feel the fresh air on my face I wheel round, bend down and ram a yellow plastic wedge under the door with a swipe of the crowbar.

The merry-go-round comes to an abrupt halt. I step right, where there's a regular door for wheelchair users. It opens outwards. I hammer the other wedge into place beneath it.

We run for our hearse. Laban weaves through the traffic, ruthless as an ambulance driver.

We pull up at the kerb outside the Radiohuset. There are lots of cars, and police too.

Two security guards wearing headsets check the guests. One is in uniform, the other, in a suit, is the man in charge.

The uniformed guard steps towards me. For a second, reality and all the plans I have for it are jarred out of place as though by some hallucinogenic intervention. Standing in front of me is the handsome young man from the Defence College car park at Svanemøllen.

'I couldn't sleep,' he says. 'After your kiss. I lay there all night, floating above the mattress.'

One must be prudent with one's kisses. It may well be that one dishes them out in the manner of gratuities. But to a romantic heart, a single one may be as good as the overture of *Romeo and Juliet*.

A couple of police officers approach. The situation is slipping from my hands. But then the mood changes. Subtly, yet unmistakably. Thorbjørn Halk is standing next to us.

Thorbjørn Halk is more famous than Bohr was in his day. Bohr never had the benefit of massive media coverage. Even if he had, it wouldn't have interested him. Thorbjørn Halk is the first great quantum-physical celebrity of the information age.

I take him by the arm and hold on tight. He tries to wriggle free, but cannot. We move forward. The throng parts, the doors open and we are inside.

We step into the lift. Only now do I realise that my ballet prince is with us. We ascend, and when the door opens Thorkild Hegn is standing a metre away from me.

He is surrounded by henchmen. Not two or four, like at the Ministry of Foreign Affairs. Ten or twelve.

He doesn't look surprised.

'Susan. You've been making things difficult for me.'

'We would have been taken away,' I say. 'But by whom?'

'By me.'

His voice is luxurious, now as then. Warm, vivid, sonorous and deep.

Hegn moves aside and my father steps into view.

He takes off his hat. His hair is reddish-blond, with not a hint of grey in sight. He must be seventy, but looks twenty years younger. At least.

He opens his arms. And before I know what's happening I find myself where every little girl wants to be, even if she happens to be forty-three years old: in her father's embrace.

He steps back and considers me at arm's length.

'Susan. Susan.'

He speaks my name slowly, trying to build a bridge across thirty-five years of time, to identify the name and his recollections of an eight-year-old girl with the woman now standing in front of his eyes.

Authority is a peculiar phenomenon. The room has fallen

323

silent, all activity drawn to a standstill. There may be between forty and fifty people around us, all with their particular roles to play in an important event that is already underway. Yet everything has ground to a halt.

In that silence, my ballet prince steps forward.

'I should like to ask for your daughter's hand.'

All eyes are on him. His words may have been valid in Shakespeare's day. But even by the time my father was a boy they must surely have fallen from circulation.

My father gestures, imperceptibly almost, and two men emerge from behind him. A fist moves swiftly in the region of my beau's kidneys and instantly he sags, white as a sheet, his legs buckled beneath him, and the two men whisk him away by the armpits.

My father ushers me forward. We go through a door, and in our wake people follow. We step over snaking cables duct-taped to the floor, circumventing a TV crew before stepping out onto a balcony above what used to be the concert hall, now a storage facility with boxes stacked everywhere.

We continue up a flight of stairs to the roof. Behind us come Hegn, Thorbjørn Halk and Laban.

Falck-Hansen is standing waiting for us. Expressionless, he stares at Laban and me.

At close quarters the balloon doesn't look like a balloon at all, more like a modern art installation. The buoyancy element itself comprises at most 100 cubic metres, harnessed within a lightweight metal framework that moreover holds the sail, a thirty-metre-tall construction of man-made fibre that reflects like tinfoil and yet is partially transparent. Hundreds of ethereal solar cells are held in place by barely visible wires.

A slightly framed, enclosed cabin is attached to the harness underneath the balloon, and affixed to the bottom of it is a long keel of aluminium. The overall impression is of a slender keelboat built for racing, on top of which someone has placed an enormous beachball, and on top of that an upturned aeroplane wing.

We are the only people on the roof besides a handful of technical staff. My father steps onto the gangway and opens the door of the cabin.

'Susan, may I show you Copenhagen from the skies?'

For a moment the situation is electrified with a potential difference of about a million volts. Hegn is about to say something, but thinks better of it. A pair of technicians appear with what must be parachutes. My father shakes his head.

'Fate is on our side today. Do you believe in fate, Susan?'

'If there is such a thing,' I say, 'then we're part of its making. Like the laws of nature.'

Hegn crosses the gangway and enters the cabin. Falck-Hansen follows him, and Halk steps forward to do likewise.

My father holds up a hand.

'Sorry,' he says.

Halk senses a misunderstanding. He glares at my father.

'And who might you be?'

Another gesture, as near imperceptible as the first, and Thorbjørn is flanked by two men. They grip him by the arms, wheel round and walk him away.

I step onto the gangway in front of my father. He turns towards those still on the roof.

'You can let the press in now.'

10

THE MOMENT MY FATHER'S HANDS TOUCH THE INSTRUMENT panel, my childhood is returned to me. Not some vague recollection, or mere fragment, but in its entirety. I remember him at the wheel of our car. His hands caressing the instruments. The smell of the leather interior. The unstated bond between us. His joy at describing the physical world. It's from him my enthusiasm stems, my wish to explain the world to my twins. I remember the sound of the door when he came home in winter. The smell and the dampness of his olive-green coat when I pressed my cheek against it. The fluid softness of bearskin when he handed me his hat.

The cabin is equipped with the electronics of a jet fighter, the instrument panel as long and wide as a desk. His fingers pass over it like a musician's.

'I've been involved all along, Susan. In the construction. Unbeknown to Halk. Quite a number of details are my own. It's the first craft of its kind to utilise the balloon as an expansion tank. Altitude is regulated by increasing or diminishing the volume.'

He pulls back a lever and the vessel rises a few inches. The bracing wires tighten with a faint whistle.

The room is illuminated by the light of twoscore suns on the roof below us, the flash of cameras going off in unison. There must be a hundred reporters and photographers. Falck-Hansen, the foreign minister, goes to the door and waves. Hegn and my father ignore them.

The spring locks of the bracing wires open, and the thin cables are reeled up underneath the cabin. The balloon rises and with it the sound of applause, gradually becoming distant. Several of the cabin windows glide down, the entire windscreen retracting into the roof. It feels like we're in the open air.

I've never been in a balloon before. The first thing that strikes me is how quiet it is. On the ground, noise is everywhere: traffic, birdsong, human voices, machines. Up here the only thing audible is the whisper of the wind passing kindly over the buoyancy element, and the gentle creak of the wingsail.

The absence of all other sound creates an illusion: it's impossible to tell if we're ascending or if Copenhagen is dropping away beneath us.

My father presses a button, and somewhere below us a system of hydraulics winches in a line and we turn towards the blue-white glittering waters of the Øresund.

He takes my hand. The memories of his physical warmth come flooding back.

Most men are unable to concentrate mentally on a matter and engage in physical contact at the same time. The signals issued by the body serve to cloud any clarity of thought. The body and the mind are, in such respect, enemies. This, however, does not apply to my father. To him, determination of thought and physical touch have always intertwined.

'The first warnings came before you were born, Susan. No one remembers any more, but European biologists were vocal about the threat of pollution as early as the mid-sixties. Since then, everything's gone exponentially downhill. The scenarios of apocalypse are unfolding now, and the biological systems are breaking down. Not one intelligent journalist is unaware of this. Not one politician, not one scientist. But still it cannot be spoken out loud. And if it could, no one would listen. The media are incapable of providing any true picture of reality. The political parties are powerless even to propose what needs to be done, aware that they would never be able to sell the goods, no one would vote for them. We are all of us a part of the problem. There are no enemies any more. We can't pass the buck. What we have to do now is to ensure the best survive. You, Susan, are among the best. You, and the twins. I'm not much impressed by that husband of yours, but he's coming too. And your mother, of course. Along with her . . .'

He hesitates. His hesitation is a crack, opened by the Effect. From that crack seeps what still is unresolved in his life: his love of my mother. Part of him has remained behind in a past it's become too late to change.

'The island has it all, Susan. In the event of a nuclear war the northern hemisphere will be ravaged by a new ice age. The southern hemisphere will be untouched. When the oil runs out, we'll have renewable energy sources and smart grid power. We'll be able to meet all our own needs for food, withstand a twenty-metre rise in sea level and still have eight hundred square kilometres to live on without getting our feet wet. We've got seeds and livestock, and the technology and information to rebuild civilisation from scratch. It's not Noah's Ark, Susan, it's not the spaceship of the Jehovah's Witnesses. It's a sustainable Atlantis.'

He gauges my thoughts. He's always been able to do that. When I was a little girl we could sense what the other was thinking. One of us would begin to speak, only for the other to chuckle with glee, tickled by the synchronism of what was going on in our minds.

'When everything comes crashing down, as it will very soon, our democracies will succumb. They were always a thin veneer. Ninety-five per cent of the world's population still need to be told what to do and how to go about it. Our political institutions will be the first to go. The military and the big transnational concerns will have to take over. Visionary politicians like Jørgen here have known all along. Many of us didn't need the commission. But the commission confirmed what we already suspected. It was a kickstart for the survival plan. It convinced the politicians and business. But the plans were already there. For the transfer of power to those with the ability and the will.'

'And you're one of them, aren't you, Dad?'

'It'll be a whole new field. Fraught with difficulties. The management of power in a post-democracy. It's going to require new knowledge, if what's left of our societies is to avoid oblivion, avoid ending up in barbary. It'll take a combination of military, operative and administrative experience. We're taking a hundred and fifty men from the special forces with us to Spray Island. Army, navy, air force. A select group of my own men. A frigate. Two fighter planes. A small submarine.'

We drift out over the Øresund. I register a sense of what migrating birds must feel when they leave land. Uncertainty combined with the euphoria of wide expanses of water.

My father turns away from the instruments. There must be some kind of automatic pilot, the minute adjustments to course must come from a computer.

'Susan, you're the one who spoke to the commission members last. Moreover, you have that wonderful talent of yours. Thorkild has told me all about it. You must have made them talk. What did they tell you? What was their time frame? When was it going to occur, the final collapse?'

I've seen Copenhagen from above lots of times before. From planes and towers, from the restaurant of the SAS Royal Hotel, from the Ferris wheel in the Tivoli Gardens, from the upper floors of my department and the Panum Building. But this time it's different. From here the city seems so vulnerable.

Maybe it's the sedateness of the craft itself, the frailty of the cabin, the delicacy of the whole construction. For a moment it's as if there's no barrier between me and the million and a half people below us.

'There was no date.'

'No matter. It'll be soon, in any circumstance. You and the twins should go home, go back to work and school, and remain prepared. Within a few months we'll have you evacuated.'

329

'Why were the commission's members killed?'

'They were elderly, Susan.'

I relax into the Effect. It feels much like falling. The experience feels unfamiliar every time, unsettling even for me. Honesty is not something to which one becomes accustomed once and for all. It's a process, a new rejection every time of all that is familiar and fixed.

'They'd become greedy, had sought to profit from their ability, to sell it off like a commodity. But being able to see into the future is a much more sensitive issue than access to any thinkable secret of state. Thorkild managed them during more than forty years. But few can live with such power without abusing it. They had to go.'

'Why didn't you wait? Until I'd spoken to them?'

My father drapes an arm around Thorkild Hegn's shoulders. They look like brothers now.

'There was a difference of opinion. Thorkild wanted them kept alive.'

I know it from the labs. That magical moment at which a hypothesis is released into the world, and what until then has been but a fragile mental construction begins to find body. That's what's happening now. The dissolution of our democracies isn't just a prognosis. Both Hegn and Falck-Hansen are fading into the background. My father is the true authority.

'Who did it?'

Pain passes over his face, another torment of the past.

'I have people, Susan. Closest to me is Jason. I have trusted him blindly. He delivered the letters, to you and your mother.'

'I saw the bodies. He enjoys his work.'

Again, a twitch of anguish.

'I wanted it done properly, Susan. The way they do in the slaughterhouses. Have you ever seen it? Admirable. They insert a tube into the spinal cord. To avoid the violence of the muscular spasms. It's all very gentle and subdued. I wanted it done like that. Jason has been like a son to me. I've looked after him, Susan. As if he were your brother.'

'How touching,' I say.

'Indeed. The things I've covered up on his account. He's a psychopath, you see. Should have had his head examined. It was his fault all this began to get out of hand. Now we shall have to cut him loose.'

'He's got my children. He's got Thit and Harald. Are you behind that?'

He doesn't flinch. It's as if his ability to be shocked has long been lost. But he pauses.

'Where, Susan?'

'I don't know. He phoned me up. Said it was me he wanted to speak to.'

'We'll have him located in fifteen minutes.'

I know it's a lie.

'And then he'll be taken care of, Susan.'

'Will you do it yourself?'

'I can't. He's like my own child.'

The other two men have come closer.

'I had a dog once,' Falck-Hansen says. 'A beagle. Incapable of regulating their appetite, beagles. He could eat till he dropped. Only he never did. Drop, I mean. All he ever did was eat. And when he wasn't eating he was begging at the table. He had the most enchanting brown eyes. We couldn't say no. When his weight got to fifty kilos his heart began to pack in. He looked like he'd been inflated with a bicycle pump. Finally, I had to take him to the vet. I looked into his eyes when they put him down. He knew what was happening.'

I feel a dizziness coming on. The membrane that separates honesty from madness is flimsy indeed, and now it's about to rupture. None of the three have noticed.

'I had to stop seeing one of my daughters!'

This time it's Hegn. His eyes sparkle and glisten. Confession always prompts a release of endorphins.

331

'She got wind of what I was doing at the institute, the commission. That it ran against all democracy. She kept putting pressure on me. Eventually, I had to threaten her with the courts. Closed doors, of course. And a prison sentence. Imagine that, threatening one's own daughter with prison!'

My father has turned to face them.

'You know when you try to remember the names of everyone you've slept with, only you can't? Imagine what it's like trying to remember those you've killed. And not being able to, because there are too many. And then when you're trying to fall asleep they're all there, lined up in front of you, ready to be counted the way you count sheep, and all you can do is hope they'll give you just a few minutes' rest.'

Somewhere within their systems, they now sense the situation to be out of control. But it's too late. There is a deep and instinctive urge in all of us towards honesty. The Effect is merely a slight reinforcement of that urge.

'I've been involved in all the major political scandals,' Falck-Hansen says. 'And that's going back forty years! I've lied in court! Allowed my staff to shoulder the blame. Ruined long-standing political friendships.'

One of the great red-letter days of organic chemistry occurred in April 1943, when Albert Hofmann, in search of an effective medicine to counter migraine headaches of the same calibre as my mother's, succeeded in isolating the twenty-fifth semi-synthetic derivative of lysergic acid extracted from ergot fungus, ingested twenty-five milligrams and was catapulted off into the world's first acid trip. The men in front of me are much worse off. Hofmann retained his grip throughout. They've already let go.

Hegn takes the floor.

'What you've all told me here makes a very deep impression on me. I'm touched. And yet all of it is so little compared to what my own conscience must bear. I transformed the institute with the sole aim of circumventing the country's constitution. I withheld from parliament, and from the nation, important information delivered by the commission. And not only because it was more than they would have been capable of handling. What I really wanted was power and influence.'

There are tears in his eyes.

'It goes back to my childhood. I had five brothers and sisters. I kept the entire family in a vice. Even though my father was a naval officer.'

He gets no further. Falck-Hansen pushes him aside.

'I'm sorry, Thorkild. But listen to this: I had two sisters. I came very close to prostituting them both. I was ten, they were fourteen and eighteen. There was this neighbour of ours. He—'

My father cuts him off in mid-flow, gripping both men by the hair, forcing them to their knees and pressing their faces to the floor.

It's a violent movement of great brutality, and yet seemingly effortless. He crouches down and leans towards them. The level of his voice is unchanged by even a decibel.

'There's something we need to agree about in order to gain a realistic idea of the distribution of guilt here. The hell I inhabit, and which each and every day—'

Circumstances notwithstanding, Thorkild Hegn manages to squeak a protest:

'I've got the law behind me, Svend, the full weight of society. I can have a hundred policemen waiting for you as soon as we land. You'll be off to that new prison at Trørød before you can say *knife*.'

Falck-Hansen manages to squirm free and scrabble to his feet.

'I represent the government of this country. And as long as our democracy prevails—'

My father pulls his legs from under him. But the foreign minister brings my father down with him in the fall. They slam against the floor.

I edge my way to the instrument panel. Kronholm is directly

underneath us. The wind farm to the north. The cabin is filled with the ponderous whisper of the enormous blades of the turbines as they rotate.

I remember Jason's silence on the phone. The sound in the background. Turbine wings. He and the twins are somewhere right below.

I locate the elevator and push it forward. A subtle rush of air issues from the expansion tank. The craft dips and begins to drop. Slowly at first, then faster, the landing strip suddenly looming large.

My father leaps to his feet.

'Dad,' I say, 'what about me and Harald? Why did we almost get killed?'

We pass over the perimeter fence of the landing strip. I aim for a rectangular three-storey structure next to the hangar.

'We hadn't got you identified, dear. And Jason—'

I pull back the elevator and a whine of air comes from the tank above. I crawl onto the instrument panel. I wriggle through the opening where the windscreen should be and lower myself carefully until my feet find the running board that goes all the way around the cabin.

The eyes of the three men inside widen. Only now do they realise where I am.

'It's her fault,' says my father. 'It's the Effect.'

I point, and their heads turn upwards towards a very small, yet conspicuous rectangular plastic box attached to the ceiling.

'It's all rather straightforward,' I say. 'A small digital camera, a microphone, two lithium cells and an aerial. The radius is a few kilometres. Hegn's people installed it in our house on Evighedsvej. I made a minor adjustment. I calibrated the transmitter and hooked it up to my smartphone. Which Laban is holding in his hand. Everything that's taken place here, from the moment we took off, has gone out directly to those hundred journalists on the roof. It'll be all over the Internet by now. Laban's got the list, too. With the four thousand names on it. You're going to be television stars. In about twenty minutes, I'd say.'

Emerging from the Effect always takes time, as if it were happening in slow motion. Full comprehension of the situation's gravity will not occur for some minutes, perhaps even hours.

The one who for now comes closest to that realisation is my father. He steps towards me and leans across the instrument panel. My eyes watch his hands.

'Susan, when I left . . . when I was forced to leave. I gave you a piece of advice. Make your bite . . .'

'. . . as hard as my bark.'

'Well, you heeded my words, Susan. This is going to be a tough one, I see.'

I look down. I'm two metres off the roof of what looks like a hangar. I lean inside the cabin and thrust the elevator control back, suddenly, unexpectedly. This time I hear no sound. But above us the balloon expands. The cabin rises instantly. I let go and land on the sloping roof, rolling into the fall, finding purchase and coming to a halt. Above me the craft ascends rapidly into the sky. I stay where I am, flat out on the roof. The wind exerts its force on the wingsail, and soon the craft appears to be drifting towards the north-west, as if abandoned.

I clamber to my feet, and stand for a moment looking out in the direction of the city.

There's a trapdoor. I descend into darkness.

11

THE STAIRS LEAD ME DOWN TO A METAL DOOR, ON THE other side of which music is playing. The voice is Edith Piaf's. Various tracks are begun and abandoned. Eventually, the listener plumps for 'Non, je ne regrette rien'. I open the door.

The space into which I emerge is big enough to have contained a handball court, though square in shape, illuminated by windows in the roof. Through the windows I catch a final glimpse of the balloon.

The place is crammed with thousands of boxes, folded tarps, small excavators and other machinery, new and largely encased in packing. There are pallets on which garden tractors stand. There are pumps. At the far end of the hall, timber and building materials are stacked to the ceiling.

In the middle of it all sits Jason Alter in a wicker chair. To his left is a low, glass-topped table on which a television set has been placed. Next to the TV is a sub-machine gun with a curving magazine.

I walk towards him. He turns the screen to face me. They're broadcasting live from the roof of the Radiohuset. A man in a suit is being interviewed. The right-hand corner shows a separate split-screen view of the balloon floating above the Øresund.

'Where are the twins, Jason?'

He turns off the TV.

'You won't have heard of the caracal, Susan. The desert lynx of southern Africa, practically unheard of in Europe. There isn't even a name for it here. It was what they called your father: *Caracal*. Do you know why? Because no one ever sees the caracal. You know it's there. It lives on the red rocks of the savannah, where it will leap three and a half metres into the air to pluck a passing pigeon from flight. You might see the feathers, find the carcass, some traces. But you will never see the beast itself. And now you, Susan, have brought him to confession on live television!'

He shakes his head.

'Your father has sentenced me to death. On national TV.'

'There's a hundred policemen waiting for him when he lands.'

He clicks his teeth.

'You don't understand, Susan. The organisation is intact and will remain so. He'll carry it on from his cell. He could run a country from any prison. An empire. I've outlived my usefulness. But for the moment it's you and me, Susan. I want you to strip for me.'

He's actually serious.

'You've already bought your way back to life once, as it were, from your own prison. Now you can do so again by being nice to me. Your life, and your children's.'

His eyes scrutinise me, looking for signs of fear.

'The twins, Jason.'

He gets to his feet and goes over to a container. He opens its doors. Inside is what looks like a cross between a garden shed and a chamber for curing meat. He opens it and the light inside goes on automatically. The space is lined with smooth, high-fibre bricks and in the middle is a rectangular steel pan. On the pan sits Harald. His eyes are vacant with terror.

'This is a furnace, for cremating bodies. Brand new. We're shipping two out to the island. No one lives for ever, not even there.'

The walls are perforated. Through the holes, the gas flames will burst.

He moves on to the next container and opens both sets of

doors. Thit is seated with her back against the wall. Both twins are alive.

'From the first time I saw you, Susan, I've wanted to see you naked.'

'Close the doors so the kids won't see,' I tell him.

He thinks about it. Then does as I say.

'I only get off on independent, mature women. I've already chosen the music. Edith Piaf. She does for me what Janis Joplin does. And Billie Holiday. I wish I could have known them. Knowing me would have changed their lives.'

'*Curtailed* is the word.'

He laughs.

'You may be right. They might not have lived as long, but their lives would have been all the more exciting. More intense.'

He unzips his trousers. His erection throbs visibly.

'Start now. I'm horny.'

A very few times in my life, I've found myself confronted with a person impervious to the Effect. Such people are out of reach.

I unbutton my cardigan and step out of my skirt, into a space within myself where I am wholly focused on survival.

He puts Edith Piaf on again. I begin to writhe, though stiffly and with one thing only in my thoughts: how to move closer to him.

My means is my body. The man in front of me may be a ruthless, dispassionate murderer, but I sense very strongly the singular temptation of the female form. The might that resides in the woman's flesh.

He's about to explode as I take off my bra.

'Come here,' he says. 'Straddle me.'

I look into his eyes. And in spite of everything – the presence of the twins, the proximity of our deaths – I feel desire. Most of what we do in life we do tamely and half-heartedly, indifferent to it all. But the physical lust between the two of us here is pure and electric.

338

I step out of my knickers. All I have left, in the crook of my arm, is my bag.

'You're going to kill us whatever we do.'

I hear myself utter the words. He hears his own reply in the same way. As if the words came not from within us, but from without. The Effect is at work after all.

'It won't hurt, Susan. A little jab, that's all. Like at the doctor's.'

He tosses his head back:

'Why am I saying this?'

He leans forward quite as abruptly, and peers at his reflection in the TV screen, as if trying to return himself to reality. He straightens up again and looks at me. His erection has subsided.

'Hegn said something. About you being able to . . .'

He laughs, and his member begins to swell again.

'It's a turn-on. Like a kind of voodoo.'

'Yes,' I say. 'And there's a trance dance to go with it.'

Slowly, I begin to spin, to gyrate. All physicists are fascinated by rotation. Belly dancers. The Whirling Dervish dance of the Mevlevi. The pirouettes of classical ballet. It's the gyroscopic self-stabilisation of motion.

What I see in my mind's eye are the rotations of Magrethe Spliid in throwing the discus. And the reason I've kept hold of my bag until now is because the crowbar is still inside it.

I'm very close to him now. I move my free hand to the opening of the bag. Halfway through my final rotation I drop to my knees. And strike.

There is little sound. Perhaps it's because of his hair, the tight, peppery curls at his temples.

And yet I know his skull is smashed. Even if for a moment there is nothing to see.

His eyes are closed. He opens them and looks into mine. What I see in his face is gratitude. At that moment I understand how tight the connection is between contempt for others and contempt for the self.

He gets up from his chair. He picks up the gun from the glass-topped table.

He ought to have fallen. Physically, he ought to have fallen. I can tell that from his eyes. But those who are motivated by something from without, be it from above or from below, will always be capable of going another round.

I grip the crowbar and step towards him.

And then I stop. Part of the left side of his chest is gone. I stare into the thoracic cavity and see a pulsating lung. The diaphragm's thin sheet of muscle. The abdominal wall.

Then comes a crack of sound, sudden as a gust of wind. His body is hurled three metres to the side, yet deposited upright.

He stands there, turns his head and looks down at himself. A stubby length of artery has affixed itself to the once-white of his shirt.

He removes it meticulously with the thumb and index finger of his left hand, as if it were a wayward piece of pasta dropped from his fork. And then he falls, flat on his face, like a tree felled.

Oskar appears from the left, in an electric wheelchair, so pale and transparent it's almost as if the wheelchair is visible through his flesh. In his lap he holds a weapon.

I open the doors of the containers. I hear myself mumbling sounds without meaning as my hands investigate my children, feeling to make sure they are whole. I look into their faces, oddly expressionless. Slowly, they rise to their feet.

I put on my clothes. We walk, with Oskar in the wheelchair. Outside, the soldier from the Meteorological Institute is waiting in a golf buggy. He lowers a ramp and Oskar wheels inside. We get in.

A gate in the fence is open. We drive through it and onto the road that runs around the island. There are no people to be seen, the whole area looks abandoned. I stare at the weapon in Oskar's hands. Its blue coating. The bazooka from Kirsten Klaussen's wall.

A green boat takes us onboard.

Halfway across the Øresund, Thit and I look at each other. She answers the question I haven't the courage to ask.

'He got started,' she says. 'But I told him I'd picked up a resistant strain of gonorrhoea from Nagaland. "You're welcome to stick it inside me," I said. "As long as you realise it's going to fall off before you even get to the emergency room at the Department of Tropical Medicine." He decided against it.'

I look away.

'Mum. That must be what's meant by evolution of consciousness. Parents need drill drivers and deck screws. The next generation can get by on intelligence.'

'Yes,' I say. 'That must be it.'

The pale-faced young girl in the glass-fronted kiosk is watching TV. The moment she lays eyes on me, she grows paler still. The TV screen shows the prime minister speaking through a barrage of cameras and microphones.

The twins and I walk home. I wouldn't be able to breathe in a car. The jeep follows on slowly behind. There's hardly any traffic on Strandvejen. The city is paralysed. The cafés are full of people clustered around TV sets. I pull my scarf around my face. No one sees me, no one recognises me.

We don't bother ringing the bell at Dorthea's, we walk straight in. She's on the sofa in front of the television. We remain standing.

'It's spreading like wildfire,' she says. 'They say other European countries, and some Asian ones too, have done the same thing. Bought islands in the Pacific and fitted them out so a chosen few can survive. They say the Danish government's stepping down tomorrow. The oldest plans go back fifty years, apparently. A little group of politicians across the various parties knew all along. The chance to be among the survivors nullified all political differences. A few business leaders and scientists were informed. Some people in the arts. A number of officials. The first heads have already rolled. Two have committed suicide.'

I go through the gap in the hedge. Our house seems unchanged. At least, on the outside it does. Inside, it's traumatised. Beyond repair.

I go in. Oskar wheels into the living room and pulls up.

'I took the list of names from Falck-Hansen's office,' I say. 'You're on it. You were to head up the security forces. You were keeping an eye on Hegn, for the military.'

'They never trusted him.'

He flicks the little joystick and the electric wheelchair glides towards the front door with a whirr.

'When are they coming to get us?'

'They might not.'

For some reason, someone's left a printout of our *Time* front cover on the table. The colours have already faded.

'You never really had any significant role in this, Susan. An individual, a single family, means nothing. It may turn out to your advantage. The winds that are blowing now will mainly batter those at the top.'

I walk up to him.

'You squandered your chances,' I say.

I realise why he was able to play the homeless alcoholic so well. That, too, is a part of his truth.

I stroke my hand across his cheek. It feels like parched soil, dry and cracked.

I close my eyes. When I open them again he's gone.

I sit down at the table. Thit and Harald come in and put a pizza box in front of me. They set the table.

We eat, though the food tastes of nothing. After ten minutes an ambulance pulls up. Two men help Laban into the house. He's walking with a crutch and has stitches in his face, twenty at least.

'Hegn's people tried to stop me,' he says. 'They didn't succeed.'

We give him pizza and Coke. He gives up on both, the wounds in his cheeks too painful. I fetch him some water to sip.

'Oskar was here,' I say. 'He thinks we might have a chance.'

I pick up the car keys. Laban and the twins ask no questions.

The streets are still empty. On the road between Charlottenlund and Valby I see perhaps a dozen cars in all.

I park on Gamle Carlsberg Vej and walk the last bit of the way. For the first time in twenty years, I see no security. A strange atmosphere pervades the quiet residential streets, as if a state of emergency had been declared. Perhaps it has.

I take the key from the hollow tree stub and unlock the gate in the fence. I walk along the tree-lined driveway, up the steps and through the front door, and enter the room.

A TV set is on in one corner. A French minister is being interviewed.

I stand quietly inside the door. Andrea Fink lifts a remote control and the screen goes black. She must have heard or sensed me. I walk forward to the bed.

The white nights are close now. Although it's late, the light has not entirely yielded, but clings instead to the world.

'I thought you'd given everything away,' I say. 'But you hadn't. You packed it all up. So you could take it with you to the Pacific. Your name's on the list.'

She reaches out a hand towards me. I take it.

'Laboratory equipment, Susan. The rest has been given away. We would have set up a magnificent laboratory, you and I. Even the collider was going with us. I'd drawn up plans for a small electricity station. Fifty megawatts of hydraulic power.'

'The idea must have come to you a long time ago.'

'To Magrethe and me. Before all the others. We tried to convince Bohr, but he couldn't see it.'

343

I sit down on the edge of the bed. I feel very tired.

Her hand is as cold as ice. I pull the duvet aside and climb in next to her. I draw her frail, bony frame into mine, to see if I might transfer some of my body's warmth to her.

'We could have lived there, Susan. With our families, Laban and the twins. We could have done big science together.'

A slight shiver passes through her body. At the end of the day, no one wants to die, not even Andrea Fink. I stroke my hand across her skin. I can't make the cold go away, it's as if it has reached into her very bones.

'All that business about questioning Magrethe Spliid was a pretext,' I say. 'You wanted us home from India because you wanted me with you. You wanted us all to go to Spray Island and be safe.'

She doesn't reply. She doesn't have to.

For a moment I remain still. Alone with my gratitude, my disgust, my anger.

I feel something warm on the back of my hand, like dripping candle wax. I realise I'm crying.

Then I get up.

'I found something out,' I say. 'These last months. Something I never knew before. Do you know what's at the very deepest part of us, inside the Effect?'

She says nothing.

'Other people, Andrea. In the very deepest part of us are other people.'

I look at her one last time. In the dim light, I try to take as much of her with me as I can.

Then I turn and leave.

As I step through the gate in the fence, out onto the street, a shadow emerges. My ballet prince.

His own mother would need a voice test to identify him. His uniform is in tatters.

He stops and looks at me. His eyes tell me what his face cannot.

'Lars,' I say, 'I'm forty-three. I've breastfed two children. I've got saggy boobs and grey hairs in their thousands. You're starting out in life, I'm heading for my pension.'

'Shakespeare says this, in the hundred and fourth sonnet: *To me, fair friend, you never can be old . . .*'

A car pulls up at the kerb. It's the hearse, with Laban at the wheel. He turns off the engine, extracts first his crutch, then his legs, and draws himself upright in front of us.

'Susan, I've composed a small piece of music. About the two of us. It's kind of a serenade. The first line is: *To the stars, your eyes are wishing wells . . .*'

He starts singing. I start walking. They tag along at my sides, Laban singing in my right ear, my ballet prince reciting in the left. I hope they're too disabled to start fighting.

In the occasional house, faces appear in the windows and look out at us. Maybe it's the Effect.

Peter Høeg was born in 1957 and followed various callings – dancer, actor, fencer, sailor, mountaineer – before he turned seriously to writing. He published his first novel, *The History of Danish Dreams*, in 1988, and was called 'the foremost writer of his generation' by *Information* magazine. His crime novel *Miss Smilla's Feeling for Snow* received universal acclaim and is an international bestseller.

Martin Aitken is an award-winning translator of Scandinavian literature. Most of his work has been from Danish, including Peter Høeg's previous novel *The Elephant Keepers' Children* (2012).